THE
GLASS
FOREST

From the Chicken House

I *loved* the end of RAVENWOOD, but I just *knew* the terrible forces of glass and steel were going to seek their revenge on our beloved cast of mighty tree-dwellers. Andrew totally surprised me with his brilliant vision of worlds colliding, though, and some totally amazing pieces of intrigue. This is just awesome!

Barry Cunningham
Publisher

THE
GLASS
FOREST

ANDREW PETERS

Chicken House

2 Palmer Street, Frome, Somerset BA11 1DS

Text © Andrew Peters 2012
First published in Great Britain in 2012
The Chicken House
2 Palmer Street
Frome, Somerset BA11 1DS
United Kingdom
www.doublecluck.com

Cover and interior design by Steve Wells
Cover illustration by Steve Rawlings
Typeset by Dorchester Typesetting Group Ltd
Printed and bound in Great Britain by CPI Group (UK) Ltd, Croydon, CR0 4YY

The paper used in this Chicken House book is made from wood grown
in sustainable forests.

1 3 5 7 9 10 8 6 4 2

British Library Cataloguing in Publication data available.

ISBN 978-1-906427-47-4

To Polly, who always knew which route this book should take. And with big thanks to the team at Chicken House for their unwavering support.

The Copenhagen interpretation of quantum mechanics implies that after a while, the cat is simultaneously alive and dead.
wikipedia.org

'It's actually genius,' [says a hedge fund manager,] 'they've understood there's a sector of the market for whom nothing but the perceived best will do, and who want something more, the more expensive it is.'
Guardian, 22 Jan 2011

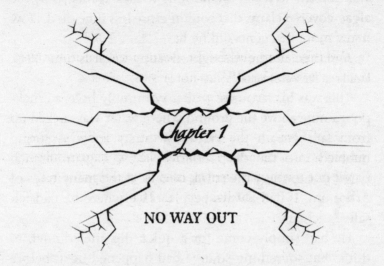

Chapter 1

NO WAY OUT

December, five days before the Winter Solstice

Ark was drowning. His arms whirled like sycamore pods, desperately trying to pull free. But the birch-weed stretched and curled like slimy fingers, wrapping tightly round his legs, anchoring him down towards the bottom of the cruck-pool. The fronds squeezed his body as if almost enjoying the drama of near-death.

He struggled and kicked with ebbing strength. Seconds flew like Ravens, but he only grew more entangled. Tiny air bubbles leaked from his nose; his lungs were nearly bursting. He threw his head back, as though by looking up he could force his way through the shoals of silver boldfish to the surface where the last of the late-afternoon light slanted down. So near, and yet too far.

Ark scanned the blurry scene, frantic now. But there

was nothing to reach for, nothing to kick against, only the algae-covered clams that couldn't care less if he died. How many more moments did he have?

And then another thought, floating towards him: *Let go, breathe in the warm liquid.* Why not?

This was his favourite winter swimming hole, a cruck-pool a mile above the ground where water was sucked up from far beneath the earth by thirsty roots. A spring bubbled into the deep hollow where a giant branch flared out to meet the trunk of one of the many trees of Arborium. It had always been a place where he had felt safe. Sanctuary.

He had simply come for a quick dip after dinner, to think. But something strange had happened next: before he had even got changed, somehow he'd tripped over an odd bulge in the bark. It had felt deliberate. Why? Then he was falling headlong. There was a rush of pressure in his ears and the weight of his woollen clothes yanked him down into the depths.

Terror clutched him. Thoughts tumbled around his head. He sensed the monstrous power of the tree reaching out to crush him like a stick of fuel. The birchweed binding him was its servant, enfolding Ark in the cruellest of bark cradles. Had the trees evolved a will of their own? He was being overpowered on home territory, by the very forest he was part of. Why, after all he had done for Arborium? What was the point now of battles won, or giant mealworms calmed, or dangerous foes defeated? All that Corwenna the Raven-Queen had taught him, all that Arktorious Malikum was destined to do would be gone.

What about the phial he wore always around his neck? Surely that would help him? After all, it contained the very essence of the trees arming themselves against attack. But it was tangled under his clothes; he couldn't reach it.

The pressure on his chest was intense. Pain glowed deep in the roots of his soul. His gritted teeth parted, ready to surrender to the spasm in his lungs.

The light above him was suddenly blocked out. Something gripped tightly around his waist and pulled hard. Mud and bubbles swirled as a blade flashed towards him through the murky grey. What now? Had Petronio Grasp come back to life, seeking his revenge? The knife slid past Ark, hacking at the twisting knots holding him down. The binding fronds writhed, furious at the interruption.

Ark was suspended in a deadly tug-of-war. His body stretched like an eel as the birchweed held stubbornly fast. Then his legs were free. He was rising, dragged up towards the light. His mouth opened as he broke the surface, gulping air, thirsty for life. A final shove flopped him down at the edge of the pool like a blanket of soggy moss, gasping.

'Wot did you fink you was doin', you stupid planker?' Mucum slumped down beside him. He was panting, his orange hair plastered to his head and his clothes dripping.

'I . . . I don't know,' Ark wheezed. 'Came for a swim . . . fell in . . .' But the trees weren't his enemy. It didn't make sense.

'Well there's clumsy, and there's plain stupid. I tell yer, mate, ever since I met you it's been trouble all the way,' Mucum grumbled. 'And that bloomin' birchweed was

like a snake in me hands. Could 'ave sworn it was alive.'
He coughed, rolled over and wiped his knife on some
fallen leaves.

'Sorry.' Ark pulled himself on to his hands and knees
and vomited.

'Oh, lovely. Did I say I wanted ter see what you 'ad fer
dinner, spewed out on the wood-way?'

Ark wiped his mouth with his wet sleeve, the taste of
bile still rising. 'No.' He tried to stand up, swaying like a
sapling. Mucum pushed out a meaty arm, steadying him.
'Thanks . . . Thanks for saving my life!'

'Well, nothin' better ter do, eh! Thought I'd find you
'ere, hangin' out in yer hidey-hole before the meeting
with King Quercus tomorrow. Lucky I came lookin' and
spotted you down there, otherwise you woulda been
crossin' the River Sticks to the Land of the Dead.' Mucum
shook himself like a dog. 'And now I'm buddy soakin'!'

Ark stared across the surface of the cruck-pool as it
steamed gently in the cold dusk. He shuddered, thinking
of the lurking threat hidden below. *Alive.* Yes, his mate had
it right.

Mucum's teeth began to chatter. 'Right, now I've done
me *wood* deed fer the day, I'm shiverin' me bits off 'ere.
Any suggestions?'

The wood-way of the giant tree they stood on creaked
slightly. But it was indifferent to the questions filling Ark's
head; questions that meant he no longer felt safe here.

'Follow me!' he said, setting off unsteadily.

'That's what I always do. And yer know what, it's a
right pain!'

Ark ignored him. A mile above the earth, the winter wind was sharper than Mucum's blade. They needed to find shelter, and quickly. At this time of evening, the wide wood-way that led away from the pool was empty, except for a single timber-goat grazing on fungus. Brush-hour was over, with most Dendrans already at home. Ark paused to get his bearings. Maybe he *had* just tripped over . . . and birchweed *was* notoriously sticky.

His hands were numb and his jerkin was as stiff as hardboard, but somehow his escape from death had cleared his vision. He looked round with wonder at the way the branches had been carved and cantilevered, creating a huge spiderweb structure that criss-crossed the great trunks of Arborium. Those engineers and carpenters of old knew their stuff. Trees had been hollowed into houses, with windows, doors and chimneys; a whole civilisation strung high in the forest canopy. And it was lit by an ingenious system of iron pipes that carried gas, siphoned from the delving roots right into most dwellings. All this, Ark thought – all the extraordinary collaboration between the Dendrans and the trees they dwelt in – was now under threat from the Empire of Maw with its hunger for wood. Back in October, at the Harvest Battle, they'd stopped the coup. But the might of Maw was only checked, and time was running out.

After five minutes of walking, hunched over against the cold, Ark stopped. Mucum looked up. 'Oh no. Yer ain't gonna catch me goin' in there!'

Ark always felt a leap in his heart as he gazed at the soaring trunk, filled with stained glass spilling colour on to the path. In the centre of a shimmering panel of green, Diana, beloved of all Dendrans, sat on a throne of leaves. Her sad smile shone down, outlined in lead. Ark crossed his hands over his chest and said a quick prayer for Victoria, his long-dead twin sister.

'What is the point of all that prayin' stuff? Now my grandma is a bit dotty, drools a little, but once in a while she does say somethin' worth listenin' to. That don't mean I'm gonna turn her into a goddess though!'

Ark turned fiercely on his friend. 'Diana . . . was . . . my . . . grandmother!' With each word, he jabbed his finger into Mucum's chest. 'And she created the whole wide-wood. A bit of respect would be nice!'

Mucum rolled his eyes and folded his arms. 'Hey, keep yer hair on. Only sayin'! I think I preferred it when you woz all shy and mousy!'

'Hmm,' Ark muttered. 'Well, if you want to turn into an icicle, you can always stay out here.' They were standing in front of the Kirk entrance. The grand arched doorway was shut, but it was never locked. He pushed the door open, and immediately he was hit with the smell of burning pine resin, thick and pungent.

The last of the evening light filtered into the main body of the Kirk, a room about fifty feet round, its carved and corbelled ceiling lost in the dusty shadows high above. Ark's eyes were drawn to the altar where another statue of Diana perched, cradling an acorn to represent the one from which the very first giant trees of Arborium had grown. There was a candle in front of it, almost burned down, the flame already guttering.

A woman knelt on the floor, her grey hair tied back and her black cloak spilling out around her like dark water. She turned at the sound of footsteps, and her wrinkled face cracked into a smile, though the two blank eyes stayed unfocused.

'You smell of damp!' she said with a light, sing-song tone. 'Are you coming to water my winter flowers by squeezing out your soggy clothes? You must have some story to tell . . .'

Ark was once again amazed at how Warden Goodwoody saw more than most sighted Dendrans. 'I *am* very wet, my Lady.' How could he even begin to explain? In this sacred space, he felt safe at last.

Mucum shuffled behind him, scratching his dirty knuckles.

'Never mind. I understand your friend does not wish to be inside such an old fuddy-buddy place of worship. But don't worry, I promise that if he goes into the store cupboard, the only miracle he'll find will be some dry towels.'

Mucum shook his head as he wandered off in the direction she was pointing in, dripping all over the polished wooden floor.

'I sense you are troubled, Arktorious Malikum. Is it not enough that, with the help of your companions, you routed the great beast and protected our holly land?'

Ark sat down on the floor beside the warden. Yes, she was right. All this he had done, and yet the trees had repaid his loyalty by trying to drown him.

'No, it is not enough,' Ark said. 'Tomorrow morning,

I must see the king. But I have no magic plan, no brilliant solution.'

She reached up to trace the contours of his face like a map, gently stroking his damp black hair. 'You are much changed. I wonder where the boy I once knew has gone.'

'I'm still here.'

'Yes. And frightened. So you should be. Truly we live in changed times. To have learned that Corwenna is as real as the tip of my nose is troubling. Corwenna! The dark Raven-Queen of myths and far-tales; the true face of nature; a storybook old crone used by mothers to scare their children into good behaviour . . . If I were to meet her, whatever would a simple old warden like me have to say? But Diana will protect us. I have always had faith . . .' She fell silent.

Ark didn't know how to answer. He had not told the warden that Diana was no goddess, but a mortal scientist from long ago, who had brought to life the seeds from which the huge trees of Arborium and the Ravenwood had sprung. Although, he thought, perhaps it was all right for Warden Goodwoody to believe. After all, Diana had believed that this tree-top world could grow from her scientifically changed handful of seeds, and it had. But right now, Ark, flesh-and-blood grandson of Diana, was simply a doubting boy come to Kirk for comfort and guidance.

Warden Goodwoody put her hands together and bowed her head as if she could hear his thoughts. 'All I have is words. You do not need to worry about your meeting tomorrow at court. Remember, every single one of those so-called noblemen and warriors goes to the bath-room just like you!'

Mucum wandered back and chucked a towel at Ark. 'That's good, that is!' he smiled as he rubbed his hair. 'Jus' think of them posh gits as they –'

'Yes!' Ark interrupted. 'I get the point.'

The warden grew serious, reaching for Ark's hands and gripping them tightly. 'But in my heart I can see a journey ahead of you. There is . . . death.'

Ark pulled away. Death. That was what had lain in the depths of the cruck-pool. He wasn't sure he wanted to hear any hints about the future.

'But,' she continued, 'you will face it, walk around it, make friends with it. In the end, it is the only way that Arborium shall be saved!'

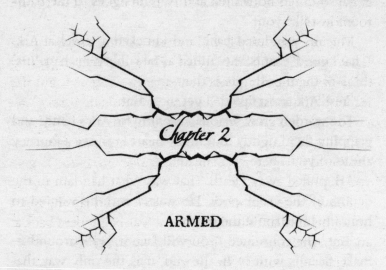

Chapter 2

ARMED

Flinty couldn't breathe. The metallic pincers closed round his throat, slowly crushing his windpipe like a walnut.

'Eurghhh!' he groaned, dropping to his knees on the frosted wood-way. It was two in the morning and the rest of his gang were sparked out in their comfy tree-cots, their dreams fermenting like the barrels of rough cider-apple they had stolen.

'Hello Flinty!' said a voice near his left ear.

'Eurghhh!' Flinty gargled again, his face turning an unpleasant shade of purple. He tried to reach into his leather boot. The hidden flick-knife, stabbed backwards, would quickly sort out his attacker.

The grip tightened. 'Concealed weapons?' A hand slipped round his ankle and plucked the knife free. Flinty heard it clatter down through the branches, the echo slowly fading towards the earth a mile below. 'It takes one to know one.'

The pressure eased slightly and a thin stream of air leaked into his lungs. 'My throat!' Flinty croaked, staggering sideways as the stranglehold suddenly slackened. But the leader of the most fearsome gang in Moss-side hadn't survived this long without a few tricks up his sleeve. And the trick that slid into his hand now was nicely sharpened.

'You don't give up easily,' the voice snarled. 'I'll give you that!'

Flinty lunged forwards. But before could rip the heart out of his assailant's body, his wrist was being bent back at an unnatural angle. 'Argh! It hurts!' he squealed.

'That's the point! Now drop it!'

It was Flinty's favourite blade, passed on by his father, who had won it in a fight in his own youthful days. It was all he had left of the former commander and there was no way he was about to lose it. He let his wrist go limp, in mock surrender, and dropped to the floor. In one fluid motion, he forward-rolled away, regained his feet and twisted round to face whoever was there. But the way was empty. All around, the bare winter trees threw silhouettes across the rutted planks, turning the highway into a path of shifting shadows.

'Show yerself!'

A cloud scudded across the three-quarter moon. On the other side of the wood-way, Flinty heard the creak of a safety rope. It was a dead giveaway. That was the thing about living high up in the canopy of the forest – every movement made a sound. 'Gotcha!' he murmured. He drew his arm back and flung the beautifully balanced knife straight at the heart of the darkness. It flew like an arrow, true in its aim.

Flinty allowed himself a smile. His would-be mugger was about to be stuck like a pincushion.

'Ooomf!' went the voice. After that, silence.

'No-one messes with Flinty!' he crowed, triumphant.

But then the shadows gave up their secret. A figure strode out, dressed in a new pink doublet and cross-gartered britches. He had shiny, oiled hair, dark eyes and one of the beard extensions that were currently all the rage among rich southerners. He looked around the same age as Flinty, but whereas the northern lad was skinny as a sword, this young man was made of rounder stuff.

As Flinty peered closer, the moonlight revealed something wrong: two wrong things, in fact. Firstly, the knife was not neatly buried up to the hilt in the lad's chest, where it should have been. Secondly, what Flinty had mistaken for an arm glinted like Rootshooter silver under the moonlight. His eyes opened wide.

'But that's . . .'

'Impossible? Not really, mate. It's called training. Here's your knife, by the way.' He handed it back to Flinty, seeming unconcerned that he was passing over a weapon. Flinty was thrown by this gesture. It showed no fear. And the arm was something else: the puffed sleeve had been cut away at the shoulder, revealing the straps and wires that held the jointed device in place. It looked wrong, horrifying, like a segmented metal worm forged in the furnaces of hell.

The elbow joint flexed, hidden cogs making a clicking sound. 'Yeah. They call it a prototype. Ugly, but it works a whole lot better than a real one.' The two pincers that passed for a hand clacked together like a cruck-pool crab to make his point. 'Only a pinch more, and I would've burst your windpipe like a rotten tomato. Good, eh?' The cruel glimmer in the lad's eyes suggested that murder would be merely an experiment to test the arm's strength. 'Petronio Grasp, at your service. Again.' He gave a mock bow. 'Well, at the service of the Mawish Empire actually.'

Flinty's brain finally began to function. This was the same piece of work who had humiliated him in front of his gang on a misty October night not so long ago. 'I thought you woz dead.'

'In which case, you were nearly just done in by a ghost, hmmm?' Petronio smiled. 'Now then. It's time to free your father.'

'What? You must be off your tree!' Flinty slid his blade back into its concealed holster. His father had gone mad, broken by the sewage rat Arktorious Malikum in the final battle at the Court of King Quercus a couple of months previously. The ex-commander was now a shambling shell of his former self, safely under lock and key in a prison on the edge of the capital city of Hellebore.

Flinty had visited his father once and that was enough. The drool that hung from his lips and the glazed eyes that stared through his son had shocked him to his core. Flinty had sworn revenge, and it would have been so easy if Ark was by himself, but the sewer boy suddenly had the weight of the king behind him. Flinty's gang might be ruthless, but they stood no chance against a king's army.

'No, I am not, as you so quaintly suggest, off my tree. Though I might be tempted to push you off it if you annoy me any more. So now I suggest you rouse your mates from their stupor. We have a prisoner to liberate.'

'What? I don't get it. My dad's . . .'

'I know what he is. It's what he was that makes him useful. He is still a compelling figurehead that some of his old followers will always rally to. And regardless of the state he's in, wouldn't you rather he was being fed some decent nosh, instead of jailbird slops?'

'Suppose so . . .'

'More importantly, I'm asking you to help me to pay back the boy who did this to your father.'

Flinty leant forward. This was beginning to sound more interesting.

Petronio continued, 'I have visited such places as would outdo any fanciful far-tale.' His eyes grew distant, his head filled with shimmering glass. He ached to be back in Maw, served by its elegant comforts, rather than stuck out here in a windy holly-hole. He looked round at the dark mass of the woods. It was so strange to think that a single twig was worth its weight in gold to an empire whose economy was in tatters, but that wasn't for Flinty to know. Petronio was here to do a job, and fear was a good motivator. 'The Empire has developed a weapon that will make every bark-brained Dendran fall to their knees and pray to their non-existent Diana! Put it this way, either you're with us, or you're dead. Your choice.'

'Oh yeah?' Flinty laughed. 'And my grandma 'appens

to be Corwenna, Queen of the Ravens.'

Petronio's mechanical arm jerked and Flinty jumped. 'You think I've come all this way to play a joke?' His voice had a menacing edge.

'Keep yer hair on, mate! Only sayin'! What kinda weapon?'

'As far from your puny collection of knives as you could possibly imagine. It is one that will suck the breath from every unwilling body. Trust me on this.'

Flinty shuddered. The boy spoke like a madman. However, from experience, Flinty knew it was not a good idea to dismiss him. 'Well. When yer put it like that . . .' The first time he'd met Petronio, he'd made a vow to get him back one day for the humiliation of being disarmed in front of his own gang. But it was rather tricky when it appeared that your sworn enemy was on your side. 'We still ain't buds though, you and me, eh?'

'Wouldn't dream of it, dear fellow. The dislike is mutual, but if you wish the future to be more exciting than this damp squit-hole,' Petronio swung his flesh-and-bone arm round to indicate the cold branch-ways around them, 'then I suggest we join forces and get cracking! Once you've discovered the delights of central heating, trust me, you will want to join the winning side.'

'Still not sure what you're talkin' about, but if it involves senseless violence – well, always up for that, me.'

'I knew you'd see sense.' Petronio smiled. 'So, senseless violence it is, then.'

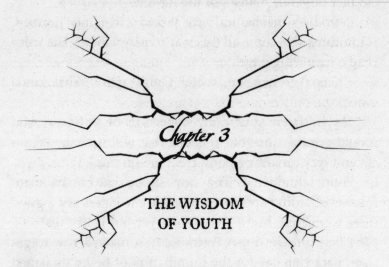

Chapter 3

THE WISDOM
OF YOUTH

Ark felt the floorboards shift beneath his feet. The wind was busy this early morning, sending gusts and eddies round the palace courtyard, teasing the white cloth on the table they sat around. Far beneath them, the four huge trunks that supported Barkingham Palace groaned and creaked in the breeze.

All through the previous night, Ark's dreams had been broken by nightmares of drowning. The encounter in the cruck-pool still confused him. Perhaps he should have told Mucum the truth, or asked the warden for advice, instead of keeping it to himself.

A cold, low sun washed over the edge of the high battlements surrounding the open yard. Beyond, the leafless branches of the forest stuck up like skinny fingers. Iron braziers filled with fiery pools of sap circled the gathering, giving off little heat. Ark looked round the circular table. The king was seated, like all of them, on a plain wooden chair, his green gown wrapped tightly round him to keep out the cold. One of his blue suede boots drummed the floor. Only Quercus was allowed to wear blue, the symbol of Arborium, for this colour represented the only crown that the trees wore: blue sky.

The king drew breath and began to speak. 'We hold this meeting in the spirit of openness. For too long our political will was carried out in secrecy, and treason flourished like a foul fungus! Thus I decreed that all future state matters should be discussed under the open sky. Now, there is much to—'

'That's all very well, your majesty,' a strident voice interrupted. The new Commander of the Armouries sat to the left of the king, looking awkward in his bronze chain mail as he fingered the hilt of his sword. His face was round and red as a rowanberry. 'But there's a difference between openness and freezin' yer galls off!'

'Good one,' Mucum sniggered.

Ark nudged him. 'Shhh!' he hissed.

Mucum rolled his eyes. He and Ark were sandwiched between a set of very sniffy Alder councillors who were doing their best to pretend that the pair of them didn't even exist. Mucum's clothes didn't help. Despite the pleading of the court, he had declined the offer of decent finery, deciding to stick with his old stained leather waistcote and a pair of grotty britches that might once have been brown. The unexpected swim in the cruck-pool hadn't even touched their griminess, and Mucum still appeared as a carrot-haired sewer worker with more muscles than he knew what to do with. The look suited him just fine.

Quercus smiled coldly. 'Commander Broadbeam, your frankness was one of the reasons I promoted you after the double-dealing of my former friend and colleague.' The king's eyes briefly rested on Ark, who winced, remembering the anger that had poured through him as he'd reduced Commander Flint's mind to a mush of hazelmeal. He knew it had had to be done. It was the Will of the Woods. But still, after all these weeks, he felt sick to the stomach at the thought of it. And where was Flint now? Languishing in prison, a husk of a man. Perhaps it would have been better had he died. Ark tore his gaze away from the king.

'As I was saying,' the king continued, 'there is much to discuss, and I agree with our new commander that it would be best done quickly before we all turn into ice carvings! So, Broadbeam, as you seem eager to speak, go ahead.' Quercus sat back and stroked his beard. From being the useless figurehead of a few months ago, he had changed remarkably. Ark couldn't quite describe it, but Quercus looked . . . younger, somehow, and sounded more . . . kingly.

The commander stood up. He was not a tall man, but the way he stomped round the boards reminded Ark of the huge timber-boar that Corwenna had once faced down. This was not a man one would want to meet in battle. 'Talk is one thing we don't have much time for. You all know about the mud-pirates who live at the base of our trees.' The commander put a thumb downwards and wrinkled his nose in disgust.

Several councillors frowned in disapproval. The mud-pirates were the scum of the earth, not worthy of discussion at court.

'Yeah, exactly,' said Broadbeam. 'I feel the same as you lot. But how would I get my morning cuppa and you lot sip your posh coffee without their smuggling skills? The Empire of Maw might be our enemy, but its far outposts still do very nicely in illicit trade with us. The point is, they smuggle rumours as well as goods.' He had their attention now. 'Now, we gave the Empire's soldiers a good hidin' last time they came here, and they ain't gonna take that lyin' down . . .'

'I am sorry to butt in here, my good man.' The king sounded positively dangerous. 'But as I remember, you – along with most of your men – were safely holed up in the North while the battle was raging here.'

'Yeah. Well, there is that.' Broadbeam's red face went even redder. 'But what I'm tryin' to say is, they're out to get us. The word is that they've got some kinda weapon that's gonna sort us once and for all. And Arborium's just one small island. A few thousand Dendrans with swords and crossbows against the massive Empire of Maw. Now I'm a bettin' man myself and I'm always up for a good fight. But even to my eye, the odds ain't too hot.'

The assembled company fell silent. Even Mucum stopped fidgeting.

'Why can't they jus' leave us alone?' growled Mucum.

The question hung in the sharp air. There was no answer. Ark let his gaze drift downwards. The boards beneath his feet were bleached of all blood, but he could still smell the faint scent of carnage. No, the Empire would not leave them alone now.

One of the councillors coughed, examining the commander slowly from head to toe, then spoke. 'So, what precisely do you suggest, young man?'

Broadbeam bridled at being spoken to as though he were no more than a young whipper-sapling. 'I suggest, sir,' he replied to the wrinkled old bag of bones in front of him, 'that we send in some of our best men as spies to find out what they're up to.'

Ark's thoughts spun wildly. He remembered the warden's words: he had been invited today by the king himself, so surely he had a right to say something? 'Er, if I might speak?'

Broadbeam's jaw fell open. He stared at the boy dressed in black. Ark's green eyes stared back, unafraid. Who did he think he was? 'Sorry, sonny. No room for pipsqueaks here.'

The king slammed his hand on the table. 'Enough, Commander! This *pipsqueak* saved my life. Have you conveniently forgotten the role this boy and his friends played in the events of the Harvest Battle, events that took place at this very spot? Do you think I made you knight them out of some senile whim of mine?' He glared at Broadbeam, daring him to answer back.

Broadbeam scowled and threw himself back into his seat. 'When we're reduced to asking babes-in-the-wood for advice, Arborium is goin' to the logs,' he muttered.

'What was that?' asked the king.

Mucum leant forward, watching intently. Usually his own way of sorting out problems was with a punch or two. But the king's voice was sharper than any sword.

'Nothing,' said Broadbeam finally. 'Let him stick his two pennies in for all I care.'

Ark felt everyone's attention shift towards him. 'I . . .' His lips felt dry as he gazed back at the high and mighty of Arborium. This was ridiculous. He'd faced the meal-worm, taken on the mighty timber-boar and helped turn certain defeat into outright victory. What did he have to fear from a bunch of old men?

'I think that the commander is right . . .'

Broadbeam sighed with relief. 'Thank you for the vote of confidence, *boy*. Now as I was saying . . .'

But Ark put up his hand. Corwenna had taught him the power of stillness. It was what trees did best. He had only to focus and he was of the trees: by Ark raising his hand and willing it so, Broadbeam's angry tongue simply stopped moving before it could rattle on.

The commander's lips strained. His eyes bulged but all that escaped from his mouth was a puff of silent frustration.

Ark continued. 'The commander is right. However, his men would be recognized instantly, whatever disguise they wore. The longer fingers are a dead giveaway, for a start.' He had their attention now. Fully-grown adult Dendrans developed long hands with a slight curl at the ends of their fingers, useful in a place where one false step meant a fall off the wood-way. It was an example of perfect evolution: with longer fingers, a quick-thinking Dendran had a chance to grab a passing branch. 'A spy needs to pass unnoticed. The Empire will be vigilant in looking for Dendran spies, so what better disguise than a treenager, when they'll only be looking for and noticing adults?' Ark held up his hand. 'See? Shorter fingers. They won't reach full size for a couple of years.' He lowered his arm and turned slowly on the spot. 'And I mean, look at me! Who would think I could possibly pose a threat?'

Mouths dropped around the table. Broadbeam nearly choked, trying to regain control of his stubborn jaw. 'You . . . must be . . . kidding!' he finally managed to splutter. 'You? You think you could go to Maw . . . ?

Mucum jumped to his feet, staring angrily at Ark. 'What d'yer mean, a treenager? If yer thinkin' of goin' by yerself, yer wouldn't stand a chance! Yer need me wiv yer, otherwise there'll be a right old mess!'

Ark smiled. He wasn't sure whether to take that as reassurance or a threat.

There was uproar around the table now, with several councillors trying to speak at once, all exclaiming about the folly of youth. But their arguments never had a chance to be heard as suddenly the early morning sun was blotted out above them. The wind lifted, picking up precious glass goblets from the table, flinging them against walls to shatter into shards. The wooden floor groaned and creaked. Every Dendran who dived for cover had the same thought, screamed aloud by one terrified councillor.

'The rumours of a weapon from Maw are true! It's too late!'

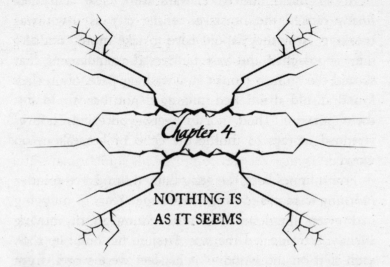

Chapter 4

NOTHING IS
AS IT SEEMS

Petronio had galloped through the night, forcing Flinty and his gang to follow at an exhausting pace, the hooves of their horses drumming on the planked wood-ways.

His father's death had been convenient. Councillor Grasp, deceased, would not miss his best horse Mercury. The silver stallion was a delight. The aerial, glassed-in moving walkways of Maw were miraculous, and the sky chariots that swooped and swirled like swallows still filled Petronio with an almost religious awe, but he had forgotten the joys of fresh air streaming through his hair, the feeling of sheer muscle pumping beneath him. Flying would have been much quicker, but Petronio did not want to reveal more of the operation than was needed to the boys of Moss-side. They were useful fodder to do his bidding. Nothing more.

At this hour, the wood-ways were clear, and they finally neared the outskirts of the city as dawn was breaking. Now they would have to take more care, and they approached the vast buttressed roundabouts that skirted the suburb trunks at a walking pace. Soon they found an old abandoned milking depot that would suit their purpose. Their horses were concealed, hooves wrapped in rags to muffle the echo of horseshoes on wood.

Five minutes later, the gang filtered through the early-morning shadows towards their target. Years of mugging had given them an invaluable education in moving silently. Petronio led the way. Despite his bulk, he took each step on the wood as if his feet were woven from feathers. Finally, he crouched down and fell still, hidden in the treescape.

He tried to ignore the ache in his long-gone arm. Fenestra had told him about the strange science of ghost feelings: though a limb might be no more, it could still feel pain, the brain reliving memories of the past. And there it was again, the memory of that moment two months ago as Ark had gripped his old hand and, by some foul magic, begun to turn it to wood. How Petronio had reacted was either insane or totally logical, depending on your point of view. Who else among all the Dendrans would dare to chop off his own arm to stop it infecting the rest of his body?

He remembered the bright arc of blood spraying into the air, the shocked look on Ark Malikum's face as Petronio was suddenly free. But it was Fenestra's modified cape, flaring out like a parachute, that had prevented certain death as they had tumbled to the forest floor far below. In a coma, he'd been smuggled out to Maw, where the surgeons had battled to bring him back from the dead. Though Petronio didn't believe in miracles, Fenestra and the technology of Maw had saved him. For that, he was in their debt.

He shook his head and focused on the present again. A drama was about to unfold, and he had the perfect ringside seat.

The prison was not the most secure site. A former commander, much reduced, was hardly an escape risk. The soldier on gate duty was bored. He stamped his feet; the boots they issued these days were pathetic and his toes were nearly numb. He was dying for a drink but he knew that if the watch-chief smelt beer on his breath, he'd be in for the lock-up. He wondered where the other guard had got to, then saw his lantern bobbing towards him through the murky light.

'Oi, Barry, where you been?'

'Doing the rounds, where do you think? This cold's getting to me. Me bladder's bursting!'

'Thanks for the detail. Anything else you want to let me know?'

'Not really. Keep a good look out for insurgents, eh? I'll be back in a minute.' The guard sloped off, the sound of his whistling fading around the corner.

Insurgents? thought the soldier. *Hah! Who would want to take on a dump like this?*

As if in answer to this silent question, a boy strode out

of the shadows, calm as you like, straight up to the surprised man.

'Hello there, how do you fancy letting the prisoner free?'

The soldier shook himself, studied the face in front of him and folded his arms. 'Ha ha, sonny. Does your mummy know you're out so late?'

'Oh dear. Didn't you hear the question? And by the way, firstly I'm not your son. Secondly, asking about my *dead* mum isn't such a brilliant idea . . . is it . . . lads?' Shadows swarmed like treacle and the lantern on the wall above the guard's head revealed that he was suddenly surrounded. He could see it was a gang of kids, but the knives in their hands bore no resemblance to toys.

''Ere, what's your game?' The soldier backed nervously towards the door, about to pull the alarm bell.

'Oh, a serious game. Very serious!' said Flinty, stepping forward.

'Barry!' the soldier shrieked. 'Now would be a good time to stop widdling abou— !' These were his last words for a few hours as Flinty lunged and decked him with a powerful right hook. The soldier slammed straight back on to the branch-way, out cold with the beginnings of an almighty black eye and a lump the size of a bloated acorn on the back of his head.

The second guard, Barry, chose this moment to enter, sword drawn and held in front of him. 'You might pack a punch, but you lot are out of your depth!' he threatened, jumping into the middle of the gang and whirling his sword competently. 'I've won prizes for my swordcraft.'

Flinty made a signal and the rest of the gang backed away. 'You do know you're surrounded?'

'Yeah? And I'm happy to share my talents with you, though it might involve the loss of limbs!' The sword scythed the air. 'Scum like you are nothing more than heads of skinny scaffield wheat waiting to be cut down to size.'

But the prison guard wasn't prepared for what was behind him. In a fierce flurry of movement Petronio leapt out of the shadows like a cruck-pool eel. There was a flash of metal and a set of sharp blades shot out from his new hand.

The guard gave a single gasp of pain as the tendon in his sword arm was sliced cleanly through. The sword tumbled through the air on to the wood-way as its owner clutched his arm to staunch the fountain of blood. Two gang members sprang forward and tied him up like a ball of string. Petronio watched coldly, then turned away. He didn't care if the man bled to death, but some shred of conscience made Flinty wrap a tourniquet rag around the guard's forearm.

One of the gang ambled over to examine the studded door to the prison, set into the trunk of a moss-covered tree. 'It's a six-lever lock. Tough one!'

Flinty wiped his hands and stood up. 'You're not going all girly on me, Stan? Too hard for yer?'

The girl simply stared back at him, the insult sliding off like water from a Raven's back. Instead of answering, she pulled a long pin out of her hair and set to work on the lock. Soon, there was the gratifying sound of several clicks. After the sixth tumbler gave way before her nimble fingers, she gave a little bow and the door silently swung open. From inside came the sound of snoring.

'What is this country coming to?' sneered Flinty. 'You'd think the guards might've 'ad the decency to 'ave stayed awake for our arrival! Get in there and tie 'em up fast.'

While some of the gang members made sure the remaining sleeping guards wouldn't be getting up any time soon, Flinty motioned to the rest to follow him. They climbed down several sets of stairs until they came to a small door, with a hatch built into it. Flinty lowered the hatch and lifted his lamp to peer into the cubbyhole. It was a plank-lined cell, with a thin covering of straw on the floor and a shivering figure curled up in one corner.

'Dad?' he whispered. The word caught in his throat. Animals were treated better than this.

Stan made quick work of the second locked door, but as Flinty strode in and looked down at his father, it crossed his thoughts that even Stan would never manage to unlock the mind that lay trapped in the broken body. Nothing had changed on the outside; the commander's fine face was still recognisable and the great, hulking bulk of him, scarred with a hundred fights, menacing as ever. But the face was empty as a beech husk. Flinty felt a stab in the guts. 'Come on, Dad, we're taking you home.'

Two of the biggest lads manhandled his father up the stairs, past the muffled cries of the trussed-up guards.

Minutes later they were reunited with their horses and galloping north. As the early sun seeped through the forest, revealing huge trees etched in white and twigs feathered with icicles, Petronio allowed himself a smile. The game was on.

As for Ark? Petronio's smile turned to a snarl as he pictured the boy who had forced him to cut off his own arm. Oh yes, he thought, squeezing his alloy pincers together. That boy's time would come, and sooner rather than later.

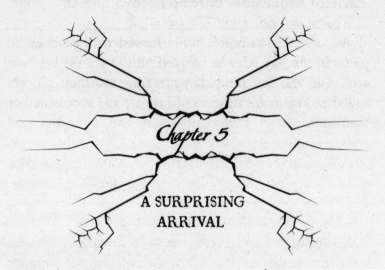

Chapter 5

A SURPRISING ARRIVAL

'**Y**ou think of me as a *weapon*. I must admit that I am flattered.' The voice was rough as tree bark as it echoed round the courtyard.

Several Alder councillors peered out from under the table where they'd been hiding. What they saw was more than a vision. They looked at each other, bewildered, uncertain what they were seeing. Some made the sign of the Woodsman Cross: *Earth Over, Sky Under, Leaves to East and West.*

The object of their fear strode across the boards directly towards the king. Black petticoats flared out from within a cloak of Raven feathers. The woman was dark-skinned, wrinkled, her mass of black hair braided with the skulls of wood-mice and shrews. 'In fact,' the voice rasped, 'such a compliment almost makes me feel young again. Now, there is no time to waste.' The tone of her words changed, sharpening like the claws that extended from each of her fingers.

The king was transfixed by vivid green eyes as the figure bore down on him. Two more steps and she would easily be able to . . .

'Make another move and you're dead!' Broadbeam stood between the unknown stranger and the king. His sword was already drawn, hovering, ready to plunge into the woman's chest.

'Oh, how very droll. Dear Quercus, it appears that your loyal lapdog is willing to die in a vain attempt at chivalry.' She turned to face Broadbeam. 'Little man, I do suggest you lower your sword. Immediately.'

Commander Broadbeam frowned. Admittedly, the woman was dressed weirdly, and those sharp fingernails were worrying, but nothing a good dose of sharpened steel couldn't sort out.

'Oh dear! Is that what you think?' There was menace now in her words. She flicked her eyes upwards. Ark and Mucum watched with satisfaction as Broadbeam took a step back, recoiling in shock. She had read his thoughts.

'Now,' continued the woman, 'my faithful companion Hedd, son of Hedd, is hungry.' She pointed to the Raven that hovered above the battlements, a dark cloud threatening thunder and lightning-quick claws. 'Unless you wish to become dinner, I once again *suggest* you lower your sword. And to put your stupid Dendran worries to rest, I do assure you I have no intention of killing your king. There are far more important threats to worry about.'

Quercus mastered his trembling voice. 'Commander, do as she says.'

Broadbeam glared at the woman, doing his best to ignore the fear rising up his gullet. Only twenty feet above, the Raven gave a sharp screech that made the hairs on the back of his neck stand to attention. Could she really control this wild sky-stallion? But he'd seen with his own eyes how she had perched on the beast's back, knees clenched, mouth fierce with the joy of power as they'd dropped straight down towards the palace. The woman – if that was what she was – had leant forward into the wind as the bird swooped down on the courtyard, claws extended like springs to land briefly on the broad planks before shooting back up into the sky. In that split second, she'd slipped expertly off her charge to catch them all by surprise.

Broadbeam knew he had no choice. His sword was reluctantly returned to its sheath.

'Nice one, Corwenna!' Mucum gave her the thumbs-up.

Corwenna turned to see Mucum and Ark standing up to greet her. 'Master Gladioli! Good to see you. And Ark.' She paused, her voice softening. 'My Ark.'

Ark hung back. He felt torn. Part of him wanted to run towards Corwenna, to embrace her. But her face had already shifted, the eyes becoming cold and indifferent as she focused on the Dendrans in front of her.

The king spoke. 'I am sorry, but did I hear your name rightly? You are called Corwenna?' He shifted uneasily in his chair. 'And you come to my court on the back of a Raven?'

'Circus tricks!' Broadbeam muttered. 'And since when

were women allowed in court?'

Corwenna's arm straightened like a spear. Sharp finger-nails hooked themselves into the commander's chain mail and the man, who was built like a scaffield bull, found himself in mid-air, his legs dangling beneath him. She pulled the Commander of the Armouries towards her as if he was lighter than a tree bud. 'I am tempted to toss you over the edge for such insults.'

It was then that Broadbeam began to understand. Her sleeve had ridden up, revealing an arm with veins that stood out like vine tendrils. This old woman could easily hurl him over the battlements.

'Please. Please!' The king put his hands up in a gesture of peace. 'He means you no harm.'

'All right,' she said, uncurling her fingers and letting the commander drop like a sack of potatoes on to the wood. 'And to answer your question, Quercus – yes, I am Corwenna, of the Ravenwood. Queen of the Ravens.'

The Alder councillors were still half under the table, gaping. 'Corwenna? My lady!' one of them began hesi-tantly. 'We thought you were a . . .'

'Myth? A chilling legend? The stuff of dark far-tales? Yes. I read what is in your mind like the veins of be-leaf. And yet here I am, breathing the same air as you.'

'The formidable Raven-Queen goddess come to life!' one of the councillors murmured in awe. Arborium was full of old wood-way shrines dedicated to appeasing Corwenna: boxes lined with dried moss, containing crude Ravens fashioned from fallen twigs. Often these were set up at the sites of dreadful accidents. Cart-crashes where a life had been crushed beneath a massive iron wheel; slippery spots deep in the woods where a Dendran had lost his footing and fallen far from the safe canopy of the trees. The shrines sprang up to avert further terror at each spot.

'Call me what you will,' Corwenna answered. 'At least it shows respect for your origins. But it comes to a pretty pass when one of your males can speak of women with such disdain!' Broadbeam was still trembling all over as Corwenna pointed a long finger at him. 'Your kind worship Diana!' She flung her arms out to indicate the palace and the forest beyond. 'Was it not from a woman that all this came to be? You have forgotten your roots. Shame on you!'

She stalked round the courtyard while Hedd, son of Hedd spiralled down towards its far side. His huge wings spread to slow his descent for landing. There was a loud thump, and several councillors jumped as the boards shook beneath their feet. But Hedd was unconcerned by what mere Dendrans thought of his presence as he perched in the far corner of the courtyard, preening his glossy black feathers and waiting for his queen's command.

'There is a way to Maw,' Corwenna said, pulling out a scroll from the inside of her cloak. She strode towards the table and leant over, letting the scroll unfurl.

The king was curious. His fingers traced the signs and symbols on the map, following the arrows that pointed west. Small triangles symbolized mountains that he'd only ever dreamed of. Beyond, a wild forest was sketched in with one word at its centre, written in black ink: Ravenwood. But it was the edge of the map that took his interest. Arborium was an island, surrounded by heaving oceans. At its far western tip on the map was a small picture of a hole in the roots of the forest, followed by a straight line that crossed the waves and vanished off the edge of the scroll. His brow furrowed. 'I have a strange feeling that events are beyond my control here. In the last five minutes, I have had to come to terms with the fact that the Raven-Queen is flesh and blood. Now it appears that she has come to us armed with a plan. Am I right?'

Corwenna nodded. 'Quercus, Councillors, loyal soldiers, all of you. My Ravens fly far and see much. But the ocean that lies between us and Maw is too wide even for their great wings. There are smugglers' boats, of course, but they are slow and uncertain. We do not have the luxury of time. There is another way – and this map, drawn out by our Rootshooter friends, reveals it. It is a strange remnant of a long-ago empire, fast, though fraught with danger.'

Quercus lifted his fingers from the map to scratch his beard. 'And you propose we send my soldiers through this –'

'Tunnel?' Corwenna interrupted. 'No. Your soldiers will not do. Arktorious Malikum has already explained why.' Corwenna's long fingers snatched the map from the table and rolled it up. 'And now he is coming with me.' Her gaze rested on Ark.

He felt it once again, the heavy weight of expectation. Why couldn't he just go home and cuddle up with his little sister Shiv? But the Empire would not leave Arborium alone. It was greedy for wood. If he didn't act, his home – and all the homes that lay high up in the trees – would be gobbled up, gone. Ark knew he had no choice.

'Eh! Wot about me?' Mucum jumped in.

'And his loyal companion, of course,' Corwenna added.

Broadbeam raised his arm. 'But your majesty! How can you . . .'

The king cut him off. 'Oh, please shut up, Commander. I sometimes wonder why I promoted you.' He turned back to Corwenna. 'You are asking me to trust you?'

'Yes.' The Raven-Queen met his eyes as an equal. 'I am.'

'Good speech,' Mucum butted in. 'But if we're done wiv the words, I reckon we should get the flock outta here.' He pointed at Hedd, who was impatiently scratching the floor with his claws.

Corwenna nodded. The time for talking was done.

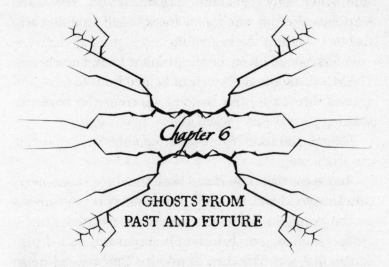

Chapter 6

GHOSTS FROM PAST AND FUTURE

Petronio was happy to let Flinty carry the former commander on his horse as they cantered over the boards and out of the city. He thought briefly of how his own father had tried to save him from the Raven in the Harvest Battle; the pathetic look on the councillor's face as he had reached out to his son. The timing had been almost beautiful. A helpful little shove from Petronio, and Grasp senior was snatched by the Raven instead. Without that act of self-preservation, it would have been Petronio rowing across the River Sticks to meet his death.

He pulled his cape closer round him. The day was bitter, the sun blotted by a covering of grey clouds. Riding with his new arm was difficult, but not impossible. The pincers that made up his right hand were remarkably sensitive, like servants under a king's command. If he thought *Open!* they snapped wide; *Close!* and they ground shut with a force that almost frightened him. How could a machine read his mind? And Fenestra had promised him that this was only the beginning . . .

A fork veered off to the left from the main branch-way. The wood itself was covered in lichen. Parasite ferns and grasses thrust up from the ruts, slowing the horses to walking pace as they picked their way through.

'Where you takin' us?' demanded Flinty.

'You'll see.'

And what they saw made horses and Dendrans nervous. The wood-way widened, rotten safety ropes flapping in the wind. In front of them lay a deserted hamlet. Houses with sagging balconies looked down on a distant square that was dark even at midday. They paused by an abandoned toll-house jutting out across the wood-way. Shutters slammed in the breeze, making the horses shy.

'I don't like the look of this,' Flinty muttered.

'And I don't care whether you like it,' Petronio countered. 'The point is that any good and holly Dendran will know well to avoid this place.' He pointed in at one of the toll-house windows. Flinty leant over the neck of his horse to peer in. The main room was quilted with cobwebs. There were cupboards filled with plates, sinks that had last seen water a hundred years ago and rotting beds that contained only resting shadows. Across the kitchen table two chairs faced each other, pulled back slightly as if the inhabitants had simply gone for a walk and would return at any minute.

'A plague on all your houses!' Petronio shouted.

'What?' Flinty turned his horse round. This place was

giving him the creeps, and the bloke with the metal arm was jabbering nonsense. Now that Flinty had his father and his gang around him, maybe it was time to get out.

'Something I read somewhere, a long time ago. If you knew the basics of science, and I'm sure you don't, then you'd know that the plague virus that killed these peasants is long gone. It is only superstition that survives.' Petronio wrinkled his nose in contempt. 'Now follow me.'

Flinty scowled but did as he was asked, urging his horse forward. Slowly he became aware of an odd sound, a distant buzzing. Then, as they moved towards the darkness filling the village square, his mouth fell open. The dark in front of him was not made of shadows, but metal. There was a creature – if it could be called that – squatting there like an enormous spider, jointed legs resting on the planks. It towered above them, its huge body emitting a humming sound, like bees but smoother. There was a grinding noise and a door appeared in its belly. White light shot out as a set of steps was lowered to the ground.

'Buddy Holly!' Flinty gasped, his hands trembling as he held the reins and tried to control his horse. His fears weren't helped by the sight of three figures descending the steps. They had arms and legs like Dendrans, but they were dressed from head to foot in white – even down to their shoes, their tight-fitting gloves and the masks that covered their faces.

One of them turned to Petronio. 'Is the patient ready?' The accent was strange, unwoodly.

'As ready as he'll ever be,' Petronio sighed. 'Do you think you can do this?'

'What do you take us for? It's a simple surgical procedure!'

Flinty and his gang stared, wide-eyed and silent, as they tried to take in not only the figures in white but the glimpse into the innards of the metal monster. Long tubes of glass, filled with light, threw a sickly sheen over the walls inside the creature, and there were racks of gleaming knives and strange metallic tools.

'I ain't letting my dad go in there!'

'Oh, for Diana's stupid sake!' Petronio growled. 'Your father's brain is currently no more functional than a scaffield turnip. I was an apprentice surgeon once, and my best advice based on Dendran knowledge would have been a course of blood-sucking leeches. Now, do you wish to hear your father's voice again?'

The hulking shape of Commander Flint slumped over the back of his son's horse like a side of meat. His only sound had been an occasional gurgle.

'But wot they gonna do to 'im?'

Petronio smiled. 'Why, rebuild . . . I mean *repair* him, of course!'

Flinty pointed at the figures poised on the white steps. 'And these buddy foreigners can do that?'

'Only one way to find out, isn't there?'

Flinty bit his bottom lip, thinking. He laid a hand on his father's huge shoulder and took in the lifeless weight of him. Finally, he gave a sharp nod. 'Stan, Daz. Sort it.' The commander's body was hauled off the back of the horse and dragged towards the men in white. Flinty spat on the ground. 'He's all yours. But if you mess up, you'll have us lot to deal with.'

Faced with a bunch of grimy-looking teenagers, dressed in black and armed only with knives, the lead surgeon almost laughed out loud. He could feel the shape of the g-gun concealed under his armpit. It would wipe out these barbarians instantly, though that would be against Fenestra's orders. 'Thanks a bunch!' he drawled. 'We're gonna make him good as new, I promise!'

Half an hour later and they were riding hard again, heading north. Rain had settled over the trees and the protection of summer's leaves was long gone. Petronio had managed the first two steps of the plan with ease. Now he hoped that Flinty's right-hand girl Stan was as good as her word. The meeting they rode towards was crucial.

It was mid-afternoon by the time they approached the spot she'd set up, an old abandoned scaffield not marked on any map. The rain had grown heavier, soaking them all and turning each hoof beat into a dull splash. There had been a few close calls on the now slick and greasy woodway. Though the horses were bred for these branches, there was no divine law that would prevent a missed step and the dangerous slide off the edge into oblivion.

They passed a couple of empty trunks, door frames bleached by wind and the seasons, sinking under a cloak of ivy. Ahead of them, the path narrowed, forcing the riders to slow and then stop.

'Are we nearly there?' Petronio asked.

Flinty nodded. 'The scaffield's a few 'undred yards down the way.'

'Then this is as far as you go,' said Petronio, as he swiftly dismounted and tied Mercury's reins to an overhanging branch. Water dripped off his cape. 'Is my safety guaranteed?'

Stan stared through the drizzle, trying to ignore the monstrosity that bulked out from Petronio's shoulder. 'That's funny, that is. Safety and my dad don't mix. But if yer want somethin' doing, Sergeant Grain and his mates will do it, fer a price. Oh, but a word of advice: when yer meet him, look him in the eye. His good eye.'

'What do you mean?' Petronio asked.

'You'll find out. And I'd watch out for his sidekick, too – Pontius. That one's a nutter. The story goes that he took down a Raven once. Even I wouldn't wanna meet 'im down a bark alley, if yer know what I mean?'

'No, I don't.' Petronio was impatient to get on. His pincers delved into his doublet and pulled out an obviously heavy purse. The arm flicked forward and the pincers clacked open, flinging the purse through the air.

Flinty caught it, felt the weight of it, opened the drawstring and peered inside. A frown furrowed his face. 'And wot about me father?'

'Oh. When he's ready ... when he's ... *well* again, I shall bring him to see you. That's a promise. But for now, take this gift as a gesture of the Empire's gratitude.'

Flinty's greed finally won over his doubts. 'Proper gold, that is. OK, you lot, we're done. Let's be off. Looks like a celebration tonight.'

'I'll let you know if you're needed again.' But even as Petronio spoke, the gang faded away into the drizzle, leaving behind only the soft jingle of harnesses. He was alone, the brambles criss-crossing the ancient path ahead of him. He picked his way carefully along for several minutes until he could see a door ahead of him, hanging by a single hinge. To his left and right, great walls of woven hazel led off into the distance, indicating the boundary of a giant scaffield.

These were the marvels of Arborium. Gigantic hundred-acre platforms, suspended between trunks and angled towards the south to soak up the sun. A thousand generations of ground-up Dendran bones and composted leaves had created the soil that grew the crops to feed the kingdom. But before Petronio could contemplate the engineering achievements of his ancestors, he felt a painful pricking in his back.

'What the . . . ?' he gasped.

'It's called a sword, sonny boy!' a voice rasped. 'And if I were you, I'd be sayin' a few prayers to Diana before it sticks into yer guts!'

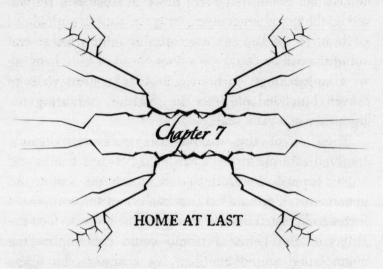

Chapter 7

HOME AT LAST

Ark paused on the branch-line. A settlement of shanty homes was strung between the branches all around him. It was a world away from the straight lines and perfect planking of Barkingham Palace: here, houses were bodged together from rough boards, treepaulin and reworked iron. Chimneys puffed away, filling the air with the scent of wood-smoke and pine resin. As the dusk came on, the gas-lighters set to work and the whole suburb, clinging to the skirts of a single tree, began to resemble a swarm of flickering fireflies.

He took a step off the safety of solid wood on to a thin, swaying ropewalk. The rope creaked, and somewhere nearby a pigeon squawked. In front of him rose a small, domed dwelling. The roof was made of treepaulin, the stitched-together harvest-leaves that kept out rain and wind. Truly, Diana gave her bounty. Once the leaves were tanned and oiled, they were more durable than leather and could be stretched over a lattice of bent twig poles.

He lifted the flap of the treepaulin and ducked down out of the cold.

'Arky-Parky!' A curly-haired little girl ran straight towards him and launched herself through the air, knocking him over.

'Shiv!' he cried. She was growing up too fast. 'How's my favourite sister?'

'I've got new socks!' She disentangled herself and pointed at the bright red socks on her feet. 'Quirky gave 'em!'

'Quercus,' Ark sighed.

'What I said! Quirky!' she giggled.

Ark looked round. The moth-eaten blankets had gone and the walls were now lined with sheepskin. There were logs in the basket, and the wood burner glowed in the corner, filling his home with a fuggy, welcoming warmth. Since the battle, the king had tried to insist on Ark and his family moving to court, but the Malikums had refused. This was home and it would do them fine. But Quercus had done his best to reward them: now there was enough food for them and all the other workers down here, deep within the canopy of the forest. Some of the injustices of the past were being swept away. It was a start.

'All right, son?' His father lay by the fire, looking perkier than he had in ages. Though he was still confined to bed with a muscle-wasting disease, proper medicine had helped clear up the cloudiness in his eyes, and regular meals had worked wonders.

'I'm not sure, Dad. I can't stay.'

'Off to see Her again?' Mr Malikum was still uncertain of Corwenna. A creature who could abandon two orphans in a wind-blown nest?

'I guess so . . .' Ark looked at his feet, trying to avoid his father's gaze. And he did still think of Mr Malikum as his father, the one who had brought him up, taught him the ropes.

'Ah, you've come a long way from being the plumber's lad who first came to work with me. Remember that first toilet job?'

'Oh please, Dad, not that old chestnut.'

'I gave you a spanner and you got a bit too enthusiastic. The look on your face as the fountain of squit sprayed all over you!' Mr Malikum began laughing and ended up coughing.

A curtain was drawn aside and a figure bustled in. 'Now look what you've done, young Arktorious. Once you get your father laughing, see what happens?' Mrs Malikum was carrying a steaming pot. 'Now wash your hands in the basin and let's see if we can fill that skinny frame of yours . . .'

'Mum,' Ark interrupted. 'I haven't got time.' He gently took the pot away from her and laid it on the table. 'I need to leave.'

She put her hands on her hips and stared at him. 'Leave? You've only just arrived!'

'I know.' Ark couldn't meet his mother's eyes. How could he explain to her that he had no choice? The battle they'd won back in the autumn had only been the beginning.

Mrs Malikum was still wearing the same third-hand dress she'd had for years. The king's finery was not for her, although Ark noticed that she'd hidden her grey hair well with red rowanberry dye. And the scent that clung to her skin was surely oil of roses, which could only be a gift from the king.

'I suppose you're going to see your feathered friends.' Even though the Ravens had saved Arborium, she would not have the Ravenwood mentioned by name in her household. She could not bear to think of the danger her boy went into, or who it was he saw there.

Ark took her by the shoulders and bent to embrace her. 'You know this will always be my home. And you shall always be my mother.'

But her lips were pursed. 'That's that, then. A fine rabbit stew gone to waste! And where are you off to now? Do you intend to take on the Empire single-handed?'

'Of course not. But we do have to find out what they're planning. And the only way is to . . . go there.'

'Go there?' It was too much. Mrs Malikum pushed Ark away and threw her arms in the air. 'But you're only a boy!'

'Calm down, my love!' Mr Malikum grunted. 'There's bristle on his chin, and what's more, there's heartwood in his soul. Diana has looked after him this far. Without our boy, the country would have been lost.'

Mrs Malikum allowed herself a tiny proud smile through her tears. 'Hmmm . . .' she said, fiddling with her fingers.

Shiv sensed that something was going on. She clung on

to Ark's legs. 'I won't let you go! Not never!' she cried.

'I know, little Shiv, I know.' He remembered the cruck-pool. If he'd let the birchweed take him, all this would have been lost.

'Will you take nothing from us?' his mother demanded.

'Only your blessing, if you'll give it to me.'

Mrs Malikum reached up and kissed his forehead. What had happened to the fourteen-year-old sewage worker of a few months ago? 'Diana speed you, my son!' she whispered in his ear.

'And give 'em all holly!' his father said, raising his cap in salute.

Shiv wailed as Ark retreated towards the door flap. He felt a terrible longing as he uncurled her tiny fingers and gently pushed her away. 'I'll come back soon, I promise.' It was a lie. The Empire was more dangerous than a den of wolf spiders. There was no guarantee of return.

As he stumbled along the ropewalk, his last sight of home was Shiv's tear-stained face pressed against the resin window and her big eyes watching her brother vanishing into the dusk.

'Oi!' The voice from the shadows startled Ark. Consider-ing the size of him, Mucum could move as quietly as a knot-mouse when he needed to.

'Do you actually *want* me to go off the edge?'

'Nah. Just keepin' you on yer toes, mate.' Mucum joined Ark on the wood-way. 'How'd it go?'

'Fine,' said Ark. What other answer could he give?

'Where is he?' Night was always the perfect disguise for the Ravens, though it could not hide the familiar foul stench of carrion.

'I thought you woz the one with the oakus-crocus powers. Use yer eyes!'

In front of them, the wood-way widened, but the path was blocked. Something large stirred in the darkness.

'Ah!' said Ark. He never knew whether to speak aloud to the mighty beasts or whether to let them read his thoughts, as he could read theirs. 'Greetings, Hedd, son of Hedd.' His voice rang clearly, more for Mucum's benefit than the bird's. There was no answer except for a slight shuffling of feathers, but now the darkness took on shape. A massive beak, catching the glint of a far-off gas lamp; the feathered bulk brooding as it perched on the wood-way. Earlier that day Hedd had flown off with Corwenna while Ark was left to say his goodbyes to his family. Now he was back to transport Ark and Mucum to the Ravenwood.

Mucum cleared his throat. 'Got some news fer you, though it don't make sense.'

'Go on.'

'Commander Flint – well, the brain-dead bloke that woz the commander – someone surprised the guards and freed 'im, early hours of this mornin'. Afternoon shift only found out on swap-over.'

Ark felt troubled, remembering what he'd done to break the commander's will. 'But why?'

'Dunno. But it's not like he's gonna be doin' any traitor stuff again, not in his state. Anyway, time to skedaddle.'

'I guess so.' Ark was still thinking. What possible threat could the former commander be? He was no more than a shell of his former self. He shrugged his shoulders; it was a puzzle, but there was no time to think about it now. 'OK. Let's go. Now, what do you say, Mucum?'

'Oh, not again. Do I 'ave to?'

Hedd, son of Hedd fixed him with a beady glare that implied it would be easy to rip out Mucum's throat with a single claw-swipe.

'Oh, all right then.' Mucum addressed himself to the massive Raven. 'We woz wonderin' – me and Arktorious 'ere, that is – wevver you fancy takin' us back to your pad?'

The bird didn't move. It cocked its beak to one side, a single black eye drilling into Mucum.

Ark was amused. 'Trust me, even the birds of the Ravenwood know the magic word, which you appear to have forgotten.'

'Magic word? Oh, give me a break!' He sighed and turned back to Hedd. 'Please . . .' he finally grumbled.

It worked. A wing flicked out to rest on the wood-way, giving the boys easy access to scramble aboard. Ark sat in front, his knees comfortably wedged round Hedd's back. Without waiting to see if they were holding on tight, the Raven flapped once, twice, three times. The downdraught created by the huge wings bent back the nearest branches and lifted the bird out of the woods and up into the evening sky.

'Whoa!' shouted Mucum, holding on to his mate for dear life. 'Never gonna get used ter this!' But even he felt exhilarated as the stars spread out above them and the bare tree-tops of Arborium glided past below. Soon the lights of the city were left behind, and there was only a freezing wind blurring their eyes as they headed west towards the mountains and the Ravenwood.

Ark felt Hedd's heart beating deep inside his magnificent breast, the warm blood coursing through his body, the homesickness that drew the Raven back towards his brethren like a surging arrow. How long it seemed since another Hedd had carried a frightened boy towards an unknown future. Ark frowned. The Ravenwood had been terrifying, yes. In the end, it had been the making of him, and yet the thought of returning to that dark heart of the woods still filled him with uneasy anticipation.

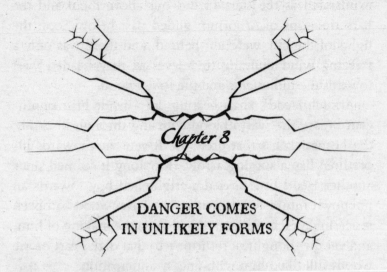

Chapter 8

DANGER COMES IN UNLIKELY FORMS

From behind, the point of the sword pressed hard into Petronio's back, the sharpened iron tip slicing through his padded jacket and his white woollen shift.

Petronio was more amazed than frightened. The path was littered with the detritus of the forest, but he hadn't heard a thing, no snap of twig nor tell-tale crump of leaf.

'Strangers are not welcome round 'ere.' The sword cut lightly into skin to make its point. 'Specially not fat, spying runts.'

Petronio felt a trickle of blood down the inside of his shift. Annoying. Getting bloodstains out of wool wasn't an easy job.

'If you're the best the king can send, then this country is going to the logs. Any last requests before I skewer you?'

'Yes.' Petronio spoke slowly, almost whispering the

words as the blade threatened to push deeper. 'Take . . . me . . . seriously.'

'Oh. Ha buddy ha!' But the man's laugh was cut short as Petronio suddenly lunged forwards. It was a perfect move. The soldier was caught off balance and he too toppled forwards, though with a lopsided grin on his scarred face. The silly boy was making it even easier for him. Now, with his sword following through, he could impale the spy face down on the wood-way and leave him to wriggle like a moth on a pin.

But Petronio had already twisted away from the sword in a sideways movement, and as he did so, he sent out the signal to his new arm, to the minute gears and levers that were primed to respond to his thoughts. He felt the thrill of adrenalin course through his body like the strange electricity of Maw. Even for a prototype, the surgeon's creation was impressive: the arm had a life of its own, moving far faster than flesh and blood.

Petronio turned back to face the man. Pincers sped through the dusk, straight towards the sword, grabbing it expertly midway up the shaft. He concentrated, watching in fascination as his new contraption ripped the sword from the soldier's grasp, almost taking a couple of fingers with it. But it was not enough. The man must be shown who was boss. *Break!* he thought. And his bidding was done as the pincers treated forged iron like a sheet of paper. The sword was crumpled up and tossed on to the wood-way between them.

There was a stunned silence. Petronio rose to his feet and dusted himself off. 'I did say you should take me seriously.' He loomed over the soldier, who was backing away on all fours like a beetle, nervously eyeing the arm.

'Wot kinda monster are you?'

'One who has been through the wars and survived. Surely you, who have fought all your life, would understand?' He could smell the man's fear, see the sweat soaking through his padded undercote. The chain mail covering the upper part of his body was rusty. If this was the best the Armouries had to offer, the plan was in big trouble, thought Petronio. Then again, the man had managed to creep up on him in utter silence . . . 'Come,' he continued. 'I am here for the meeting. It would not do to keep your master waiting.'

The soldier scrabbled to his feet, flexing his fingers to see if they still worked. 'Right. I knew that. But I 'ad to make sure.'

'Of course you did. No harm done, eh?' Petronio smiled.

'Suppose I'd better show you in, then.' The man kept his distance as they picked their way through scratchy brambles towards the door.

The abandoned archway into the scaffield revealed two more men, with swords drawn, skulking in the thick grass. The three soldiers now formed an escort, tightly bunched round the boy their leader had said was to be treated 'carefully'. A path had been trodden through, weaving around a strange mix of small trees that had taken root in the shallow compost of the scaffields: silver birch and sycamore, plus wrinkled fruit trees, their pears and apples long eaten by the wasps. Much of the old infrastructure of Arborium had been abandoned when the population had shrunk with each wave of the dark plague centuries ago. This scaffield, once a place of produce, was now a forest within a forest.

At its heart, in a recently-cut clearing, stood Sergeant Grain, Stan's father, with a group of men. His breastplate was also rusty, his hose stockings torn and beginning to sag. But the face was in even worse repair. One eye was moon-pale, with a jagged scar running from the deformed lid all the way round to a cauliflower ear. The other eye swivelled round to fix on Petronio.

'What you looking at? Something wrong with my face?'

One of the men stepped forward threateningly. Big was not the word: this Dendran was a towering tree trunk. All eyes swivelled to fix on him as he cracked each of his knuckles in turn with a sound like dry leaves crunching. The sword at his side looked almost tiny, and the meaty hands that were clenched and ready looked quite capable of pounding Petronio's flesh into jelly.

'Easy now, Pontius,' said the sergeant, raising his arm. 'Let the boy answer.'

A low, dissatisfied rumble issued from the giant's chest and he stepped sullenly back. An uneasy silence fell. Petronio, remembering Stan's words, wondered if the brutish Pontius really had dealt with a Raven. He wouldn't be surprised. And why did he keep staring at him like that? It was unnerving.

But it was the sergeant he was here to deal with. Petronio swallowed and willed himself to look the leader in his one good eye. 'No. Nothing at all.'

A knife appeared in the sergeant's hand. The blade was as rough as his pock-marked face. 'Good, 'cos it's the only face I got. And if yer don't like it, I'd happily stick this knife so far up yer insides you could use it to cut yer curly-wurly beard.'

Petronio got the message. Even with his arm, he was outnumbered. Better to stay polite. 'Sorry.' The word felt wrong in his mouth.

The blade vanished. 'Nuffin' to apologize for, we're all friends 'ere. Eh, lads?' Several of the men grunted. 'After all, he's a walking pay-day, I do believe! With attached codpiece!' The leader's words had the desired effect as a ripple of laughter passed through the assembled group. Only Pontius stayed silent, his eyes still staring at Petronio with menace. 'Though I'm not so sure about that thing that's sprouting from your shoulder,' the sergeant continued. 'Does it live?'

Petronio considered the question, allowing the pincers to move slowly apart. 'Only when I want it to.' He sensed some of the men fingering the hilts of their swords, staring at him as if he were some foul creature from deep within the roots.

'Ah, I think I am growin' to like our young man. He's certainly got guts.' The tight mouth of Sergeant Grain sharpened to a grin. 'But before we come to business, our guest has been travellin' hard. Care for a drink?'

The soldiers parted, making way for Petronio to step forward. When his father was alive he had made the occasional condescending comment about allowing the 'young lad' a goblet of watered-down wine with his dinner. But the stone cup that was passed to him now contained a whole season in every gulp. Pressed apples, fermented and quenching his thirst, filling his belly with warmth. He drank deep and passed back the cup. 'My thanks.'

'It's not thanks we're after, mate. Go on, then.' Grain was waiting. Ten heads leant forward, wondering if the message that Stan had passed on would be backed up by hard and shining evidence.

Petronio obliged. 'I have what has been agreed upon.' He reached down to his belt.

In a flash Pontius was on him. 'Stop!' he boomed, gripping Petronio so hard that the boy almost passed out with the pain. But as the giant tore open the bag to make sure it contained no hidden weapons, he grunted in amazement. It was true . . . the bag contained nothing more than pure, unadulterated bribery. The small golden ingots spilled over the trampled grass, convincing all present that the cause of Maw was righteous.

'Very good!' said Grain, as his eyes feasted on the sight of such ripe fruit. He turned to Pontius. 'Down, boy! Down! You must forgive my bodyguard,' he said to Petronio. 'Ever since his little girl caught fever and died, he tends to be a bit irritable.'

It was on the tip of Petronio's tongue to say he didn't give a damn if the soldier holding him in a vice-like grip had lost his precious daughter, but he thought better of it. The giant Dendran stepped away and Petronio was free, though he could already feel tender bruises where each of

Pontius's fingers had dug in. However, Fenestra's lessons had been thorough; the sight of gold worked magic. First Flinty and now the former followers of the commander: they all sold their loyalty like sap-soap.

The sergeant did not stoop to pick up the ingots, but let them lie there catching the last of the light. He scratched the scar on his cheek before speaking. 'I'm a little bit concerned 'ere. Most of the lads who followed Julius Flint are either dead or whiling their lives away in squitty root-dungeons.' He glared at the woods around him. 'What if you're no more than a trick, sent by Quercus to sniff out traitors? You could be double-crossing us.'

'Even if I was,' Petronio countered, 'do you think I'd be willing to cut off my own arm to fool you?' He sighed. 'I did think it might take more than mere gold to convince you though.' He clicked his fingers and the trees behind them suddenly rustled.

Every shabbily-dressed soldier transformed into an instinctive animal, swivelling round to kneeling position as bows were heaved over backs, strings pulled taut and eight deadly arrows trained on the undergrowth. Pontius bared his teeth like an animal, his throwing knife poised and ready for flight.

'Reveal yourself!' barked the sergeant.

In the shadows of dusk, only silence.

Grain flashed a look of anger back at Petronio. 'When I've finished with you, your flesh will be mince for my huntin' dogs.' He turned to the others.

'Men!' he ordered. 'At my command!'

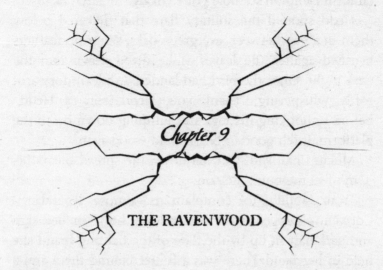

THE RAVENWOOD

Ark and Mucum were in luck: the wind that usually swirled round the great wall of mountains in the far west of Arborium was absent. All the same, they felt as if they would freeze as they burrowed ever deeper into the feathers on Hedd's back. Hedd had darted high over the sharp white summits with ease, giving a squawk of triumph as they left one land behind to descend safely into another.

The trees they coasted towards now were different. Even though Ark had been here many times now, these trees never ceased to startle him. Below them there were no straight, rearing trunks. Branches did not stick out at right angles, making them easy to carve and splice into the high wood-ways that criss-crossed Arborium. Instead, the Ravenwood spread out beneath them in a tangle of twisted trunks. It was the original wild-wood, like a childish Dendran scribble gone wrong.

Hedd spotted the solitary flare that flickered below them in a gap between evergreen oaks. Wing-tip feathers brushed against the leaves as he dived down into the dark night. Once the bird had landed, Ark leant forward, softly whispering, 'Thank you, Hedd, son of Hedd,' before unhooking his legs and jumping down on to the platform. It felt good to be on solid wood again.

Mucum half slid, half fell down the spread-out wing. 'Can't feel me bum!' he said.

'Your ability to complain is almost legendary!' Corwenna stepped from the shadows, her wrinkled skin and dark hair lit up by the flare of the flaming brand she held in her hand. There was a flutter behind them and a sudden gust of wind. Hedd was gone, called by his bird brethren to roost and rest.

Corwenna stared at Ark and nodded. 'I see you survived the journey.' Her voice was chilly, an echo of the gnarled icicles that hung from the branches around them. Ark nodded, feeling the ache in his back and bones after the long flight. So much for welcome.

'Of course you are welcome!' Corwenna snapped. It unnerved Ark every time, the way his mind was as open to her as a cracked shell, with every thought exposed to be picked over by her long, sharp nails.

'Perhaps when you were born,' she continued, 'I should have given you a skin of feathers, hmmm?' She crooked her finger. 'Come.'

The wood-way they stood on twisted and curled its way towards the nearest trunk, and was filled with gaps where knots had rotted away. A single false step could snap an ankle. Corwenna strode ahead of them, the light from her brand bobbing away into the dark as Mucum and Ark picked their way slowly behind. Ark knew that the lack of safety ropes should not bother him – if he relaxed and trusted his body, then walking the Ravenwood should be no different to home – but it was easier said than done.

The branch grew wider and ahead of them a door opened, spilling its welcome light towards them.

'Eurghhh!' Ark cried. 'My foot!' His rubber-soled shoe was stuck fast to the wood. Spread over it, and inching up his leg with a slight scratching noise, was a three-foot-long mass of brown fuzzy fur. 'Help!' Ark's voice was a high-pitched whine.

Mucum burst out laughing. 'Honestly, Malikum, considering you faced a buddy mealworm, you don't half make a song and dance sometimes.'

'But it's creeping up my leg and it's . . .'

'Gonna eat you?' Mucum bent down and began to stroke one end of the animal. Admittedly, it was difficult to tell which end was the head, but he must have got it right as the creature began to vibrate.

Despite Ark's horror, an image popped into his head of one of the many wildcats that roamed Hellebore. Some of the tamer ones liked nothing more than a saucer of scaffield milk and a good scratch behind their tufted ears. And now this creature appeared to be making a similar noise.

'Is it . . . purring?'

'Course it is! Good to hear the Malikum brain's workin' again!'

Slowly the caterpillar disentangled its hundreds of tiny legs and shuffled back down Ark's body towards the path. 'You're a lovely little thingy-wingy, ain't yer?' Mucum crooned as he stepped aside to let the creature shuffle away.

'Thingy-wingy?' Ark shook himself all over.

'Well, what do you want me to call it, the Dendran-munchin' Killer Caterpillar? Nah, me dad used to breed 'em fer their fur. Gorgeous coats for the rich gits – and I tell yer what, they cut up real nice in a stew!'

'I couldn't eat that!' Ark was horrified.

'Them legs are pretty good fried in walnut oil, nice 'n' crunchy.' Mucum licked his lips as the creature curled over the edge of the wood-way and vanished. 'G'night Mr Tasty-toes!'

As they reached the doorway, a blast of warmth met them.

'Shut the door! The winter would suck the very life from us, if it had its way!' Corwenna motioned them towards the fire. The hollowed-out room was cosy rather than grand, but the furnishings revealed how Corwenna lived. Jewels and baubles, stolen and given as gifts by her Ravens, were stuffed into nooks and crannies. The chair she sat in was covered in a throw of black velvet lined with fox fur. Fine tapestries hung from the walls, keeping out the draughts that edged in through splits in the bark. In one of them, Ark noticed, a woman with bright silver hair bent her archer's bow, crouching on a crude wood-way as a tiny golden arrow shot through the air and into the heart of a timber stag. Red thread burst from the stag's breast, representing its life-blood draining away.

'Is that . . . ?'

'Diana, the huntress. Mother of us all. Yes. And if she could see the monster that Maw has become, she would fight her way back from the Land of the Dead to stand alongside us!' The coldness had finally left Corwenna's voice; and was that the hint of tears in her eyes?

'I believe you,' Ark said, trying to pretend he hadn't seen her quickly wipe her face with the hem of her cloak.

'Sorry to butt in here, yer maj, but I'm starvin'!'

'No. I'm the one who should apologize. Words and history will not fill your stomachs.' A pot bubbled away over the fire, and a delicious smell drifted towards their noses. 'And before you worry even more, young Arktorious, I promise there are no caterpillars being boiled alive in there!' She winked at Mucum.

As Corwenna stirred the pot, she hummed an old children's song. 'We're going on a boar-hunt! We're going to catch a big one! We're not scared . . .'

Fifteen minutes later, the spicy meat-filled stew had warmed them both from the inside out. Mucum wiped his lips with his hands and gave a satisfied belch. There was a comforting smell of burning pine cones, and a slight swaying motion as the tree gave way to the winter winds. Here they were safe, wrapped up in a blanket of bark. Ark felt his eyelids grow heavy.

'Yes. Here is safe sanctuary. But if Maw has her way, it will not be so for long.' Her eyes fixed themselves on Ark.

'So once again I must let you go . . . though I shall not let you enter the enemy's lair without weapons and subterfuge.'

Mucum's ears pricked up. 'Now yer talkin'! Though I got no idea what yer mean by *sub-ter-fog*. Anyways, I 'ope yer got somefin' good fer us.'

Corwenna's face grew stern. 'Your Holly Woodsmen say that patience is a virtue. Such pomposity does annoy me sometimes. However, on this occasion they are right.'

'Yer mean we gotta wait?' Mucum whined. 'But I wanna see what you goddess-types can come up wiv! It's gotta be good stuff if it's gonna beat them Maw-ish guns.'

'How interestingly you put it. It is good *stuff*. The Ravens provide, and the trees that bore us all have their own potent gifts.' Corwenna paused. 'But the hour is late, and it's time for bed.'

'No it ain't! We gotta get going. Fings to do, world to be saved and all that ma-*larch*-y. I'm ready, me.' But even as he said it, a yawn escaped from his lips.

'Exactly,' said Corwenna. 'The day has been long enough. All shall be revealed in the morning.' She led them to their room, where two beds were prepared with feather quilts. A single candle flickered in a carved recess and a zinc basin of root-water shimmered underneath it.

'But . . .' Mucum tried to carry on even as he found himself flopping down on the bed.

'But nothing.' Corwenna's voice was hypnotic, compelling both boys to crawl under their quilts. 'Sleep now, for tomorrow the journey begins.' She blew out the candle and closed the door quietly behind them.

As Ark drifted off, his hands sought out the phial around his neck: a weapon of the trees. Corwenna had described it as a 'dark gift' when she had first given it to him, fetched by the first Hedd from the edge of the Land of the Dead. Ark had not discovered its true nature until the final confrontation with Petronio when he had used it to turn his enemy's arm to wood. Even now, he could feel the slight pulse of what the phial contained: the living essence of every Arborian tree. But what good would it do against the might of millions? And did Corwenna really have any other weapons that could take on the might of Maw? What trickery did she have up her feather-lined sleeve? Broadbeam had said the odds weren't brilliant . . .

But before he could think about it any more, sleep finally took him after a day that had begun with a king in his palace and ended with a queen in a twisted wood.

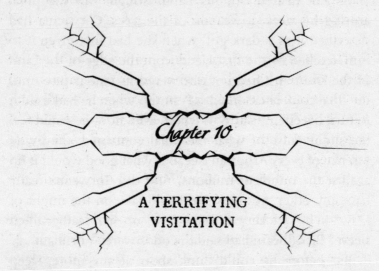

Chapter 10

A TERRIFYING VISITATION

'Would you . . . would you . . . would you . . .' The words emanated from the undergrowth, repeating themselves over and over.

Sergeant Grain felt the first flicker of doubt. Why would the enemy give their location away like this? The command to fire waited on his lips as eight taut bows swivelled towards the unseen target. Whatever lay out there was about to be slaughtered. But the voice was . . . what *was* it?

He shook his head. 'Hold!' he hissed to his men. 'And that includes you, Pontius!'

A frown crossed the soldier's face – attacking was what he did best, but the boss was the boss. The rest of the men also did as they were told, despite the ache in their arms, the itchiness in their fingers.

The voice continued. 'Would you . . . tell your men to

put their weapons doon . . . down!' The mistake felt glaringly obvious to Petronio. He wondered if they would notice.

Then a figure emerged. The bronze breastplate had been polished, though the grey velvet surcote was torn and the black boots had holes in them where wood-mice had chewed the leather away. The broad face was clean-shaven, and Grain would have known that kinked nose anywhere.

'Damn and Diana!' Grain spat on the wood. 'We thought you was gone to the logs!'

Commander Flint's eyes darted round in their sockets before finally focusing on the sergeant. 'I was . . . I was . . .' The commander bent his head to one side as if trying to shake an earwig out of his ear. 'I was not myself.'

'Yer can say that again.' Grain hadn't risked visiting, but every one of his men knew that Flint was a drooling mess. Now, the sergeant felt uneasy. The commander that stood in front of them, swaying slightly from side to side, was more bone than muscle, a gaunt shell of the man who had inspired them to risk everything for the takeover coup, to get rid of the king and earn themselves unimaginable wealth and power. Grain had been one of the lucky ones, tasked with staying behind in the Armouries to help take command once the coup had been successful. Instead, Flint's men had been taken out by a bunch of kids and Rootshooters.

'But 'ow did yer get out?'

'I had . . . help.' The eyes flicked over briefly towards Petronio.

'And you're – OK?'

'Never felt . . . never felt better.' Flint breathed heavily, each word an effort.

Petronio was glad he was no longer the centre of attention. Flint's entrance had been perfect. It had been a gamble, but it appeared that the surgeons had come up trumps – though he found the voice worrying, with the odd word standing out too obviously. Did the surgeons think this was all some kind of game? But all that mattered was for Grain and his stooges to believe in Flint. After that, anything was possible.

'Bring me a . . . torch . . . I mean, lantern.' Each time Flint spoke, his voice grew stronger.

Grain felt old reflexes spring into action. 'Yes, sir.' He turned to his men. 'What are you starin' at? He's the gaffer, right? Put yer bows down and sort out some light.' Lanterns were quickly lit and hung from nearby branches. 'Are yer hungry, sir? Me men can sort you some rations – squirrel jerky and some nuts?'

'Are you . . . kidding me? I wouldn't eat that trash if you paid me!' the commander squealed.

Petronio bit his lip. What the holly did the surgeon think he was up to? His eyes scanned the shadows behind the commander. All it would take would be for one curious soldier to root around in the bushes and their ruse would be uncovered.

'Righto . . .' said Grain, frowning. 'Squirrel used to be yer favourite, 'specially the pickled eyeballs. Yer used to crunch 'em up like gobstoppers.'

'I'm . . . I'm sorry,' said the commander. 'I am still . . .

recovering after what that boy Malikum did to me . . .'

'Yeah, well . . .'

The lanterns revealed more than bare straggly trees and wilted nettles: by the commander's side was a shining silver case with a black handle. He now bent to pick it up and stepped forward into the circle of pale light. His movements were clumsy and awkward. He laid the case flat on the ground and fumbled with the catch. 'The boy is right,' he said, as the lid opened smoothly. 'Mere gold alone will not convince you. Perhaps this . . . will.'

Nine faces leant forward, eager to catch sight of what lay within. Only Grain held back, looking round the abandoned scaffield as the early evening stars flicked on one by one. He stared at Petronio.

Petronio kept his face neutral. He knew that ultimately both he and Grain wanted the same result, so theoretically they were on the same side. But underneath those twisted scars, Petronio knew that Grain was no fool.

''Ere! Look at this, Sarge!'

Grain turned to view the contents of the case. Ten glittering balls lay nestled in a soft bed of some grey substance. The balls were each the size of a Dendran fist. They appeared to be made of black glass, reflecting back the flickering lantern flames and the looming faces of the soldiers.

'And?' said Grain. 'We've all got balls. Otherwise we wouldn't be 'ere.'

A few of the men tittered nervously. But they all felt it: there was something wrong about the case, its smooth lines out of place somehow compared to the rough bark all around.

'Very . . . funny,' the commander replied. 'To answer your question, this is what the science of Maw can offer. The size of them should not fool you: this . . . is . . . a deadly weapon.' He had most of them now. For Dendrans, accustomed to swords, the case seemed to contain black secrets. 'If each of these spheres is placed in a particular geographic location, the Quantum Trap can be sprung. In three days' time, at the Winter Solstice, when every super-stitious Dendran steps outside and makes his way to Hellebore to gawp at the moon being cut from the sky, the button will be pressed.'

'Button? What's a button got to do with anything? I got one of them on me tunic . . .' the sergeant growled.

'Oh, you people are so . . . forgive me, I forget myself again. Not that kind of button, trust me. Once the energy of the spheres is . . . woken up, activated, every Dendran within a mile's radius of each sphere will be rendered . . . ah, unconscious.'

Petronio tried to hide the smile that played round his lips. *Unconscious?* So that was the way they wanted to play it. It made sense. Even battle-hardened soldiers might blanch at the idea of outright massacre.

'How do we know it's gonna work? And more to the point, apart from the gold, what do we get out of it? And is there any danger to us?' Grain voiced the doubts of all of them.

Commander Flint responded by gently easing one of the spheres from its bed of foam. It gave off a faint humming sound, as if a hive of bees was hidden within. He cradled it in his hand. 'Oh, it will work. And what you get will be power. No more cold rations and worn-out clothes in the freezing Armouries. After all, Maw will need trained natives to help run the colony of Arborium. You shall be lords of the forest.'

'Sounds good to me!' said one of the soldiers.

'Shut yer gob!' Grain hissed.

'As for the weapon,' the commander continued, 'shall we see what it can do?' He suddenly pitched the ball high into the air. Ten pairs of eyes followed its trajectory fearfully and even Grain flinched, wondering what would happen if this Maw-made destroyer shattered on impact.

The commander's other hand uncurled and shot out to catch the ball as it descended. For a moment, no-one breathed. It was masterfully done. 'On the other hand, perhaps it's best not to experiment, do you think?'

Grain tried to ignore the trickle of sweat down his back. He was finding it hard to think straight: a leader back from the living dead, a softy southerner with a smirk on his face, and now this game. He watched as the sphere was replaced and the case snapped shut, then closed his eyes and breathed deeply, remembering former times. Flint was his superior. *If in doubt, follow orders.*

'All right. What next, sir?'

'Good. I entrust you with the case. Tucked inside you will also find ten pairs of eye goggles. You will each need one of these clever devices at the right time to cause each sphere to begin its work. A word of warning though: each glass weapon is filled with delicate insides. It's called circuitry, and under no circumstances must you let it come into contact with water.'

'What the holly is *sir-ki-tree*?' asked one of the soldiers.

'Never you mind. It's Maw-made. That's all you need to know.

'You still haven't answered the question about danger to us,' Grain pointed out.

'Ah, yes. Your, er . . . goggles. That's it, the goggles will also protect you. Now leave us, I have matters to discuss with my s—'

Petronio could hear the word almost before it was out. *Servant*. He was fuming. Buddy surgeons! Who did they think they were? He was no-one's *servant*. How dare they?

'I have matters to discuss with my . . . young friend here. Go about your work, and do not breathe a word of this. A map will be given to you, showing you where the spheres are to be placed in a ring round the city. You will receive precise instructions when we return with the final part of the weapon.'

Petronio was beginning to feel the plan might work. It would have been easier to use Mawish soldiers, but they didn't know these woods. The natural gas that the trees gave off would quickly prove fatal to outsiders who were not inoculated, and since the Harvest Battle, stocks of vaccine were running low. The help of the Armoury rebels was therefore vital to the plan.

'Right, lads!' Grain barked. 'You heard him. We're outta here.' He took the case himself. It was surprisingly light. Part of him felt like throwing it over the edge, but instead he passed it over to Pontius to carry. They filed along the muddy path and away into the night, leaving a couple of lanterns behind.

Petronio and the commander waited in silence. A few minutes passed. 'Are they gone?' said the commander.

'Yes.' Petronio crossed his arms in impatience. 'You can drop the act now.'

The commander's mouth immediately closed; the body was suddenly stock still.

Petronio walked forward, clicking his fingers. 'Hello. Anyone at home?'

Flint gave no response. His eyes became unfocused, returning to the blank stare of a madman.

Petronio peered around the back of the commander and saw a figure amble out of the darkness. His white clothes contrasted with the mottled browns of the bare bark and dead grass around them. He held a small black box with a metal wire sticking out like a sky-hornet's stinging tail.

'How cool was that? Bringing a vegetable to life. That's what I call technology!'

'You stupid little stick! If Lady Fenestra was here she'd rip your clever tongue right out by its roots!'

'Whoa there, boy. You're getting too big for your boots. I was only warming up! It's one thing remote-controlling a sky-skimmer back home in Maw, but running the software on this big brute of a Dendran was hard work.' The surgeon-programmer reached up and pinched Flint's cheek. There was no reaction. 'Admit it. I've done good. The name's Al, by the way.'

'Well listen up, Al. You fooled them, but Grain was

suspicious. Next time, less talk, more action. And perhaps I need to give you some Dendran language lessons.'

'Whatever.' The man shrugged.

Petronio suppressed a sudden shudder. The body next to him had as much life in it as a plank. 'Where is Commander Flint now? What happened to his . . .'

'His what? His soul? His spirit? I didn't know you believed in all that old-fashioned stuff!'

'I don't,' Petronio answered gruffly. Diana's prayers were best left to dumb Dendrans who didn't know any better. But still . . .

'Good. I tell you, his brain was soft as jelly when we scooped out a great chunk of it with our scalpels. Of course, we left enough behind to keep his body functioning, otherwise he wouldn't be breathing. But you'd hardly believe the technology we managed to pack in there.' Al tapped Flint's forehead.

Petronio felt queasy. He changed the subject. 'Right. What next? I assume our transport is ready?'

'Yup. The envoy's been buzzing me every half hour. She wants us back in Maw.'

'Good. I'm cold and hungry and I've forgotten when I last slept. Get your men to put Flint in hibernation for later use. Let's go.' Petronio brushed past the empty shell that had once housed Commander Flint.

It was time to return to the place he was beginning to think of as home. To Maw.

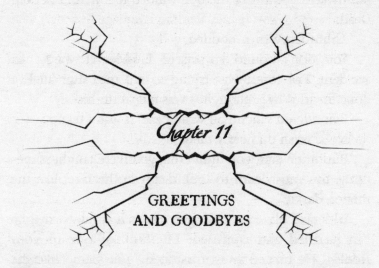

Chapter 11

GREETINGS
AND GOODBYES

Ark felt a pressure on his arm. His eyelids flickered open. The other bed contained only a crumpled quilt; Mucum must have woken already. There wasn't much light in the room, but he could still see the vivid green eyes staring down at him. He and Corwenna had the same eyes, but they were so different in so many other ways.

'How did you sleep?' The voice was surprisingly soft.

'Well, thank you.' He tried to shake off his grogginess. The feather-filled mattress was soft and Corwenna's hand felt warm on his arm. He wanted it to stay there, but then the question that had been haunting him came back.

'The night before last, I went for a swim.'

'And?'

'I don't know . . . perhaps I tripped over, but somehow I ended up at the bottom of the pool, being held down by birchweed. It was like the tree wanted me there. For ever. Dead.'

'Ahhh.' Corwenna nodded.

'You don't sound surprised! I know it wasn't an accident. The forest was trying to kill me, after all I've done for it! Why? I thought I was part of the trees.'

'I wondered when you would ask. It was a test.'

'No it wasn't! I nearly died!'

'But in the end, you didn't die; you were taught something. You must learn to look death in the face, like the mirror, darkly.'

Ark's eyes blazed with anger. 'That's helpful. Next time I'm terrified and confused, I'll think of one of your riddles.' He turned away, frustrated. 'You sound like the warden.'

'Perhaps we are two sides of a coin. But Arktorious, listen to me! When the time comes, I promise you will understand. Anyway, your companion did come to the rescue, hmmm?'

That was no answer. Typical. He looked up at the Raven-Queen, at the woman who bore him, the woman he would never call mother.

'What chance do we have?'

'Ah, chance is the word. Even I cannot know the outcome. However, you passed the test in the water.' She leant in close and Ark thought she was about to embrace him. Instead, she fingered the phial round his neck. 'You used this once before on that boy, Grasp.'

'Yes.'

'Well, if it could turn his arm to wood, who knows

what it can do among the shimmering spires of glass? It is the distilled essence of the woods. When the time comes, it shall be useful.'

Today was the day they set off into the unknown. Ark felt afraid, but how could he tell her that?

'You forget that I can read you like the veins of a leaf. And I have a feeling that within an empire of millions, there will be those who dream of more than glass. Now come. Breakfast is ready and your friend is already eager for the fray.'

Ark smiled. 'That sounds like Mucum!'

Five minutes later, he was dressed and following his nose through the warren of Corwenna's quarters. A pair of double doors lay open and bright winter sunlight streamed on to a balcony that struck out from the edge of the trunk. The small platform was lined with iron railings, forged in the shape of quills. Beyond, the Ravenwood sighed and shifted in the morning light. Strange bird-calls echoed in the distance and Ark had the sense that there were watching eyes hidden in the evergreen leaves.

At the table, Mucum was already tucking in. 'This is the life!' he sighed. 'Porridge with wood-honey, and there's smoked cruck-pool trout fer afters.' Ark sat down as Mucum poured him a glass of thick liquid from a carved ash-jug. He sniffed, then sipped: pear juice, the sweet remnants of autumn.

It was then that he noticed the pair of knives side by side in the middle of the table. The white bone handles were carved to fit a fist, and the shining brown blades curled like claws. Their honed edges glittered.

'Not bad, eh? Your old lady told us we was gonna be armed!' Mucum picked up the knife and tested it against his thumb. Instantly, a line appeared with drops of blood beading the edge. 'Buddy Holly!' He stuck his thumb in his mouth. 'Don't want the Ravens to sniff out me blood! Well, I reckon these'll happily slice a few Mawish wind-pipes, though I ain't so stupid as to reckon a coupla blades will take out a whole empire . . .'

Before Ark could answer, there was a sudden squeal of delight. The knives were not the only surprise. A tall figure in white stepped shyly through the doorway.

'Flo!' shouted Mucum.

'Moi loverly boy!' Flo sang as she ran eagerly towards him.

Mucum jumped up and held out his arms. Though the Rootshooter girl was bald as an egg, those fluttering eyes did for him every time. He grabbed her in a boar hug and twirled her round. 'Where you bin, girl?'

'Why, yow know me. Oi've been preparin'.' Flo was slightly out of breath, her usually pale white skin flushed. She looked back at Corwenna, who had emerged from the shadows to observe the reunion. 'Now, before Oi tell yow what Oi've found out, give us a kiss!'

Mucum's face went red. He gently put Flo down. 'Not 'ere!' he whispered.

'Why? Dost thou not care for me any more?' Her large, owl-like eyes threatened to spill over with tears.

Mucum panicked. ''Course I do. It's not that. It's jus'. . . well . . .'

Corwenna was amused. 'Of course, if you don't kiss

her, I could always feed you to the Ravens, hmmm?'

'Righto, yer maj. When yer put it like that I guess I got to . . .'

'Kiss her. Yes. Or else we shall never get anything done!'

'Fair doo-doos,' Mucum muttered. 'Come back 'ere then!'

Ark looked on, feeling a strange mix of emotions: happiness for his friends mingled with something else that he would never admit.

It was Flo who pulled away. 'Good-oh!' she said. 'That was what Oi needed after moi long journey. Now Oi be famished. Let's be 'avin' some grub, if yow please!'

'I do please!' said Mucum, clearing space on the table and pulling back a chair for the elegant Rootshooter. Soon, the bread rolls, porridge and trout had vanished, the last of the honey was scooped from the bowl and the jug of juice was drained to the dregs.

'I am truly feeding an army!' Corwenna muttered as she began clearing away.

'Let me help,' said Ark.

'No,' Corwenna insisted. 'Today, I serve you. After all, it is I who shall stay here, safe in my snug while you travel through the deeps.' She looked at Flo, a question in her eyes.

'Moi lady. Do not worry,' said Flo. 'Our scouts have been to the very edge of the island and found what the legends spoke of. And Oi can tell yow, it be as real as the warmth in moi loverly boy's hand!' She reached out to grab Mucum's hand and hold it tight.

Ark realized his earlier instinct had been right. Beyond

the balcony, there *were* watching eyes. Hundreds of them. Shadows had shifted, and the Ravens now revealed themselves, perched rank upon rank, arrayed through the canopy like a library of feathers. He felt the weight of the flock, its sense of brooding power. Already, many had been lost at the battle in the autumn. Now, they waited upon him, Arktorious Malikum, to ensure their future was not wiped out altogether.

In the middle of them all, Hedd, son of Hedd balanced on the stump of a lightning-scarred trunk. The bird's thought rang out, clear as Kirk bells:

These knives, our gift to you, tree-boy.

Ark opened his mouth to reply, then realized he had no need of speech. These birds could read his mind like the Wood Book. He had only to think and they would know:

I thank you.

Hedd tilted his beak to one side, a single eye staring down at Ark.

Dark is way ahead. Beware shine of glass. Hold truth in your hand.

Hedd had spoken. Obeying some hidden signal, each Raven gave a single sharp screech. Ark blinked as the mighty birds rose and wheeled away.

He reached out to the middle of the table and picked up one of the knives. It felt comfortable in his hand and incredibly light.

'Bird bones are filled with hollow cavities,' Corwenna explained. 'That is the miracle of their flight, and why you don't see Dendrans flapping through the air. As for the blades, their glitter is not for show. Flo and her Root-shooter friends have ground up the dust of diamonds mined from deep beneath the forest. All their skills have been used to turn Raven claws into weapons even Mawish soldiers would be afraid of.'

Ark lifted the blade, turning it until the sharpened edge caught the sun and sent small beams flickering through the forest. He'd seen the damage that Mawish guns could inflict. How could mere knives be of any help?

'You will find out,' Corwenna answered his unspoken thought. 'There is nothing they cannot cut through.' She handed Ark and Mucum a pair of finely-tooled leather holsters, each embossed with a Raven wing. 'I have packed food in your knapsacks. Follow me now.'

'Blimey,' said Mucum, stuffing his knife into the holster. 'She don't hang about.'

They all ran after the Raven-Queen, following a winding route that led through endless doorways and up and down various sets of rickety stairs. How could one tree contain so many hollow spaces? They passed through an ancient ballroom filled with spiders' webs. High-arched resin windows punched through the bark to let in light. Ark was sure he could hear the echo of long-ago dances. Had Diana actually twirled round in this very spot?

'She did!' Corwenna called back. 'And I was the girl peeping in through the keyhole, jealous of all that late-night laughter!'

Finally, they arrived at a windowless wooden cave. A heavy iron chain was looped over a wheel in a pulley system that hung from the ceiling. A large wooden basket, with a wicker gate in the side, was attached to the chain. Below it was a hole in the wood, dark and deep.

'Oi tell yow,' said Flo, pointing to a hand-winder bolted to the side of the basket, "twas 'ard work comin' up from the deeps. It be yowr turn now, moi boy!' She smiled at Mucum.

'You what?' he frowned.

'Yow be havin' the chance to use 'em magnificent muscles of yowrs. What goes up must come down, eh? And we be travellin' by the roots!'

'You mean I gotta get inside that flimsy thing?' He remembered the last Rootshooter lift he'd been in and gulped.

'Yow worry too much. This be a slow and steady one!' She pulled open the wicker gate and stepped on board. The basket swayed slightly. Flo took a flint-tinder from within her white robes and sparked up a small lamp attached to the side of the basket. 'We'll be fine.'

Corwenna pushed a small leather pouch into Ark's hand. He opened it, fingering the flat discs of wood hidden inside. 'I don't understand . . . ?'

'In Maw, what you hold in your hand now is wealth beyond imagining. Apparently, elm burr is almost priceless.'

Mucum peered in. 'A bunch of polished twig bits? You must be kidding.'

'No!' said Corwenna. 'Where you are going, these carved coins will open doors and make many minds do your bidding.'

'But what's this?' Ark pulled out a small, intricately carved wooden butterfly. The wavy grain of the wood gave the illusion of fluttering wings.

'This is a gift that shall be given. And she who wears it will help you see to the heart of the matter. The perfect subterfuge.'

'Diana save us!' Mucum muttered. 'Not more bloomin' riddles!'

'This is no riddle, but it might be an answer. You invoke the name of my mother, but she was not alone in her quest to make Arborium come to life. I have dreamed that the spirits of those she worked with live on.' Her face set itself in an impassive mask. 'Go now,' she said, her voice suddenly as rough as a Raven's squawk. 'The Will of the Woods be with you.'

'And with you,' said Ark, mumbling the old Holly Woodsman words without even thinking. He slipped the butterfly back into the pouch. 'Stick this in your cruck-sack,' he said to Mucum. 'Let's get going.'

They stepped carefully inside the basket. Flo closed the gate and they held on to the sides as Mucum began turning the handle. The chain gave a protesting screech, but inch by inch, the pulley moved round and the basket began to descend.

Ark leant out of the edge of the basket, looking up to where Corwenna knelt, her green eyes trying to hide their apprehension. Slowly, as they inched down towards the roots, her face faded into the distance.

The journey had begun.

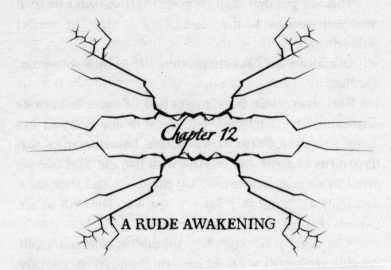

Chapter 12

A RUDE AWAKENING

Randall Jarrett felt her mattress begin to buzz. 'Give me a break!' she muttered, curling her pillow round her head and trying to jam it into her ears. The buzzing continued, and even worse, the whole bed began to tilt slowly sideways. Randall's fingers gripped the edge of the bedstead, determined to hold on, but by the time the bed reached a forty-five-degree angle she knew she'd lost.

She finally let go and slid in an ungraceful heap to the floor. There wasn't even a bump, as her mother could easily afford the fake memory-wood planks that gently gave way to the contours of her body. 'OK, you've made your point,' she sighed, slowly standing up and stumbling towards the wash-basin that slid out from the wall. In keeping with current fashion trends, the glass bowl today was frosted pink, adding a rosy glow to the dull room.

'Thank you, mistress. I take that as a compliment.' Each

word issued from tiny speakers embedded in her moulded wristband.

'Yeah, right. How they ever managed to program sarcasm into you, I'll never know.' She bent to scoop up some water from the basin, trying to rub the sleep from her face. There was a metallic smell to the liquid that even the best filters couldn't hide.

As she straightened up, she studied herself in the mirror above the basin. Unruly red hair tumbled down past her shoulders, a nightmare to comb. And there was definitely a spot lurking right on the tip of her chin. She reached for a tube of concealer and dabbed some on while turning to one side to look at her profile. She had inherited her mother's sharp looks – the angular face, the eyes clear as cut glass, the lean body.

'Do you wish to know the weather report, mistress?' The voice was as smooth as the blank walls that seamlessly lined Randall's bedroom. The scientists had explained that there were two speech modes for her prototype Personal Virtual Assistant: via wrist speaker or directly through the tiny sound chip implanted in her ear. Mostly she preferred to hear the voice out loud.

'I can see for myself, thank you,' said Randall, turning round. The fourth wall of her room was one single sheet of glass through which the sun streamed. Her eyes flicked over the city that spread beneath her. Skyscrapers two kilometres tall sprouted as far as she looked, twisting and twirling round each other like ballerinas frozen in awkward poses. A network of walkways and shimmer-avenues joined the buildings together. Every surface winked and glimmered, catching the morning sun and throwing its rays back and forth. Apparently, the architects of Maw had copied the shapes of the mythical trees and vines that had supposedly covered this very land thousands of years ago. To an outsider, it would be dazzling. For Randall, it was simply a bunch of tricky angles and enticing overhangs.

At least the glass wall was soundproof, and because of her mother's job, they were rich enough to live above the no-fly zone. Otherwise, she would have been deafened by the jam of the vert-taxis that moved up and down between various buildings, the hover-buses and the endless commuters stuck in the morning crush-hour. Randall leant towards the mirror again, quickly swiping her lips with the latest colour, rowanberry red. The Gloms were always making up weird names. What was a 'rowanberry' supposed to be, anyway?

The view reflected in the mirror unexpectedly vanished. She turned to see that some stupid businessman had illegally hopped his lane to fly above the rest of the traffic, and was now stalled, stationary outside her window. He was a typical air-head: balding, with a paunch that deserved its very own Merc-capsule. And he had the nerve to ogle her through his windscreen.

Randall smiled sweetly at the man and gave him a very interesting hand signal. 'What a glass-hole. PV, we appear to have an unexpected visitor.'

'Yes, mistress. Dealing.' Unwelcome traffic was like spam; a nuisance to be got rid of as quickly as possible. Randall watched in amusement as an invisible sonic wave bounced from the edge of her building and straight into the businessman's comfy capsule. The man's eyes went wide in shock and his leer vanished. She couldn't hear his scream of pain as he put his hands over his ears, but the effect was successful: the vehicle went into automatic, quickly dropping away to rejoin the crowded airways further below.

'I suppose I ought to say thank you.'

'It's my pleasure,' PV answered. 'Now shouldn't you be getting dressed for school?'

'Get a life, PV.'

'I do not know what you mean, mistress. It appears – even to my own insufficient neural networks – that I think, therefore I am. To summarize, I have a life already.'

'Oh, save us!' Randall muttered. She sometimes wondered whether her Personal Virtual Assistant did have a mind of his own, though. All his functions were contained in a small glass cube attached to her keyring and wirelessly linked to the touchscreen on her DNA-integrated wristband. Perhaps if she unclipped the cube and stamped hard on it, it would stop his hectoring voice once and for all. But something stopped her. PV was company, of a kind. Randall could go days without seeing her mother, and even when they did intersect, Fenestra would only give her daughter a hard time about missed homework and unsuitable clothes. As for Randall's father, Gabe Jarrett, he was long gone; too busy seeking out a newer, younger model of Lady Fenestra. All he had left her was a name.

Randall shook her head. She wouldn't put it past PV to

have created a secret backup stashed in a silicon vault deep beneath Sharkley's Bank. After all, he was a one-off, super-advanced, prototype model, not even available on the market yet. He was in a completely different league from any of the other basic virtual assistants out there. But why did she even refer to PV as him? He sounded male, but that was only voice modulation.

Randall had had enough of him for now; she could do without the nagging this morning. She tapped the 'silence' mode on her shiny wristband.

'But mistress . . . mistr . . .' The voice crackled once and then died. What did PV know? School was not part of her plan today.

Randall took off her pyjamas and held them out, waiting impatiently for the wash-chute to open up so she could throw them in. 'All-in-One! The Calvin Shine!' she said aloud. The wall identified the voice command and reconfigured itself into a drawer containing the folded body suit. As she slipped it on, she admired the way it hugged her frame. It was windproof, breathable and even had built-in shock protection in case she fell. And it was black. What was it someone had said once in a vid-mag she'd been skimming? *Black is always the new black*. Lastly she slipped on a pair of rubber Shimmy-Shoos. Where she was going, her luxury wooden platform boots might look fantastic but would be downright dangerous.

She grabbed her packsack out of the drawer. 'Shut it!' she commanded. The drawer obliged, becoming a blank wall again in the blink of an eye. Randall reached under her bed to pull out the hidden bits of kit she'd need:

spools of rope, extending hooks and a couple of alloy insta-ratchets in case she got stuck – though Randall Jarrett had never got stuck in all her fourteen years. She stuffed her tools into the various pockets woven into her body suit.

She slipped out into the corridor, ignoring the background hum that all buildings in Maw gave off. The dull, glowing floor beneath her feet shifted slightly. This high up, on floor five thousand and thirty-two, the winds that roared through Maw ought to snap the glass structures in half. But glass itself had become part of the evolutionary process, as her boring teachers had told her too many times. Now the substance that formed the core of her home listened to and respected the wind, flexing and bending like rubber. You could master nature, but her forces were still to be heeded. Despite hurricanes and whirlwinds, no building had fallen in Maw for over a thousand years, since the last great crash of twenty-nine.

As she crept down the corridor, Randall could hear voices coming from her mother's study. Another political meeting, no doubt. That was all her mother ever did these days, aside from her trips abroad. Randall could feel the call of the outdoors, her fingers itching to take on the new route she'd been dreaming about all night until PV had so rudely woken her up.

She checked the pocket tucked under her armpit. The tiny hoverfly-cam lay nestled there, fully charged, anchored by fine wires and ready to film and upload her latest escapade. Her mother might be the Envoy of Maw, but Randall was the queen of the glass canyons, and her free-climbing films, with her identity suitably disguised, regularly had over a billion hits.

The voices paused and footsteps stalked towards the study door. Randall felt her heartbeat speed up: she didn't have time to make it down the corridor. Any moment now and the door would swing open to reveal a daughter not dressed as duty dictated. Randall could almost see the haughty eyebrows raised, the frosty stare of disapproval, the mouth polite but pursed, already storing up the screaming match for later.

But Randall couldn't move; she was frozen to the spot like the ridiculous glass statues that lined the rooftop pleasure gardens in the city centre. She'd be grounded, and all her climbing dreams shattered into shards.

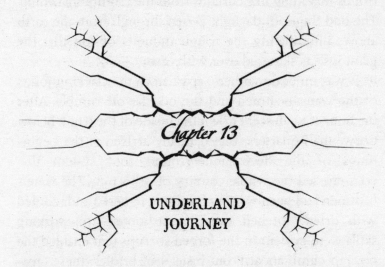

Chapter 13

UNDERLAND
JOURNEY

'**A**re we nearly there yet? Riding on the back of an over-grown insect ain't exactly my idea of fun!' Mucum shouted. His voice echoed round the massive root tunnel.

'Oi don't think my loverly companions loike yowr tone of voice,' Flo shouted across from her own water-boatman.

'Yes,' Ark joined in, 'and aren't you always the one who says go with the flow?'

'But me bum hurts!' Mucum whined, saddle-sore after hours of travel.

'That's a bummer!' Ark smiled, unsympathetically.

Mucum groaned. Ark and jokes did not mix.

'Stop moaning and look at the view!' Ark was enjoying himself. This was a different country they were travelling through now. A hundred feet above them, bark-bats screeched as they flitted through bright phosphorescent fronds that hung like curtains from the crumbling ceiling. The odd finger of daylight poked through from the earth above, illuminating the rough mounds of soil that the giant insects skittered over with ease.

It was quiet down here, apart from the clacking joints of the water-boatmen and the odd far-off rumble. After the hour-long descent down the inside of the trunk below Corwenna's quarters, they'd finally arrived at the beginnings of the deep underground root system that criss-crossed the whole country of Arborium. The water-boatmen had been waiting for them, tethered and saddled with dried, stitched moss. Rootshooter iron-working skills were evident in the forged stirrups that enabled the boys to climb aboard, but instead of bridles, these creatures were controlled by holding on to their feathered antennae. With six legs each, they didn't exactly canter, but lolloped off towards the west and the point indicated on Flo's map.

After a couple of hours, Ark couldn't stop thinking about what lay ahead. Two foolhardy boys with a couple of knives daring to try and break into Maw? It was madness.

'Why, will yow listen to that?' Flo said suddenly.

Snatches of sound floated down the root towards them.

'What's there to sing about down 'ere?' Mucum growled.

The words became clearer, punctuated by the sound of marching feet:

'High-ho! High-ho! 'Tis off to dig we go,
Dressed in suits,
We doive through roots,
We dig for ore,
Yow know what's more ...
It's fun! High-ho! High-ho! High-ho!'

Flo urged the insects into a gallop until the source of the singing was revealed. In front of them, a Rootshooter working party squelched through the mud in their bare white feet. Over their shoulders they carried pickaxes, and their bald heads shone out like shiny mushrooms. They were all even taller than Flo, their pale, thin bodies squeezed into rubber diving suits.

''Ow's it goin', Flo?' shouted the leader of the group as Flo slowed down to a trot.

'It be good, Mojo!' Flo replied. 'Yow off for the iron?'

'It be tin today, cousin! Them lot up top must have their fancy plates 'n' tings,' the woman sniffed. 'Warghhhh! Won't thou stop for a gossip?' The woman had an even stronger accent than Flo.

'Sorry cousin, Oi be forgettin' moi manners!' She pulled gently on the antennae of her insect and slowed to a stop. 'Yas. Them Dendrans do be odd, living up in the windy canopy!' Flo laughed, smiling at Mucum.

''Ere! Yer not talkin' about us, are yer?' Mucum frowned.

'Who, moi?' Flo smiled. 'I only be joshin'!'

The Rootshooters put down their pickaxes and stared at Ark with their big moony eyes. 'And this be the boy what touched the mealworm and mined 'is slimy soul?

'I did,' Ark answered quietly.

'What about me?' Mucum butted in.

'Yas!' one of them agreed. 'Thou be his brave companion what covered our enemies with great plops of poo!'

Mucum smiled proudly. 'Yeah! Squit-cannon. Sorted them out, I tell you!'

'Ahhhh!' they all sighed admiringly.

Mojo pulled out a curled-up twig that had been strapped to her back. It was a spiral about a foot across and hollowed out, its knobbly circumference stripped of its bark and decorated with white chalky swirls that resembled a root system in miniature. 'This then be our dreaming gift to yow!' She put one end of the instrument to her lips and began to blow.

One by one, the other Rootshooters closed their eyes and began to hum along to the single-noted drone. Even Flo joined in as they clicked their long fingers to a hidden rhythm. The music soared, turning into the buzz of summer bees nosing through the wildflowers that edged the scaffields, the beat of wood-cricket wings, a dance of all that was strong and good.

Even Mucum was silent, carried away by the deep woody murmur that bounced round the tunnel. Ark felt it then: the strength of a thousand Rootshooters, vibrating round the roots and soaking into them.

Minutes passed. Maybe hours. Even the normally fidgety water-boatmen stood still. Finally, the humming faded away into the dark. The rest of the Rootshooters picked up their tools and strode away down a root that branched off to the right. Mojo let the drone die away, then tucked the instrument away behind her back. 'Diana's blessing be yowr guide. All our kin will keep these two boys in our hearts.' She stopped and looked round. Ark wondered if she was waiting to hear the trees speak, but all he could hear was a small crumble of soil far above. 'Yas.' Mojo nodded. 'Moi-thinks the trees do have faith in yow.' Her eyes rested on Ark. 'The forest be as alive as yow and moi! But Oi thinks yow know that, boy.' Her eyes dug deep into his, as if she was mining his deepest thoughts.

'Thank you,' said Ark, though he wasn't sure what for.

'Time Oi got diggin'!' Mojo said. 'Good-day, kin!' She bowed to Flo and loped off into the dark.

'What? Is she family?' Mucum asked, still feeling slightly disorientated.

'All be family down 'ere. But Mojo and I go back a lornnng way. She be moi tenth cousin, thirteen toimes removed.'

'If everyone's family, how d'yer know all their names?' Mucum scratched his ear. 'It would do my head in!'

'It be in moi blood, loverly boy. If one Rootshooter dies, we all feels it instantly, be we north, south, east or west. Then we gets together and has a send-off like yow've never seen. Enough drink to wish 'em spirit over the River Sticks and enough tears to make one of yow cruck-pools . . .'

Ark was dizzy with it all . . . the miracle of this other world, this under-wood. Most Dendrans in Arborium had no idea at all about the lives of Rootshooters as they never encountered them, despite relying on their iron for the pipes threading through the trees for water and sewage. *As above, so below.* One could not do without the other.

'Anyways!' said Flo. 'If toime flies, so should we! Giddy-up, girls!' In answer to her command, the water-boatmen sprinted off.

Half an hour later, Flo sniffed the air. There was a definite tang of salt. 'We be there soon enough, boys!'

Though the going had been flat for some time, the root began dipping down at an alarming angle.

''Ere. What's goin' on?' Mucum was almost thrown off as Flo pulled hard on the antennae of her water-boatman and all three insects came sliding to a halt.

'Trust me. We be goin' to the deeps now. Only pray there be no puncture in the roof above.'

'Why?' Mucum looked nervously upwards. Instead of the flit of bats, there was now the steady *drip, drip, drip* of water.

'Because thou dost not want to be drownded!' Flo laughed.

A drop landed on Ark's face. He wiped it with his finger, then licked it. It was salty. 'Is that what I think it is?'

'Yas, Ark of the Woods. It be so.'

Ark nodded. 'You see, Mucum, it's the sea.'

'See what?' Mucum asked, confused.

'A lot of water. Miles of it. Bigger than any forest, deeper than any root. Tucked away up in the trees of Arborium, we Dendrans have no real idea of what lies outside our leafy world. The sea is just one of those things, and trust me, if that lot comes gushing in, we're very, very dead.'

'Oh. Gotcha. Thanks for that cheering thought.'

Flo lit three lamps that had been hanging like bells off the edge of her saddle. 'The way be picky and steep, but moi western kin assure me this route be not flooded.' Her confidence did nothing to reassure them as she tweaked the antennae of her water-boatman and her lantern bobbed away down into the darkness.

'After you, mate!' said Mucum nervously.

'Hmmm . . .' said Ark. But it wasn't as if they had a choice. The way inside the root was steeper than any trunk-stairs, but by leaning back and letting the six legs of each insect do their work, it was only a matter of minutes before the path became less sheer. The air was warmer, almost humid, and the slope downwards was becoming more gentle when Ark saw that Flo had come to a stop ahead. As he drew closer, he saw why.

The root had been sliced in half by a smooth, circular wall that blocked the way. Its surface was oddly pale and completely unmarked. No lichen, no fungus, not even a clump of deepweed.

Mucum groaned. 'It's a dead end.'

Ark agreed. The wall looked unnatural. Corwenna had told them that their blades would cut through anything, but he had a feeling they would barely scratch this surface. They were stuck.

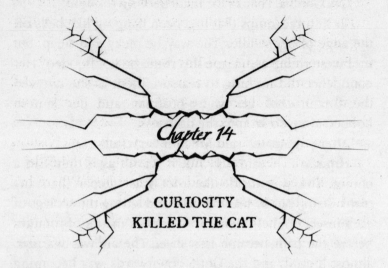

Chapter 14

CURIOSITY KILLED THE CAT

Randall panicked, her eyes roving the corridor, searching for a means of escape. The footsteps were almost at the study door and she was trapped.

Despite being in silent mode, the wristband gave a single, soft buzz. 'Not now, PV!' she hissed. Maybe her so-called assistant had managed to override the voice cut-out button and summon her mother. She wouldn't put it past him.

But the buzzing continued. What did PV think he was playing at?

Oh! It was staring her in the face. Of course!

A cupboard stood beside the door, its old-fashioned curly handle now beckoning. It was a priceless piece, made of real kiln-dried oak, its slightly warped shape strangely out of place among all the straight lines. As quietly as she could, Randall turned the handle and stepped inside. She held her breath and waited for her mother to expose her hiding place. Maybe PV was winding her up after all.

But nothing happened. The footsteps faded away and the voices on the other side of the wall resumed. Randall breathed in through her nose, finding the musty smell that surrounded her oddly comforting. The cupboard was empty, only there to impress when important visitors came round. There was plenty of standing room inside.

She flicked her wristband. *Let there be light!* Where had she heard that phrase before? The screen brightened and there was the symbol of a smiley face beaming at her. She could have sworn the liquid-ink winked at her. Her fingers quickly spelt out a short message:

Thanks. I owe you one.

The screen response came back instantly. *It was gladly done, mistress. Though please, next time you try to silence my voice function, do so gently. Even electro-neurons are sensitive!*

Randall smiled. Maw was becoming a strange place when a machine could choose to add an exclamation mark to its communication.

The glow of light from her wristband suddenly reminded her of something. She reached up and felt her way along with her fingers. Yes. It was still there, high up at the back of the cupboard, the finger-sized hole she'd discovered when she was little. Her mother had left a chair near the open cupboard, and Randall had been exploring. Later, when she had asked about the hole, Lady Fenestra had explained how such ancient planks were cut from trees, and told her that these cross-sections contained tiny windows where former branches had been – knot-holes. Randall had been fascinated, and imagined that if she could stare through the hole long enough, she would see the long-gone forest it had come from. Instead, there was only the smooth outer wall of the study, blank and beige.

As a geeky youngster, it had taken her only half an hour and couple of tools filched from the tech-store to drill through the wall on the other side and to insert a thin, flexible length of eye-scope. It was said that curiosity killed the cat, whatever that meant, but her mother was always so private that it had become a habit for Randall to try to find out for herself what happened behind closed doors.

However, to an eight-year-old, endless meetings about rebellions in the far outposts of the Empire were beyond dull. She'd quickly grown bored of her spying game, and the scope had lain forgotten for years.

Now she was bored again. She wanted to hit the outside, get climbing before the predicted afternoon winds came slamming in from the east. She stood up on tiptoe and pressed her left eye against the knot-hole while tapping out a remote command signal on her wristband. She waited for a reply, wondering if the old tech would still work.

PV vibrated softly. *Is this wise, mistress?* scrolled across the screen on her wristband.

Oh, for Frame's sake! Randall ignored the message, hoping that he would do as he was told for once.

A line of dots crossed the screen, the equivalent of

shrugging shoulders. The scope finally activated and the study on the other side of the wall swung into focus.

Her mother was standing by the balcony, the glass doors open. Her trouser suit was nipped in at the waist, the tailoring harsh with angular shoulder pads and sharp pleats running down the front of the legs. The colours were sober for this time of the morning, though of course the suit would adapt as the day went on, easily able to switch to a dazzling palette to impress at bright dinner parties and expensive political functions.

As adornment, Fenestra wore only one piece of Oak-couture, a single strand of flawless mahogany pearls draped round her elegant neck. It was worth a hundred times the yearly salary of a lower-floor citizen. Randall couldn't help being impressed by her mother's cold beauty.

It was Fenestra's birthday tomorrow. What to buy the woman who had everything? Randall had been searching on Tree-bay for ages, scrolling through umpteen designer burr-brooches and twig-tiaras. PV had helpfully informed her that most of them were fakes. To find something Lady Fenestra would approve of – that would be a miracle.

The study was completely different in appearance from the rest of the apartment. Aside from the view, every wall was covered from floor to ceiling in ancient wood panels. There was even a fireplace in the corner. Ridiculous! Log-burning was the sort of showing-off only billionaires could afford.

But Randall's eye was caught by a second figure. Why was her mother hanging out with a boy? The teenager in question was seated at one end of a long wooden table. His face, framed by black curly hair, was the colour of her mother's rich pearls, but surprisingly compelling. The beginnings of a beard had been trimmed into a vertical rectangular stripe that was currently all the rage in town, and in his ear he wore a shiny chunk of haematite. But he still looked out of place, his bulky body squeezed into a three-piece suit of grey molten wear, its smooth liquid-like substance pinstriped with metallic thread.

She looked again, fiddling with her wristband to zoom in the scope. The boy's right arm rested on the table, though arm was the wrong word. The jacket sleeve could not quite disguise the over-sized mechanical limb that sprouted from his shoulder. It was unnatural, ugly. Couldn't the boy's parents afford some decent prosthetics? The pincers on the end were the most disturbing part, appearing to have a life of their own as they clacked together.

The next shock was what the boy's mottled brown eyes were staring at. Randall adjusted her scope to follow his gaze. Something crawled slowly across the table. She felt a sick lurch in her stomach.

Lady Fenestra finally spoke, and the scope's built-in microphone carried the sound wirelessly to the tiny implant in her daughter's ear.

'I take it the surgery was successful?'

'You already know it was,' said the boy, his voice dismissive and petulant. 'Flint is a commander once more, though now he's what the surgeon calls "remote-controlled". And the weapons are primed and ready to go.'

Randall wondered what they were talking about. It sounded like more boring military waffle. Though how could a teenager be involved?

'Good. Time is short. You are invited to witness the Quantum Trap tomorrow morning. Its capabilities, as you will see, are lethal. Should the trial be successful, you have three days before the Winter Solstice, where the majority of your fellow countrymen will finally be dealt with . . . as it were.'

In her hidey-hole, Randall mouthed the words to herself: *Quantum Trap*. It sounded clinical, cold. But before she could think about it any more, her mother continued speaking.

'Now, as you see,' Fenestra pointed at the table, 'in the matter of your arm, we have made progress. Chemically, glass is a liquid. We have simply exploited its properties. The movement co-ordinates have been smoothed out and its potential, if I might be modest enough to say so, is staggering.'

The boy scratched his beard and looked away towards the window. 'It's a finger.'

From her hiding place inside the cupboard, Randall shuddered as the thing crept round the table like a see-through worm.

'Yes, it is a finger. But please, do not underestimate what it can do.' She pulled a glittering object from the bag that hung at her side and placed it on the table. 'Diamond is the hardest object known to mankind. We use it to edge our drills and saws. Strange to think that this tiny stone started its life as an ancient leaf on a tree before falling and being crushed to carbon.'

'Please, spare me the science. I'm not a complete dunce.'

Fenestra arched her sculpted eyebrows. 'I wouldn't dream of suggesting it. Now watch.'

Randall also watched as the finger paused, then balanced on end as if sniffing the air. Its complete transparency somehow made it all the more horrifying as the finger scratched its way across the pitted surface of the table towards the diamond, then slowly but surely curled round the stone. There was a grinding noise, then a sudden crack.

A look of fear crossed the boy's face, quickly replaced by a mask of bored disinterest. But Randall was in awe as a shower of diamond dust shot up towards the ceiling, each flake glittering as it fell back to the table.

Fenestra continued. 'Soon, we will grow it into an arm which you will be the first to try. And if the graft takes . . . if my researchers can find a way to attach the liquid glass to skeletal DNA . . . we shall cultivate an army that will be invincible!'

Instead of being bored by her mother's endless political games, Randall now felt uneasy. Who was this boy with the mechanical arm and strange accent? Why was he here nodding at talk of a Quantum Trap? And if Maw already ruled the world, why did they need an army forged from glass?

Her head was spinning and the cupboard a dark and confining prison. She had to get out.

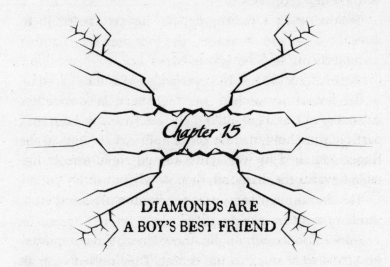

Chapter 15

DIAMONDS ARE
A BOY'S BEST FRIEND

'Look yow!' said Flo, proudly.

'I'm lookin', girl, and there's no way through,' Mucum replied.

'No. Yow must use 'um eyes. Look yow!' she said again, her voice rising in sing-song pitch.

That was when they saw it, glittering right in the centre of the wall. Like the multi-faceted eyes of the water-boatmen, it reflected the lamplight and threw it in a hundred directions.

'It be diamond!' Flo explained finally. 'And this be the entrance to the old diamond mine from before times.' She leant forward in her saddle and pressed the shining stone with the palm of her hand.

There was a small click. Instantly a crack appeared, zigzagging from floor to ceiling. The wall gave a soft hiss and then split, the two halves slowly sliding apart into hidden recesses.

Following Flo's prompting, the insects carried them over the threshold. 'And this,' she indicated the chamber around them, 'be yowr way to Maw!'

Both Ark's and Mucum's eyes widened as they gazed up at the cavern that arched over their heads. The root had been dug out, and behind it their lanterns picked out rock walls glinting with tiny points of light. Ark thought of the diamonds in King Quercus's crown; how small they seemed now, compared to the scale of this.

Flo dismounted and walked towards the nearest wall, stroking a square panel with her long white fingers. The chamber flooded with light. Above them, three rectangular strips were stuck to the ceiling. They pulsed with an inner glow, as if they were filled with fireflies. Ark was confused.

'And before yow ask, that be 'lectric what helps us see!'

'And what the holly is that?' Mucum pointed at a platform built into the far wall. It was about twenty feet high, with steps leading up to it. On top of the platform, resting on a pair of dull, metallic tracks, was a glass structure in the shape of a smooth rolled-up scroll, only a hundred times bigger. The tracks led off into a dark hole.

'That be transport! Now, come orn. Yow ain't got all day.' Flo stood at a smooth black table. As her hands moved over its surface, glowing letters and numbers oozed and shifted beneath them like a mass of wood-ants. Then the capsule lit up like a lantern.

'Them steps moight be a bit rusty, but they war good enough when Oi tested 'em last week.'

'You've been here before?' Ark's head was dizzy with it all.

'Yas. Them stories were true all right. Way before the Empire of Maw, them old explorers from across the ocean had found a fault that ran deep under the earth. They were greedy, like root-rats, sniffin' out rare stuff. And what be rarer than a stone what shows off like the sun? And how does 'un get from A to B? Steal a bit o' sunlight and stuff it in a battery-powered capsule: that's what that glass thing is up thar. Transport. Loike ridin' in the inside of a Raven what's see-through and with no wings . . . only much faster, see?'

'I don't see nuffin'!' Mucum growled.

'Never yow mind. Yow must trust me, like yow trusted the Raven-Queen, yas? Oi've been dustin' and polishin' and even found 'em old book-manuals to tell us how to get it workin' again. And as far as Oi can see, there be just enough juice left in 'em ancient batteries to get yow there. Now, enough of the talkin'.' Flo turned away to tether the water-boatmen, stroking their shiny scales and cooing to them. 'That's my oochy-coochy!'

She reached into her shoulder bag to pull out some dried seeds. Ark tried not to shudder as giant mandibles reached out and gently picked the food from her hands to crunch it up. 'Good girl!' Flo said, stroking one of their antennae. 'We be goin' home soon,' she sighed.

'Hang on a sec,' Mucum said. 'Whatcha mean, goin' home?'

'Aw, moi sweet and handsome, hast yow not worked it out yet?' she said as she shepherded her friends towards the platform stairs.

Mucum's face dropped. 'Nah! You're not coming with us? But we're a team, right? You and me . . . and I guess old wonder-worker here might be useful too . . .' Mucum flicked his thumb towards Ark.

'And Oi be tall and bald and would stick out in Maw loike an iron filing in a bowl o' porridge. And Oi be needed to follow the manual and "program" the route from that there table-thing. Anyways, a part of me is travellin' with yow!'

'No it ain't!' said Mucum, his lower lip drooping.

'Take out yow knives!'

Ark was puzzled, especially as the Raven-claw blade he pulled from his bag was now glowing as if lit from within.

Mucum felt his own blade. 'It's warm!'

'Yas. Tis a gift from Mojo and from all of us! Tell moi, boys, what creature did yow think of when they made their dreaming?'

'What, that song back in the tunnel?' said Ark.

'Yas.'

'Bees,' said Mucum.

Ark was surprised; that was what he'd been thinking of too.

'Yas. Bee dance. But bees be not only jolly. When threatened, what dost yow think they do?'

Ark remembered when he was six years old, having a June picnic in the scaffields with his parents. A bee had flown into his hair and he'd tried to run away but couldn't stop the constant pain. After screaming and tears, Mrs Malikum had finally gently freed the little creature to fly off while cradling her wailing son.

'Sting?' he said.

'Yas. And that is what yowr weapons can do if need be. Sting with all the strength of the root-dwellin' stumble-bees. We Rootshooters dreamed it, and so it come to be.' There were tears in Flo's eyes. 'Put yowr knives away. 'Tis toime to be off . . .'

They had reached the bottom of the stairs by now. Up above, the capsule began to hum.

'Oh, squit,' Mucum said. 'I thought you woz comin' all the way.'

'And Oi knows it . . .' Flo squeezed Mucum's hand, then pulled gently away. 'It be one minute to take-off. Quick now. Press the small diamond in the door of the capsule and strap yowrselves in!' Already, she was striding back towards the table, her fingers reaching out to work whatever magic lay within it.

Ark slowly climbed the rusty stairs, but Mucum hung back, unsure. 'See ya!' he shouted towards the retreating Flo.

'Sooner than yow can blink yowr gorgeous eyes! Take care!' Flo sang back.

At the top of the platform, the capsule loomed over them. A cold wind blew in from the hole that the tracks vanished into.

'This is hazelnuts!' said Mucum.

Ark nodded. 'Yes. To think, we could have stayed as poorly-paid sewage workers and stood by as the whole country was taken over.' He pushed the small stone set into the curved glass door of the capsule. The door swung slowly upwards to reveal a compartment with two rows of two seats.

'Never seen nothin' like this!' said Mucum, peering in suspiciously.

'Well, might as well get on with it.' Ark stepped forward, and fell inside with a jolt as the whole capsule lifted suddenly off the rails and hovered about a foot above them.

'Holly Moly!' Mucum exclaimed. He peered underneath the suspended cylinder but could see nothing. 'It's jus' floatin' there! T'ain't natural.'

'Twenty seconds!' Flo shouted.

'Come on!' said Ark. He was on his feet, feeling the capsule sway slightly.

'But what's at the other end?'

'Maw,' Ark replied simply.

'And what have we got to defend ourselves? Two glowing knives and some manky bits of wood. I don't like the look o' this!' Mucum said.

'There's a lot of things you don't like. But if you don't get in, I might be leaving without you. Much as I'd like to save the whole wide-wood by myself, I admit your help would be appreciated.'

Mucum sighed, jumped up and scrambled in. As he did so, the transparent curved lid closed automatically over them. They were sitting in a giant glass tube with one end pointed at the unknown. A black surface, similar to the table that Flo stood over, lay in front of their knees. Numbers flashed across the surface.

10 ... 9 ... 8 ...

'Are you strapped in?'

Mucum slumped into a surprisingly comfortable seat. He could feel the material moulding itself to the shape of his back as he pulled a shiny belt across his lap.

3 ... 2 ... 1 ...

'This ain't gonna . . .' were the last words Mucum uttered before an invisible force threw them back into their seats. The capsule shot forward faster than any arrow, straight towards the dark tunnel mouth.

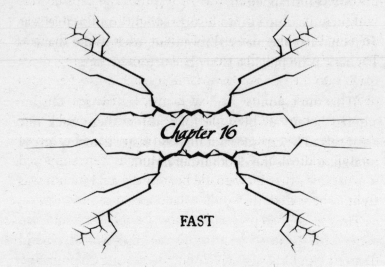

Chapter 16

FAST

'I want my mum!' Mucum screamed as the capsule hurtled through the darkness.

'Wha-a-t?' shouted Ark. Perhaps in the ancient past the capsule had been well sealed. But now, after what seemed like hours of being trapped inside, sharp streams of freezing wind cut through the tiny gaps in the doors, turning their transport into a whistling whirlwind.

Ark couldn't even bend his neck to see his friend in the bucket-seat beside him. The walls of the tunnel were perilously close, but it was the speed that was truly terrifying as the capsule accelerated through the deep underground earth-fault.

Ark's eyes flicked to the combination of numbers and letters flashing on the flat black surface in front of his knees: 3,000 km/h, 3,300 km/h, 4,000 km/h. As the numbers crept up, his body was pressed further and further back into the seat. His mind was racing too. The capsule was wingless, and had no feathers to force the air beneath to do its will, so how did it fly? Flo had talked about the sun. The sun powered the trees of Arborium, helping them reach into the sky, but how could it reach down here into deep darkness and use its heat to propel them forward?

Ark remembered the machine that had hovered above the battle at the palace, spilling out its poisoned cargo of foreign soldiers. Now both he and Mucum were supposed to trust this other Maw-made boat of the air. Mucum was right to be scared; they didn't stand a chance in holly.

The capsule had powerful lanterns at the front, and two cones of light now illuminated the underworld around them. It would have been slightly less stomach-churning for both of them if the journey was straight, like the wood-ways of Arborium, but these chasms deep beneath the ocean twisted and turned like a wiggly hazel branch, and there were no reins to help with steering. Ark and Mucum were nothing more than helpless passengers as their transport took on a life of its own.

'What if there's, like, creatures down 'ere? Big 'uns, like that mealworm?' Mucum shouted.

'Don't worry!' Ark yelled. 'I think we've met the local wildlife already!' He pointed at the front glass screen, already smeared in a pus-coloured splat of insect bodies.

'Squitting Dell!' Mucum suddenly wailed. A sheer wall of white crystal reared up, hundreds of feet high, ready to smash them to smithereens. Mucum squeezed his eyes closed, but Ark stared in amazement. As the crystal cliff blotted out the view, the capsule swung them round to the left in the nick of time, so tightly that Ark's insides almost turned to scrambled scaffield eggs. He had a feeling they weren't out of the woods yet, though, and he was right. Moments later, they were flying straight towards a gigantic waterfall that poured from a hidden lip of rock far above. Their lantern beams picked out the glitter of the foaming spray. Even here, from half a mile away, they could hear a roar louder than any thunderstorm.

Mucum was ashen-faced. Ark tried to remember the old prayers, mouthing them silently: *Yea, though I walk though the valley of the shadow of lost breath, I will fear not winter, for thou art with me, thy twig and thy oak branch to comfort me.* But he was far from the reassuring presence of the trees. What abilities did he have here? His hands had stopped arrows falling from the sky, but could they turn back the weight of a million tons of water?

He remembered how he had reached into the mind of the mealworm. Perhaps this machine had a mind too? If he reached out to whatever presence lurked deep inside, maybe he could steer them out of danger. He was Ark of the Woods, victorious in battle! If Commander Flint's mighty pride could be broken, surely this shining beast could be tamed? He willed himself to focus on the panel in front of him. But the capsule ignored him, bucking like a leaf in the wind as it aimed straight at the heart of the waterfall.

Ark tried again, slowing his breathing, his thoughts creeping like ivy as they tried to decipher the workings of the infernal device. His mind followed the source of energy behind the super-fast fans that pushed the capsule forward, finding veins: circuits thinner than the tiniest threaded root, pulsing with light and energy. Was this the 'lectric that Flo talked about? His mind dived towards the core, the heartwood of the machine. But there, at the centre, was nothing but a roaring rush of zeros and ones, tumbling over each other so fast they blurred in his mind. How could he talk to such a creature?

The numbers on the table in front of them crept higher: 6,000 km/h, 6,500 km/h, 7,200 km/h. At this rate, and with the whole capsule groaning at the seams, they would soon be ripped apart.

There was a popping, whooshing sound, then silence. Water briefly covered the screen before being forced to the sides. Even the wind dropped.

'Whoa!' Mucum grunted. 'What 'appened? Tasted me brekkie a few times again there!'

'Thanks for that! Think we've passed straight through the waterfall.' Ark was exhausted from his failed efforts to communicate with the capsule. He shook his head to try to clear his thoughts. What drove the thing was alien to him. This was not Hedd, son of Hedd, but a different sort of bird, bred by the ancestors of Maw. He had been defeated; all he could do was surrender. 'I think we're getting near.'

''Ow d'yer work that out?'

'Look.' Below them, a pair of shining metallic tracks disappeared into the distance. The walls they slid between were now smooth, wrapped around the capsule like a pea in a pea-shooter. Anything outside the glass was a blur. And although the numbers indicated they were still travelling at a terrifying pace, they both felt almost no sensation of motion.

'This is *Maw* like it. Get it? *Maw* like it?'

But before Ark had a chance not to laugh at Mucum's terrible joke, there was an almighty, shuddering bang. Ark was dimly aware of the front part of the capsule crumpling inwards. The windscreen shattered and dagger-like splinters scythed the air. Something warm gushed from his cheek and down into his mouth. It tasted like a mixture of iron and salt. He knew that odd flavour. What was it?

He cried out in shock as a memory flitted through his head: the dark, drizzly night on a slippery branch when Petronio Grasp had cut him, and the sudden battering wind as a Raven had soared out of the night to claim its clot of flesh, drawn by the perfume of his blood.

Then Ark's mind shut down.

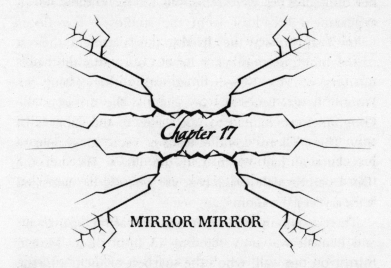

Chapter 17

MIRROR MIRROR

Randall shut down the scope, though she couldn't rid her mind of the sight of the glass finger dragging itself across the table. She slipped out of the cupboard, glad to be free of its confining darkness. She needed fresh air.

Her Shimmy-Shoos made no sound as she stalked the corridor. Each door except her own bedroom door was wired to Fenestra's computer. Even if she went into the kitchen for a milkshake, somewhere in her mother's database there would be a record of her opening the fridge. It was a pain. Her few friends were able to come and go as they pleased, but Randall was stuck with a mother who was paranoid.

Fenestra lectured her frequently about 'subversive elements': people who wanted to undermine and disrupt the way the Empire was run, people who would 'do anything to destroy the financial structure of Maw'. Often her dull speeches were rehearsals for the endless screen appearances broadcast from the studios a few floors below. That was why they lived in this apartment: the rest of the building, number 1 Babel Court, was the headquarters of Pox News, broadcasting throughout the Empire. It was Fenestra who sculpted the messages the Conglomerates wanted to put across to the subjects of Maw. These 'Gloms', as the heads of each Conglomerate was known, had nicknamed the Envoy Fenestra the 'Din-Doctor'. *Make enough noise and eventually the masses will believe anything,* the Gloms laughed.

There was only one other way out of the apartment, and Randall was now standing in front of it. 'Mirror, mirror on the wall, who's the sharpest of them all?' she murmured. The mirror said nothing, a blank sheet reflecting her thin body and pale, frowning face. If she stood there long enough, the scan should automatically start.

Nothing happened.

She reached down to her wristband, and with a flick of her finger restored PV's voice function.

'PV? What's going on?' she asked.

'Oh, mistress!' the machine sighed. 'You are aware that the security protocols have been updated again? The mirror doorway will not open as it has done before.'

Randall turned her head back down the corridor. There was an ominous silence, then she heard movement. The meeting in the study was clearly over.

'PV! Listen!' she hissed. 'Has a shielded system ever beaten you? You're a one-off; the one and only PV in existence. Those other lowly virtual assistants are primitive;

ancient, with hardly any functions at all. You're the best bit of kit there is!' Ever since Fenestra had given her the glass cube, Randall had been constantly amazed at how it responded and what it could do. Even flattery was worth a try.

'Mistress. I appreciate your faith in me . . .' Was that a hint of pride in the normally smooth voice?

'You can do it, PV!' Randall whispered, eyeing the study door as the handle twisted downwards. She had virtually the same genetic map as her mother, she reasoned, so as long as PV made sure the scanner found no significant differences, she was in with a chance.

The door was beginning to open. Randall knew it was too late; once Fenestra strode out of the study and saw her daughter challenging the mirror on the wall, Randall would pay, big time.

But PV worked his techno-miracle just in time and the mirror glided silently to one side, leaving a large oblong gap. Randall leapt through, hoping she hadn't been seen as it slid shut behind her once again.

'That was close!' she muttered, leaning back and trying to control her breathing.

'Not quite, mistress. I calculate that you had another 0.34 seconds before eye contact would have been made.'

'Hmmm . . .' she said. 'I owe you one.'

'One what, Miss Jarrett?'

'Oh, never mind.'

The room she was now standing in did not appear in the architectural plans of their apartment. No cams were installed and the single sheet of glass that covered the far wall was one-way. It let natural sunlight stream in, but from the outside it appeared to be part of the outer wall of the building.

The reason for its secrecy sat on two long tables running the length of the room. Randall always found the smell cloying compared with the comforting tang of the city. The tiny dwarf-trees repulsed her. Each grew in a small circular tray, roots hidden beneath a layer of perfectly raked gravel. Some had a scattering of small fallen leaves, sprinkled like rusted filings, artfully arranged around their shrunken, twisted trunks. Other trees reared up straight, with branches that sprouted at right angles, evergreen needles hiding the revolting odour of miniature pine cones. The whole room was like a sci-lab experiment in miniatures gone wrong. What if these stunted monstrosities could move? Would they try to strangle her?

Randall licked a drop of sweat from her upper lip and spat it out. A forest inside four walls. The thought of all this stuff growing and moving made her feel queasy. Living wood? Ugh! And it was more than illegal. If the broadcasters in the rest of the building found out, they'd be screaming about traitors from within. But as her mother was virtually untouchable, the laws of the Empire did not apply to her.

'You know we should not linger, mistress. Though this is the only unseen way to the outside, I deduce that your mother may wish to show her visitor her most prized possessions?'

PV was right, as usual. The crippled thug from pod-knows-where was welcome to this place. Fenestra had never even thought to share what she considered treasure with her own flesh-and-blood daughter. *Treasure.* Maybe that explained this vault. Money really did grow on trees; if Randall snapped off a twig, it would keep her in a steady stream of designer footwear. But if so much as one leaf was out of place, Fenestra would find out. This was her pension fund as well as a dangerous obsession. To Randall, it was only an exit.

'Yeah. Let's get going.'

She ran towards the small air vent built into the far glass wall, kneeling down to release the catch. The vent swung outwards, letting in a blast of icy-cold air. She put her hands on the edge and looked down. The scale of it always made her dizzy, a sheer wall of glass curving away for at least two kilometres before vanishing into the smog of the traffic far below. A thin sheen of ice-crystals covered the glass. She'd have to be careful today.

'Brrrr!' said PV.

'Oh, really, PV! Just because you have temperature sensors, it doesn't mean you can shiver.'

'Sorry, mistress. I am programmed to respond to the weather.'

But Randall wasn't listening. She was determined to use as few as possible of the tools tucked into her suit pockets, and her only concessions to the weather were the thermo-gloves she quickly pulled on and a pair of goggles which she slipped over her head, adjusting them to filter out the sun's glare. Her breath made miniature clouds in front of her face.

'Time is short, mistress!' PV urged, his voice re-routed into her earpiece.

She nodded. The mirror loved Lady Fenestra and would let her through instantly. Randall's right hand reached up and found the tiny ledge above the air vent. Her fingers dug in as she let the rest of her body swing free of the opening. With her other hand, she swung the vent shut.

This was what she lived for, the lone girl dangling by her fingertips three-quarters of the way up the tallest tower in Maw. The wind sliced past her ears as she sniffed deeply, inhaling the wonderful clean, metallic perfume of the city, mixed with the subtle spicy smell given off by the slabs of super-coated glass that clad the jungle of buildings around her. Here was danger. If her fingers weren't strong enough, she'd soon be tumbling down the sheer wall she clung to. It was one slide she would never survive. Wonderful!

'Mistress! Be still! Your mother and her guest have arrived!'

She tried to slow her breathing. One movement and the glass would amplify the sound, alerting them to her presence. Randall was now effectively blind: she could not see in, but her mother and the boy could see out. And if they did look, they would see her hanging in mid-air, her body splayed against the outer wall.

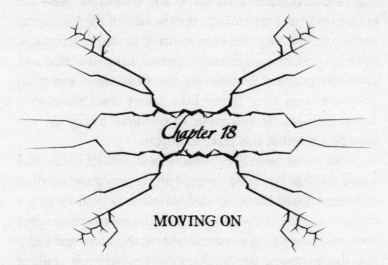

Chapter 18

MOVING ON

'This is beyond *be-leaf* . . .' said Petronio.

'Is that one of your Dendran jokes?' Fenestra arched her sculpted eyebrows.

'No. Seriously. To take trees and . . . make them small . . .' Petronio was uneasy. What diabolical science would it take to squeeze the whole of Arborium into a room this size?

Fenestra mistook his comments for admiration. 'I admit there is an art to it. My pruning shears are sharp and these trees respond well to discipline.'

'I bet they do,' Petronio murmured.

Fenestra was almost purring as she leant over one of the pine trees and clipped a few needles to make the shape more pleasing. 'But of course, you come from a land of woods and take them for granted. Here, as you well know, the trees have long since become the stuff of history. Children read about them in books, just as they read about dinosaurs. As far as the masses of Maw are concerned, trees are extinct. For the sake of the Conglomerates maintaining absolute control of the economy, it must stay that way.' Fenestra turned from the tree and suddenly gripped Petronio by the shoulders. 'And what you have seen here is my little secret.' Her violet eyes bored into his. 'If you wish to continue living, do not breathe a word of this place to anyone.'

'Yeah . . . of course.' Petronio shook himself, rather like a dog that has just been shouted at. He was growing tired of being treated like a pet and Maw was beginning to get to him too: the constant hum as if the rooms themselves were carrying on quiet conversations; the unnatural light; the sharp angles; the unchanging temperature. Still, at least it wasn't as cold as Arborium.

Petronio looked away from Fenestra, and nearly bit his tongue. There was a figure on the other side of the glass, stuck to the vertical surface like a black, overgrown beetle. Long hair splayed out in the wind; goggled eyes stared back at him. He instantly took in the shape of the body that indicated it was a girl.

Fenestra had been too busy showing off her tiny trees to notice anything else. Should he alert her to this intruder? Had they been overheard? But something stopped him. What was it?

Then it came to him. Fenestra had mentioned a daughter with wild red hair. She had hinted that the relationship was fraught, that her daughter was difficult to handle. In that instant, Petronio put two and two together and made a decision. He wouldn't give the girl away. Not yet, anyway. He knew all about difficulties with parents . . . besides, it might even prove useful to hold this bit of knowledge about the envoy's only child.

'Hadn't we better get on?' he said, smoothly slipping away towards the mirror door. 'After all, we don't want to keep your employers waiting . . .'

'Yes. Of course.' He could tell she was annoyed; her most precious pets were being ignored.

'After you!' he said, as the gap appeared in the wall. He risked a glance back at the window, but the shape had vanished.

'Meetings. Ha! That's all the Gloms ever want,' muttered Fenestra as she stalked past Petronio down the hall. The mirror slid silently back into place, trees replaced with blank reflections. 'They should let me get on with my work . . .' she looked at Petronio, '. . . our work. To go back to Arborium was brave, young Grasp.'

Petronio smiled. His father, Grasp senior, had never praised him once in his miserable, short life. 'It was the obvious thing to do. And we need Sergeant Grain and his men on side if the plan is going to work.' The countdown was on and Petronio was itching to get back to Arborium, to see the look on Quercus's face as he begged for mercy.

'No ifs this time. Once you see what our quantum engineers have created, you will be glad you chose the winning side.'

'I already am!' said Petronio. He meant it. Ever since he'd overheard the conversation between his father and Fenestra, there had been no going back. 'You keep mentioning the Gloms. Who are they?'

'Oh. The Conglomerates are run by businessmen and women with too much money and not enough brains to know what to do with it. It's my job to see they get what they want and to find the most practical way to achieve the goals of the Empire: profit and growth.'

Petronio didn't understand half of what she'd said, but the word profit chimed nicely with his own ambitions.

Fenestra stared at the door in front of them, then kicked it with her high-heeled shoe. 'Shardy workman-ship! Open, damn you!'

The door grudgingly vanished into its recess.

Petronio was impressed. The door led straight to the outside, but instead of a sheer drop, a glass tunnel reached out into thin air.

'No need for flying,' said Fenestra. 'My travelator will get us there in minutes.'

The glass was so clear, Petronio could see the long drop into the bowels of the city. Dendrans took living high up for granted – but how the holly, he wondered, did this ropewalk of crystal work? The thin bridge ran straight as an arrow, easily spanning the vast distance between their building and its neighbour. He looked up, trying to see what supports or cantilevers enabled its construction. Nothing but air. Even more confusing was the way that at this level, the next building must have been a quarter of a mile away, but further up, it leant towards their tower like a half-toppled tree trunk. Maw was a lopsided shimmer-ing jungle, truly topsy-treevy.

'Come along, young Grasp of the woods!' Fenestra took a single step and there she was, gliding away from him without moving her feet. Petronio was amazed all over again each time he saw one of these moving walkways. Fenestra's private travelator, constructed to a higher specification than its public counterparts, was especially impressive.

'Come on, get on board!' Fenestra shouted, laughing. She was already twenty feet ahead, and quickly drifting further away. Petronio hopped on to the glass, wobbling slightly as he found his balance. The slight rippling motion in the transparent floors was always disorientating at first, but then there was the now-familiar exhilaration of being carried through the sky without wings or hooves. Moving floors . . . who had thought to invent such beautiful laziness?

A little later, Petronio stood slightly behind Fenestra as they finally came to a halt in front of a pair of smooth doors. After the travelator they had taken a glass lift that had rocketed up to the top of the tower, bursting through a layer of cloud. 'Now remember,' whispered Fenestra, 'we are about to meet the so-called chief executives of the Conglomerates. A bickering bunch of bawling babies, but there you have it! My job is to soothe their fears, and yours is to stay quiet.'

The door opened and they were ushered in by a secretary who tried not to look at Petronio's arm. Finally . . . the seat of Maw's power. What a long way he had come from the boy he used to be, smoking stolen cigars in a utility room.

Apart from the door they had come through, the circular room they now entered had a 360-degree view, the city spread out far beneath them. The room was floored with thick oak planks, blackened and warped with age. The diamond-shaped glass table that filled the room's centre looked out of place in this setting, as did the nine seated men and women staring up at him. He wondered for a moment why they were so obese – but then, this was a brave new world of *travelators* and *lifts*. No walking needed. Their loose-fitting robes, emblazoned with the logos of the brands each one represented, made his eyes ache. He noticed how some of the names oddly seemed to hark back to the trees: *Oaky-Kola, Bud*.

'Shouldn't the boy be in school?' The man who spoke was evidently the boss of something called Eezy-Cheeze. Glowing by-lines flickered up and down the sleeves of his robe: *One squeeze and you'll be tasting heaven. Buy two, get a virtual cow to add to your online farm, FREE!* The man's heavy-lidded eyes had already dismissed Petronio, his puffy fingers drumming impatiently on the polished table.

'I am capable of speech,' Petronio said.

There was a shocked silence.

'Oh, the one-armed savage boy understands me!' The man turned back to his scroll-screen and yawned with distaste.

Petronio wondered how deep his knife would have to dig through the folds of fat before it found the man's heart. He stared back at him, his gaze unblinking. He'd expected army generals, not this preening gathering of peacocks. 'I do question why you would insult the only *boy* capable of doing your dirty work and delivering the glass spheres as you have asked.'

The man looked up sharply and drew breath through his teeth.

'Ladies and gentlemen, please,' Fenestra interrupted. 'My young colleague is entirely trustworthy. He also respects your aims in this situation.' She turned to Petronio. 'Don't you?'

Petronio nodded. He remembered the lesson his father, the late Councillor Grasp, had taught him: *Know your enemy.* And though this lot weren't his enemies, they certainly weren't on the way to becoming best buds either. He was glad to see that the mechanical arm seemed to make them nervous.

Eezy-Cheeze ignored Petronio, concentrating on Fenestra. 'Envoy, my associates put their faith in your methods last time. You failed. Instead of victory, all that you brought back from that cursed island was a damaged member of the Dendran species. And now we are being asked once again to trust you. The economy is in freefall. We need results!'

The others murmured in agreement.

'Lord Far, I admit to the setbacks,' Fenestra replied. 'But the essential components are in place. My team are ready to demonstrate the weapon's capability tomorrow morning. There is some risk involved, so I would perfectly understand it if you did not wish to see it first-hand.'

Lord Far? thought Petronio. Perhaps the name was accurate. These Gloms lived in a land of far-tales and make-believe. But they were also Petronio's route to power and riches far beyond any Arborian dream.

'Are you implying we might be frightened?' the man

spluttered, his soft cheeks turning a shade of mottled red. 'In the cut and thrust of high finance we have all faced far greater dangers. We look forward to seeing you there tomorrow.'

As one, the Gloms turned back to their screens. One of the women tapped her screen irritably. 'Point of order three, as I was saying, there have been some problems with mould in our Woodstock reserves.'

Already, the secretary was holding the door open as the lift waited. Evidently they were dismissed. Petronio felt like he was a five-year-old back in Acorn school, made to stand in the corner when he'd *accidentally* stuck a compass point through a fellow pupil's hand. Served her right for calling him fat. Compared to this lot, he was skinny as a twig.

'As I said before,' Fenestra muttered as the door shut behind them, 'a bunch of spoiled brats, though it doesn't do well to annoy them. And I thought I told *you* to stay quiet! You must learn to master your temper. Now then, we will talk further on the way back, and then I have work to do. If my lazy daughter bothers turning up after school, I shall let her show you the sights.'

The sights? Petronio felt he had seen enough for today, particularly as the lift zipped down the side of the building. The miles of twisted glass blurred in front of his eyes and the pap that passed for breakfast in Maw swilled horribly around his guts, threatening to spew all over the shiny interior of the lift.

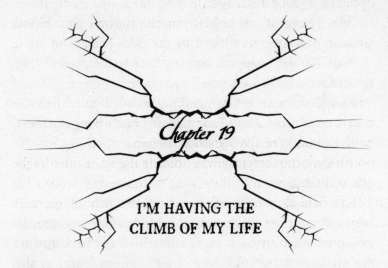

Chapter 19

I'M HAVING THE CLIMB OF MY LIFE

'Clear!' said PV.

'You sure?' The outer glass gave nothing away. There could be a crowd inside for all Randall knew.

'I am not programmed to make mistakes, mistress! Your mother and her colleague have exited.'

'And they didn't see me?' Randall could hardly believe her luck.

'According to my infra-red input and audio sensors, the boy made eye contact for 5.65 seconds, then suggested that he and your mother leave.'

'Thanks for the info. Next time, leave out the hundredths of a second though, OK?'

'But accuracy is my primary function!'

Randall ignored the peevish tone. She was confused. The boy with the artificial arm had discovered her but said nothing. What did it mean? She didn't like the idea of being seen by a stranger.

'May I suggest you begin your climb now? Your blood circulation has been reduced by the cold. I calculate . . .'

'No!' Randall snapped, coming back to the present. 'No calculations. Until I ask you.'

PV fell silent, as though sulking. Randall could feel the ache in her arms. How long had she been hanging there on the outside of the window? It said something for the hours she'd put into training that her grip on the ledge was still firm.

She hauled herself up to sit on the tiny ledge, and began flexing her fingers, then rubbing them together to get some warmth back in. Finally, she leant back against the glass, sucking cold, breezy air into her lungs as she feasted on the view. Out here, perched high in these windswept canyons the way the falcons of old had perched in the trees, was where Randall felt she was most herself. Here was the only place she was truly alone, despite being surrounded by millions of lives.

In the distance, a flock of pure white c-gulls wheeled and turned, their screeches bouncing and echoing round the arching towers of Maw. Out here, on the other side of the glass, Randall could see more clearly how they twisted and spiralled upwards, competing for light and sky.

She smiled. She pitied the faceless drones hidden in the offices piled one on top of the other. The morning work shift had already begun, the hum of crush-hour traffic now easing off far below her. Once transported to their various brand-named buildings, the many million wage slaves would spend their dull days scurrying about at their mundane jobs in perfectly comfortable temperature-adjusted zones. Nobody in their right mind went outside, apart from Randall.

But beneath the shiny veneer she already understood how the Empire was run. Business was about calculating ways to kill off the competition. Nothing beat taking down a Conglomerate, chewing it up and then spitting out the pieces. They were welcome to it!

She pulled out an energy bar and tore off the wrapper with her teeth. It was formulated from derived sugars and salts to give the exact amount of slow-release adrenalin. As for flavour, it was an oblong of mushy blandness.

Randall dropped the foil wrapper, but even before the wind had a chance to carry it away, a recyclo-van appeared out of nowhere, hovering primly as it sucked the offending bit of rubbish into its mouth. 'Tut! Tut!' came the pre-recorded voice. 'Don't throw it away! You have two days to pay. And have a nice day!' A slot opened in the side of the vehicle and a segmented arm stretched out to stick an adhesive enforcement notice on her shoulder.

The little van zipped off again, but not before Randall had given it an interesting hand signal. 'Tut! Tut! to you too! Dumb machine!' she said, ripping the ticket from her shoulder and shoving it in her pocket. She swallowed down the last of the bar. Time to go.

Randall twisted round and reached up with her right hand for the familiar gap. It was the start of a known route, worked out from hacked and downloaded architects' blueprint plans. No matter how hard the architects competed with each other to make their buildings the smoothest, there were always tiny cracks and joints within the surface of any structure. And Randall's fingers were like nano-spiders, searching out every nook and cranny as she began to haul herself up the sheer wall towards the sky.

Half an hour later she had reached the jutting spot she was looking for, at a point where the curved façade of a neighbouring tower leant over within only a few metres of Randall's building. The skyscraper that housed Beeching Incorporated was almost close enough to reach out and touch. Almost, but not quite. She'd spent hours last night avoiding homework as she worked out the difficulty rating. It was a particularly tricky position that had so far defeated her. She didn't need PV to tell her it was a 'nine', or maybe even an unheard-of 'ten'. However, if she went for the move, and landed it, she would win more online praise in five minutes than her mother had given her in a lifetime. And as for what lay beyond this impossible twist? Uncharted territory. Brand new slopes asking to be conquered. The thought of it made her skin tingle.

'All right, PV. You can stop with the silent treatment now.'

'I do not know what you mean, mistress!'

'Yes, you do. Now, calculate the distance,' she said through gritted teeth. The tip of one foot was dug into a rain-duct and a single hand gripped a length of cable. She was almost horizontal, suspended from an overhang that shouldn't have been mathematically possible.

'The gap is 3.6 metres. As commanded, I have not included hundredths in my measurement.'

'Golly gosh. You want me to say thank you?'

PV didn't respond to the sarcasm. 'Your insect's video feed is now activated and ready to film the manoeuvre. Though, might I say, mistress, I estimate only a fifty-six percent possibility that you will survive the jump.'

'I didn't ask for your opinion!' Little silicon squirt, she thought. Who did he think he was? But the odds made her heart beat faster. Easy to use a filament gun to fire a rope across, or any of the other tools tucked into her packsack. But the neighbouring building was temptingly near.

With her free hand, she reached gently into the pocket under her armpit. Her fingertips felt the flutter of tiny wings. Taking care not to crush them, she slowly extracted the hoverfly-cam. It rested on her outstretched palm, iridescent wings unfurling to catch the morning sun in a dazzle of colour. Stereoscopic eyes stared at her as the Maw-made insect waited, attached by thin wires.

'Off you go, little fellow!' she smiled. 'Plenty of distance shots and close-ups, please!' Two antennae quivered in the equivalent of a *yes*. The makers had even built in a pleasant-sounding chirrup to go with it.

'And make me a star!' she whispered, though the biting wind snatched her words away. The hoverfly paused, then bent its gleaming legs. One spring and it took off into the morning sky. Quickly, it began to buzz round Randall, taking a series of videos that PV would later cut, splice and edit together into a fast-moving film.

'Here goes!' she shouted, tensing her thigh muscles, uncurling her fingers and leaping out into empty space.

*

Stuck at a desk behind the glass wall of the opposite building, a trader yawned at his scroll-screen. It told him that Hedge-Fund futures were dipping. The fabled Hedge, said to be the last remnant of a time when trees had covered Maw, and now securely protected by rocket-proof glass on the roof of the largest bank in the Empire, had only grown three millimetres in the past six months. With Compost up, and sunlight in good supply, the forecasters had promised four millimetres. They were wrong. So much for financial wisdom . . . still, the trader thought, if the good subjects of Maw wanted to take a bet on it, he was happy to take their money.

Meanwhile, the handhold Randall was reaching for was only millimetres away. Her mesh gloves brushed the outer wall as her fingers stretched to reach the grip-point. But PV's calculations had failed to factor in weather considerations. Ice crystals were one danger, but frost pockets were the hidden killers. Her fingertips curled into a ducting crevice as she bunched her fist against the side to provide traction. She might as well have stuck her hand into a bucket of oil. There was nothing to hold on to and her arm instantly came free.

Something flickered at the edge of the trader's vision. He looked up, and his mouth fell open in shock. No way! He must have drunk one too many Buds last night . . . otherwise how could he explain the vision of a goggled figure in black flying through the air towards his office? Its arms flailed round and round, then it fell from view.

The trader closed his eyes, then opened them again.

There was nothing there. Perhaps he just had a migraine coming on.

PV was right, again. The percentages were against Randall and now she was freefalling through the December sky. The hoverfly kept up with her, wings buzzing away as it filmed her descent. Oh yes, it would make a *shatteringly* good film.

Randall was about to achieve the biggest hit of her short climbing career. Her suit had built-in shock protection to stop bones breaking from a height of up to thirty metres. But two kilometres? She was as good as dead.

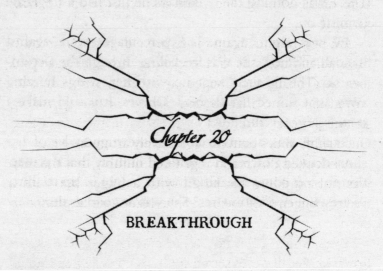

Chapter 20

BREAKTHROUGH

'Wakey, wakey, rise and shine. Though you don't get much shine down here, buddy boy!'

Ark's head felt muzzy. Maybe it was a dream: the ghosts of the Land of the Dead calling out to him. But the sharp pain in his cheek was still there, and whatever kept prodding him in the ribs hurt like holly.

'Off me . . .' he mumbled, his words slurred.

The prodding continued. 'Yeah. Gonna let you live just long enough so we can hang you high. Serve you right for gatecrashing our little gathering!'

Ark slowly opened his eyes. Flickering candles spun around him and straight walls veered off into darkness. He screwed his eyelids shut and tried again. 'Where . . . am . . . I?'

'Oh, that's good. The Gloms have sent in a coupla bumbling spies and one of them sings *Where Am I?* Holy

Lord of the Woods!' The voice snarled. 'You ain't foolin'
no-one!'

Ark began to focus on the figure that swam in front of
him: pale white skin and wiry grey hair. The man was
lean as a plank and dressed in a patchwork coat with
woven-in colours that blinked on and off like eyes. Grey,
stained britches extended all the way to the man's feet.
Once-shiny shoes danced aggressively around.

Ark looked down and registered numbly that the man
was not prodding his jerkin with a finger but with a
curved dagger. One push and the blade would plunge in
deep.

'I've come . . . I'm not . . . a spy.' Ark tried to hide his
fear as shrew-like eyes stared at him with disbelief. Had he
survived the journey to Maw only to have some *walnutter*
finish him off? 'Mucum! Where's . . . Mucum?'

'The other spy? He's out of it.' Thin lips curled into a
sneer.

'What do you mean?'

'Dead, dried up, extinct, like the seeds of all the trees,
get my drift?'

'No!' Ark wailed. 'Can't be . . .' He slumped back. The
news was as heavy as a Rootshooter's hammer.

'Aww! Poor boy's all alone now, well ain't that a
shame?'

Ark barely heard the taunt. Him and Mucum. Bickering, laughing, facing down sewer-rats and guards armed
with swords. Diving down into the deeps. Wielding the
squit-cannon like a weapon of war when the battle was
nearly lost. They'd faced everything together. They'd even

finally made it into the bowels of Maw – if that *was* where the capsule had crashed. And now, just when Ark really needed him, he was gone.

Ark suddenly knew how Flo must have felt when her father Joe had fallen from the battlements. He was alone again, without even Corwenna's voice to guide him. He tried to swallow, but the dust clogged his throat and hot tears blurred his eyes.

Then something sprouted deep inside him, greater than the grief that splintered his soul. If he, Ark Malikum, still lived, then maybe Arborium was not yet lost. Mucum, great lumbering pain that he was, wouldn't have wanted him to give up. What would he have said? *Think, mate! That's what yer buddy brain is for! Thinkin' things through.*

So, first things first. Had he lost his knife in the crash? No, he could feel its warm comforting glow as it nestled in its sheath under his armpit. He remembered the drone of Mojo's instrument and the humming Rootshooters. But even if they had filled the blade with their power, he wouldn't have time to grab for it before the man skewered him like a timber-boar, and it would be the same story if he tried to reach for the phial.

Time to work out his surroundings, see if there was anything that might help him. He was no longer strapped to his seat; someone had pulled him out from the cracked and crumpled shell of the capsule. He was lying on the floor next to it, surrounded by a halo of glittering glass splinters. He glanced to one side. There was a hole smashed in the wall like a ragged wound.

The room the capsule had crashed into was long and

thin, supported by rows of pillars that reached from the floor to the ceiling only a few feet above his head. The walls were impossibly straight, but covered in strange writing, as well as drawings of . . . trees! They were everywhere, crude outlines of branches and leaves painted over the dirt-stained ceiling and floor. Ark was reminded of his little sister's stick drawings. But there was no sun shining through this flat forest; instead, the scene was illuminated by long, thin cylinders of light similar to those in the diamond mine.

Ark switched his gaze from the drawings. There were other figures clustered round the man who held him down, all staring at him with hate in their eyes. They were also dressed in tattered clothes. Some of them wore what looked like silk vines tied around their shifts and their coats had mis-matched buttons. The women wore short petticoat skirts that would have been freezing in Arborium's winter.

'That's right, have a good look round. It'll be your last. As I'm sure a good little servant of Maw like yourself knows, this shrine is breakin' every law under the high-up sun. But the Gloms are playin' you like a fiddle. While they're toying with their Woodstock investments, the city is dyin'! Well, we can't have you reportin' us to the envoy, now can we?' The blade pressed harder, easily piercing the black leather of Ark's jerkin.

'I don't understand what you're saying.'

The hand holding the knife stayed steady. 'You know, you talk odd for a spy.'

'I told you, I'm not a spy. I'm from . . .'

'. . . the secret police. Yeah.' Ark saw a fleck of spittle on the man's blistered lips.

'You must believe me!'

The man's eyes narrowed. It was evidently the wrong thing to say. 'What d'you know about belief?' he spat. 'I *believe* you've entered our holy place intent on doin' us poor Levellers harm. It's our dream to bring the trees to life once more. But the Gloms want to get rid of us and our seeds like we're vermin. Anyways, you already know all that. And seein' as you don't believe in prayers but only worship profit, I think it's time we gave you final mercy. All I can say is it'll be quick – that's a first-glass guarantee!'

The crowd had been silent so far, but now they jostled to get a better view and began to jeer.

'Take him out, Jed!'

'It's the only way!'

'We have to protect the seeds!'

Here, in this dim basement, far from the cradle of good green leaves, there was no mercy to be found.

The blade began to press home. Ark shut his eyes. He had promised his family he'd come back, that he'd take Shiv in his arms once more and cuddle her tight. That promise was about to be broken.

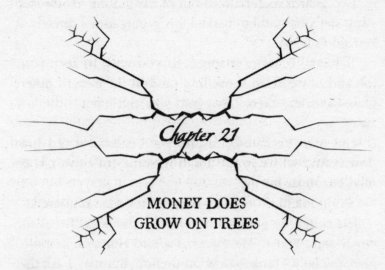

Chapter 21

MONEY DOES
GROW ON TREES

'**P**lanks! Stacks of them,' said Petronio, stating the obvious.

The dimly-lit cavern stretched away into the distance. Each plank was about twenty feet long and an inch thick. They had been sanded smooth and then laid out on padded rubber cross-struts. Petronio craned his neck up, trying to take in the stacks looming hundreds of feet above him. It was like a library, shelved with wood instead of books. And the scale of this storage space was mind-loggling. 'How many?' he asked.

'I don't keep count, but about five hundred and forty-five thousand, according to the Gloms,' Fenestra replied.

It seemed a strange way to treat a load of ancient timber. Even though Petronio understood how valuable wood was here, he couldn't quite get used to the idea. He leant forward to touch one of the planks.

Two guards materialized out of the gloom. 'Please step away, sir!' one of them barked, his g-gun aimed directly at Petronio's heart.

'Soldier!' Fenestra snapped. 'If you wish to keep your job and not end up shovelling sand in the eastern desert glass-factories, then I suggest you put your little toy away!'

The man hesitated, unsure. But Fenestra stared him down. 'And while you're about it, some coffee would be nice. No sugar for me.'

'Do I look like a blinkin' barista?' the man muttered.

His colleague grabbed him by the shoulder. 'Do as the envoy says, Frank.' He turned back to Fenestra. 'I apologize, my lady. Frank is new on the job. But may I ask that your boy not touch the stock? Our employers would have a fit if they found out you'd even been here.'

'Of course!' said Fenestra. 'Silly me. I merely wanted to the lad to understand.'

'Which I do. You *have* already explained it.' Petronio rolled his eyes.

It was with a sigh of relief that the claustrophobia of the heavily-guarded vault was left behind and Fenestra ushered Petronio into an office filled with welcome, real sunlight from the far glass wall.

'Sit,' Fenestra said.

Petronio hated the way the chairs in Maw instantly expanded as he sat down, moulding to the contours of his buttocks and back. It was unnerving.

There was a knock on the door. The same soldier who had pulled a gun on him five minutes before now bore a tray laden with two steaming glasses and a bowl of sugar. The man was obviously resentful, almost dropping the tray on to the low table between them.

'Will that be all, ma'am?' he said through gritted teeth.

'Yes. But if I find you've spat into the coffee, I'll have you defenestrated.'

Only last night, the envoy had told Petronio how her family had come by their power and surname. In an ancient struggle between warring factions, one of Fenestra's forebears had thrown his enemy out of a window. That was what defenestration meant.

The soldier's eyes widened with shock. 'Wouldn't d-dream of it . . . ma'am,' he stuttered.

'I'm glad to hear it,' she said. 'You can go.' She waved the now-trembling soldier away and turned back to Petronio. 'You have coffee in Arborium?'

'Smuggled,' said Petronio, ladling in sugar and taking a series of gulps. The taste was smoky and sweet, like caramel. 'But by the time it gets through to us, it's usually been cut with chicory. Buddy mud-pirates. I could get used to this stuff, though.'

'It's time I told you more details about the – erm – facts of life.' Fenestra appeared uncertain as she fingered the mahogany pearls round her neck.

Petronio almost choked on his coffee. 'Are you joking? What do you think I learned in medical school?'

'Well now, it's true that I am capable of humour.' She smiled, and Petronio felt his cheeks flush. Her teeth were perfectly white, the lips redder than any holly-berry. 'But don't worry, young man. I refer, of course, to the financial facts. You need to understand how this glittering empire pays for itself.'

Not another lecture. Petronio tried to suppress a yawn. His mind drifted back to the room with the tiny trees. He wondered again about the girl on the other side of the glass, swinging one-handed like a sycamore pod. She was probably having more fun than him.

'. . . and that's when the value of wood began to sky-rocket.'

'Sorry, what?'

Fenestra sighed. 'At least do me the honour of pretending to listen.'

'Apologies, my lady. Didn't sleep well.' He took another sip of coffee and tried to ignore the sun's rays bouncing off the bare walls.

'I see I shall have to start at the beginning again. Right, what is money?'

'Is that a trick question?' Petronio thought of gold. Its glitter. The weight of it.

'Here in Maw, money is only a concept. Once it was based on the stocks of gold that countries kept in their vaults. Our primitive ancestors printed words on their bank notes. They were a promise to pay the bearer of the paper a certain amount of gold. It was based on faith alone.'

Petronio was puzzled. In Arborium paper was for scribbling on or wiping your backside.

'But the countries of old were expanding, and the forests stood in their way. Land was more valuable when built on, so the trees began to shrink in number. All this commerce had an unintended side-effect: once the last tree had been cut down – to make way for the foundations of a new bank, as history tells it – people gradually realized that burning leftover wood was a waste of a valuable resource. Slowly, timber itself began to gain in rarity value.' Fenestra paused.

'Go on!' said Petronio, his boredom vanishing like morning mist. Although he already knew some of this, it was starting to make more sense now. He took a sip of his drink, admiring the tiny heat elements in the cup that kept his coffee steaming hot.

'At first,' Fenestra carried on, 'you could pick up a plank at a hovercar-boot sale for a few copper coins. Logs were still available for next to nothing. To think of it!' Fenestra sighed.

'But why didn't they just plant more trees?' Petronio cut in.

'I'm getting to that. Be patient. Business saw an opportunity and began to buy up the remaining stocks. That was when the real wood-rush began. For you see, after the cutting down of the last tree, something else was discovered: no new trees would grow. What little open ground was left was poisoned, turned to sand, totally polluted; the last seeds were found to be sterile. It didn't matter what means were tried. Nothing. So, with no new trees, antiques were dug out of cupboards. Boxes and pallets were carefully taken apart and hoarded away. Chairs and tables were sawn up to make brooches and twig-trinkets.'

'Of course, the governments at the time didn't stand a chance. They were already in debt to business and the early Gloms of long ago saw an opportunity. Call it evolution, if you like, but a takeover of the government by the Conglomerates was the natural next step. Wood was now so valuable that whoever controlled the Woodstock controlled the world. The Gloms made it their business to dominate ownership of the stocks of wood. And thus the Mawish Empire was born.'

In Petronio's mind, cogs whirred into place. 'So because a bunch of businessmen bought some planks, they ended up running the show!'

'That is too simplistic. But yes, the nine major Conglomerates each have an equal share in the one vault that contains the majority of the stock. It is our Holy of Holies and, as you just found out, well guarded. Few are blessed with the opportunity to see it.'

'So that's what you've just shown me?'

'Yes. Fort Knots, the Empire's treasure chest. And that, as you know, is why your little island is so important. We don't yet understand how Arborium managed to stay hidden for thousands of years. Our scientists talk of an ancient viral worm that crawled through our cyber-cloud, creating a blind-spot that no satellite or fly-by craft could see through. But whatever happened in history, it is the future we must take charge of. If anyone else were to get hold of Arborian wood and flood the markets in Maw, the value of the wood in Fort Knots would drop to next to nothing. Can you imagine? The Conglomerates would collapse and the economy they control would be destroyed. No! We must have command of Arborium for ourselves; keep its valuable trees under lock and key. We discovered it. It is ours!' Fenestra raised her hand and slammed it on to the table with such force that hairline cracks zigzagged across the surface.

Petronio jumped, startled. First she had shown him a glass finger crushing a diamond, and now here she was with icy fire in her eyes, talking wildly about piles of wood. It was better just to nod and smile, he thought – it didn't really matter so long as it all led to the downfall of Arborium and his own personal rise.

'Tomorrow morning, the Quantum Trap will be ready for its final test. It is also my birthday tomorrow, and I cannot think of a better present. As the Gloms said, I cannot afford to fail twice. If your commander lets me down, you might not be so useful to me any more.'

The threat hung in the air like the particles of wood dust that hovered under the dim lights of Fort Knots. Petronio shrank back in his seat. What could he say to a woman whose ancestors delighted in tossing enemies out of high windows?

'My lady,' he said, swallowing his pride, 'I am yours to command.'

'Yes, I know!' she smirked, and at that moment Petronio hated her for it.

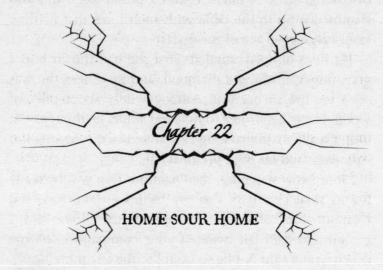

Chapter 22

HOME SOUR HOME

'**M**iss Jarrett! Miss Jarrett!'

Randall's head was clanging. Why wouldn't they leave her alone?

'She's alive!'

'Yup. Eyelids fluttering. Pulse good.'

'Flaw, get her to talk.'

'Miss Jarrett, can you hear us?'

Her body felt like one big bruise. So much for the anti-shock properties of her Calvin Shine suit. She tried wriggling her fingers.

'Nothing broken, mistress!' PV said quietly. She hoped he was right as she reluctantly opened her eyes.

'Lucky for you we were working this particular sector.' The woman who spoke to her looked familiar. She was dressed in a quilted body warmer that might have once been white but was now brown with bird droppings, grit and the grime of a million windows. 'Drink!' She put a bottle to Randall's frozen, blistered lips.

Randall took a sip. 'Hey, Flaw,' she croaked, finally recognizing the window cleaner she had met once before when out climbing. 'How you doing?' She hauled herself up and looked round. The plasti-platform clung to the vertical walls and was low-sided, like a stretched-out baby's cot. As hidden magnets slowly pulled it up the side of the building, the two other cleaners leapt up from where they were crouching over her and quickly resumed their jobs. They swayed in perfect synchronized motion, wiping the windows with long telescopic rods in a rhythmic back-and-forth action.

'Fine,' said the woman, pulling a few loose strands of hair into her brown ponytail. 'I was keeping up with my quota when I saw you tumbling through the sky. I had the controls in my hand and was able to shift the platform fast enough to catch you. But it was touch and go whether you'd end up splattered down in the dark canyons. Can you move?'

'Yeah.' Slowly, she rolled over, took a deep breath, then staggered to her feet. She gripped a side-rail, feeling the dizziness subside. The city dazzled her eyes, indifferent. The twisted spires appeared to be leaning over her and laughing. Today, they'd nearly beaten her.

'You saved me.'

'Thank the seeds. Perhaps I was meant to catch you.'

Randall frowned. 'What do you mean, *thank the seeds*?'

'Nothing, Miss Jarrett. Only a phrase.' She peered nervously up at the hoverfly-cam. 'Is that thing still filming?'

'No,' said Randall. 'It's only programmed to shoot the

exciting action bits. Boring talk isn't anyone's idea of good viewing.'

'That's good.' The woman turned back to her hand-held control. 'We'll drop you off on the next floor up. You're very lucky. Be more careful next time.'

'Oh, I will be – tonight. Nobody's conquered the north face of the Beeching Building before. I've been planning it for ages.' According to the cloud-gossip that Randall was tuned into, only one free-climber had ever made the attempt. The resulting film had been fuzzy but heart-stopping as the wild winds that blew around the upper reaches had plucked the boy from near the seven thousandth floor. He had tumbled down like a vase knocked from a shelf, slowly shrinking out of shot. Randall shuddered. 'The glass slopes may be vicious. But nothing's going to stop me making the first unaided ascent.' Randall could see the concern in the woman's face. 'Don't worry. I'll be fine. I know what I'm doing.'

The woman reached out a hand to stroke Randall's hair, then stopped herself. 'You might think you do, but what if one day no one's there to break your fall, like we were today?' A few minutes later, the platform glided to a halt outside an air vent hatch. 'You can make your way back in from here,' Flaw sighed. 'But tell me, girl, why do you do it?'

As Randall leant over to work the latch-lock, she turned to peer up at the blue haze of sky. 'Because it's the only time I feel free.' Randall trusted Flaw not to tell on her. She was only a lowly worker after all, with no proof.

'That's what we dream of,' Flaw murmured. 'Log-speed you.'

'Thanks Flaw. I owe you.' And with that she was wriggling inside the fire escape. Randall knew that once she was alone, PV would start lecturing her about the danger she'd put herself in, but right now she was too tired for it. 'Sleep!' she muttered, the only total command that PV could not override. The buzzing stopped. Peace at last.

As Randall took the boring, indoor route back, she wondered about Flaw's odd words. Nobody really talked about *logs* unless they were in a position to invest a few million. It was strange.

Later, after she had updated her status without mentioning her fall, she headed out to look for something to give her mother for her birthday. On the outskirts of the consumer district a street vendor tried to sell her a pair of fake green Leavi jeans, but Randall was more interested in the tiny jewelled wood brooch displayed in his fold-out case.

'That's top designer stuff, darling! One hundred percent Firberry! The perfect present for yer boyfriend. Or fer you, 'cos you're so pretty. I can do you a special price.'

Randall was furious. 'It's not for my boyfriend!' she snapped. 'And don't call me darling.' She held the golden-coloured brooch up to the harsh light, examining the miniature carved knot at its centre. 'This piece of trash is a counterfeit splinter of common pine! Firberry? My Glass!'

The man did his best to look offended. 'Don't you swear at me, missy. You couldn't afford it anyway. Now listen, little girl. Does your mummy or daddy know you're skivin' off school?'

'I've no idea. But seeing as my mother is the Envoy of

Maw, shall I get her on-screen so you can have a chat with her about your illegal business?'

The man instantly changed tack. 'Sorry, miss. No offence!' he whimpered as he slammed his case shut and scurried away. It didn't make Randall feel any better. Why did she even bother to remember her mother's birthday? The most she'd get in return for whatever gift she found was one of her mother's pretend smiles before the present was quietly slipped into recycling. Randall pushed her hands into her pockets and headed to the locker in the gym where she stored a hidden stash of school clothes. She exchanged her climbing gear for her school uniform and several minutes later, let herself back into the apartment.

Fenestra was waiting for her. And by her side was the boy, staring at her with recognition in his eyes. 'A good day at school, my dear?' Her mother's cold lips brushed the side of her cheek.

'Fine.' Randall pulled away, wincing at the sudden stabbing pain in her back. The affection was only for show. Anyway, Fenestra was welcome to check up on her attendance. According to stats reports, Randall was a model pupil. Elementary hacking. At least she'd learned something in her fourteen years.

'I'd like you to meet our guest who is staying with us tonight. Petronio Grasp. My daughter, Randall Jarrett.'

The boy put his mechanical arm forward then realized his mistake. Awkwardly, he shifted round and presented his real hand.

'Pleased to meet you,' said Randall without meaning it. The contact was brief, his fingers surprisingly warm.

'He has come from the far suburbs on a matter of . . . business.' Fenestra pressed a finger to her ear. 'Yes,' she said. 'Give me five minutes.' She turned back to her daughter. 'I have calls to attend to. Perhaps you could take Petronio on a little tour before dinner?' She strode away down the hall, leaving only an uncomfortable silence.

Half an hour and several travelators and lifts later, Randall and Petronio sat at a table by the edge of a glass pool of water. The pleasure gardens were the great wonder of Maw. The domed structure that contained them, easily five kilometres in radius, was cradled between four huge towers on a web of pulsating glass fibre-filaments. Clear canals criss-crossed the transparent paths, lined with shimmering grit to stop people sliding over the edge into the crystal water. Dotted around were trees and bushes, built out of fir-bo glass and finished off by the finest craftsmen in fetching shades of brown and green. The pleasantly warmed air was filled with the cries of children sliding down helter-skelters that wound around engin-eered holo-trunks. It was a world within a world.

'Is anything real up here?' Petronio toyed with his glass.

'What do you mean, real? Like your arm?'

The boy smiled. 'Point taken! I guess without your technology, I'd be fairly armless.'

'Oh. Funny.' She was glad to be sitting down. Her thighs were sore from her climbing escapade earlier. But tonight, she'd tackle the north face. This time, she'd win.

Petronio eyed up the gigantic dome that soared over them, a barrier against the harsh chill of winter outside. 'They made a rubbish job of the trees.'

'Some people like them. And at least they don't smell.'

The boy's eyes grew distant. 'Where I come from, the leaves are as big as a man and tougher than leather.'

'I thought you lived in the suburbs.'

'Ah, yes. I mean the, erm, statues of leaves. Never mind.' Petronio used his real hand to take a slurp of his Oaky-Kola. He grimaced. 'Brown, fizzy and sweet. Disgusting.'

'You don't have to drink it!' said Randall. Who did he think he was? She grabbed a candy Treet from the bowl in front of her and popped it in her mouth. The silence stretched out. A flock of albino-white crows wheeled above them. 'The birds are real, even if the park wardens cull any that aren't pure-bred. And the flowers actually grow. The display is famous throughout the Empire.'

The flower bed she pointed at was tilted up to catch the far-off sun. And the garden itself, with its groves, grottos and perfect tinkling waterfalls, was a mechanical marvel. From morning to night, it rotated on its hidden axis to soak up every ray of available light.

'It's still fake!' Petronio growled. 'A ton of flowers planted out so that all the petals make a picture of an oak tree!' As he spoke, a gaggle of tourists from the far eastern suburbs gathered by the display to take pictures. 'Everything's about the trees – the drinks, the food, the pictures – but there isn't a real one for five thousand miles – unless you count those blooming dwarves your mother has hidden away.' He turned and stared at Randall meaningfully.

She gasped. 'What do mean?'

'Oh, don't look so shocked. I saw you on the outside of that secret room, clinging to the glass. But you needn't worry, your secret's safe with me. Well . . . it is, so long as you do me a favour.'

'What? How dare you! What sort of favour?'

'I want you to let me know what your mother, the envoy is up to.'

'Unbelievable! You want me to spy on my own mother?' Randall nearly choked on her sweet.

The boy clacked his pincers together and studied them carefully. 'Of course, I could tell her where I saw you earlier today.'

'That's blackmail!' This boy, with his arm of metal and sneering mouth, made her feel sick.

'Got no choice. I need to look after number one, i.e. me. If I don't succeed in my task, she could have me killed, easy as blinking one of her painted eyelids.'

'She wouldn't do that!' But Randall wasn't so sure. She thought back to the times she'd overheard conversations about 'dealing' with enemies.

'Are you kidding me? You're her daughter. Even you must know the meaning of the family name.'

'It's a story!' Randall protested. But in her heart she knew he was right. She stood up. 'We'll be late for dinner,' she said coldly. It was all tumbling round inside her head. The glass finger, the talk of armies, this strange boy who was trying to imprison her with his commands. Pod the lot of them. Once she'd eaten, she'd make her excuses and head out. She wondered if her mother would even miss her if she slipped and fell.

She took a deep breath. Out there, beyond the dome, the sky was calling to her once again.

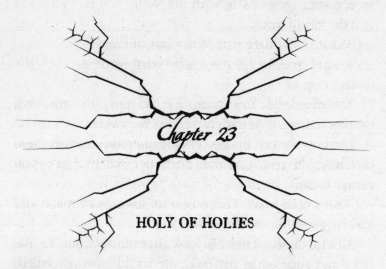

Chapter 23

HOLY OF HOLIES

Ark felt the space between one breath and the next. It stretched out like a summer's day, high in the canopy-cruck-pools of Arborium. Ark and his friends diving and splashing like pine-porpoises, desperate for the sun to stay longer; sharing a meal with his mother and father; throwing a giggling Shiv up into the leaves; Corwenna and the Ravens. All these thoughts and more flew through his head as he saw the blade begin its journey towards his heart.

The wind murmured in the tunnel behind the remains of the capsule, and carried on that breeze Ark felt a sudden faint echo of Corwenna's voice. *Be still. Time is what you make of it.*

She was the Raven-Queen, but even with her power, her words could not carry for five thousand miles, could they?

Be still. Look close.

The blade his attacker held was Maw-made alloy, etched in swirling patterns that reminded Ark of a snail shell. The hand that gripped it was determined.

Look close.

The handle! Ark recognized it instantly. The top of it was carved in a sliver of oak, and as he stared at it Ark saw the journey of this hidden jewel, smuggled across the seas by trading pirates. What was nothing but the wind's plaything, a mere fragment of twig in Arborium, became a commodity in Maw, traded on the black market for gold and silver.

All this Ark registered between one breath and the next, and even as the knife slid through leather, sliced the cotton of his shift and nicked the skin between his ribs, he was gathering himself. His mind was now also a blade, slicing away the scared boy. This was no time to be terrified. Wood was there to do his bidding.

Mucum would no doubt have made a joke about it: *It wood do, woodn't it?*

Ark breathed in, closed his eyes, then opened them again, staring straight at his attacker. As he did, the knife sprang from the man's grasp as if covered in burning hedge-log prickles. It spun up through the air before landing with a clatter on the hard floor.

Anger rose in Ark like a tide of sap as the shocked man backed away, cradling his own hand as though it didn't belong to him. One thought. Ark knew that was all it would take. One thought and he could crush this man's mind like an acorn . . . this man who had laughed about his best friend's death. He felt the twitch of a smile. Yes. It would be so easy.

It was delightful to see the sheen of sweat on the man's forehead, the fear that now invaded his eyes and crept like a vine over his shaking limbs. He couldn't break eye contact with Ark, no matter how much he tried. Ark didn't even need the phial that hung around his neck. There was a roaring in his ears, the strength of a whole forest packed into his small body. 'Come on then!' he screamed, his words thundering between the pillars, pushing away the crowd like the backdraught of a Raven's wings.

'Eurghhh!' A groan echoed round the angular walls.

Ark stopped, blinking slowly. Somehow he was no longer lying down, but standing. Figures cowered nearby, arms raised in the air for protection.

'Eurgh. Argh, me head. What 'appened, mate? You're not frightenin' folks wiv all that oakus-crocus stuff, are yer?'

Ark shook himself, the vision of the forest that had flooded his mind receding. The blade on the floor was only a knife with a wood-tipped handle. Nothing more. The throbbing behind his eyes faded, like the sun over distant cruck-pools.

'Is that you? You're . . . not dead?' Ark asked uncertainly, turning towards an overturned seat that had been ripped free and flung against the far wall.

'Do I sound like a buddy ghost? Reckon I was out fer the count there though. Now, it's great fun hangin' round upside down, but 'ow about unstrappin' me . . . please?'

Ark fumbled with the catch and Mucum rolled out from under the seat, swaying slightly as he stood up.

'Dizzy . . .'

'Take a breath!' said Ark.

'Wotcha think I'm doin', stupid?'

Ark beamed. If his mate was insulting him, then he was still very much alive. 'I thought you'd . . .'

'Walked the plank? Nah. Anyways, what would yer do without me?'

Ark felt tears behind his eyes.

Mucum punched him on the shoulder. 'Don't go blubbin' on me, right?'

'Of course not!' Ark wiped clumsily at his eyes. They'd come a long way since he'd bumped into his workmate on the wood-way last autumn.

Mucum shook himself, made an unpleasant gargling sound and spat noisily on the ground. 'That's better.' Then he looked round at the strangely dressed group staring at them. 'Erm, so where are we? And what's all this lot about? They don't look like a bunch of new best buds to me.'

'You could put it like that.' They were still two boys against a crowd, even if it was a mob that was suddenly wary, unsure of the boy with the strange power in his hands.

The man who had held the knife at Ark's throat was slumped against a wall, but now he staggered to his feet. 'Kill the spies!' he rasped. 'There's enough of us to overpower them.'

The figures looked at each other, unsure at first, then

they began to close in, fists clenched. There were indeed too many of them, and Ark's reserves of energy were empty.

'Do something!' Mucum squeaked. ''Cos we are seriously in the brown stuff!'

But Ark had nothing left. He was emptied out, with a headache throbbing between his eyes that threatened to cleave his skull apart like a log. The crowd would swarm all over them like marching wood-ants. They'd come all this way and for what? To be killed by a seething rabble in a chamber of hand-scrawled trees.

'The Raven-claw blades!' Mucum had already grabbed his and was swinging it in a threatening circle. Ark fumbled for his own blade, feeling the warmth of it in his palm, but he had no idea how two tiny weapons would stop an angry mob.

There was a hissing sound and a rectangle of light appeared in the far wall. From within the painted forest, a figure stepped forward from the light and strode briskly through the crowd. Everyone stood still as he passed.

'What's going on?' The voice was low and commanding.

Ark's attacker wiped the sweat from his forehead. 'Spies, Remiel. They broke in. Don't worry, I have it under control.'

The man, Remiel, had skin as dark as midnight fungus. Under his close-cropped curls, a pair of bright, searching eyes scrutinized Ark and Mucum. Unlike the others, he wore a loose white robe. It was impossible to tell his age, though despite the lack of wrinkles Ark noted that his eyes shone with age and wisdom.

Remiel cast his gaze over the broken capsule, taking in

every detail. 'Hmmm. Let us ask some questions first. Would spies smash their way in with what looks like an ancient mining capsule? And since when has the Empire used children to do their dirty work, Jed? It might pay for you to look more closely. So, why are they here? Spies? Maybe. But it is also possible they are here for another purpose. Whatever their intent, we must discover it, yes?' His tone was gentle, each word carefully chosen. But to Ark it was obvious who now held the power in this underground chamber.

Remiel turned to the two boys. 'Please, put away your weapons. We mean you no harm.'

'Oh yeah? We surrender so you can do us in?' said Mucum.

'I give you my word.'

Silence hung in the air.

Ark looked steadily at the man. Then he turned slowly and nodded to Mucum, who shrugged his shoulders.

'Your funeral, mate!' he muttered as he reluctantly slid the knife back into its scabbard. 'Well, both our funerals, actually.'

It seemed Jed wasn't going to give up that easily, though. 'But this one,' he said jerking his finger towards Ark, 'tried to kill me!'

One of the crowd whispered something into Remiel's ear.

'I see. But perhaps it was self-defence. It appears *you* were about to execute him! Am I right?'

'This is our sacred shrine. They're infidels! The punishment was just.'

'Hang on a sec,' Mucum butted in, an idea forming in his mind as he gazed at the painted trees on the walls. 'I've no idea what a hinfidel is in your neck of the woods, but maybe this might convince yer.' He fumbled in his cruck-sack. ''Ere you go!' he said, as his hands unfurled. A pile of wooden shapes nestled in his palms. The top one, the smallest, was carved in the shape of a butterfly. He handed it over to Ark, who balanced it perfectly on the edge of his thumb, swinging it round for all to see.

There was a deadly hush as the crowd fell silent, their eyes soaking up the sight of the polished grain shining under the dim lights.

Ark wondered if he could make the butterfly come to life. Even dead sapwood had a soul. That was how he'd stopped arrows in mid-flight. The thought alone was overwhelming. What was he capable of? Corwenna's gift was beginning to make sense.

'So what?' said Jed. The crowd ignored him.

'It's Him! Look what he holds in his hand,' one said.

'He is here!' said another.

'It was foretold, the living frond of the forest!' said a third.

The feeling of the crowd had changed from hatred to awe. But why? And what did they mean by Him?

One by one, except for Jed and Remiel, they all dropped to their knees.

Mucum put his hands on his hips. 'Oh, buddy save us. 'Ere we go. Looks like yer got yerself some new followers. Can I jus' remind them that you were once a squitty sewer boy?'

'Thanks for that, Mucum.' But his friend was right. Ark felt uneasy with this new reaction. He was used to fear and danger, sneering and scorn. This deference was also strangely threatening.

Jed had lost control of the crowd, and he didn't like it. 'Yeah, but them bits of stuff could be fakes.'

'"Yeah, but" nothing, Jed. You know they are not. This young man holds a whole world in his hands. And have you truly forgotten the story of the boy who would rise again, like sap bringing forth a new spring; bearing a winged creature in his hand, carved from sacred wood? Do you not recall how the legend tells of a revolution of freedom in this blighted land?' Remiel's voice rose higher. 'So, was it your decision to dispatch his soul to the River Sticks without my authority?'

Jed stayed sullen and silent.

Ark almost stuttered as he spoke. 'Um. Please, everyone, get up. I don't know who you think I am, but I don't think . . .' His gaze wandered across the walls and his mind clicked into focus as he registered what he saw. Of course; now it began to make some sense. They were surrounded by paintings of trees, and he was a boy born of the branches, holding real wood in his hands. Was this why Corwenna's parting gift had such an incredible effect on those in front of him? There had to be some kind of connection.

He slowly handed the butterfly back to Mucum. There was an audible sigh from the crowd, as the shapes and the carving vanished back into the pouch.

Ark turned to Remiel. 'The River Sticks? You have drawings

of trees all over these walls. And yet, my every instinct tells me we are in the Empire of Maw?'

'Very observant. And the fact of your accent should have told Jed that you were not from these parts. He who looks about him with such surprise and uncertainty has travelled far.'

'Yer could say that,' Mucum butted in. 'We're Arborian, born and bred.'

Several figures in the crowd gasped. 'The fabled kingdom of trees!' they whispered to each other. 'Words have come to life!'

Ark looked sharply at Mucum. 'The whole point is not to give ourselves away, remember?' he hissed. 'Not tell the first people we meet where we've come from!'

But there were tears in Remiel's eyes. 'It is true, then?'

Ark softened at the sight of such a response from Remiel himself. He hesitated, then nodded.

'All these years, we have believed, though not seen. The small amounts of new wood that still circulate on the stick-market had to come from somewhere. But the tales of trees taller than skyscrapers? Maw's law-makers would have us believe that this is illegal superstition; that the timber that remains is only the scraps of long-dead forests . . . I apologize for my friend's rudeness. I am Remiel, and you are . . .'

'Hungry!' said Mucum.

'That one doesn't talk like the companion of a mythical hero!' Jed grunted.

Mucum bunched his fists. 'And if you don't shut yer face, beanpole, I won't act like one neither. I won't forget wot you nearly did to my mate!'

'Easy. Easy!' Remiel broke in, putting up his hands. 'You must understand that we meet here as *Levellers* – those who worship nature in the form of once-living trees. For us, even to speak of a real wooded world outside these walls is seen as heresy, punishable by death. Now come, there is much to discuss of why you are here. You are our guests. Oakley!' He beckoned to a shorter man.

'At your service, sire!' Oakley was short and weather-beaten, with a greying beard, gruff voice and a face like a crumpled pippin apple. 'Come on, you lot, get out of the way. Guests are tired and starvin'. They need feeding, not worshipping, eh? Come on then, you two, we'll make our way to the hub and I'll do you some hash browns and eggs, washed down with plenty of coffee. How does that sound?'

'Sounds good!' said Mucum. 'I'm always up for a good nosh, me!'

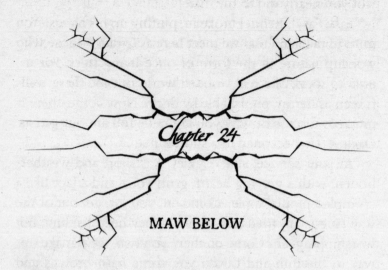

Chapter 24

MAW BELOW

As Ark and Mucum followed Remiel through the illuminated doorway, Ark turned back and stared in puzzlement. 'It's a blank wall! What happened to the door?'

Mucum swung round and gaped. 'How did yer do that?'

'Not by magic,' said Remiel, looking at Ark, 'simply a holographic illusion that makes an entrance appear as a solid wall. As I said, worship of living trees is a subversive act punishable by execution. This branch of our church must stay hidden.'

Oakley stood by Remiel's side like a bodyguard. He lifted his arm. On his wrist, a metallic band beeped twice. 'Clear, boss.'

'Good.' Remiel turned to the boys. 'It appears we are safe, for now. The Gloms don't usually bother sending patrols down this far into the basements. But we must move fast – the way you are dressed is an instant alarm signal.' He turned to lead them away down a passage that grew increasingly warm as they walked along it. Overhead lights spluttered and fizzed and the pitted floor was filled with scum-covered puddles.

'Why is it wrong to honour the woods?' Ark asked as they scurried to keep up. He thought of Warden Goodwoody, and the incense-filled Kirk cradled high in the canopy.

Remiel paused in front of a set of semi-transparent fluttering strips that hung from the ceiling and blocked the way ahead. 'If any of us are caught carrying images of trees, or attempting to grow seeds, or even heard talking about the promised land of leaves, the Gloms will snuff us out. Timber is only a product to be traded. If we were able to grow trees again, it would upset the money markets.'

'That's totally conkers!' said Mucum.

But Ark understood. And what was more, it meant that what Corwenna had given them was currency. He stayed silent as he looked up into Remiel's eyes. Unlike Jed, who had been left behind to clear up the crash site, there was something about this man with skin as dark as Rootshooter coal that Ark wanted to trust. Maybe, he thought, their journey into the unknown was not a complete folly after all.

'Yes,' said Remiel. 'The time of revelation is close. There is plenty to discuss after we have eaten.'

'I recognize that smell!' Mucum said, sniffing. He wrinkled his nose like the expert he was. 'Squit. Loads of it.' He sniffed again. 'And ammonia? Lovely stink. Almost makes me miss the sewage station.'

'Seriously?' said Ark.

'Nah. Life's been a lot more fun since we stopped shovellin' the sticky stuff! But what's that sound?'

As Remiel pushed his way through the strips, the screeching grew louder. Mucum and Ark had no choice but to follow.

'Welcome to one of the many factories of Maw!'

The stench caused Ark to gag.

'Chickens!' Mucum shouted, stating the obvious.

There were what looked like a hundred birds stuffed into each mesh cage, squawking and shrieking. The cages themselves were piled on top of each other, higgledy-twiggledy. It was a building formed from living birds. Ark tried not to look as they walked between two stacks of cages that towered hundreds of feet above them, but he couldn't help it. Some of the poor creatures had been trampled and lay rotting at the bottom of their cages. Others had pushed their heads through the thin mesh and were slowly strangling themselves. For these birds, sunlight was unknown and the air they breathed was rancid. This was no scaffield farmyard. Ark felt their pain beating against his heart like the hammering of a wood-pecker's bill.

'Maw is hungry!' Remiel shouted above the noise. 'Therefore its billions must be fed.'

Finally, they reached the other side of the stacks, and pushed their way through another set of fluttering strips. The scenery changed. Instead of dark gloom, intense white light poured down in a flood from high overhead. Mucum and Ark had to shield their eyes. In front of them lay a green jungle filled with fine dewy mist.

'Hydroponics!' said Remiel. 'A mix of water and chemicals used to grow plants. There is no open land anywhere in the Empire of Maw. It's all been built on. Apart from the eastern deserts, the whole continent is now one big city-state. But basement space is cheap to rent. And our solar kites that fly high above the atmosphere trap sunlight and feed it down here into these dark spaces.'

'Are those tomatoes?' Ark asked. 'They have no smell.'

'Yes. And there are peppers, beans, all the vegetables we need.'

'But what about soil?' said Mucum, shuddering.

'Long gone!' Remiel sighed, as he bent over to pluck two small tomatoes to give to Ark and Mucum.

Mucum bit his in half and grimaced. 'Tastes of mush!' he said.

'Yes,' said Remiel. 'Ancient corporations poisoned the land with many kinds of pollutant. In the end, it was only good for using as foundations to support the city above us. The earth itself may have gone bad, turned toxic, but business found a way of growing profitable plants in water trays, with special chemical nutrients and systems to keep the roots from drying up. It is efficient, but the results are, as you say, somewhat bland.'

Mucum abruptly came to a standstill. 'Somethin' wrong 'ere! Listen up!'

'What?' said Remiel.

Ark watched nervously as Oakley deftly pulled a

weapon from his tunic. He'd seen arms like this before, in the battle at Barkingham Palace. The gun was clear as water but more deadly than a mere liquid could ever be.

Oakley swung his weapon round. 'What is it, boy? What can you hear?'

Ark peered around, seeing nothing except a wall of green, freckled with red peppers. The only sound was the soft hiss of sprinklers. 'What is it, Mucum?' he whispered.

'Nothin',' Mucum finally muttered.

'Nothing?' Remiel looked genuinely puzzled.

'Yeah. Nothin'. No bees buzzin'. No skylarks risin' and singin' their little hearts out. No fir-crickets chirpin'. This place might be green, but it's dead.'

A mixture of emotions passed over Remiel's face. Then he sighed. 'Oakley, stand down. For all you could shoot would be a dream.' He turned to Mucum. 'These creatures you speak of have long gone into legend. But the way you speak of them fills my old heart with hope. The guardians of long ago who built our shrine knew that you would come one day. Now, I hope you're hungry, we're nearly there.'

He veered left, pushing his way through a forest of hanging purple grapes. 'Up you go!' A ladder was cleverly concealed among the twisting vines. Oakley shinned straight up it and Remiel bowed to Mucum and Ark. 'After you.'

'How do we know it's not a trap?' said Mucum.

'It isn't,' said Ark before Remiel could reply. 'I think we're safe.'

'Safe?' Mucum blustered. 'Since all this ma-larch-y

kicked off, I've forgot the meanin' of the word.'

'Sorry, sir. My friend here loves to whinge.'

'Yes,' said Remiel, trying not to smile. 'And he's very good at it.'

''Ere, yer not laughin' at me, are yer?'

'Wouldn't dream of it!' said Ark, as he clambered up the ladder. Mucum continued grumbling as he reluctantly followed behind.

Once through a raised trapdoor, they found themselves in a surprisingly airy space. It was a circular room with translucent, smooth walls that let the outside light filter in. Oakley was already busy in what was obviously a kitchen area, cracking eggs and pouring them into a pan. The floor was covered in a hotchpotch of rugs. There were chairs, a table and in one corner behind a curtain, a sleeping area.

'Pull up a seat,' said Remiel.

Ark looked warily at the chair in front of him. He could see the grain in the spindles, but when he bent to touch one, it felt wrong. 'It looks like wood, but it isn't.'

'Exactly. A bad copy,' said Remiel as he strode over to sit down behind the large rectangular table that dominated the room. His hand stroked its stained and battered surface as if it was alive. 'But this, on the other hand, is the real deal. It was handed down through the generations. If I sold it, I could easily afford to live in one of the penthouses high up above us. Eat first, and then there's much I have to ask you.'

Oakley put down two full plates and steaming glasses that filled the room with the scent of coffee. Soon they were tucking in. 'Good ter see you lot got knives and forks and plates, like we do back 'ome.' Mucum licked a tiny bit of yolk that had escaped from the side of his mouth.

'One can buy Eezy-Cheeze in a tube, but nothing beats a proper breakfast, especially after a difficult journey. Isn't that so? Now, it is time to tell why you are here.'

Ark took a sip of the sweetened coffee. He could taste a hint of cinnamon. 'It's a long story,' he said.

'And we have all the time in the world,' Remiel answered. 'Unlike my rather foolhardy colleague Jed, I have faith that you are not spies.'

'Actually,' said Ark, 'we are. Only we don't work for Gloms, whoever they might be.'

'Yeah, been meaning to ask, who the holly are the Gloms?' Mucum asked.

Remiel frowned. 'They are the kings and queens of this empire, whose subjects only worship one goddess: not the prophet Diana, but Profit, and his dark consort, Loss.'

'Well that don't make no sense!' said Mucum. 'Yer talkin' a bunch of Lumber-jumbo!'

It was Ark's turn to speak. 'We too are subjects of royalty. We come on behalf of King Quercus of Arborium and Corwenna, the Raven-Queen.'

Remiel and Oakley listened in awe as Ark began to paint a world where trees were giants, cities cradled within their high branches. By the time he had finished the tale, tears streamed down Remiel's face.

'It's all true, then,' he muttered, more to himself than to Oakley. 'Our prayers have not been in vain! But how was it that the capsule crashed straight into our holiest place?'

'There are those who might say there are no mere coincidences,' Ark replied. He thought back to Corwenna's last words to him. How could she have had an inkling of where they'd end up? 'But how will we get back home?'

Remiel motioned to Oakley. 'See to it. As they came, so they must be able to return.' He turned back to Ark. 'We have a whole network of scientists who support us. They will help to repair the travel capsule.'

Ark shook his head in wonder. 'Scientists like . . . Diana?'

'And that, my friends, is the most amazing part of your story! For the Levellers are descended from a long-long-ago group of scientists who saw the way the world was going. The last tree had been cut down, but they had already been gathering seeds, ready for the second growing. Many seeds were sterile, though, dead before they could dream of the sky because of the chemicals that had leaked into the ground. But some were saved and science was used to alter their properties. Though the world was awash with greed, these few wise women and men saw that if they could create a green lung for the planet, and hide it from view, then one day, maybe, Eden would be restored. One of their number had to sacrifice all, leave her family, pretend to die. The others used the computing means at their disposal to hide every trace of her journey to a rocky island where the seeds could be planted.'

Ark felt a great heaving in his heart. Corwenna had already told him what she knew of this story. 'You mean Diana!'

'Yes. But though we believed in the tale with all our souls, you have come to us today and told us that Diana did succeed in her journey to that once-barren island, that her dream came true. Stuck as slaves down in the basements, or cleaning the windows of the rich, we began to wonder if those ancient pictures of trees meant anything or if they were mere myth. Now, you are concrete evidence, arriving at a time when our own spy has heard rumours of a new weapon called the Quantum Trap. So far, we have not found a way to confirm the rumour. Now I think it may be you who holds the key!'

Ark almost caught hold of Remiel's thoughts. Corwenna's training was rooting itself deep down inside him. In the last few months, he'd begun to be able to read what lay behind spoken words. He knew that right now, Remiel was thinking of Corwenna's gift, hidden in a pouch in Mucum's crucksack. 'Your thoughts have turned to something we brought with us?' he asked.

Remiel looked at Ark with wonder. 'Yes, Ark of the Woods. They have indeed. And you,' he turned to Mucum, 'I have a feeling that you are no mere companion. Am I right?'

'Yeah!' said Mucum, almost blushing. 'He'd be permanently down a squit-hole without me.'

'Indeed,' said Remiel, rubbing his chin. 'And how are your lying skills?'

Mucum frowned. 'Well, I'm up for a good night's sleep, jus' like anyone else . . .'

Ark smiled grimly. 'He doesn't mean lying down! He means lies. Like your brilliant excuses for being late at the sewage works . . .'

'Oh right! Well, yeah, I can talk the hind leg off a

branch-donkey, if that's what yer mean. Why?'

'And how are you with heights and climbing?'

'Yer losin' me 'ere,' Mucum growled.

'I certainly don't mean to. But it strikes me that with your natural skills, as well as with that carved butterfly hidden in your pouch, you might come in very useful – if you are willing to do something very difficult and dangerous.'

'Difficult and dangerous. Now yer talkin'!' said Mucum. 'Tell us more!'

'Patience. All will be explained to you.' Remiel's face grew serious. 'If Fenestra has her way, all that our ancient ancestors worked so hard for, all that is now your forested home, shall be destroyed!' He slid open a drawer from his desk and took out something that resembled transparent paper. He unrolled it, revealing colours and numbers pulsating within, and began moving his finger across the surface. There was a soft purring jingle and then a voice rose from Remiel's wristband.

'Yes, master?'

'The situation has changed. I need a report from you. Please transfer all recent information to the screen imme-diately. Then we shall plan.'

'Understood, master.'

'What the holly was that?' said Mucum, looking round the room to see who'd spoken.

'That was our faithful virtual servant, the only one of his kind, made by our scientists and installed somewhere he might prove very useful. We call him our Personal Virtual Assistant, but you can call him PV for short.'

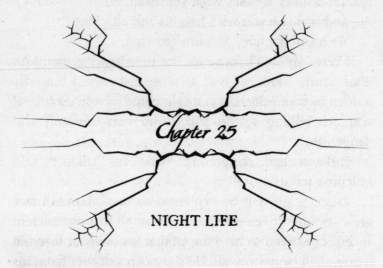

Chapter 25

NIGHT LIFE

Randall looked up at the stars. Amazing to think there was nothing between her and the heavens above: no triple glazing, no protective dome, nothing to stop the light waves travelling at their incredible speed to paint this light-spattered picture.

All thoughts of the mechanical-armed boy and his cunning words were scoured away by the freezing wind. It blasted in sudden gusts around the far corner of the building. This time, the jump had gone according to plan. PV had already played it back through her goggles in slow-mo. The hoverfly-cam had captured the shot of her perfectly, flying like a bird. The background of the filming was stunning, revealing the city transformed by darkness. At this late hour, the lights that shone out through the millions of windows formed their own blinking constellations. The city was truly decked out in diamonds.

'How much further?' she grunted, feeling the strain in her feet as her toes curled into invisible crevices.

'Close, mistress.'

'Close? You're supposed to be the expert in numbers, PV.'

'Mistress, I was trying to please you by approximating a sense of distance rather than the exact figure itself.'

'Whatever!' she muttered, hauling herself up centimetre by centimetre.

'Four point two metres exactly, which at your current travelling speed indicates an arrival time of approximately forty-three seconds.'

This was the holy grail. The enormous Beeching edifice, with its curling overhangs, and glass abutments sharp enough to slice off fingers, was the last unconquered peak, the highest of them all. She thought back to the boy who had lost his life in the earlier attempt. 'This is for you!' she whispered, her right arm swinging up to find the final handhold. Randall Jarrett Fenestra was about to land it, big time. She'd be a star, burning in her own cyber-firmament.

'Come to check out the view?' asked a voice. It was a boy, sitting back, swinging his legs over the edge of the roof.

'What?' Randall gasped as she negotiated the last overhang and flopped into the shallow gutter that ran round the summit. The roof was where tidy architecture was able to let down its hair. Air-con units were piled in messy cubes and cables ran everywhere in an overgrown tangle. A thin line sliced up into the sky, flickering with pulsating light. At its top, hidden to human eyes and near the edge of the atmosphere, a single solar kite would be floating. She'd seen the vids – several hundred square kilometres of solar panels, floating high above the planet and soaking up the sun's energy, enough to feed the thousands of offices, malls, and apartments below.

'How the hell did you . . . get up here?' Randall said as she tried to get her breath back. She already knew the answer. The boy's suit wasn't branded; she could even see a few tears in it and his bulk threatened to rip the rest of it. But it was classic climbing kit. This orange-haired boy with a smirk on his face was no rooftop engineer.

'Same way you did, girl.'

'But that's . . .'

'Impossible? Nah!' The boy flexed his long fingers. 'I've been sussing this route out for months. Tonight looked like a good one!'

'I was going to be the first to ever reach the top. How do I know you didn't take the lift, wriggle up through an air duct or something and change into your gear when you got up here?'

'You must be kiddin'. I'd be laughed out of town. The unwritten code of the free-climbers?'

'Till Death do us fall!' they both chanted at the same time.

'But I've never seen footage of you climbing.'

'Well, the fing is . . .'

'What?'

'The wind took my fly-pram a while ago.'

'Your what? Fly-pram?' She wondered if the boy had a

speech impediment. Although maybe it was simply his odd, strong accent.

'Uh . . . fly-cam. So I lost all the feetage . . . footage before I even had a chance to upload it. I don't bother trying to film no more.'

Randall couldn't help feeling relieved. 'So you've got no proof of this climb tonight?'

'Nah. Glory's all yours, babe. You earned it and you filmed it.'

'But you did it first. You could tell on me.'

'Honour among thieves, eh? But listen up, you know I got here first. That's enough for me. Jus' glad I made it in one piece. It's Mawesome, ain't it?' The boy sat and stared at the view, eating it up like a kid in a candy store.

Randall felt confused. She'd never met another free-climber face to face, preferring the assumed names of the message boards. This monolith of glass belonged to her. And why would he so easily give up on instant fame? 'You talk strange.'

'Maw's a big place, girl. Ever heard of the 'burbs? We can't all afford to wear what you do. What's that suit of yours called?

Randall shrugged. 'Calvin Shine Sleek-Look.' Then she turned to the air in front of her. 'You can stop filming now!' she commanded. The buzz softened and she felt a soft flutter of wings as the fly-cam landed in her sore hand.

'Wow! Amazing. What is it?' the boy asked, staring.

'What make, you mean? Sharda. It produces fantastic pictures.'

'I bet,' said the boy. 'Name's M . . . Morris, by the way.'

'I'm Randall,' she replied, not sure if she should shake hands with a strange young man three kilometres above the earth.

Two small lights began to wink on the boy's chest.

'What's that?' Randall asked.

'Nothing.' The boy turned away, as if shy.

'Please. Show me?'

'OK. So long as you promise not to tell anyone.'

Randall was now doubly curious as the boy shifted towards her again.

'Look. I run a few lines to pay the school fees and me mum's health bills. If me dad found out, he'd kill me, 'cos kids ain't supposed to deal in this stuff.'

Randall nodded, instantly understanding why. The small burr of wood pinned just inside his tunic was carved into the shape of a butterfly. The skill behind it was obvious, down to the two winking antennae. And unlike the strange *plankensteins* actually growing in her mother's vault, this bit of wood was dead. More than that, it was treasure.

'It's the real thing. Carved from smuggled elm,' he said, proudly.

'You don't need to tell me that. I'm not stupid.'

'Never said yer were. But this little beauty's gonna pay me way through college, ain't yer?' He lifted a stubby finger to gently stroke the antennae.

'Ahem, mistress?'

'Machines don't cough! What do you want, PV?'

'But mistress, it is what *you* want that I am thinking of . . . your mother's birthday tomorrow?'

'What?'

'You have been looking for a present, have you not? And . . .'

'A present? Oh! Yes, of course. Perfect!' She lifted her wristband and waved it towards the boy. 'PV. Scan it!'

'Oh, yer got one of those shard-di-da virtual assistants. That's all right for you posh lot.'

'Excuse me, young sir,' the modulated voice replied. 'Not only do I bear no resemblance to those common assistants, being a prototype superior in every way, I also happen to be an expert in brand verification. In a world of shoddy knock-off goods, one can never be too sure about the genuine article!'

'You invisible little piece of chip, if yer tryin' to insult my reputation, I'll shove your memory right back up where the sun don't shine.' Mucum was really getting into character now.

PV ignored the insult. 'Scan complete, mistress. It is an original Vivienne Webwood and would make a most worthy gift for . . .'

'That will be all, PV.' Randall cut in, before he could give her identity away. 'Merris, I want to buy your brooch.'

'The name's Morris. And did say I was sellin'? Highest bidder. That's who this little beauty will go to. No one else.'

Randall was finally in her element. He might have out-climbed her, but when it came to the cut and thrust of finance, she'd learned from the best. 'Oh, trust me. I have access to funds that would make your eyes water. You'll not only pay off your college fees, but be able to afford a new designer climb-suit every week for the rest of your life. Or two. Or three. In fact, the sky is totally the limit.'

The boy paused. 'Well now, when yer put it like that, maybe we can talk business after all.'

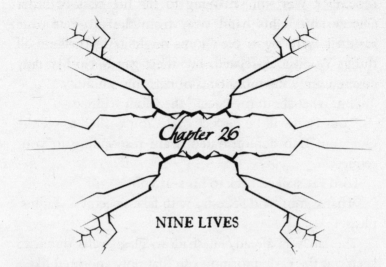

Chapter 26

NINE LIVES

Petronio stared at the cat. It was obviously a pampered pet, its white fur groomed to within an inch of its life. Lord Far, the Glom that Petronio had hated on first sight, was scratching the creature's ears with his stubby fingers. The resulting purr filled the small, close atmosphere of the laboratory.

'There, there, my little processed slicey-wicey!' the man murmured.

'Please step away now, sir!' said Fenestra.

'Why, envoy?' he sneered.

'Well, when I activate the holding force field, I assume you wish to keep your arm attached to your body?'

Petronio wondered if Fenestra was having a subtle dig at him. After her earlier threat, he wouldn't be surprised. The stump of his arm was itchy today, the weight of the attached mechanism tiring his muscles. Whatever her motive, it was still satisfying to see the boss of Eezy-Cheeze snatch his hand away from the cat. Petronio's instincts were right: the Gloms might be experts on all things Woodstock-related, but their gaudy clothes only covered up fleshy mountains of moronic stupidity.

'But what about my Pucci?' the Glom whined.

'Your Pucci will be perfectly safe. You wished to see the Quantum Trap demonstrated. I am responding to your request.'

Lord Far stalked back to his seat with a huff.

'Thank you!' said Fenestra with fake sweetness. 'Lights, please!'

The lab was already in shadow, glass walls tinted to keep out the early morning sun that now appeared like a black disc hovering over the far edge of the city.

All nine Gloms were seated on a raised dais to the left of the chamber. In front of them, under the spotlight, the cat prowled on top of a circular podium about two feet across. Each time it got too close to the edge there was a sudden spark, followed by a yowling screech. The force field worked: kitty wasn't going anywhere.

Ten feet to the left stood an exact replica of the podium. But instead of a cat, there was a small, sealed glass dome with a rubber tube attached to one side.

Apart from the tiered seating, the lab was entirely empty. The only hint of what was about to happen lay in Fenestra's hands.

Petronio's mind wandered. He found himself thinking about Fenestra's daughter. The defiance in Randall's eyes as he had threatened her was almost exhilarating. But it was her lips he kept picturing, the way they pouted as she flounced away from him. And he wished the girl could understand him. His actions were for self-preservation. With someone like Fenestra, he needed safeguards. For now, he was still useful to her. But afterwards?

The Envoy of Maw turned to her audience. 'What I hold within my palms is the future.' She carefully unfolded two objects and placed one of them over her eyes.

'We have delayed important meetings in order to come to watch you put on a pair of glass goggles?' The Glom's voice, already squeaky, now soared into the higher registers.

'If you would cultivate patience, I will explain.'

The other Gloms shifted in their seats. Some had already unfurled screens and were catching up with market reports. But Fenestra did not seem bothered. 'Look through the glass darkly and all shall be revealed.'

'Ooh, I am scared!' Lord Far guffawed. 'Our great envoy showing off her latest look, and my cat on a stage. Sweet Cheesus! Our Empire will reign victorious . . .'

The laughter of the others was cut short as Fenestra turned her icy gaze away from the Gloms and towards the podium. The cat had also grown bored, curling up in a ball with only the occasional flick of its tail to indicate it was displeased with its new temporary home.

'Suck out the oxygen in the vacuum chamber!' Fenestra commanded, clicking her fingers. She gripped the second object, something black and shiny, and held it in front of her, before turning to look once again at the cat.

Petronio had been told what to expect. But instead of

looking at the experiment, his eyes were drawn to Fenestra. She wore a long dress that was understated and sober, the colours muted for business. It was the brooch that caught his eye, so lifelike he wondered if it was about to take off. He knew that wood was precious in Maw, but it was still strange to see a carved piece of it pinned to her shoulder, especially something carved with such finesse.

'On a count of five!' Fenestra said. There were five short beeps. Then nothing. The Gloms were not amused.

'And that's it?' Lord Far roared. 'Get rid of that damn force field! Come on, Puccikins! We have more important matters to attend to . . . ' But as he stood up and bent down to pick up his scroll-screen which had slithered to the floor, the rest of the Gloms fell into a deadly hush.

'I knew you'd fail!' Lord Far said, pulling himself upright with an effort. 'Perhaps it's time we thought about appointing a new envoy . . . Oh! Wha— what's happening to Pucci?'

Petronio was also astounded. No amount of talk could prepare for the vision that unfurled in front of them. Pucci was still on the podium. But what appeared to be an exact replica of the cat was now clawing at the inside of the glass vacuum chamber.

'Watch closely, my good *colleagues*!' said Fenestra. 'The principle behind the mechanism of the Quantum Trap is very simple. The act of my looking at the cat through these vision integrated goggles has triggered the weapon. I see, therefore I create. Your eyes are not deceiving you. Puccikins is in two places at once. You could call him a copy cat.'

A smile lit up Lord Far's fleshy lips. 'Ah! Wonderful. Two for the price of one! The possibilities are boundless! I humbly eat my words, envoy. Your job is secure!' he crowed sarcastically.

'Wait!' she snapped. 'If the cat is in two places at once, and one of those places has had all the air removed from it, then . . .'

The man's smile turned to horror. The replica in the vacuum chamber was struggling for breath. It even stood up on two legs, pathetic claws trying to cut through sheer glass. But all eyes were now on the original cat, which also appeared to be in the same agony.

'Yes. Despite being surrounded by the good, filtered air we all pay our metered bills for in Maw, Pucci is also suffocating, and will soon die.'

'No! Stop it! You promised my Pucci would be safe!' screeched Lord Far, tears rolling down his plump cheeks. 'I beg you. Stop.'

'But sir! You asked my scientists to devise a weapon that would take the lives of Arborians without damaging their priceless trees. I am simply demonstrating it in action, on a mere cat.' Fenestra paused, locked in eye contact with Lord Far. 'You do wish to witness exactly how it works? No? Ah well, as you wish.' She tapped her finger on the black object, jabbed at something on a scroll-screen to her side and pushed the goggles up on to her forehead. The replica cat in the vacuum chamber instantly disappeared. 'That is the short-range function you have just seen, for individual targets only,' she continued as Lord Far rushed to the platform and plucked up a very dazed-looking Pucci.

There was a moment of stunned silence, then one of the Gloms stood up and clapped her hands together. The others followed suit, and the room filled with quick applause and congratulations.

'You must forgive my little deceit!' Fenestra said when the Gloms finally quietened down and Lord Far was staring at her with hatred. 'The cat was always going to be spared. However, this trial is merely a tiny taste of the terror that will be unleashed on the barbaric Dendrans. This was the last test. The weapons are already in Arborium. All they are waiting for is the final coding stream, contained within this memory key.'

The envoy held up the thin, shiny black stick. To Petronio, it resembled a large splinter, something that would burrow in deep and do its work well.

Fenestra continued. 'Once this key is delivered to Arborium and uploaded into the case that contains the glass spheres, the Quantum Trap will finally be ready. On the date of what they call their Winter Solstice the spheres will be activated and the trap will be sprung. I need not bother you with the precise details. All you need to know is that significant numbers of Dendrans shall find themselves both where they are, and simultaneously orbiting in outer space. Needless to say, space is simply a larger version of this vacuum chamber!' She pointed to the empty glass container on the podium. 'With no air, the Dendrans will struggle, then suffocate – quickly, as we just saw. Any who survive will soon be rounded up. And then, the trees shall be ours!' Fenestra paused for effect and smiled, before continuing. 'In the wrong hands, such an amount of wood would destabilize the economy. That is why we must have control. Of course, much of the forest will have to be culled and burned to control stock and to avoid any danger of the market being flooded, but the rest will be preserved, guarded and carefully harvested, with the best branches and burrs sold off gradually. Your share prices will skyrocket!'

Petronio sat back. He was impressed. The weapon worked. And even better, as far as he was concerned, Lord Far had been totally humiliated.

The Gloms were beginning to rise, wanting to ask further questions, but they were interrupted by a sudden flashing of red lights and the sound of buzzing alarms that filled the lab.

Fenestra frowned, tapping her earpiece. 'We have a security breach? A spying device? How is this possible?'

Petronio also frowned, recalling how he had asked Randall to spy on her mother. She couldn't cause something like this, could she? Even if she could, he reasoned, he would simply deny any connection. He folded his arms, pretending boredom and waited for the panic to subside.

'It's obvious!' spat Lord Far. 'Who else would betray us but a foreigner!' He pointed his finger straight at Petronio. 'The traitor is right in front of you!'

The eyes of the Gloms were on him and even Fenestra stepped away from him as though he were infectious.

Petronio was always quick on his feet, and fast to think. But as he jumped up, soldiers were already pouring through the door, and his chest lit up with a flicker of red target spots as a hundred g-guns were aimed at his heart.

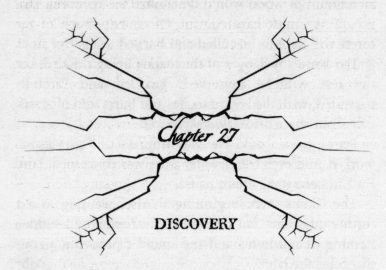

Chapter 27

DISCOVERY

Ark and Mucum stared in mute horror as Petronio Grasp walked straight towards them, bathed in the blood-red glow of flashing lights.

'I can tell you one thing,' Petronio stated calmly, ignoring the guns bristling like hedge-log spikes all around him. 'I'm not the spy round here.' The metal arm reached up, pincers opening wide like a jaw, ready to chew its prey into tiny pieces.

'No way! It can't be. He's alive! And he can see us!' Mucum gasped, backing away towards the middle of the room.

'Returned from the dead!' Ark muttered. 'Impossible!'

Remiel spoke. 'This is evidently a nasty surprise. But remember, though we can see in and watch what is happening on screen, we cannot be seen. The 3D webcam hidden inside the butterfly's antennae gives us an extraordinary window into wherever the Envoy Fenestra goes. This is unfortunate timing. I had hoped for longer before the cam was discovered . . .'

The screen relayed pincers closing in fast. They shut with a clang, inches from the brooch. In the lab Petronio bent forward and stared straight into the two tiny lenses quivering above the insect's carved wings. 'Mmm, I wonder . . . what can you see, little beastie?' he whispered.

In Remiel's hidden home, Ark peered down at the screen, feeling the force of the gaze crossing the space between them. Of course, he told himself, Petronio could only see the brooch itself and could have absolutely no idea who might be using it to spy on the proceedings. But nonetheless, Ark felt sick, as though the enemy he thought had died was standing near enough to breathe on.

Ark remembered the battle back in October, recalling how he had gripped Petronio's hand and pierced it with the Raven quill to deliver the poison that began to turn the boy's arm to wood. It was such a shock to see Petronio living, moving, speaking. But even worse than finding that Maw had saved him was seeing the Empire's in-fir-nal contraption attached to his shoulder. What monstrous magic was it that could replace an arm with a machine?

Petronio's voice shot crystal clear through the speakers embedded in Remiel's screen. 'Shoot me if you wish. But first check a little hunch of mine. It's easy for me to spot the wood of my former Arborian home – and when I recognize it, I have to ask myself what it is doing in this room. Right there!' He pointed and all faces swivelled into view. 'Just see if your security breach lies inside the pretty brooch the envoy is wearing!'

There was the sound of rustling cloth, and a sudden shocked intake of breath, so close to the tiny microphone in the wing that it almost blew the speakers.

'He's a liar!' Lord Far shouted as the weapons surrounding Petronio wavered. 'A double agent desperate to save his pathetic forest!'

Petronio appeared remarkably calm, turning away to address his would-be attackers. 'I haven't been here long. But back in Arborium, I was trained from a young age to have a sharp eye and it is the reason I am alive today. When I walked in here this morning, I noticed that trinket of Lady Fenestra's. It's very much like the fine carvings of home. In fact, not like, it is. However, in Arborium, I've never seen a carving embellished with such fine glass eyes. Glass so jewel-like it is only found in Maw. As I said, it's a mere hunch, but let's at least put it to the test? I assume your security forces must have something they can use to scan the brooch and check if it is indeed the source of the breach?' Petronio's question was followed by silence.

Fenestra was the first to speak. It was strange for Ark to hear, but not see the woman who had already nearly destroyed his home once before. He heard her swallow. 'This is an outrageous suggestion! My daughter gave this designer piece to me for my birthday only this morning.'

'Is that so?' said Petronio. 'Well, happy birthday, envoy. My hunch is beginning to be confirmed.'

'What?' spat Fenestra. 'What can you possibly mean?'

'Only that, as I said, I have a sharp eye and a well-tuned

ear. If I'm right, and based on what I've seen of your relationship, I won't be surprised to find that she'd be more than happy to sell you out!' Petronio swivelled round to peer into the tiny glass eyes. 'Isn't that right, Randall?' he jeered.

'Close, but not close enough,' Ark murmured.

And now there was a different sort of battle going on, one with weapons far sharper than the shards blasted from a g-gun.

'How dare you?' Fenestra screamed. But there was a slight quiver in her voice, a tiny pause of fear. 'Do not presume to judge my daughter as being anything like YOURSELF!'

Remiel's hands gripped the table as he stared at the screen displaying the scene unfolding in front of them. 'We must shut off the signal. Otherwise they can trace us!'

By his side, Oakley shook his head. 'PV is the best, my lord. By the time the signal bounces round a few hundred relay stations, they might well assume we are on the moon.'

Remiel frowned 'But they are aware they are being observed now!'

'Yes, and we need to keep listening for as long as is both possible and safe. Agreed, PV?'

'Yes,' came PV's voice from the speakers in the screen. 'I have complete confidence in my programmed abilities.'

'What about the girl?' Mucum asked. 'I was the one what conned her good an' proper. It's not her fault she's gonna be fried!'

There was a burst of static fuzz. 'I have not computed

that consequence,' said PV.

Ark wasn't concerned about the fate of a lone girl though. The trial they had witnessed was a mere glimmer of what Arborium was to suffer in less than two days' time. He thought of his family, of all the families perched like birds high up in the trees, a whole way of life wiped out. But what could they do to stop it?

On-screen, the stand-off continued.

Finally Fenestra sighed. 'Run the scans.'

A member of the security forces stepped toward her holding a small box in one hand. At the same time, the Gloms backed away from the envoy, as if ready to disown all knowledge of her.

A machine-like answer came back immediately. 'A webcam is functioning. Please destroy immediately.'

'Too late!' said Lord Far. 'And may I remind everyone that we have not yet established if the foreigner is involved.' The anger that blazed in his eyes as he glanced first to Petronio, then towards Fenestra was fuelled not only by the way his cat had been used, but by the threat to business. 'And I want my best systems hacker to crack this thing and follow the trail! Now!' he screeched, stalking right up to Fenestra and pointing his bloated finger straight into the cam. 'Whoever you are, we are coming for you! The might of the Empire will crush you and I shall personally make sure your heads are preserved in the marketing section of our museum to show what economic traitors look like!'

Remiel recoiled from the leering face filling the screen. 'It's time the signal disappeared.' His hand reached under the desk to flick a switch. Lord Far faded until all that was left was a shadow on the thin scroll.

'What do we do?' said Ark.

'We must analyse all the possibilities and then act accordingly,' the voice called PV answered.

'Oh, great!' Mucum muttered, 'So we sit round like scaffield pigs waitin' for slaughter while Mr Nothing 'ere, who we can't even see, works out how they're gonna hunt us down! Perfect!'

Petronio ignored the taste of bile in his mouth. Only moments ago, he had been certain that he was about to be lacerated by filaments of glass. The injustice of it rankled. For once, he was innocent. Betraying the Gloms would serve no advantage. The brooch really had been a hunch, a bluff even, a whiff of instinct. Mind you, it was sharp instinct that had saved him in many back-street brawls before. He also had to admit that there was a small pleasure in seeing Fenestra squirm, especially after the way she'd treated him. Though he still wasn't convinced how Randall fitted into the theory he had spun. He pondered again on his threats in the pleasure gardens, not really believing the girl was capable of taking things this far. Her dislike of her mother was real enough, of course. Petronio remembered his own action in pushing his despised father into the path of a hungry Raven. Maybe Fenestra was wrong and Randall was exactly like him: not bothered about betraying the bond of blood.

'Envoy, hand it over!' Lord Far was now clearly enjoying himself.

'My daughter is innocent!' Fenestra protested.

'If that's the case, then let my man prove it!'

By his side, one of Lord Far's geeks was already fiddling with a grey box, unhooking wires, his fingers a blur as they danced over a sequence of buttons. There was an eager look in his eyes as the fragile butterfly was placed into a glowing cradle at the bottom of the box. Numbers fluttered across a small screen as the man frowned in concentration. 'Already offline, boss.'

'Do I care? Find the source or find a new job!'

'Don't worry. I'll deal with it!' The fingers continued with a life of their own. Petronio was envious. Would his promised glass arm be able to replicate human movement? Though now he'd accused Fenestra's daughter, maybe that promise would be broken.

'Getting there . . . no matter how high they build those firewalls, I'm jumpin' them.'

'Which means?' asked Lord Far.

'This! Even though I can't track the signal itself, I've run a search on the girl. Oh yes, you won't believe what I can find out. I've cross-matched all cloud images of her, even ones she's deleted. And our own spy-cams and fly-cams are everywhere. So, check this out!'

The numbers vanished from the screen to be replaced by a grainy video image.

'Oh no!' Fenestra exclaimed as she leant over to look. 'It can't be!'

But it was. Though the shot was out of focus and taken at night, the action was clear. It was a rooftop. A boy with orange hair unpinned and handed over a wooden brooch to a girl. Randall.

'Freeze it!' Petronio commanded. 'Can you get a better picture of the other figure?'

'Yeah! Of course – it's called zooming!' The picture expanded on the screen.

'How the holly . . . ? Arborium is here!' Petronio said slowly, in disbelief.

'What do you mean?' Lord Far demanded.

'That imbecile of a boy is called Mucum and his best mate happens to be Arktorious Malikum, a grotty little sewage worker.'

'So? Two teenage Arborians. Should we be scared?'

Petronio paused, remembering Ark's grip on his hand. 'Yes. We underestimate them at our peril.'

'Now tracking,' said the geek, more to himself than to anyone else. 'DNA traces from the brooch . . . might be able to pick them up if he's touched any sensors on doorways . . . Aha! Got him! He's been somewhere in this vicinity. Very recent match.' He beamed, expecting praise.

Lord Far only nodded. 'Yes. We shall flush them out.'

The geek continued staring at the screen. 'OK. Am now finding the girl. All real-time images searched. Mmm. She's not tried to hide her whereabouts at all. There she is, asleep in her bed! Is she dumb or what?'

Fenestra stood quite still, doubt appearing like fine cracks on her forehead. 'My daughter. I can't believe that . . .'

'Believe what you want, envoy. But she will answer our questions!' Lord Far was in command now. He turned to the other Gloms. 'Who knows what their plans are? They could be working with the Leveller tree-rorists. We must move fast. Double the protection round Fort Knots and summon Special Branch.'

There was a hushed silence, interrupted by one of the Gloms. 'Special Branch? But we only use them in the case of national emergencies!'

'What do you think this is? Time they earned their outrageous bonuses. If Arborium thinks it can goad us, it had better beware our response!'

Petronio watched in satisfaction as the Gloms got to work and began summoning troops. His fake arm ached, ready for action, ready for sweet revenge.

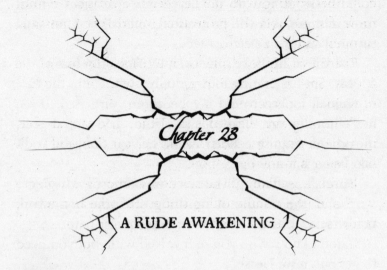

Chapter 28

A RUDE AWAKENING

'**M**istress, wake up.'

'Why? School's boring. Even you know that.'

Her wristband buzzed insistently. 'Mistress. Please wake up now. You are in danger.'

'Oh, shatter me! My mother's going to tell me off again! Like I care any more.' Randall had spent half the night putting together the film of her exploits. The hardest part had been the summit sequence, and deleting all evidence of the boy's legs as she finally hauled herself on to the highest roof in Maw. The final footage looked fabulous, and she'd fallen asleep dreaming that the stars in the sky had woven themselves into a crown to float slowly down on her head. Now she was exhausted and her hair felt greasy.

'Stop annoying me!' she grunted, pulling the pillow over her face.

'Mistress. If you do not leave this apartment within three minutes, you will be arrested, interrogated, possibly tortured and then electrocuted.'

Randall sat up. 'Joke time over, PV. That's not funny.'

'Nor am I intending to practise my wit.'

Randall looked round her bedroom, surprised to see her climbing suit cleaned and already laid out. A soft, melodious ringing echoed inside her ear. 'Oh, for Pod's sake, who is it now?'

'Randall . . . darling.' The voice was almost a whisper.

'I'm in the middle of finishing off some homework before school.' She'd never been called *darling* before.

'I don't know who you're involved with, but you need to get out, now. Please.'

Sleepiness vanished. Randall was shocked. Had her mother just tried to stifle a sob?

'I don't understand.'

'Don't lie to me. The brooch. They found out!'

'Found out what? It's an original Vivienne Webwood, cost me a fortune! I thought you liked it.'

'And the cam hidden inside? Oh, please. What do you take me for?'

'What cam?' Randall was confused. 'What are you talking about?' Then slowly, something dawned on her: the lumbering lad on the roof, the easy coincidence of events. Surely not . . . ? But who was he? How could he have known where to find her? And why plant a cam inside the brooch?

'We can talk later. Use your usual exit, through the bonsai trees. And find somewhere safe.'

'What? How do you know I . . . ?'

'That you've been skipping school? That you are one of the best free-climbers in Maw, with your skills sung throughout the cyber cloud? I *am* your mother, Randall. And now the Gloms are after you. They are sending in Special Branch. Trust me, please . . .'

The secret police? The thought made her shudder. It wasn't only companies they took down. 'But all I did was cut school!'

'They think you are a traitor. And you know how they deal with insurgents!' Randall did. Now she was scared. She spun round and dived into her clothes. Then a thought occurred to her. 'How did you know, PV?'

Her wristband fell briefly silent before replying. 'That is a question for another time, mistress. They have arrived on this floor already and are about to enter with force.'

Randall was already peering down the corridor. She heard a loud crash and splintering as the front door yielded. There was no way she would make it to the mirror. Decision time. She sprinted to the cupboard. It had worked once before. Maybe she'd be lucky.

Even as she pulled the latch closed and crouched in the darkness, heavy footsteps stamped straight past. It was a poor hiding place. Once they discovered her bedroom was empty, they'd come looking.

Randall's pulse raced. Overhangs and close climbing scrapes were easy compared with this. Timing was all she had left. The intruders didn't have eyes in the back of their heads, or so she hoped as she gently lifted the latch and peered out. The bedroom door was shut. She could hear tearing sounds and grunts of dissatisfaction. She eased her way out, then bolted down the corridor, trusting that PV would play his part.

The mirror was already sliding open as she ducked through, sprinting between the trays of stunted trees.

'Stop!' a voice shouted.

'Oh, glass!' Randall muttered. She worked the catch on the escape window. 'PV, shut the door!'

She stood on the ledge of the open window, feeling the cold morning air swirl into the room, and heard something behind her.

A pair of kevlon-armoured police stood at the entrance to the secret den, staring at her with their bright blue eyes. The contact lenses that made their pupils glow contained laser-guidance systems. The g-guns held firmly in the palms of their hands were primed, ready to slice her like toast.

They paused, taking in the law-breaking sight of tiny forbidden trees, and their mouths dropped open, before the smaller of the two managed to tear his gaze away from the branches to address the matter in hand. 'Miss Randall Jarrett Fenestra. You are in breach of bye-law six hundred and five, namely that you abetted and aided traitors to Maw and did wittingly help them to spy on restricted business practices.'

'You do talk funny!' Randall replied. 'Bye now.' With that, she let her weight topple her slowly backwards. All her years in free-climbing might or might not pay off, she reasoned. It was a crazy plan. Randall knew it was a matter of do or die. But she certainly didn't want to hang round for a cosy chat, and nor did she intend to end up as a splatter of blood and bone smeared over some buttress far below.

At the same moment, a shard of crystal glass passed close, singeing one of her eyebrows as it shot harmlessly through her hair and into the sky behind her. What she didn't see was the tiny glowing splinter that had detached itself from the main projectile. Small as the tip of an eyelash, it now neatly attached itself to a strand of her hair. Even as she tumbled straight down, a c-gull without wings, the splinter was already emitting a high-frequency sound.

The ratchet rope cinched to her belt and attached to the window catch above her spooled out as she fell past acres of vertical glass walls. One hundred metres; two hundred metres. As the freezing wind threatened to turn her hair into braided icicles, Randall wondered if the Special Branch operatives would snip the cord. No, of course they wouldn't. They wanted her alive, for *interrogation*.

Her body arched as the thin skylon rope stretched to its half-kilometre limit. The belt around her waist abruptly pulled tight with a g-force that must have been up to 3G. Randall's stomach was squeezed tight. Her spine jarred. She didn't even have enough air in her lungs to scream out in pain. At least she had eaten no breakfast to up-chuck into the abyss below. She bounced a couple of times, hoping her body wouldn't slam into the side of the tower. Then she was swinging like a pendulum, her feet and arms brushing past the indifferent walls of the building.

She had no plan, only to get away. What had the boy with the orange hair sold her? Had she been so easily fooled? Now she was on the run for her life. The jump had been clever, but not clever enough . . . Too soon, others would be zooming through the air in a flypod. She was trapped.

'PV. Help me.'

'Mistress. This has been caused by my actions.' Was that guilt she heard in the usually smooth metallic tones? 'However, I have summoned help. Look!'

'My lady, we meet again!' The stained platform scooted across until it hovered only just beneath her. The woman in the grimy brown body-warmer and hat reached forward to steady Randall's swinging on the rope.

'Nguh! Flaw? How did you know I was here?'

'Can't explain. Must act quickly. Here, I'm unclipping you. This is a cleaner's uniform. Put it on! Now!'

Randall didn't usually like being told what to do. But this was different. She picked herself up from where she had landed on the platform floor. 'I don't understand!' she said, dazed.

'Reasons will not save you! Go on!' Flaw thrust a quilted top and trousers at her. 'And be quick about it.' As Randall put the uniform on, the woman lunged towards her with a wicked-looking blade in her hand.

'What are you doing?' Randall whimpered.

'Trying to make it look like you kept falling, you spoilt fool!' Flaw hissed as she cut off Randall's belt and let it flutter away down into the city depths. The platform lurched sideways against the nearest wall. Before Randall knew what was happening, a hat had been pulled roughly over her head and an extending mop shoved into her hands.

'Get to work!' Flaw commanded.

Randall was too stunned to do anything other than what she had been told. Seconds later she heard the buzz of electric motors descending behind them. The glass in front of her gave a perfect reflection of the hovering flypod, with porthole guns trained on the platform. Randall kept scrubbing the window as if her life depended on it. Which it did.

She waited for the loudspeakers, the order to put their hands against the wall, the round-up. Subjects of Maw were always being 'disappeared.' Up until now, Randall had never taken notice of protesting mothers blitzing the cyber-cloud with their protests. Now she was tasting true fear for the first time. How could Flaw even try to fool them?

But instead of barked orders, there was only the sound of whirring blades fading into the distance.

'You can stop pretending now!' Flaw hissed.

Randall looked at the smeary mess in front of her. 'I don't think I'm much good at it anyway.'

PV's voice cut in. 'We must hurry. Remiel's lair has been discovered. He has asked us to meet him at charging station 326. It is halfway along the safest route . . .'

'What the . . . ?' Randall was bewildered, but PV continued speaking over her.

'Mistress, it is not you I address, but Flaw. Please stay silent. As I was instructing, it is halfway along the safest route to the underground shrine. According to my status reports, the engineers are close to repairing the vacuum train. Flaw, it will be better if I guide the girl myself. You must return and warn the rest of the Levellers to activate all security protocols and stay hidden.'

'Remiel always said you were a marvel, PV. How you can seem to be in several places at once is nothing short of a miracle,' Flaw murmured, pulling Randall towards her and gently kissing her forehead. 'I have to go. Log be with you.'

'*Log be with you?* What do you mean? In the last twenty minutes, I've woken up to find that I'm accused of being a traitor, that I'm wanted for questioning, that maybe even my mother doesn't believe me and that my whole sharding life has gone. And now you're chatting away cosily with my PV about vacuum trains and shrines, and someone called Remiel!' Randall dropped the mop and blinked her eyes to try to stop the tears. 'What's going on? Will someone tell me, please?'

Flaw took the girl and enfolded her in her arms. 'There, there,' she said soothingly. 'Once you're out of here and safe, all will be explained. We're sorry you became involved. Truly.'

Randall couldn't even remember the last time her mother had stroked her hair. And now a mere worker, who seemed to know much more about what was going on than she did, was comforting her. It was all a mess, and somehow she was stuck right in the middle of it.

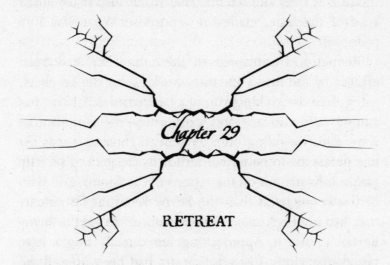

Chapter 29

RETREAT

'**I**s this the only way?' Remiel pleaded. He looked away from Ark and Mucum and round the hub. On the walls hung framed sheets of printed paper. 'The last pages, from the last books . . .' he murmured.

PV's voice issued from Remiel's wristband. 'There is no choice and no time. They are closing in.'

Ark still could not get over the concept of a voice, a being, that had no body. Corwenna had always said there was more to the whole wide-wood than meets the eye. The Empire and its technology had proved that. But PV felt different to the cold machines that throbbed within the walls of every building in Maw. Ark sensed something else in him. Did he dare to try to reach out to PV with his mind? He could speak with his thoughts to Corwenna and the Ravens. But PV? Yet according to the Raven-Queen, Ark himself was born of the woods: a living breathing mixture of trees and science. That would also make him a kind of machine, made for a purpose. What was PV's purpose?

Remiel had explained to them how PV had been created by the finest scientists working for the Levellers, using the existing blueprint of a basic virtual assistant but adding revolutionary and extraordinary functions that were mind-boggling even to Remiel. Their idea was for this prototype to be tested out for its capacity to secretly gather information on the actions of the Gloms. And who better to test it on than the Envoy Fenestra? Of course, they had not been able to risk attempting to get the envoy herself to use it. Approaching her directly might have raised suspicions. Instead, Fenestra had been offered the use of the only newly-created Personal Virtual Assistant for her daughter, as a sort of advanced toy. Naturally, she had only been told of a few of its exciting new capabilities. So she had no idea that while PV was communicating directly with Randall via her DNA-integrated wristband, there was a second controlling wristband that PV's glass function cube was linked to: Remiel's. Neither was Fenestra aware of PV's ability to connect wirelessly with just about all forms of technology he was put into contact with, without being traced. So, while Randall did not necessarily see enough of her mother to make her a useful direct spy, every time she entered her own personal code into the security system of their home, at least PV could slip silently into Fenestra's closed household network. Ark had understood very little of what he had heard, but enough to appreciate that this PV was something special.

'What about the daughter?' said Remiel, interrupting Ark's thoughts.

'She is alive. I am bringing her.' The voice was calm.

'Good.' Remiel grabbed his screen, rolled it up and secreted it within the folds of his robes. 'Oakley, you know what to do.'

'I'm preparin' a nice welcoming party, boss.'

'Good.' Remiel was distracted. 'Mucum and Arktorious. You have the information you came to find out. What do you intend to do with it?'

Ark felt overwhelmed. 'We have to destroy the Quantum Trap . . . stop that thing from ever being used. Otherwise, all of our people will be . . . no more.'

'Right,' said Mucum. 'Business as usual then, huh? Us two with a coupla knives against the massed armies of Maw. Easy buddy peasy, I don't fink.' He frowned. 'We might 'ave pulled it off last time. But we ain't on home scaffield-turf now, mate.'

'As Levellers, we can go to ground,' said Remiel. 'But now they know about you, there is nowhere in the Empire that is safe.'

'Might I make a suggestion?' PV interrupted.

'We're all ears,' Mucum said sarcastically.

'It might be possible to disrupt the weapon at the point it is triggered. The probability is only forty-two percent, but the odds against you breaking into the labs and destroying the machine are nine point five percent.'

'Could you talk in some kind of language these Dendrans will understand, PV?' Remiel sighed.

'Yes. If I accompany these two young men to their

place of habitation, we might have a chance of stopping the Quantum Trap before it is initiated. Remiel, this cannot be done by these two alone. You will need to hack in and disrupt the mainframe. There will be possible loss of life.'

Remiel sighed. 'I have found that paradise exists, and that the forested land is no dream.' His face grew hard. 'So I won't have a bunch of greedy businessmen destroy it. But how can you accompany them, PV? Even assuming that I could still link to the functions housed in the cube, I can't go as I'm needed to co-ordinate everything from here. Neither can I simply peel off my own wristband as it is genetically coded to work only when on my person, just as the girl's is . . . ah, the girl. She needs to be hidden, yes? I wonder. Hmmm. Could she be persuaded?'

'I calculate the likelihood of persuasion to be less than twelve percent. As for my operating mode, though I can communicate through any available system, my main functions are backed up in the glass cube on Randall's keyring in exactly the way your scientists created me: for the purpose of spying on her mother, the envoy. Thus, in answer, I would indeed be able to accompany the young men, if the girl Randall were with them.'

'I'm not quite following all this,' Ark broke in. 'Do you mean we run away back to Arborium?' He felt the phial round his neck, and sensed a green, coiling anger stirring deep within him. But what could he do? Summon the Ravens? Turn weapons to wood and smash them to splinters? Unlikely. He was one small speck among billions who no longer even believed in living trees.

'A tactical retreat!' Remiel answered. 'Giving you the only possible chance of finding and destroying the weapon before it is used. Oakley has found our best engineers to repair the mining capsule. The technology was more than antique, but they are nearly there. We need to hide you until tonight, though this might prove difficult. Enough talk. Action is what's needed now!' He took one last look around the room that he had called home, briefly pausing to stroke the desk before indicating the raised trapdoor near the far wall. 'After you,' he said.

Ark followed Mucum down the steps and back into the jungle of greenery, feeling dazed. They'd only been here since yesterday and already they were fleeing.

As they pushed through the hanging bunches of oversized purple grapes and melted into the sterile foliage, footsteps could be heard clanging back up the steps. There was a small bang and a puff of smoke rose towards the lights high above.

Remiel crouched among the thick roots of the pepper plants. 'They're in. Give them a few more seconds . . .'

Oakley's face was tense, the wrinkles on his forehead compressed in concentration as a gnarled finger hovered over his wristband.

'Now!' he whispered.

There was a quiet pause, then a sudden *whoomph* that sucked the air from their lungs. Ark and Mucum looked up to see swords of flame stab into the air above them. There was a single scream, cut off by the sound of wrenching metal as the whole hub began to sway, then slowly topple backwards, the vines that disguised the building ripped out by their roots.

It reminded Ark of a tree-fall he'd once witnessed as a child. An old tree that had been weakened by the winter storms had been creaking ominously for weeks until the council finally had the sense to evacuate the neighbourhood. But the event itself was like a funeral, crowds of onlookers mixing in with those whose homes were under threat, all straining against the safety barriers to watch. It only took a single gust and the whole tree began to fall backwards in slow motion, wood-ways ripped like paper as a whole suburb crashed away into the forest. Even the birds fell silent as the forest mourned one of its own.

Ark remembered the nightmares later, imagining he was a child left behind in one of the houses as the living room sloped away and walls turned to floors, tables and chairs flying forwards to crush him.

A shove against his shoulder brought him back to the present.

'Got what they deserved!' said Oakley as he pushed Ark away from the scene.

'May their souls rest in peace.' Remiel led the way through the undergrowth, footsteps muffled by the soft drench of sprinklers. 'There'll be more coming soon. Follow me close.'

They walked single file, leaving the flames and the burnt-out hub far behind them. Minutes went by and still they hadn't been discovered. All they could hear was the background hum that was everywhere in Maw, like the laboured breath of some gigantic machine. Despite all this space, Ark felt hemmed in. The scale of this single room dwarfed the massive scaffields back home. But scaffields tilted towards a real sun and were touched by genuine breezes. The air in here tasted of metal and the unwavering light from the ceiling above hurt his eyes.

It was as they stepped across a gravelled walkway that their luck ran out.

Remiel's hands were already in the air as a g-gun dug into his robes, aiming at his chest.

'What have we here?' the soldier drawled. His adaptive armour had done its job. Aside from the weapon and the sneer on his face, the man was a stalking camouflage job, decked out in shades of green. With his free hand, he spoke into his wristband. 'Got three of them. But no sight of the orange-haired one.'

'That'd be me!' Mucum snarled, leaping out from behind the soldier, his fist connecting perfectly with the man's nose. An instant spray of vivid red coated the nearest green leaves as the soldier crumpled.

'Thanks!' said Remiel, arching his eyebrows. 'Where did you spring from?'

'Lucky it was me what was last in line. Spotted 'im easy. Crept round the side and behind 'im. Good to know I still got what it takes!'

'When you've finished congratulating yourself,' Oakley growled, 'we have company!'

The plants behind them erupted with the sound of crashing soldiers. Ringing shots sent up sprays of gravel between their feet as they scrambled sideways between rows of plants.

'They're not shooting to kill!' Remiel panted. 'Doesn't
. . . make . . . sense.'

And then it did. There was only one direction they
could go in, with the soldiers forcing the pace. The
tightly-packed row of beans they were walking between
finally came to an abrupt end. In front of them, a solid
glass wall reared up towards the cavernous ceiling. No
handholds to climb, no doors to escape through. It was a
dead end.

All four turned to see the ranks of soldiers fanning out
around them in a semi-circle, weapons pointed.

'Any ideas?' Mucum muttered.

Ark shook his head. He'd made arrows drop from the
sky. But these alien weapons would not listen to him.

'We could go out in a blaze o' glory. Yer know, charge
'em with our knives.'

'I admire your courage, young man!' Remiel said.
'However, perhaps we must bow to the inevitable.' He
closed his eyes.

But what prayer could save them now?

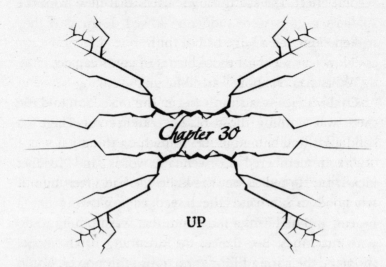

Chapter 30

UP

'Close your eyes!' Oakley murmured.

'I'm no coward!' Mucum snapped, staring straight at the soldiers and their weapons in defiance.

'Never said you were!' Oakley replied. 'Only we're about to have a bit of flash, bang, wallop! And get those special knives of yours out too.'

Ark turned his head sideways, catching the brief glimmer of a grin from Remiel's faithful servant. What was he up to? They had no choice but to trust him. As they obediently shut their eyes, Oakley pulled a small grey canister from a pouch on his belt. There was a click, and a fizz.

Shots rang out, and the air exploded round them.

'Wakey! Wakey!' Oakley shouted. 'Time to get to work.'

They opened their eyes to a changed scene. The air was filled with fog, an instant wall to baffle their attackers, and the mist still pouring like milk from the canister had a second effect. The see-through shards that flew from the soldier's g-guns were suddenly slowed down as if they had encountered a huge ball of fluff.

'Now let's see what those blades of yours can do, eh?'

'What you on about?' said Mucum.

Oakley's face was almost lost in the mist. 'You told me there was nothing those blades couldn't cut. There's a solid glass wall behind us. Do something about it!'

Ark remembered Corwenna's words and instinct kicked in. He pulled out the knife she had given him. It felt good in his hand, the honed edge glowing like a beacon and he heard a faint hum that was nothing to do with machines. Bee dance, the dreaming of the Root-shooters, their song filling these gifts with power. Would it work? Only one way to find out.

'Mucum, start at the top and slice away from me!'

Mucum grabbed his own knife and gripped it in his large fist.

'On a count of three!' said Ark. 'One! Two! Three!' They both raised their arms and stabbed the sheer wall at a point a few inches above head height. As the blades met the glass, there were sparks and something like resistance, but then the points punctured the surface as though sliding into frozen butter.

'Blimey!' said Mucum.

'Now cut along your side!' Ark commanded.

It was hard work forcing the knives to move sideways, but once they dragged the blades downwards the diamond-tipped blades slid through the glass like they were slicing bread, creating an instant door shape. The shouts of confused soldiers lost in the fog echoed behind them.

'What now?' said Mucum, panting.

'Over to you,' Ark replied. 'Push!'

Mucum turned sideways, gritted his teeth and used his shoulder to shove against the solid wall. There was a scraping sound, then a splintering crash. 'Buddy Holly!' he exclaimed. 'That's more like it!'

The gaping hole that beckoned was their escape route.

'Go! Now!' said Remiel. However, the fog was already thinning.

Mucum turned and saw the fading mist. 'Quick! Where does this lead?'

They stepped through, crunching over shiny splinters, and found themselves in a long, enclosed space with glass walls rearing all around them. Mucum stared, bewildered. 'There's no way out! We're trapped! Where are we now?'

Oakley spoke. 'We're at a point where two basement systems of different buildings intersect, but they separate into individual towers up above.' He pointed to what looked like a grimy open glass box standing against the opposite wall. He pushed Mucum and Ark towards it. 'Get in there,' he muttered.

The four figures crammed themselves inside as running soldiers headed towards the shattered doorway, taking aim through the last wisps of fog.

'Do somethin'!' Mucum squealed.

'Naturally!' said Remiel, reaching out a finger towards a softly glowing button protruding from the wall.

'Hold on tight!' Remiel shouted as the floor of the box

shuddered. Ark and Mucum's knees gave way as the whole thing catapulted them upwards.

'Much as we'd like to stay and be shot,' Remiel yelled down as the first soldiers scrambling through the archway beneath them slid from view, 'we have other, more pressing matters to attend to!' He turned back to Mucum and Ark. 'Service lift. Very old. Very basic, but thankfully still working, even if the door won't close.'

'Argh! What was that?' Mucum clapped his hand above his right ear. His palm came away sticky and red. 'Bloomin' roses! I've been hit!'

As the lift swayed, Remiel reached forward and with expert fingers probed the side of Mucum's head.

'Ow!' Mucum cried.

'Ow is good,' said Remiel. 'A scratch. Nothing more. Though I didn't know that the companions of mythical gods bled.'

'Will yer leave out all that oaky-croaky stuff! This ain't no bleedin' scratch!'

Ark smiled, relieved. If his friend was complaining, that meant he wasn't too badly hurt. He tried to steady himself as they hurtled upwards much faster than any Rootshooter lift. 'I can't believe we did it!' he said.

'Teamwork!' Oakley smiled. 'But we ain't out of the hoods yet!'

Walls zipped past. Ark thought of the basements that they had just escaped from, musing on how the sub-levels were like the roots of the trees at home. They provided the structure and machinery that supported the towers high above.

'The rich only want pleasing views and prefer to hide the grubby business of commerce in the bowels of the city,' said Remiel looking down. 'Delivery systems, bakery warehouses, heating, ventilation, generators and whole ghettos of laundry slaves to keep their sheets pristine and white. Why do any of the workers below need to see the light of day? As long as they are fed and watered, the system works. Such division makes me sick in my soul.' Remiel looked into Ark's eyes. 'This is why we believe that the way of the trees offers hope.'

'Don't put us on a pedestal!' Ark replied. He thought of the shanty settlements deep beneath the canopy of home, drowned in shadow and far from the sun. He thought of the Rootshooters. Since the battle, Quercus had promised that things would change and they had already begun to. Ark hoped there would still be Dendrans left in Arborium to carry on those changes.

Suddenly they burst out of the dark enclosed space and into intense sunlight as glass towers twisted away from each other. The lift continued climbing up the outside of its building but now winds whipped past the open side.

'Elms Bells!' said Mucum, clinging on and taking in the view that was filled with shimmering towers that twisted and curled their way up into the sky, 'It's a bloomin' forest.'

'A glass forest!' Ark muttered, as they rose ever upwards. And yet these sky saplings had no leaves, no timber-goats scrambling round to find the tastiest fungus, no scented breeze filled with the smell of bark and root. This endless city was both beautiful and ugly.

'I thought the Rootshooter lifts were good, but this is conkers!' said Mucum. 'Where we goin'?'

'Up!' said Remiel. 'Not all those in high places are corrupt. There are those who are willing to help us.' The lift gave a jarring clang. 'What in the name of Bark was that?'

'Trouble,' said Oakley, as the lift ground to a halt.

There was a bell-like ping. As the outer doors finally shuddered and closed with a grating sound, other unseen doors between them and the building itself suddenly slid apart. Mucum fell backwards as he had been leaning against them. He picked himself up hurriedly and they all peered into a long glass corridor, like a slightly translucent snake, vanishing into the distance. There were closed doors on either side and silence from the rooms beyond. But what came round the corner towards them from the far end was trouble indeed.

'Oh, great,' said Mucum. 'We're gonna be sliced to smithereens this time!'

But Oakley was already on the move, pushing open a hatch in the roof with a clunking thud. 'Come on, you lot. A massacre ain't the result we're looking for!'

The soldiers were a good hundred yards down the corridor but they didn't seem to be in a hurry. Ark was the last one to pull himself up through the hatch. Once he staggered upright he knew why the soldiers were in no rush: the wind that threatened to knock them off the tiny lift roof was mercilessly sharp. And Ark had a horrible feeling of vertigo. It was one thing running along a mile-high branch to escape an attacker. But that was familiar.

And all that time ago, a length of rope had saved him. Now, the four of them were perched on a precarious nest, edging back towards the sheer wall behind them, trying to keep from toppling off the sky-high edge.

The wall above the lift was solid glass. Mucum grabbed his knife, preparing to see if they could do what they had done earlier. But Remiel shook his head.

'Even if you could cut through in time, where would it lead? Straight into close firing range of the soldiers.'

Ark felt his smallness. Once they fell, this city would swallow them in its greedy maw. No wonder the soldiers felt they could take their time.

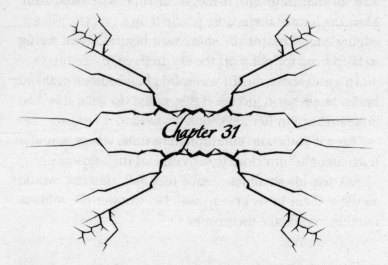

Chapter 31

'I'm freezin' me hazelnuts off 'ere,' said Mucum, squinting into the wind.

'The least of our worries,' Remiel murmured. 'PV?'

The voice that emanated from Remiel's wristband was almost blown away by the breeze. 'Did the master pack safety parachutes?'

'I'm afraid not.' Remiel turned to the boys. 'It appears that our time has come. We will be questioned, then killed. You do understand that?' Hope faded from his dark eyes as he stared at Ark. 'Unless the woods that you come from have other secrets not yet revealed?'

Ark could sense the soldiers nearby. Soon they would enter the lift and aim their weapons upwards. Surrender was inevitable. But a voice inside his head was speaking. Had they come this far to give up so easily? He thought of the Rootshooters who had used stitched-together leaves to swoop and soar into battle. What did they have to hand? Nothing but what was around them.

Think! said the voice inside his head again. *I said that you would have to face death.* This time it had a familiar lilt. Even from this distance, he recognized it. Could Corwenna really catch the wind and let it carry her thoughts over thousands of miles? Ark looked around frantically. The sheer face of the sky-building that the lift clung on to like a beetle was impossibly smooth. Even if they tried to climb it, the soldiers would be able to pick them off like target practice.

Ark knelt and looked over the edge of the roof they were standing on. In some ways, he thought, Maw resembled the Ravenwood. Its jumble of glass was truly higgledy-twiggledy. No tower reared straight up; there were twisted kinks and turns, enormous angled abutments and ledges that stuck out from the rearing, shiny trunks of the buildings. Then he spotted something.

'Look!' he shouted.

Oakley was already kneeling beside him, peering down as the vicious updraught threatened to tear his beard off.

The ledge Ark pointed at was about three hundred yards below them, a flat glassy triangle pointing outwards like an arrowhead.

'And?' said a puzzled Oakley. 'Are you proposing we fly?'

'Sort of,' Ark replied, trying to ignore the fear rooted in his guts. But before he could say anything else, an amplified command floated up to them.

'By order of the Corporate Justices of Maw, you have thirty seconds to surrender any weapons and climb down into the lift one by one!'

Remiel clenched his fists, then released them. 'It would be braver if we jumped. Once we are in their hands, their methods of torture will ensure we betray all our good and loyal comrades.'

'What?' said Mucum. 'Do ourselves in for the greater wood? What about Arborium?'

'My boy, there are many other lives that sway in the balance. And it is those believers who we must have faith in, for maybe they will find a way to save your country. Perhaps PV will be able to persuade Randall of our cause and she can travel to your country alone.'

'The percentages are low, master. But I shall keep calculating the best options.'

'Thank you, PV.' Remiel looked down as if ashamed. 'As for the rest of us, it's too late.'

Mucum frowned. 'This can't be it. It don't feel right to give up without a fight.' He turned to Ark with a catch in his voice. 'It's been a good run, mate . . .'

'Oh, for Diana's sake!' Ark interrupted. 'There's no time for doom and gloom!' Quickly he pulled off the leather necklace that hung round his neck and lifted the phial he carried to the sunlight.

The others could just glimpse murky movement within the small stoppered bottle. Whatever lay contained within writhed with a life of its own.

'What is it?' asked Remiel.

'The Will of the Woods!' answered Ark.

Sunlight appeared to have a strange effect on the phial. It began to pulse, and despite the cold, Ark felt a sweat break out on his forehead as he cradled it in his palm. Even with the threat of g-guns only a few feet below them, this tiny phial seemed infinitely more dangerous.

'Will you trust me?' he asked as he pulled the stopper from the bottle.

'We have no choice!' answered Remiel.

'Then on the count of three, we jump, one after the other. Do your best to aim for the ledge below us. Leave the rest to me.' Even as he spoke, Ark knew that just as Remiel had said they had 'no choice' but to trust him, so he had no choice but to trust in the compressed power of the woods contained within the phial.

'Ten seconds and we start firing!' A soldier's voice carried up a tinge of hard annoyance.

'Three . . . two . . . one!' Ark led the way, hovering at the edge for a moment, then leaping like a crazed timber-boar into the unknown.

Mucum wasn't so sure. But if he was going to die, he decided, he might as well enjoy the ride. 'Life's a beech!' he screamed as his legs carried him off before he could stop them.

The other two were mesmerized by Ark's words. What did they have to lose? Everything and nothing. Remiel and Oakley ignored the voice of the soldier counting to ten and quickly followed in the slipstream of Ark's mad words.

Four bodies tumbled uselessly through the air, their velocity increasing as they sped towards their fate.

In a passing hoverbus, a child pressed her nose against the window.

'Mummy! Flying people!' she squealed.

'Of course, dear!' her mother murmured, barely looking up from the glowing spreadsheets on her lap. 'Such pretty daydreams!'

What the little girl didn't see was the tiny drop of liquid that Ark had shaken from the phial round his neck before he jumped. The drop dived where he had sent it, an insignificant sparkle whose aim was utterly true.

Ark knew that what he was doing was beyond logic, rationality or understanding. It was pure intuition, like when he'd pricked Petronio's hand with the Raven quill and delivered a single drop from the phial into the thug's bloodstream. The result had been equally impossible. All he had to do was believe . . .

In his mind's eye, he guided the drop until it splashed on to the far ledge below them. Then, as the glass zoomed up to meet them with its sharp and shimmering edges, Ark focused every thought on conjuring life in this sterile place – even though all that lay below them seemed to be certain death.

The drop made contact, the murky grey liquid changing colour to a minute inkblot of vivid green. Like spilled paint, the colour spread across the ledge and out of it roots began to stir and soft leaves to unfurl. The hard ledge sprang instantly to life with a carpet of growing vines.

Thus, at the moment of impact, instead of shattered bones and crushed bodies, there was merely a soft 'whump' as each of the four landed and were cushioned by yielding leaves.

'Holly's boils!' Mucum grunted as he bounced once, then settled on the lush greenery.

'This is beyond my capacity to analyse!' agreed PV.

Once the shock had drained away, they each slowly regained their feet, noticing a strange sound around them.

'What's that noise?' muttered Oakley, still amazed he was alive. 'I hear humming!'

Ark beamed. 'I think it's the vine leaves, simply happy to be alive.' He didn't know how he'd done it, but he was glad, even though without soil, the mirage of growth would soon wither and die.

'And so are we all!' said Remiel, swaying unsteadily among the soft vines. He looked up to see the soldiers far above them peering over the edge of the now tiny lift. 'It looks like we escaped!'

'You reckon?' The voice was gruff and angry as another soldier appeared only ten yards away on a fire escape at the edge of the vines. His g-gun was aimed straight at Ark. 'Backup needed!' the man blurted into his wristband.

Ark should have felt fear, but he could feel the vitality of the vines surging through him. So instead his mouth formed words that were either brave or stupid. 'I suggest you put your weapon down. Slowly.'

'Ooh! I am scared. Threatened by a puny teenager! Now shut your gob and step off the weird green stuff. All of you!'

Ark's smile grew wider. 'Fetch!' he said, talking to the

seething mass of vines as if it were a favourite pet.

A tendril shot up out of the leaves.

The soldier wavered. 'What in Shard's name . . . ?' But before he could squeeze the trigger, the vine tendril leapt forward, wrapped itself round the gun and ripped it from the soldier's grasp.

'Good catch!' said Ark.

The vine wagged the gun in the air like a happy tail, then tossed the weapon over the edge to clatter harmlessly down into the shadow canyons far below. Before the soldier could even respond, other tendrils tangled round his body until he was trussed up like a cruck-turkey.

'Good one, mate!' Mucum was dumbfounded.

'Thank you!' Ark gave a bow in reply.

'Yes, I congratulate you too, but now we must leave!' said Remiel, scouting the way ahead.

'Come back 'ere!' the soldier shouted hopelessly as they stepped past him on to the fire escape and into the building.

Ark was the last to leave. He knelt and stroked one of the leaves of the vine. 'Thank you!' he whispered. Already the leaves were turning mottled and brown, the soft branches flaking. He felt sad. This short-lived plant was dying for them. A worthy sacrifice, but a sacrifice nonetheless.

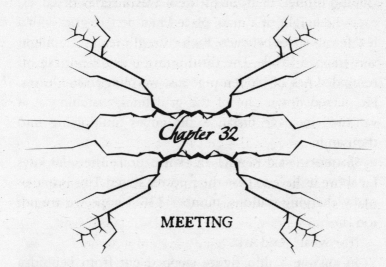

Chapter 32

MEETING

Their journey now had to be extra cautious. They couldn't risk attempting to travel upwards any more and so made their way carefully down. PV did his job, warning them of routes that had vid-cams. They used service lifts and fire-escape stairs as they delved back into the roots of the city, finding that deeper appeared to be safer. Oakley lifted a small floor-hatch to reveal a tiny service tunnel under their feet, filled with cables, pipes and glowing wires. As they crawled down, the background hum of Maw grew louder.

'Where are we going?' Ark asked. They were all sweating, the large metal pipe running at their side almost too hot to touch.

'You'll see,' said Oakley.

Ten minutes later, Oakley lifted a latticework grille above their heads and they all clambered out of the sloping tunnel. In front of them was a series of cubes, each the height of a man, placed in a perfect grid with a few feet of space between. Each cube glowed as if sunlight was trapped inside. The thrumming noise they gave off reminded Ark of hidden pigeons, warbling in the leaves. He peered down one of the grid lines, watching as it vanished into the distance, the cubes multiplying into thousands.

'Batteries,' said Remiel, in explanation. 'The solar kites far above us have to have their power stored. This is one of many charging stations, number 326. I hope we are not too late.'

'For what?' said Ark.

In answer, a thin figure stepped out from behind a cube. The girl had red hair and pale, almost clear eyes filled with cold suspicion. Ark couldn't help staring. The clothes she wore hugged her skin as close as bark, revealing a lithe, muscled body. Was this the girl Remiel had spoken of?

The girl returned his stare, a haughty look that reminded Ark of the Envoy Fenestra. He could also sense her tiredness and confusion. He almost felt sympathy, until he remembered that she was part of Maw.

The girl turned to Ark's companion, eyes widening in shock and recognition.

'You!' Randall spat, pointing her finger at Mucum. 'You were the one who sold me out!'

'Sorry, darlin'. Nothin' personal!'

'Personal?' she shouted, 'Whatever foul plan you had has shattered all over me from a great height! According to the Gloms, I'm guilty of spying on the Empire and being a tree-rorist. But I'm not the spy.' She took in the tall figure, robed in white. 'Are you some sort of leader of theirs? Whatever plans you've made don't stand a chance. When my mother gets hold of you lot, I'll look forward to watching the execution.'

'Bravo! A fine performance!' A young man emerged from the shadows. 'You almost convinced me of your innocence.'

An angry look crossed Randall's face. 'I *am* innocent. If you've been working with my mother, you should know that. Now, get these undercover agents arrested!'

'Oh,' said the young man, stroking his trimmed goatee beard. 'How very droll. Your acting skills are most amusing.' Petronio was doubly pleased. Whether the girl was innocent or not was not his concern, so long as suspicion did not come anywhere near him. The rather clever device attached to one of the hairs on her head had proved its worth. Lord Far's technical advisor had been able to track Fenestra's daughter with ease and thus she had been the unwitting bait to spring this trap. And what a catch!

Petronio stepped slowly and deliberately towards Ark, his lips tightening, his mind filled with thoughts of revenge.

Ark was shocked at the boy's confidence. The last time he'd seen Petronio in the flesh he'd been kitted out in a showy doublet and colourful britches. Petronio had also been unconscious, his life-blood leaching into the court-yard boards of Barkingham Palace. Now Ark could see the boy's Maw-made grey suit, woven through with shining metallic threads. He could also see the terrible appendage attached to his right shoulder. Instead of fingers, pincers clicked like the claws of a cruck-pool crab.

'You should have died!' Ark said.

'I suppose I should. But now you find me alive and well. No thanks to you.' He bowed mockingly. 'At your service, Malikum. Or rather, not. I'm at the service of Maw now.'

'You've sold yourself and our homeland to the highest bidder!'

'What did you expect? You took my arm. But I have been re-armed now, literally.' He took another step closer.

Ark flinched as the metallic limb flexed. It was like a serpent made of cogs and gears, coiled and ready to strike. Out of the corner of his vision, he saw Oakley and Remiel also moving forward and he wondered what chance they might have together.

'Oh, I do love those calculating green eyes of yours, Malikum. Always trying to think one step ahead. Perhaps the four of you combined could take me out. But really, did you honestly think I'd come here alone?'

Ark knew in that moment that Petronio wasn't bluffing. The shadows were not empty but teeming. Glints of g-guns flickered in the dark depths.

A man emerged, striding awkwardly forward to stand alongside Petronio. He was dressed in a shapeless shift to disguise his bulk. Ark was fascinated to see snails of shining words crawling up and down the clothes in a never ending circuit:

Eezy-Cheeze! A slice a day keeps health bills away!

The man wore a permanent sneer on his sweating face. 'And this is our revolution! Pathetic! A girl who really should have known better,'

'But my lord . . .' Randall broke in.

'My lord nothing!' the man hissed. 'Do not interrupt me or I will have you shot.'

Randall pressed her lips tight. This was no telling-off from a wound-up teacher.

'As I was saying; here is our ill-thought-out conspiracy – the girl, two foreign teenagers and a scruffy Leveller with his misshapen shortass of a servant!'

'Yeah, fatso? Not looking so handsome yourself!' Oakley said defiantly, clenching his fist, ready to answer the insult.

'Do not stoop to his level!' said Remiel.

'Oh, now that is funny!' said the man. 'I'd be have to be a contortionist to stoop to that one's level.' He stared at Remiel as though he was an insect stuck on a pin. 'I had heard that you still lived. Sorry to say it's not for much longer.'

'Yes,' Remiel agreed. 'It appears that our luck has run out. Though trust me, the trees will have their revenge, Lord Far.'

'That's what I love about you Levellers with your stupid dreams of living trees and even dumber ideas of bringing Eden back here. A forest in Maw? Whatever next?'

A few soldiers sniggered.

'Well,' Lord Far continued, 'your dreams are about to be shattered, or should that be splattered – with blood.'

'Sir, might I interrupt?' Petronio's tone was soft and oily. 'As a reward for finding the true spies, may I claim the boy for myself?'

Before he even had an answer, true to his surname, Petronio grasped the initiative. In three short strides he closed in on Ark and before Ark could think of a single lesson Corwenna had taught him, the fake limb shot out, pincers opening to encircle his neck.

'Arghhh!' Ark struggled but could barely make a sound as his breath was squeezed out by the slowly closing claws.

Mucum sprang towards Petronio, flicking his knife out of its holster. 'You little traitor. I'm gonna gut yer like a boar.'

'What a quaint and old-fashioned weapon!' Petronio said, ignoring Mucum as his mechanical hand worked its dark wonders.

Mucum paused, knife raised and saw suddenly why Petronio wasn't worried. Several wavering dots, glowing like fireflies, danced round his chest: the laser-spot aims of multiple g-guns.

'How amusing!' said Lord Far. 'Such loyalty is almost becoming. Now, put the knife down!' He waved his arm towards Petronio as if granting a royal decree. 'Yes. If it is your pleasure to finish off the Arborian spy, you have my permission.' Then he turned back to the soldiers. 'What are you waiting for? Take the rest of them out, including the girl who betrayed us in the first place. A fourteen-year-old, high-born infiltrator? What is the Empire coming to?'

'Wait!' The voice was sharp and strident, tinged with

panic. A woman ran out and clutched at the folds of the big man's robes.

As Ark felt his life-sap beginning to drain away, his dimming eyes vaguely recognized her. Instead of the Holly Woodsman disguise, her clothes now were angular, long and sharp like the towers she called home. 'You promised! My daughter was deceived. It's obvious she is innocent of all this. And you gave me your word!'

'Lady Fenestra! Would that be the same word you gave me in assurance that my little Puccikins was also safe?'

'That was a cat! This is a human life! Have you no mercy? And anyway, the cat was spared.'

'My dear envoy. As we have said many times together, it's not personal. It's business. The Empire must protect itself. Your daughter knows too much. As the saying goes on the trading floors, *too much knowledge can be a bad thing*. No hard feelings, eh?'

Randall looked at her mother. 'You gave me away!' Her eyes brimmed with tears.

'I had no choice but to let them trace you, my darling. They told me the only way to save you was by finding you. It turns out that I am the one betrayed. But I must bow to the markets.' She gave a little curtsey towards her employer and then strode out . . . straight into the line of fire. Even as Lord Far was raising his arm to signal to the soldiers to do their job, Fenestra had stopped, standing right in front of her daughter. 'I am a mother, not an economic machine. You'll have to take me down first!' Her eyes were fearless, defiant. G-guns wavered and were lowered. There was silence.

'It sounds as though you are in league with our enemies!' spluttered Lord Far. 'This situation needs to be contained, dammit!' He jabbed his finger at the soldiers in the shadows. 'Do as I command,' he screamed.

The soldiers wavered. A single voice spoke out. 'But she's the envoy, sir! It goes against all our training, sir!'

'And business decisions overrule all protocol! Kill them *all*, unless you wish to be tried for treason!'

Ark could feel his last breath leaving his body. His best bud Mucum was frozen to the spot, feeling like a coward. Remiel held Oakley back and tried to accept what fate was bringing to them, and Randall cowered in her mother's arms.

But before Lord Far's order could be obeyed, there was a loud fizzing noise and the vast chamber was plunged into gloom.

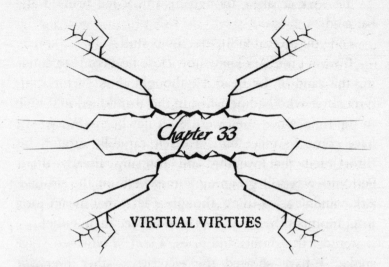

Chapter 33

VIRTUAL VIRTUES

Ark wondered why he could suddenly breathe again.

'Stupid hand!' Petronio hissed. The pincers had gone slack and loose, the whole mechanical arm falling uselessly to his side.

Ark staggered, sucking welcome air into his lungs. 'Traitor!' he gasped, trying to clear his thoughts. There was no time for the knife or the phial. Instead, all his pent-up rage went into his curled fist, slamming into Petronio's stomach with a force that knocked him backwards. The soldiers were in disarray, their targets vanishing as the glow faded from the giant cubes around them.

'Hold your fire!' shouted Lord Far. 'They're going nowhere. The system backup will bring on emergency lights in under sixty seconds.'

'What's happenin'?' whispered Mucum as complete darkness descended. 'Are yer still wiv us, buddy?'

'Yes,' Ark croaked, though his throat felt bruised and battered.

'Did you do that killin' the lights stuff?'

'It wasn't me.' Ark knew how close he'd come to entering the Land of the Dead. He thought about Victoria, his twin sister who had perished in the abandoned nest high in the trees when they were both newborns. Would she have come to meet him? He felt carefully around his throat, felt the swelling and bruising already there. Petronio was still groaning somewhere on the ground. Ark couldn't see a thing, though at least that meant for a brief moment their attackers couldn't see them either.

Amidst the shouts and cries, a soft, modulated voice spoke. 'I have shorted the electrics. Gather everyone quickly and follow my instructions.'

Ark wondered if the voice was speaking inside or outside his head. Corwenna could talk without moving her lips, sending her thoughts directly into Ark's mind. Was PV able to do the same? It didn't really matter, so long as he listened to what the words told him. His senses were on alert in the complete, liquid darkness.

'Get off me!' came Randall's voice. Ark heard a sudden thwacking sound, then Randall fell silent.

Somewhere nearby, Lady Fenestra screamed, 'My daughter! My daughter!' over and over as if speech alone could save her.

Following PV's whispered instructions, Ark stretched out his arms until he brushed against the familiar bulk of Mucum. He grabbed his arm and veered to the left. 'Follow my leader!' he whispered.

'Ain't a game!' hissed Mucum.

'I know, but we're still against the clock. Just try not to trip over anything.'

'Left by seven steps. Take ten steps forward.' PV's instructions were exact. Ark let his feet guide him. In front he could hear Oakley's laboured breathing and Remiel's faster, lighter breaths. The noises of confusion faded quickly behind them.

'We out of the woods yet?' Mucum grunted.

'Don't know,' Ark puffed. A glimmer of light that revealed a doorway ahead also illuminated the outlines of the other two moving swiftly towards it. 'OK. Now we run!'

They flung themselves through the door, away from the charging station, straight down a set of dimly-lit stairs. Ark saw now why Oakley was breathing so heavily: Randall was slumped, half-conscious and groaning, over his back. They clattered ever downwards, but already their ruse had been discovered and footsteps echoed behind them. Shots rang out down the stairwell and glass shards splintered round their heads.

'Time to do our laundry?' Remiel panted.

'That would appear to be your most advantageous probability,' PV agreed.

'You what?' wheezed Mucum as sounds of pursuit thundered above and behind them.

Remiel came to a sudden halt, pressing a button on his wristband. As the others careered into his back, a smooth metallic square at their side slid open to reveal a small black hole. 'This!'

Mucum bent forwards and sniffed deeply. 'Oh yeah! Recognize that pong anywhere. To an old sewer-hand like me, the whiff of stinky underpants is practically perfume!'

'Less talk!' said Remiel. 'Feet first is best. After you.' He stood aside.

Oakley unshouldered the groggy girl and fed her legs none too gracefully into the hole, letting gravity do its job. Then he grabbed the top edge of the laundry chute and in one quick motion, bent his legs and swung himself through.

'Jus' like old times, eh, sliding down them Xylem tubes?' Mucum grinned as he squeezed his bulk through the tiny opening. 'Whee!' The sound of his voice vanished into the inky darkness. Ark clambered quickly into the hole and let go. Suddenly, he was sliding round and round in a speeding spiral, Remiel's feet not far above him. He remembered the time he had gone diving with the Root-shooters. Another journey into the unknown.

Flump! Ark's thoughts were broken by a landing even softer than the instant jungle he had conjured from the phial. He rolled sideways, narrowly missing Remiel's arrival.

'Twigs alive!' shrieked Mucum. 'Good to know you civilized lot stink as bad as Dendrans!'

They floundered through various soiled garments that the rich of Maw could not be bothered to wash themselves. The great basement laundry room was warm and damp. Workers, with their heads bent, moved between piles and seemed oblivious to the new arrivals. The mist hanging in the air reminded Ark of foggy autumn mornings on the wood-way, and he suddenly felt dread-fully homesick.

Oakley already had Randall over his shoulder again, but her eyes flickered open.

'What's ... what's going on? I've been kidnapped!' she said weakly, as she tried to free herself. 'Help! He's a madman!'

But the laundry workers in their stained overalls ignored her. They were dotted round the mountain of clothing, using the devices on their wristbands to check each item before chucking them into high-sided trolleys. Once the trolleys were full, they trundled across the floor towards distant swing doors where even more steam hissed out.

Oakley let go of his grip on Randall and she slid to the floor. She rolled on to her knees, then stood, swaying slightly. 'I'm Randall Jarrett Fenestra, daughter of the Envoy of Maw, and these are illegal tree-rorists!' she screeched.

'Ooh-er. Miss Rich High-and-Mighty in a spot of bother? Now you know how the other half feel most of the time!' said one of the workers, pausing to spit on the ground to make his point. He turned to Oakley and winked at him. 'All right, Cedric?'

'OK. Been better.'

'Cedric?' said Mucum. 'What kinda name is that?'

'A good one!' growled Oakley. 'You got a problem with it?'

'Nah, mate. All oaky-doaky with me!'

Oakley turned back to Randall. 'Sorry, Miss Jarrett.

Friends in low places. Have as many tantrums as you want but this lot will keep their traps shut.'

Randall backed away. 'How dare you speak to me like that! When Lord Far understands the truth of the situation, you'll pay!' she hissed, rubbing her head where Oakley had knocked her out earlier.

'But it was Lord Far who ordered you shot,' Remiel interrupted, removing an undergarment that had wrapped itself round his leg. 'We saved your life.'

'No, you didn't. If that orange-haired glass-hole hadn't fooled me with the brooch, I'd be off for another day free-climbing instead of this.' Randall's eyes darted from side to side, looking for a possible escape route. But two huge laundry workers had already moved to block the only door.

'Yes, indulging your hobby while your mother sets out to destroy the last and only natural habitat in the world,' said Remiel. 'It's good to see you have a conscience. Trust me young lady, if you go back, you might as well sign your own death sentence.'

'I don't even know what you're on about. But I do know that thanks to you, all my vids, my gear, my online friends, my everything is gone!' She pulled the small glass cube from her pocket. 'And you, PV. What's going on? You seem to be able to chat cosily with him as well as me.' She looked mutinously at Remiel. 'I thought you were my friend!'

The cube was like a miniature version of the batteries in the charging station. As Ark peered at it he was sure he could sense movement within.

'You never treated me as such, mistress.' PV's voice leapt from her wristband.

Randall fell silent. 'Yeah, well, that's 'cos you're a machine – and a lying, deceiving one at that,' she muttered, wondering what would happen if she dropped the cube and stamped on it. Suddenly the fight went out of her. 'What do I do now?' She hid her face and gave a heaving sob.

'Come with us,' Ark said gently.

'Where?' Her voice trembled as she sank to the ground and hugged her knees. All the while, her mind was working furiously. Her mother had taught her that every difficulty was merely an opportunity in hiding. Perhaps, she thought, there was a better option than making a run for it. Easy to fool this lot. She'd been lying to her mother for years, but PV was another matter. His sensors in the wristband could pick up even the slightest change in pulse. She'd have to play it very carefully if she was going find a way of turning the situation to her advantage.

'To a land where trees don't grow in rooms, but reach for the sky. Arborium. Unless we stop the Quantum Trap, all that we are fighting for will be destroyed.' Ark thought back to Remiel's unlikely idea that PV could help them if they got back to Arborium. But PV was attached to Randall and needed her DNA coding to function fully. It was the way he was built. Yet without PV's know-how, they might not be able to stop Maw's awful vengeance. Ark's mind whirled in circles and kept coming to a halt at the same point: the girl had to be part of the package and it was up to him to convince her. If not, they'd have to take her forcibly.

'You mean, leave everything behind? You make it

sound so easy. And why should I care about a bunch of branches?'

'You will when you see the whole wide-wood. Haven't you ever dreamt of scaling bark instead of glass?'

Randall pretended to hesitate. She knew they were right: she was no longer safe in Maw. But if she went along with their plans for a while, she might get enough information to clear her name, and her mother's; prove her worth to the Empire. She made her decision – she'd been accused of being a spy. Well then, that's what she would become.

'It doesn't look as though I have any other choice.'

'We're the good guys,' Mucum pitched in.

'Hmm. Just because you saved me from the g-guns doesn't mean I've forgotten who caused this in the first place.' She stared meaningfully at Mucum with narrowed eyes.

'Come on.' Oakley sounded impatient. 'There's a train to catch!'

'And a forest to save,' said Remiel. 'PV, I marvel at your quick thinking. The power cut was sheer genius!'

'Yes, my neuro-circuits are functioning adequately,' PV said modestly.

Ark felt dizzy with it all. They'd been up. They'd been down. They'd been pursued every which way. Now, they were dug even further into the sub-basements of Maw and the sheer weight of the city pressed down on him. He'd be glad to leave. The shock of having found Petronio alive was almost as bad as the bruising round his neck.

'You're not going to tie me up like a prisoner?' Randall

demanded. She knew she shouldn't appear to give in too easily.

'No,' said Remiel. 'That is how the Empire treats those who disagree with them. You are free to do what you wish.' He turned and beckoned the others to follow him.

Randall shrugged, pausing long enough to look indecisive. Then she ran through the now-open door to catch up. 'This is crazy!' she panted, jogging alongside.

'I do know how you feel,' Ark said, his own breath coming in gasps. 'Same thing happened to me. One day I'm unblocking a toilet and the next, my life is completely topsy-treevy. Perhaps it was meant to be?'

Randall glanced sideways at the strange boy with his brown skin and vivid green eyes the colour of the leaves in her mother's vault. The way he had looked at her when he'd asked her to go with them was oddly compelling. For a moment, she doubted her plan for deception. However, the seed of resentment grew stronger each moment she thought of what she was losing. Destroying all that she lived for was not *meant to be*! How dare he! Such a pathetic excuse was only for the superstitious. She thought of what her mother had taught her about superstition, but the thought instantly conjured a picture of her mother standing in front of her to shield her from the guns.

'But we're leaving my mother behind,' she blurted out. 'She tried to save me.'

'The Envoy of Maw is not our problem!' Ark snapped. 'Sorry, I know you're her daughter, but it's thanks to her that we're here. Besides, I'm sure the Empire will not dispose of one of its most useful assets.'

Randall took a deep breath. 'I suppose you're right. How's your neck?'

'I'll live.'

'Funny, it was my mother who made me show that brute Petronio around. Should have trusted my instinct. The *glasstard* sold me out.' Her jaw tightened even more thinking about Petronio and how he had used her for his own ends.

'Yes. That's what he does.' Ark clenched his fist. Grasp's time would come.

Half an hour later they stopped abruptly in front of a blank wall.

Remiel lifted his wristband. 'Jed?'

'Yeah, boss?'

'Have the repairs been successful?'

'Only one way to find out.'

Remiel lowered his arm and turned to the others.

'It looks as though we will shortly be saying goodbye. This is it.'

Oakley shuffled awkwardly, then roughly patted each boy on the shoulder. 'Do what you gotta do,' he said gruffly.

As the holograph that disguised the wall was switched off and the two doors slid open, Mucum turned to Ark. 'So, if the train's oaky-doaky, then we're really off home again?'

'Yes,' said Ark. But instead of joy, all he felt was an overwhelming sense of doubt over what lay ahead.

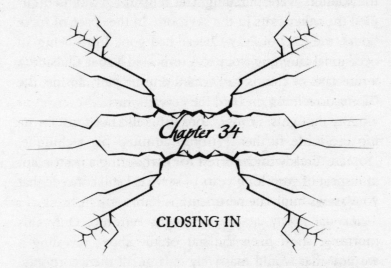

Chapter 34

CLOSING IN

Petronio was furious. 'All your advanced technology outwitted by a bunch of numbers that seems to have a mind of its own? How is that possible? What went wrong?'

Lord Far stroked his plump cheek. 'This is the first time that a virtual assistant has gone native. Perhaps it was infected with a virus? But the core programming of all Maw-made machines contains code that ensures they cannot act against the Empire's interests. It's an unusual development for that code to be overridden.'

Petronio felt a dull ache under his ribs. The sewer-rat had escaped his clutches once again. And he'd been so close, savouring every sensation as the pincers had squeezed closer. So much for mechanical know-how.

Lady Fenestra sat shackled on the other side of the table, her usual haughtiness vanished like the gang that the soldiers were pursuing. The remaining Gloms occupied the other seats in the skyroom. In the space of mere hours, the CEO of Eezy-Cheeze had gone from being an occasional laughing stock to a respected leader. Outside, a whitewash of clouds had wiped out the view. Inside, the Gloms now hung on Lord Far's every word.

'Any thoughts, Envoy?' Lord Far could not resist twisting the knife further. Petronio admired his technique. 'You are already under arrest for harbouring a traitor. But in respect of your long years of service, I still concede that your views might be pertinent.'

How the mighty are fallen! thought Petronio. Only this morning, she'd been the star of the show, revealing a weapon that would massively enlarge all their corporate fortunes. Now, the shadows under her eyes were heavy, and her usually firm jaw quivered.

'Do what you will,' Fenestra said. 'I know my daughter had nothing do to with this. And so do you!' This last accusation was aimed at Petronio. 'I saved your life, gave you a new limb, took you into my house and this is how you repay me?'

Petronio felt a brief twinge of something. Guilt? But it was instinct that had led him to the brooch. Besides which, his first concern had been to avoid being taken as a traitor himself, and in this instance he knew it was not he who had sold out Maw. 'The footage showed your daughter meeting with Malikum's brute of a sidekick. How could I ignore real evidence?' he replied defensively. 'And the fact that she's gone with them proves the point.'

'She had no choice! It was either that or be executed!'

One of the Gloms spoke, ignoring Fenestra's outburst. 'Lord Far, we admire the way that you uncovered this plot and the tracking device did indeed lead your hacker-in-chief to the charging station. However, as we all know, they now appear to have gone off-grid. We have lost them!' The complaint was a challenge.

'All is not yet lost. Trust me. I have received information that the spies will attempt to escape to their homeland in an ancient mining capsule. Apparently, there is a route that lies deep under the ocean that divides Maw and Arborium. This is the way they managed to pass all border controls to enter into Maw.'

'How do you know all this? And why have we never discovered this impossible-sounding security breach?' The woman who spoke, the CEO of Views International, took a sip from a glass of bright green liquid. As the drink touched her lips, it covered them with tiny rainbow sparks. Petronio had tried a can of Heaven-Sup earlier. It had looked good, but tasted foul.

'Patience,' said Lord Far. 'The most important information concerns their intentions. If they reach Arborium, their aim is to stop the Quantum Trap before it is deployed.'

'Two teenagers?' the woman smirked.

'. . . who have managed to evade capture several times in the course of this day. Is your memory that short?'

'So . . .' She and all the other Gloms waited for the answer.

Lord Far tapped out a series of numbers on his scroll-screen. There was a short pause, before a voice echoed out.

'Lord Far? Anything I can do for you?' The voice was

both oily and ingratiating. It reminded Petronio of his father's tone when first dealing with Fenestra.

'My dear man, your approach was very much appreciated; your suggestion most helpful. Is the package in place?'

'Depends . . .' the voice said. There was a slight crackling sound.

'Of course! It does all come down to value at the end of the day. I promise, there is a plank currently residing in Fort Knots with your name carved into it.'

'Right. Well, not as I don't trust you or anything. But perhaps you could send over the proof of ownership?'

Lord Far raised his eyebrows. 'Naturally.' His fingers moved in a blur over the screen. There was a soft ping. 'There. Satisfied?'

'Yeah! I'll be buyin' myself a Hovermerc, new clothes, a holiday and . . .'

'I would love to hear all about your planned spending spree, but could we get on with the business at hand?'

'Certainly, my lord. Anything for the man who pays. I'm setting the activation code right now. Give them plenty of time to get far, far away underground and then . . . BOOM!' The sudden shout nearly toppled the Gloms off their seats.

'Who was that?' said Petronio. The last time he'd intruded on a meeting of the Gloms, he'd been dismissed as an irrelevant outsider. Now, he'd earned the right to ask questions.

Lord Far rolled up his screen. 'That was a little splinter dug deep into the dark-grained heart of the Levellers. He was good enough, or rather greedy enough, to seek me out earlier this afternoon with a proposal. An unforeseen but useful tool. No more. No less. When his work is done, he shall indeed be given a plank . . . to walk off.'

'Bravo!' said one of the Gloms.

'But Randall is with them!' Fenestra shouted, trying to stand, despite the gleaming shackles that kept her in her seat.

'Exactly!' said Lord Far. 'Either you are with us, or against us. Your daughter has made her choice. So have I.'

Petronio watched Fenestra's face crumple into despair and tried not to feel disturbed. He had to be careful himself. Lord Far was a ruthless operator. As soon as Petronio was of no further use, they might well do the same to him. It was a valuable lesson.

'Good day, Envoy!' said Lord Far as Fenestra was hauled away by a pair of burly security men. The door slid shut on the sound of her shouting and he turned back to his screen. 'Now, shall we find out a little more about what this Jed person has planned?'

The repaired capsule was much smaller than before, so it was more of a squeeze for Ark, Mucum and Randall to fit aboard. Ark peered out at the crowd of people who had gathered and had a sudden idea.

'Mucum! The bag, quickly!'

'All right. Keep yer hair on!' Mucum extracted the soft leather pouch and handed it over.

Ark's hand felt around inside, before closing on his prize and holding it out to Remiel.

'It can't be!'

'It is,' said Ark. 'And in our land, nothing special.'

One of the Levellers gasped. 'An acorn!'

The response was automatic, everyone chanting in unison. 'The seed of all that was and that shall be!'

'There's more!' said Ark, lifting the leather necklace over his head and removing the stopper from the phial. The cushion of vines he had created up in the glass towers would undoubtedly have withered by now. But he might be able to do something different. A single drop landed on the tip of the acorn. There was a slight hiss and a curl of smoke rose up. Then, like the miracle it truly was, there was a crack in the side of the seed and a small green shoot poked its way through.

'Tend it well!' said Ark. 'For this is the birth of a growing revolution! Oh, and we might as well leave these here too.' He tossed across the whole pouch containing the remaining shapes of Arborian wood.

There were tears in Remiel's eyes, and awe among the assembled Levellers. He gripped the boy firmly by the shoulder. 'Your Diana go with you now!'

'Your Diana!' Ark corrected him.

'Yes!' Remiel agreed. 'Till we meet again!' He leant over to embrace Ark. 'And Randall, without you and PV playing your part, there is only tragedy ahead. I hope Arktorious has convinced you of our cause?'

Randall paused. The trick with the acorn had her worried. There were plenty of con-artists in Maw: the Gloms couldn't run the Empire without them. But the green shoot that flared out new leaves like a candle flame appeared to be real. 'Yeah. I'm on board. No choice really.'

The transparent curved lids slid shut above them with a smooth click. Ark worked the console in front of him. The capsule rocked slightly, then began moving slowly down the hastily rebuilt track. He turned back for a last glimpse of the far shrine and the flock of candles lighting up the pictures of pretend forest.

'Is this safe?' said Randall. Climbing outdoors, she had the illusion of control. In this tight space she felt trapped.

'Nah!' said Mucum. '*Safe* ain't what I'd call it. Think of it like fallin', but horizontal-like! Anyway, you can always go back there to be shredded to mulch!'

'It's going to be all right,' Ark said. 'I promise.'

Randall swivelled round and stared at him. 'Really?'

Before he could answer, they were all thrown backwards as the capsule shot down the rails and took off. Engineered tunnels gave way to jagged rock fissures and soon the capsule was bucking and twisting like high branches in a gale-force wind.

Cocooned in his seat and held tightly by a harness of spun glass, Ark wondered if the information they had found out would be enough to help save Arborium. There was still so much to do; so far to go. He was tired. Tired of running, tired of being brave, tired of dredging deep within himself to find the strength to carry on. Despite being thrown from side to side, he began to drift . . .

Master Arktorious!

Ark woke instantly. To his left, Mucum was snoring, revealing teeth in need of a good twig-brushing. To his right, Randall had her eyes closed, her head moving to the sound of muffled music. He couldn't get over how PV could talk and play a whole orchestra of instruments at the same time.

Master Arktorious!

Ark glanced at Randall's wrist. The sound of the Personal Assistant's voice did not seem to be coming from there. *What?* he thought. *How are you speaking to me?*

I have not been able to deduce the logic of it, Master Arktorious. But your mind, like mine, appears to be able to move beyond its body.

Yes! PV had it right. But Ark was confused. He'd only ever communicated with Corwenna and the Ravens like this. It felt strange.

I agree — though I do not have the circuits to register 'strange.' But there is a more pressing matter. I have detected a timer as well as traces of chemicals on board.

Which means?

I overrode the initial function of the timer shortly after launch as it seemed unnecessary to the journey. However, it appears to have reactivated. I am currently analysing the nature of the chemicals. This combination is usually used to—

PV's communication was cut dead by an intense flash of white light, followed by the loud BOOM! of an explosion.

Ark lay still. Liquid trickled from his eardrums and there was a searing pain in his chest. Mucum's face hovered above him, a gash on his forehead, and Randall was struggling with her harness. They were both shouting, but the sound of their voices was slowly fading away.

Ark thought of his little sister Shiv, and of his father resting in the cot-bed by the fire, and his mum forever worrying. Flames licked around the cabin as the capsule nose-dived. Inside Ark there was no reserve of energy, no hidden trick of the trees he could call on, no whispering encouragement from Corwenna. Only blackness.

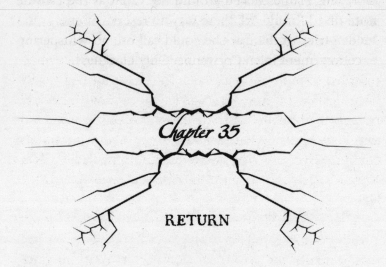

Chapter 35

RETURN

The bank of cloud loomed ahead of them like a grey city, puffed up on its own pride.

'Pressure dropping. Blind spot ahead. Going into guided function,' said the pilot.

'How interesting,' Petronio replied sarcastically. The journey had been smooth so far, the flypod soaring over the smooth ocean through a perfect blue sky. Even though he'd made the trip before, he couldn't get over all the water below them, a five-thousand-mile divide between Maw and Arborium. He hoped the pilot knew what he was doing. He didn't want to end up in the forbidding sea below.

The view vanished and they were flying through thick cloud. 'Have you taken your dose of vaccine?' said Petronio. 'I don't want you dying on me once we land in Arborium.'

'Do I look dumb? 'Course I have. We all have,' the pilot

answered. 'Pod knows how those trees of yours evolved to keep out us foreigners by giving off that poison gas stuff. But they ain't gonna get me!'

Petronio had already stopped listening as his mind returned to more recent events. The sewer rat had finally been dealt with. Revenge tasted good, though it would never bring back his arm. The thought of Ark dead caused him to wonder. What would life be like without his cunning adversary? The answer came immediately: *easier*. Now his task was to make himself indispensible to the Gloms.

It hadn't taken much to water the seeds of doubt already planted in their minds. So, although Fenestra had masterminded the plan so far to 'acquire' Arborium, once she had been removed, sobbing, from the room, Petronio had seized his chance. He had reminded the boss of Eezy-Cheeze that it was he, Petronio Grasp, who had played his part in resurrecting Commander Flint; that the bribery of willing Dendran soldiers could not have taken place without his negotiating skills. Surely it was obvious that he was the inside man for the job? And who knew, he insinuated, whether Fenestra had been playing a double game all along, what with her law-defying miniature tree collection that had so scandalized the Gloms when they heard of it. Could it be that her sympathies actually were with the kingdom of Quercus? Of course, Petronio knew that Fenestra was a loyal subject of the Empire. But casting suspicion suited his purpose perfectly.

His words had poured into Lord Far's ears and what took root had produced results. Fenestra had been forced to hand over the memory key, the last component needed to complete the Quantum Trap. The small black stick now nestled in Petronio's pocket. Amazing to think of the power it would unleash. So, here he was, accompanied by two soldiers of Maw who had been to Arborium before, along with a pilot for the flypod and Al, the surgical technician who had manipulated Commander Flint on his previous trip. The technician was only a servant and the soldiers, Heckler and Koch, knew which way the wind blew. He was no longer some teenage boy to patronize but a young man with influence! Petronio lapped up their sudden respect. And now that Ark and his oafish oak of a companion were out of the way, it was time to prepare the Quantum Trap.

Petronio's satisfying thoughts were interrupted as a massive black shape loomed out of the clouds, almost colliding with them. He glimpsed a large, pupil-less eye fixing on him for a short instant before the shape vanished again.

'Whoa! What the shimmering heck was that?' The pilot's voice registered panic. 'Systems can't make head nor tail of it!'

Petronio knew only too well. 'Buddy Ravens!' he muttered. 'Last thing we need.'

'Ravens? Shard! Them big birds?'

'Yes. And those beasts will happily tear this tiny craft apart with a single set of claws. So go into stealth mode, now!'

'I hear you!' the pilot responded, his finger jabbing frantically at the screen in front of him. The computer showed an image of the solid flypod appearing to fade suddenly into its surroundings. 'OK, we can't be seen.'

Petronio was still worried, though. His pulse raced, alongside his thoughts. How the holly had the Ravens found them in this thick cloud? It had been the same at the Harvest Battle, as if somehow the Ravens were being remote-controlled.

Heckler stared intently at the screen. 'I think we're in trouble,' he whispered. 'Remember, Koch and me saw those things in the battle before. We were among the few survivors who escaped. How's their hearing?'

'Excellent, I'm afraid,' Petronio mouthed back. 'So, unless your technology can outwit them . . .'

The lights inside the craft had already dimmed and the sounds of the engines faded to a disguised hum. Everyone attempted not to breathe as they all scanned the windscreen, peering through the thick fog.

Petronio tried to stop his arm twitching. That damn virtual assistant had fused several of its circuits when it shorted the power back in the charging station, turning his arm into a floppy wood-eel. Even though the technicians had repaired it, it hadn't been the same since. Now it had a life of its own, clicking and whirring at precisely the wrong times – like now. He felt Heckler and Koch's unease, the way they tried not to look at it.

'Can't you shut that thing up?' the pilot whispered.

'I'm doing my best!' Petronio answered, trying to think the appendage into submission. Though Fenestra had explained how it functioned, the idea that his thoughts could control its movements was still unnerving.

The arm gave one final jerk, then fell still.

Silence wrapped itself round the craft. The black shadows that prowled the sky appeared to have gone. All that was left was the clouds.

The pilot relaxed in his seat. 'Hah!' he said. 'Flying savages could never beat a Maw-made flypod in stealth mode!'

His confidence was shattered by a sudden *Whump!* Petronio was thrown forward, the harness digging deep into his shoulder. In the force of impact, he bit his tongue and felt blood welling inside his mouth.

'Contact! We have contact!' the pilot screeched. 'Port engine down. Starboard engine 73 per cent and falling. We're losing power!'

The craft yawed wildly from side to side. Through the cracked windscreen and thinning cloud, Petronio saw what had happened. A Raven had flown straight into them, and had paid the price for the mid-air smash. Its wings flopped uselessly as its body plummeted down.

Serves you right! thought Petronio, gripping his seat grimly.

The pilot clenched both hands around the joystick in front of him, willing the flypod to respond. 'Systems recalibrating! On-board functions rebooting.'

The clouds thinned into wisps. As the view revealed itself, the pilot gasped.

It was Al, the technician, who spoke for everyone. 'That's bad. Real bad. So many of 'em!'

Even through thick glass, the sound of screeching filled the cabin. The craft was surrounded by a flock of Ravens, easily a thousand strong. It was as if a thundercloud had been torn to shreds, the air pulsating with black streaks of lightning.

The pilot's eyes widened.

'Do something!' Petronio hissed. Being invisible wouldn't help them now. The Ravens were obviously agitated, sensing the intruder in their midst, beady eyes searching for a glint, a clue to home in on.

'Do I look like a miracle worker? Going into evasive! Though on a single engine, the probability of getting through unscathed is low.' The pilot kept his eyes glued to the windscreen as the flypod flung them in a tight arc right through the middle of the flock.

Petronio's stomach lurched as they were thrown from side to side: metal flotsam of the sky. How could the on-board computer guide them through this jungle of feathers and scything claws? The stealth shields were irrelevant now. One more impact and they too would be spiralling down like the Raven they'd hit earlier. If the flypod couldn't find its way out of this fluttering maze, they were out of luck.

Petronio ignored the rising nausea. In just over thirty-six hours, the Quantum Trap was planned to go off. Had he come this close to realizing his dream, only to be taken out by a bunch of sharp-beaked brutes?

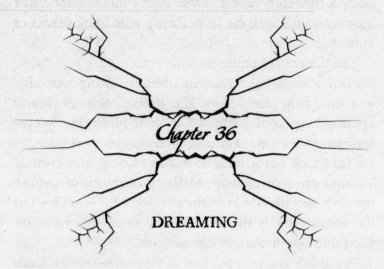

Chapter 36

DREAMING

Ark heard the sound of lapping waves and the far-off roar of tumbling water. He opened his eyes.

'Where am I?'

Silence.

The boat he lay in floated on a vast expanse of blackness, pulled by unseen currents. There had been a crash, flames. But it all blurred like the mist that hovered above the strange lake. His raised his hand to his face, exploring cold skin. There should have been gashes, bruises, burns. And yet he was unmarked.

The current that guided the small, open-topped skiff grew stronger. He could sense a waterfall ahead of him. His heart longed for it more than anything in the whole wide-wood. Perhaps he had already crossed the River Sticks. What was Arborium and its struggles now, but an unimportant, fading dream? In front of him was a greater adventure. Beyond the lip of the lake, hidden behind the tumbling wall of spray, was a drop that went down for ever . . . and after that, peace.

Another craft glided out of the mist, its prow slicing through the black depths like paper. The sail was shredded and the green paint on its hull peeling. A single, feeble lantern hung from the mast, shedding a soft glow on the figure sitting at the tiller. Her laced bodice, petticoats and stockings were grey, melting into the mist.

'Arktorious. Arktorious Malikum!' The voice was like the husk of a beech nut, soft and furred.

Ark stared in shock at the vivid green eyes, the nut-brown skin and the tumble of black hair. 'Who . . . are you?' he stuttered.

'You know the answer. Look deep to your roots!'

An image came to him. An abandoned nest high in the trees. Two wailing babies, left to the mercy of wind and rain. Orphans of long ago, their cries heard by a passing plumber. One lived, cradled by the love of the Malikums to grow into a boy called Arktorious. The other, exposed too long to the cold, took fever. Died.

'Is it you?' There were tears in his eyes. They felt wet. Real.

'How I've missed you all these years, brother mine.' Her tears now matched his, just as her eyes formed a mirror to his own.

'Vic . . . Victoria?' It was almost too much to say the name, as though his heart might split into kindling if he spoke it aloud.

'Yes, my twin, my living dream, the brave one who

still has much to do!'

'But you're taking me home now? Yes? Over the edge!'
Ark reached out to grip the side of the other boat.

The girl's smile was sad, her silence as deep as the lake
beneath. She raised her long, thin arm and pointed
behind him, away from the waterfall.

'No! I'm coming with you.' Ark stood up. He would
jump into her boat. But the girl clicked her fingers and a
wind rose like a wall between them, tipping him back the
way he had come.

'You must return!' Victoria said, steering her boat away.
'It is up to you now.'

'Don't leave me! Wait!' He looked round for a paddle,
for anything to follow his twin sister. He bent his knees,
ready to jump into the water and swim the ever-growing
gap. But before he could move, the current grabbed hold
of the boat, spinning it round and round and round . . .

Ark heard the sound of lapping waves and the far-off roar
of tumbling water. He opened his eyes.

'Where am I?' he said, with blistered lips.

There was smoke and flames, and a deep throbbing
pain in his chest. He looked down. His once-white shift
was stained and wet, but where he expected to see red,
there was green. And the vivid stain was shrinking even as
the pain faded.

It made no sense; the injury was fatal. He could see the
sharp strut that had sheered off the capsule and sliced
straight through him. It was still lying at his side, glittering with blood. But he could see something else too. The

phial that Corwenna had given him rested against his cotton shift, a tiny drop leaking from the stoppered top, and he could feel it as well. The liquid that had almost killed Petronio was soaking deep into him, sparking his failing body back to life. Was this, he wondered, what it was like to be a tree: to feel the sun, distilled and running through your veins like fiery liquor? He blinked, and the stain had vanished, leaving only a small rip in the cloth.

He could move. He wasn't in pain. But there was no time to dwell on miracles.

'Ark, mate? You OK? Buddy Holly, thought you was a goner!'

Though the capsule was still in one piece, it swayed violently from side to side, and the engine casing was covered in flames.

'In fact, reckoned we was all goners. Umph!' Mucum was thrown against a seat as the capsule pitched to one side. 'What the bark 'appened?'

Randall spoke, her voice very quiet. 'We seem . . . to be floating . . . on a river, a fast one . . .'

'Flaming buds! Is we crossin' the River Sticks?'

PV piped up, the smooth voice bouncing round the smoke-filled capsule. 'If I might provide information. There were explosives on board.'

'Betrayed?' Ark said. 'Surely not . . . who would . . . ?'

'That is beside the point! My sensors have detected a secondary, backup device that will shortly detonate. Also, there is a waterfall ninety-two point three metres ahead of us. I calculate the craft and those inside it will be . . .'

'Yeah, machine-features, we get the point!' a wild-eyed

Mucum growled. 'We're gonna be served a portion of unhappy-ever-afters!'

Randall was still staring though the cracked and smoke-blackened glass. Mucum clicked his fingers in front of her face.

'Oi, lady. You wanna live? We gotta make a move, pronto!'

'What's there to live for?' she said quietly. 'I've lost my mother, my home, everything. And it's your fault.'

Ark and Mucum turned at the same moment to see the flames crawling greedily up towards them. Mucum spun back to face Randall.

'Look. I can keep sayin' sorry. Fat lot of wood that's gonna do now. You wanna sit there, be a piece of whining fried chicken, yer welcome to it! Me? I'm outta here. Fast.'

The capsule gave a sudden lurch and water poured in, sloshing round their feet, rising quickly to knee level. However, the cold seemed to shock Randall into action. 'OK, big mouth. How do we get out?'

The capsule tilted and Mucum fell against the section that formed a door. 'Mmmf . . . just get this . . . open . . . oh . . . . pus-buckets! That buddy explosion has jammed it.'

'Use your legendary strength!' Ark cried.

Mucum grabbed the handle again and heaved so hard the veins almost popped in his arm. 'No use, can't shift it. Try some of yer oakus-crocus!' he yelled.

But Ark was now staring straight ahead at the waterfall, his thoughts filled with the face of his twin sister. Had he really seen her? She had died as a baby, so how could she grow into a girl? It didn't make sense. He must have dreamed it. Yet he wanted to see her again. So, if he did nothing, gave up, they would be reunited . . .

Randall was also staring at something: the partly-shattered console. 'I've got it! Sit down,' she shouted. 'Now!' She pushed Ark back into what remained of his seat and jumped into her own. 'You too, meat-for-brains.'

Mucum was so shocked he did as he was told, though not without muttering. 'How the deck is havin' a nice little sit-down goin' to . . .'

'Oh, shut up. Have you never heard of ejector seats?' Randall's training from years of free-climbing had kicked in. All those near escapes where she'd had to think on her feet or face a fatal drop. Now she knew exactly what to do. 'You wha—' Mucum began.

He never had a chance to finish his question as Randall leant forwards and pulled hard on a small red handle in the middle of the console.

There were three simultaneous explosions. Ark's image of his sister vanished and he felt himself being thrust up, his hair flattened and cheeks pulled back by incredible force. It was lucky that the cavern the river ran through was so high. Otherwise, they would have been skewered by the stalactites that hung down like sharp fingers from the roof.

Small parachutes flared out above each soaring seat and the three of them hung, suspended in mid-air. Ark could hear buzzing. He thought it was the aftershock until he glanced sideways. Each stalactite was covered in a carpet of tiny, pale white flowers and above the blooms there hovered swarms of buzzing bees. *Stumble-bees*. The

Rootshooters had spoken of this wonder-ground miracle. Every bee was born blind, using the smell of the pollen to guide it to the feeding grounds. But once they sipped the sweet liquid, a transformation took place. Their tiny bodies used the nectar to produce light, which now trickled like honey across the cavern. And it was this light that, in turn, fed the flowers. One could not live without the other. Was this what the Rootshooters celebrated in their bee-dreaming song?

Ark's slowly descending chair swung gently above the river. Further off the capsule was sucked over the foaming lip of the waterfall. As it vanished into spray, a flash of light and a muffled popping made the rock tremble. A back-draught from this second explosion caught the parachutes, spinning them sideways and downwards until they landed with a bump on the cold, wet shale of the underground river bank.

'Gnnerf!' said Mucum, having been tipped forwards on to the ground with a mouthful of gravel.

Randall leapt up the moment she touched down and stood over Mucum. 'Get up! You sold me down the river, you stole my life and still I saved your miserable backside. You owe me!'

'Guess we do,' Mucum mumbled, hauling himself on to his knees. 'But right now, we gotta find out where the holly we are. How far d'you reckon we travelled?'

'Possibly not far enough,' said Ark, grimly.

'Meaning?'

'Master Arktorious is right. I have detected vibrations,' came PV's voice.

'You what? So a bunch of "vibrations" is gonna get us now?'

'Well, they are approaching closer,' said PV, 'and might I suggest that your intelligence is unsuited to speculation.'

Mucum turned to Randall. 'Is that thing insultin' me?'

Randall stroked the glass cube inside her pocket. 'Let's just say that for a set of sophisticated circuits, he's a good judge of character!'

But Ark was in no mood for jokes. He could see a fissure in the cavern wall, gaping like a sharp jagged tear at right angles to the river. It was from there that the vibrations came towards them, with a sound like compressed thunder.

Behind them lay the river, flowing fast towards the foaming waterfall.

'They must have sent back-up,' Randall said nervously, retreating step by step towards the water. 'What Lord Far has started, he'll finish. I should have known: the Empire never gives up.'

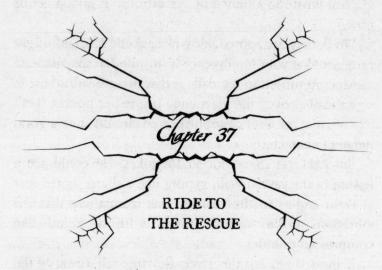

Chapter 37

RIDE TO
THE RESCUE

'Holly's boils!' Mucum shrieked, rooted to the spot.

'What the shimmering heck is *that*?' said Randall, edging further along the bank.

'Flo!' cried Ark. And into the cavern cantered a looming water-boatman, with Flo astride its back.

'I be yowr cavalry come to the rescue, missy!' she sang, pulling on a rope that brought two more of the creatures into the cave behind her. But her eyes were not on the stranger, Randall. Flo leapt off the huge insect and bounded over the slippery shale towards Mucum. 'Yow be returned moighty soon, moi brave hero.'

As Flo flung herself at Mucum, the coiled-up tension inside Ark's body released itself with a snap. He felt tired, hungry and grimy, as if all the greed of Maw needed washing off. As for visions of hidden lakes . . . what was he thinking of? These were his friends, living and breathing.

Flo's beautiful big smile yanked him right back into the present. 'But I don't get . . . how did you find us?'

Flo pulled away from her embrace of Mucum. 'A little birdie told me. Well, a moighty big birdie actually. And though she might never say it 'erself, Corwenna was sore worried for yow.'

'What?' said Mucum. 'The old witch 'oo sent us into danger in the first place has got feelings then?'

'Yas,' said Flo, without smiling. 'More than thou can ever know.'

She rushed back to her steed and her long white arms delved under a leather flap on the saddle. 'Yow be wanting some nosh after yowr journey. Then yow can tell all, eh?'

'I'm sorry,' Randall interrupted, 'but will someone tell me what's going on?'

'Warghhhh!' said Flo. 'Oi be forgettin' moi manners. Tis Oi who should be sorry!' The tall girl gave a bow. 'Moi name is Flo, and Oi be of the Rootshooters: them that live in the roots of the trees and mine 'em minerals for Dendrans up top.'

Randall frowned, her eyes travelling from the top of the girl's bald head all the way down her long legs to the rough boots she wore. The only trees she'd ever seen were the tiny twisted specimens in her mother's vault. 'I don't get it. How can you live in the roots of a tree?'

'Why, very comfortably, thank yow!' Flo smiled. 'And who dost thou be?'

'Randall. From the Empire of Maw. On the run, I guess.'

'Well, though thou be from that accursed place, yow be welcome! Any friend of these goodly lads here is a friend of moine. Two did leave and three has returned. Yow can tell all in good time.' Flo handed out some brown lumpy sticks.

'Eurghhh!' Mucum muttered. 'I know you lot are into recycling, but I ain't gonna be eating any of the brown stuff!'

'What does yow think Oi'm feeding yow? Why, that is hilarious! Nibbling on ka-ka? Whatever next! Naw, this be home cured worm-sausage. Very tasty.'

'Worms!' said Mucum. 'Oh well, that's fine then!'

Ark was far too hungry to refuse. He took a bite, chewing and swallowing quickly so as to taste it as little as possible. 'It's not bad. Kind of spicy.'

Randall watched him nervously, then tried a small corner. She grimaced but didn't spit it out.

'That be the ticket!' said Flo. 'Now, come all, we've got a long journey.'

'Mistress, I am also in need of sustenance!' said a smooth voice from Randall's wristband.

The nearest water-boatman turned its head from side to side, its six legs skittering on the cavern floor. Flo's eyes opened even wider than normal. 'Who be that? Is there yet another?' she said, looking round.

'Oh, don't mind him, I mean it,' said Randall. 'Meet my virtual companion, PV.' She pulled the keyring out of her pocket. The far-off light of the stumble-bees washed over the tiny glittering glass cube, making it sparkle.

'What manner of thing be thou?' Flo asked in awe. 'It is a mighty small see-through body yow have!'

'Yes,' came the voice, 'in your eyes, I imagine I appear

strange. But according to my sensors, I have also never come across a being like you.'

Flo slapped her forehead in glee. 'That be a very clever answer. Well, there's more to the wood than meets the eye! But what manner of food dost thou eat?'

'Sunshine!' said PV. 'My batteries are running low.'

'Aha!' said Flo. 'If yow wish to ride with us, I can supply yow with beams aplenty! 'Tis deep night in the wood above, but with Diana behind us, Oi reckon we might make a nice meeting with the dawn.'

The glass cube was tucked away and Mucum demonstrated to a reluctant Randall how to get up on to the back of one of the waiting water-boatmen. 'This is just weird!' she complained. 'I'd rather climb a building than climb up on this thing.'

'Yeah. Gives yer an idea 'ow we felt turning up in Maw. Jus' grab those feathery things.' Mucum pointed to the pair of antennae sticking out of the creature's segmented head. 'And use 'em for steering.' He then hopped up behind Flo.

As the water-boatmen picked their way out of the cavern, Ark's head swam with questions. Everything was happening so fast. If Corwenna had felt something of what was about to happen before the strange time of his passing across the lake towards his sister, then she must have got Flo to act immediately in galloping underground to find them. That also meant that they were not far from home.

He watched Randall ahead of him. It was clear she was uneasy balancing on the strange beast and he could guess her fear of entering into unknown worlds. Only a few months ago, he too had been taken away from all he knew that was safe to a place where every step he took was tinged with the unknown.

During the ride, Mucum told Flo the story of all that had happened. She made all the right noises and slapped her thigh with glee when she heard about Mucum acting the part of a free-climbing brooch smuggler.

'Don't look so pleased!' Randall broke in, furiously. 'His stupid fibs cost me my whole life.'

'Oi am sorry, moi girl! But trust moi, when yow sees what we're fightin' for, then maybe yow will understand.'

Randall set her mouth in a grim line and stared straight ahead. What day was it, she wondered? Had she really not been to bed since the moment she had woken up to find everything changed? She was so tired. The rhythm of the boatmen was quite soothing and she was dimly aware of passing through chasms of quartzite and fissures where seams of yellow gold zigzagged down the walls like lightning. She had fallen into a doze in the saddle when the air changed and the salt tang that indicated they were still under the ocean slowly gave way to a deeper, loamy scent.

A sudden jerk woke her. The path ahead of them climbed steeply, weaving between mounds of fallen earth and hanging fronds that brushed over them like empty gloves.

Ark saw that she was awake. 'The root system!' he said. 'The great, living foundations of the forest.'

'You mean we're inside a *tree*? Impossible!' She shuddered, wondering if Ark and his foreign friends had technology that shrank them all down.

'*Impossible* is precisely what I thought when I first saw your towers of glass,' he told her. 'Perhaps we are both learning to change our ideas of what is and is not possible.'

Gloom was gradually replaced by stray shafts of light, criss-crossing with the flight of bark-bats, their roosting chambers disturbed by the noise of stamping feet. And then, an opening, seemingly carved into the end of the root tunnel, with light spilling down ahead of them.

'Oh, wow!' said Randall, beginning to understand Flo's earlier words as they passed through from inside to out. Her breath made tiny clouds as the insect that carried her slowed to a stop. The covering of snow was blotchy, unable to hide what looked like a mass of huge, writhing worms as the roots wove their way across the forest floor. She craned her neck upwards, trying to take in the trunks that towered and twisted above her like skyscrapers of wood. From the snippets she had overheard her mother tell of Arborium, she had imagined a filthy forest full of barbarians intent on destroying the Empire. And even though she had been told by Ark that the trees here were vast, she hadn't been able to picture their scale. These living monsters were thousands of times larger than the stunted growths in Fenestra's vault. She felt a brief flash of something like terror, but it gave way immediately to awe. She sniffed. Was the smell really that disgusting? No, it was . . . fresh, clean. But she did seem to be suddenly out of breath. That was odd; the water-boatman had been doing all the work, not her. 'This . . . is . . . unbelievable!'

she gasped. As thoughts tumbled, Randall's fingers moved unconsciously, itching to check out handholds, work out routes.

'Plenty of good climbin' 'ere, girl!' said Mucum. 'Though it's a long drop if yer fall . . .'

'Here be the early sunshine. Your little friend better eat it up, good and proper!' said Flo.

Randall pushed up her sleeve to let the slanting rays rest on her wristband, and also pulled out her keyring.

'Mmm!' said PV. 'That is most pleasing!'

'Mmm? What kind of . . . word is that? You . . . worry me, PV!' Why did her lungs feel so empty? Yes, the air was different, but everyone else was breathing it too. It didn't make sense.

'But mistress! My logic circuits are capable of learning modes of speech. And I do believe this sunlight has a charging capacity I have not experienced before.'

But Randall wasn't listening. 'I . . . I'm finding it hard to . . .'

'Mistress!' PV interrupted, 'I detect that your blood pressure is plummeting, your immune system is in overdrive and your nervous system is showing signs of shock!'

Ark twisted round in his saddle. 'Are you all right?'

'No . . . not really.' Her eyelids fluttered and she felt her lungs and throat tightening. Fingers slipped from reins and she slumped forward on the saddle.

'What be the problem?' Flo cried.

'I cannot ascertain the cause,' PV broke in. 'It appears my mistress is suffering a severe reaction to an unknown antigen. If nothing is done, her heart will stop beating within ninety-eight seconds.'

'By all that is wood and holly, I should have realized!' Ark leapt down and ran to the now unconscious girl. 'She's from Maw. She's allergic to the trees!' He caught Randall just as she began to slide off her steed. Bringing the daughter of Lady Fenestra to Arborium hadn't saved her life after all: exposure to the trees was a death sentence.

'You'd better fink of somethin' quick, buddy, or she's a goner!' Mucum said.

'Really helpful,' Ark muttered through tight lips. Already Randall was lying on the ground, her rasping breath growing more shallow moment by moment. What would Corwenna do? What could *he* do? It was their fault she'd been brought here in the first place. No prayer would save the day. And as PV said, time was short.

He scanned the towering trees above. To him, they were sanctuary; to this foreign interloper, they were weapons.

'We do need the medicine that those of Maw do use for protection,' said Flo, kneeling next to Randall. 'But we don't have none!' she sighed.

'Wait!' Ark felt something: a small flutter as if the tiniest leaf had spoken aloud. His fingers moved to the phial round his neck, quickly lifting the leather thong over his head and unstoppering the phial. The bottled essence of the trees was pure poison for some. It had nearly done for Petronio, turning his arm into a living, sap-filled branch. But Ark hoped that a smaller dose, given in opposite circumstances, might act differently. There was only one way to find out.

He knelt down and touched a tiny drop to Randall's pale lips.

'What dost thou do?' Flo cried. 'It will kill her!'

'No,' said Ark, though he wasn't sure.

The forest held its breath. Even the water-boatmen sensed something, their usual skittishness calming to a standstill. Ark was aware of how close he was to Randall, and it was a strange feeling. He had to focus, send all his will, all that he had learned into the hope that she would . . .

'Urgggh!' Randall grunted, her shoulders convulsing. Her eyelids flickered open. 'Where . . . what . . . ?' Her eyes were unfocused and her whole body trembled.

'Whoi!' Flo cried in joy. 'Thou be back in the land of the living!'

'My scanning reveals that my mistress's heart rate is within functional parameters,' said PV.

'What happened?' Randall shook herself and sat up. 'I was . . . I saw things . . . two huge birds and water . . . so much of it . . .' She put a finger to her lips, rubbing the trace of green liquid. She turned to Ark. 'You . . . saved my life?'

Ark backed away, blushing. 'No . . . it was the trees.'

'Buddy brilliant! Quick thinking there, mate. Though I must admit it gets annoyin' the amount of times you pull off this kinda jiggery-oakery stuff. So, crisis over, are we out of 'ere or what?' Mucum asked.

'Are you strong enough to stand?' Ark forced his hand

forward and helped Randall to her feet. 'We still have a long journey ahead of us and our current mode of transport will not do.'

By now, colour had crept back into Randall's cheeks. 'But how did you do it?'

Ark paused before answering slowly, pointing to the phial. 'I used this, the essence of all that we believe in. It is both boon and bane. In your case we were lucky. It worked like the vaccine your people have used before. It seems the trees have need of you after all; you are now protected from their deadly gases.' Ark stopped and glanced up, as if hearing some far-off sound that the others could only dream of. 'Ah. They are here.'

'Who's here?'

'Look!'

It was hard enough for Randall to take in the giant trees that had walked out of legend into reality; harder still to comprehend that those trees had nearly killed her too. But what seemed to perch far above them now made the hairs on the back of her hand prickle like static. Could birds be that big? These were not the manicured albino crows of the Empire. Briefly, she remembered her vision while unconscious. But in the dark place that had – only moments ago – nearly taken her into death, the birds had been white . . .

Ark saw the serried ranks of roosting Ravens, camouflaged in the shadows of the misty morning. He closed his eyes and sent his thoughts up into the freezing air. *Hedd, son of Hedd, how is She?*

As if in answer, one of the great birds screeched once,

its thoughts stuttering into Ark's mind as if frozen by the season. *Queen wept on your leaving ... must not tell.*

I promise. After all they'd been through, the evidence that Corwenna truly cared made a difference.

'What do we do now?' Randall asked.

Ark sighed. 'We're only halfway there. Time for another journey. The Ravens will take us.'

'Ravens? You *what*? Let me get this right. I nearly died just now. My butt is killing me after riding on the back of these *roaches* for ages. Some proper shut-eye would be great. But instead, you want me to get on the back of an oversized flying mutant!'

'Yes.' said Ark. 'Exactly. Though I wouldn't call any of them mutants to their faces. They might rip your tongue out. Or much worse.'

Randall looked to see if he was joking. He wasn't.

Mucum grinned. 'Trust me, Randall. All yer gotta do is 'old on tight.'

'Trust *you*?' she replied.

'Yeah, well . . .' Mucum fell silent.

'Welcome to Arborium,' said Ark. 'This is my home, our home: the land that your Empire is so desperate to destroy. So, unless you want to stay down here by your-self, this is where we go up. Are you ready?'

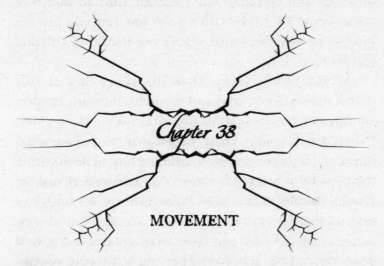

Chapter 38

MOVEMENT

Petronio swept his finger along a panel of lights in the small grey box in his hand.

Commander Flint's left arm rose up.

Petronio tapped a single light.

Commander Flint's fingers curled into a fist. All this time, the face was blank, the eyes staring straight ahead.

'You're the technical expert. How do I make him speak?'

'Check out the groove on the side, and press hard!' Al stood by in his white coat, a smirk on his face.

Petronio looked around the abandoned scaffield beyond the outskirts of Hellebore. It was the perfect testing ground. The jungle of dead winter grasses and twisted apple trees was covered in a muffling coat of snow. The wind was up, the sky grey and grim. The great buttresses and beams that supported the ancient platform were groaning and creaking. Any Dendran with an ounce of sense would be inside with a good fire. Petronio just felt glad to be anywhere that wasn't the inside of a flypod machine.

He was feeling lucky. After all, hadn't they already defied the reach of wings and claws this morning? Superstitious Dendrans might have given thanks to the goddess Diana, but Petronio knew better than to believe such nonsense. It was expert programming buried deep within the flypod that had guided them through the dark mass of Ravens. Despite their inborn killer instincts, the birds had no idea that the craft had quickly accelerated out of their reach. Once the pilot had taken time to calm down, he'd gone on and on about whether the self-repair systems would do their job. But the final landing had gone without a hitch. And now that they were back, Petronio had a job to get on with if the plans of the Empire were to succeed.

It was a good conclusion all round. Ark was dead, the Ravens outsmarted and Quercus snug in his palace with no idea what was coming.

He lifted the box towards his mouth, felt for the groove and pressed his thumb into it. 'I am your leader!' he said.

The box converted each syllable into code and sent it wirelessly to the module embedded in the body in front of him. Commander Flint almost instantly moved his lips. 'I am your leader!' He sounded like the commander of old, the battle-scarred veteran who had led the Armouries through both war and peace.

'Well, Al,' Petronio smiled, 'it looks like we're on to a winner!'

'Well, Al,' the commander parroted, 'it looks like we're on to a winner!'

Petronio took his thumb off the side of the box and stalked towards the now-still commander. 'Did I say you could speak, dumbo, eh?' The eyes were vacant, empty as the field of snow around them. 'Yes, not so clever now, eh, logs for legs!' Petronio reached up and slapped the commander's cheek.

A look of alarm crossed the technician's face. 'Hey, sonny! Careful with it. There's a lot of expensive circuitry in there!'

'I am merely letting this piece of meat know who's boss.'

'Right,' said Al, frowning. 'Whatever you say.'

'Exactly. Whatever I say.' Petronio liked the feeling of being boss. 'Right, Al. Sergeant Grain and his lot are on their way. No fancy business this time. You've been given plenty of info about the commander's character and I hope for your sake that you've got your script to hand. One slip-up and my arm might get the urge to snap a few limbs.' Petronio handed over the grey box.

'All right, Grasp. Keep your hair on, eh.' The technician's eyes slid away from the hunk of metal sprouting from Petronio's shoulder. He retreated towards the orchard behind them. The snow was a useful disguise: in his white coat he vanished into the whiteness, leaving Petronio alone with the shell of the commander, waiting.

'Well, Flint, let's play the game to the end.'

Flint stood like a tree, silent.

Petronio felt the itchiness of his woollen shift, smelt the faint tang of the urine used to bleach it white. The britches cut into his thighs and the leather boots were already soaked through and caked with mud and snow. Changing into Arborian clothes had felt instantly uncomfortable. The suit he wore in Maw had sat on him like a second skin, the smart fabric shrinking perfectly to his size. But it wouldn't do to look outwoodish here, not yet. He didn't want to spook the soldiers.

A high-hare sprinted across the snow, its ears stuck up like twigs. Petronio licked his cold lips. The food in Maw was no better than mush. He pictured a hare stew, cooked till tender in a casserole of Boardo wine. Once Arborium was in his hands, he'd make sure that the supply of animals was preserved. Like the timber itself, they could become a valuable commodity.

There was a rustling farther off and Sergeant Grain stalked into the clearing, flanked as ever by the giant Pontius and eight other men.

'Greetings, sergeant. I hope you are well.' It wasn't Grain who worried Petronio, but the monster by his side. The case containing the Quantum Trap weapons looked tiny tucked under his over-developed shoulders.

Ever since Petronio had first met Pontius, he had been aware that here was one Dendran who was possibly a match for his Maw-made arm. He'd even had visions of the pincers trying to close round those enormous biceps. One flex of muscle and Petronio could imagine the alloy mechanism shattering. Still, he thought, they were all supposedly on the same side for now. And he had other, more important matters to focus on.

The sergeant's good eye rotated in its socket to fix on Petronio. 'I'm squittin' freezin', as it 'appens, and wondering what the holly I'm doing talkin' to you, *boy*! Surely our leader can speak for himself, eh?'

Despite the cold, Petronio felt sweat break out on his forehead. So far, the commander hadn't even moved. *Come on!* he thought. Grain was welcome to his insults, so long so he got the job done. Payback would come later.

The other soldiers, in their rusty chain mail and torn hose stockings, formed a raggedy circle, swords in their sheaths, crossbows strung over their backs, wary as badgers, sniffing the air suspiciously.

Just in time, the commander came to life, moving awkwardly on the spot. Petronio heard a small clicking noise. 'You are not . . . talking to him. You are talking to . . . me!' The voice was spot on, both sneering and superior even though the delivery had odd, unexpected gaps. 'But as this *boy* represents our . . . paymasters from the Empire of Maw, I suggest you give him due respect!'

Petronio was both relieved and pleased. He pulled a leather pouch from his doublet. However much he gave out, it would never be enough. He mused on the sound of the word 'Maw'. Each time he heard it spoken aloud he smiled inwardly as he heard 'more'. *More* was certainly the only way to feed greed and treachery. The heavy chink as he lobbed the pouch towards Grain had the desired effect of deflating tension.

'You have the . . . case?' the commander asked.

'Pontius,' Grain muttered. 'Bring it out.'

The soldier brought the case forward, keeping it well away from his body as if he was holding a burning branch. He placed it at the commander's feet, its smooth lines looking out of place in the mess of leaves, twigs and frozen mud.

'Time to explain how this is going to work,' Commander Flint continued. 'Right now, the weapon is . . . not armed. The boy will see to . . . that.'

Petronio acted on cue. The memory key was already clutched delicately in the pincers that made up his right hand. He took a step forward, trying to ignore Pontius's dull stare. He crouched down by the case, looking for the slot that Fenestra had told him about. It was cleverly concealed in the handle, a thin gap that was almost invisible.

Petronio had wanted to make a show of it. Hence the use of his Maw-made arm. He willed the mechanism to push the key into place.

'Damn and Diana!' he muttered under his breath as the key dropped from the pincers into the slushy ground.

Nobody spoke. The envoy had promised Petronio an arm that would move like liquid glass, but he was still stuck with this clumsy contraption. Humiliated, he used his real forefinger and thumb to pick up the key, shoving it into the slot and giving a sudden twist.

They all heard it then. A humming sound, like a billion bees trapped in a bottle. A flock of starlings flew into the air, twittering in alarm as they soared into the mist. As Petronio held the case, he could feel it: all that power, squeezed in tight. He thought back to the experiment the Gloms had witnessed in Maw. Once this case was triggered, a far greater force would be unleashed.

The humming faded as the soldiers shifted uneasily. Even Pontius frowned, the wood-way creaking under his bulky body.

As Petronio stood up Commander Flint spoke. 'Undo the case.'

Petronio did as he was instructed, flipping open the catches.

'The task is in front of you!' Flint's voice growled as the ten glass spheres were once again revealed, nestling like deadly dark suns in their cradle of grey foam. 'Tomorrow is the Winter Solstice, the shortest day . . . of the year. As you know, nearly all Dendrans will flock to the centre of Hellebore to celebrate and be right where we want them to be. Even the rest of the Armouries have been invited down. I assume you have . . . wisely made sure your families are kept up north.'

A few heads nodded. This part of the plan was already known.

'Good. You ten men will each take one of the spheres to its allotted spot on the outskirts of the capital, forming a ring around the city. The case itself will be taken somewhere central.' The commander flicked his head towards Petronio.

Yes. Petronio had the exact location in mind. Risky, but perfect. And it required a certain boldness.

'The weapons must be primed and timed exactly. Your signal will be the ringing out of the Kirk bells that toll for five o'clock in the morning.'

Al was working the commander's voice perfectly. Petronio was impressed. The time issue bothered him a little, the reliance on primitive clocks. But these soldiers would feel uncomfortable wearing Maw-made time bands on their wrists and they'd grown up hearing the passing of hours with clangers on bells, not beeps on watches, so it was best to stick to what they trusted.

The commander was issuing his final instructions. 'Once you have put on your specially adapted eye goggles, you will be ready. Take out your sphere and place it carefully down. And I warn you now. The spheres must not come into contact with water or they will be rendered unworkable. '

'Yeah, yeah,' grunted one of the soldiers. 'You told us that bit before. Just cos' we're hard as planks don't mean we got no brains.'

The commander rotated his head to stare hard at the man with dark, almost blank eyes. 'Firstly, you address me as sir. Secondly, if you let the sphere entrusted to you come into contact with even a drop of dew, I will personally nail your hands and feet to the wood-way, then use my sword to rearrange your insides. Once the Ravens smell your blood, and they will, you can watch as they feast on your guts. Do I make myself clear as glass?'

The soldier gulped. 'Yes, sir! Sorry, sir. Meant no offence, sir!'

Sergeant Grain glanced down at the spheres in the case. 'Where's the what-d'you-call-it? The trigger?'

'That's the clever part. With the aid of the goggles, your

eyes are the trigger, though the case itself will relay the destructive energy released from the spheres all round the city. On the fifth chime of the bells, you must stare at the sphere.'

'You what?'

'The Empire is more than a source of gold. It has machines that can create miracles. Look deep into the spheres, *through the goggles*, and they will unleash their darkest secrets. Every Dendran caught in the collective force field will be . . . knocked . . . unconscious for about twelve hours. This gives you plenty of time to bring in the rest of your men to take over, ensuring a coup that is bloodless and swift.'

Petronio wondered if they would swallow the lie a second time. When the Quantum Trap created a double of every living body and made it float in airless orbit high above the planet, then all Dendrans in the capital Hellebore would suffocate, even while surrounded by fresh air. Almost every single one of them, aside from a few in the outlying settlements. Dead. And the ten willing traitors setting the spheres in motion? Petronio knew that the goggles would actually only activate the spheres, not also protect anyone from their effect, as they had been told before . . .

'And so, to the future!' the commander continued. 'Not only will the Empire pay you well, as you already know, but the cold days and nights in the Armouries will be left behind, I promise you. You shall lead a life of luxury, and do what good soldiers should always do.'

'And what's that, then?' Grain asked. 'Remind us.'

'Run the show. Collaborate with the Empire of Maw. Be at the heart of power.'

'Well, Commander, when yer put it like that, what are we waitin' for, eh?'

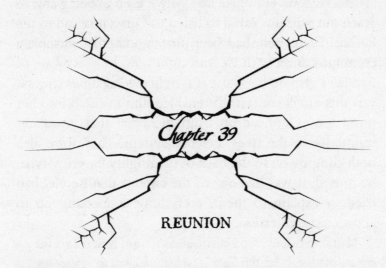

Chapter 39

REUNION

Hedd bore Ark and Randall west towards the mountains. One of his kin-sisters carried Mucum and Flo. Both Ravens had been steadily climbing higher, battling the freezing currents of air. Ark could feel his face going numb and was aware that Randall's grip around his waist was beginning to slacken. 'Don't go to sleep! You'll fall!' he shouted, but the wind whipped away his words.

Can't feel my legs.

'If you fall off, there'll be a lot more you can't feel!'

Can't feel my legs . . . heights shouldn't scare me . . . who is this boy I'm holding on to? . . . so strange but . . . something . . . those green eyes . . . see into me.

Ark was shocked and not only that, he felt embarrassed, as though he had been caught eavesdropping. He seemed to be hearing her jumbled thoughts, whirling like sycamore pods. How? He had grown used to being able to reach out with his mind to listen to Corwenna and to the Ravens. Then there had been that moment of unspoken communication with PV. And right now, he was aware of Randall's grip on his waist as it tightened again. Perhaps it was this direct contact that enabled him to reach into her mind too? Or the drop from the phial that given her immunity to the trees' defence system? They were also both clinging on to the back of the mighty Raven. Maybe, he mused, it was like one of the circuits that Remiel had tried to explain to them, everything connecting up to allow communication.

Must keep focused . . . get information . . . report back to Lord Far . . . save my mother . . . but this place . . . so beautiful. And the strange boy . . .

Ark's guilt about hearing evaporated. REPORT BACK?' BETRAY US? WE SAVED YOUR LIFE!

Ark felt a jolt run through Randall's body. For a moment her fingers fell slack and the wind almost pulled her from the bird's back.

What the shard are you doing in my head? Are those your thoughts? Am I hearing your thoughts? Can you hear . . . argh . . . The wind that had been whipping around them changed tactic, transforming into a howling roar. They had flown into a whirlwind, an invisible hand that now tossed them through the sky. The two birds strained to keep level, their wings almost bending backwards in the force of the storm, but they were struggling; just feathered flotsam at the mercy of the elements.

Ark dug his fingers deeper into feathers and squinted sideways. Beneath them the trees had vanished, giving way to snow-covered rock. Ahead, great peaks reared up savagely.

We're going to die! Randall's arms clutched tensely round his waist.

No. I don't know.

Oh, come on, wonder-boy . . . you made an acorn grow and . . . you seem to be jumping about like some nano spot-welder inside my head . . . surely you can . . . do something?

It was a challenge. Ark knew that. But what could he possibly do? They were being tumbled like leaves. He turned away from Randall's thoughts, burrowing deeper into feathers to feel Hedd's distress. The great bird laboured with the extra weight, heart hammering like a woodpecker's beak. Ark glanced back. The other Raven was also caught in the maelstrom, its wings beating helplessly as it was pitched from side to side, while Mucum and Flo held on grimly.

Hedd's screech pierced the gale. He lurched sideways then dropped like an autumn acorn in a downdraught that sent them plummeting straight towards one of the rearing stony outcrops.

Ark had learned to make arrows drop from the sky. But the wind was an alien element, unknown, like the Empire of Maw. He could not command it to be still. A memory surfaced. Deep down in the roots as Rootshooter Joe looked on in awe, Ark had walked towards the monstrous mealworm and put his hand on the belly of the beast. Instead of instant, devouring death, there had been calm.

Calm! That was it! He dug his hands even deeper beneath the feathers of Hedd's back. Fear was pushed aside as thoughts flowed through him like chlorophyll, down his arms and out though his fingertips:

You are Hedd, son of Hedd, Lord of the Ravenwood. The trees are beneath you and the sky your servant. Can a mere breeze defeat you and your kin-sister? Will such great beasts allow their pride to be brushed away?

Both Ravens still plummeted towards the steep slopes, wings flailing against the whirlwind.

Ark clung on, braced for impact, but in the space between one breath and the next, his thoughts were permeating deep into Hedd's dark heart. As the rock rushed up to meet them, as the mountain opened its cold white mouth to swallow them up whole, Hedd gave a tiny flick of his tail feathers and flared out his wingtips. The other bird followed suit, flock instinct making it act the perfect mirror. At the very last moment both birds turned so tightly that feathers brushed against stark rock. Then they were circling round and up, each wing-beat stronger as they rode the air towards the cruel crags.

Ark felt Randall shaking behind him.

You talked to it . . . you . . . calmed it! You did it!

Maybe. Ark was too exhausted to even think any more.

Hedd gave a great squawk of triumph as they flew up and over the circling necklace of lonely summits to leave behind one land and pass into another. It was as though the mountains were a natural wall, for the wind that had nearly smashed them into splinters was suddenly absent. They soon crossed the snowline, flying high over a very different kind of forest. As the low winter sun peered weakly through the clouds, the two Ravens spiralled down, descending towards the Ravenwood. The snow-covered platform was barely visible below them, but already Ark's keen eyes had picked out a darker shadow waiting in the whiteness.

Wings bent back and up, acting as brakes as claws skittered over the frozen surface. They skidded to a halt and Ark tried to stay calm as he slid down the wing that Hedd pushed out, landing on the platform with a soft thump. He held out his hand for Randall. She climbed down, her eyes refusing to meet his. *What is this place . . . and oh . . . who is SHE?*

Ark let go of her hand and the contact was broken. 'You'll see,' he murmured. He turned to Flo and Mucum. 'Are you all right?'

'Apart from nearly up-chuckin' me breakfast, thinkin' we was goners – again – oh, and bein' log-tired, I'm fine!' Mucum growled. Flo smiled faintly, swaying to find her balance.

'You have done well,' Corwenna rasped, shuffling forwards into the daylight, her dark face etched with concern. Ark was shocked at how suddenly shrunken and old she looked, as if in the short time they had been away, centuries had passed. She reached out a wavering hand to stroke his dirty, blood-smeared face.

'My Hedd is grateful to you.'

'It was instinct. Nothing more.' He felt confused. Corwenna was usually cold and commanding. What had happened to her?

'You ask the question. I give you the answer. You are part of me and my strength went with you. You have survived the journey to Maw and now, even my good bird Hedd and the wind that bears him must bow before you. But such achievement comes at a cost.'

'You're speaking in riddles again.'

'Does it matter?' she snapped, drawing her hand away. 'What have you found out?'

Ark hated the way Corwenna's mood could change. In that moment he wished he was home. Real home, with Shiv bundled into his arms and his mother cooking up dinner. The burden of everything he still had to do weighed too heavily.

'We have brought back information,' Ark replied slowly. 'But not enough. We have only until tomorrow. One day, to stop every Dendran gathering in the city for the Winter Solstice from being killed.' *And what for?* Ark thought, but didn't say. *A pile of timber!* It was madness.

'Yes, time is short,' Corwenna muttered, 'and their greed grows strong and tall like our trees. But you must also know, something has come before you. My border patrol sniffed it out. It was foreign, sharp and fast. One of my feathered kin died before she had the chance to fly out of the way.' Her voice was sour now. 'The Maw-made bird vanished into thin air. But they smelled its thick metallic scent as it sped away.'

Ark had seen the flying crafts of Maw, zipping between buildings like soulless kingfishers. He wondered who had been inside this particular one, but knew the answer with all the instinct of ancient hate. 'Petronio,' he muttered.

While Ark and the woman spoke, Randall shivered with cold. Her body reeled from the journey, her mind trying to take in not just the strange land, but the even stranger boy who could click open her mind like a screen-file and pore over its contents. Her plan to find out enough to expose them all to Lord Far had been laid bare. What would the boy do? And why had they made the hazardous journey to this old, wrinkled crone woman with tiny skulls braided in her hair? The woman turned to stare back at her with unnaturally bright green eyes: so similar to Ark's but without any softness. Randall shrank under the gaze.

'Why are you scared of me, child?'

'I'm not a child and I'm not scared.'

'No, you are the proud daughter of one who seeks to destroy the wild-wood and all that we believe in. And you, spoilt brat of Maw, are hoping that – who is it that you think of – Lord Far? That he will look more kindly on you and your mother once you supply him with infor-mation. Yes?' As she spoke, the old woman appeared to transform. Her stooping spine straightened until she towered over Randall and her voice no longer wavered, but reverberated through the trees.

Randall reared back as though from being punched.

'Oh, don't look so surprised. I too can read you as easily as the moth-eaten Wood Book. And I ask you, is my home a product to be consumed, then hidden in deep, airless vaults? Would Maw reduce us to *planks?*' Corwenna's leaf-green eyes bored into her like a mine-drill. Her fist thumped a branch at her side to make her point. As if in answer, there was a deep rumble that set the whole wild-wood vibrating.

'I don't . . . I don't know,' Randall whimpered.

'Your fear is justified. I may be old but I am not stupid. If a tick tries to suck the blood from my body, there is no time to practise *forgiveness!*'

Corwenna's words beat like wings round Randall's head. The power behind them forced her into a crouch. She looked up, but Ark, Mucum and Flo made no move. Corwenna's bunched fist uncurled and Randall gasped to see the long fingernails black and glossy as the Ravens' plumage, each sharpened to a wicked point.

The mad woman strode straight towards her, with hands like claws reaching forward.

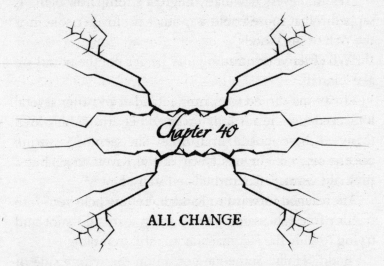

Chapter 40

ALL CHANGE

'Stop! Stop it now!' Ark roared, standing between Randall and Corwenna, though no-one had seen him move. 'If you let your dark heart rule your actions, you'll be no better than the killers of Maw!'

Randall was on her knees, the cold snow soaking into her body, tears streaming down her face as she looked up at Ark. How had he moved so fast? But what chance did a boy have against those sharpened claws?

'It's true,' Randall whispered, almost to herself. 'I was going to do what I could to sell this country out. So just let the hag finish me off. What else do I have to live for?'

Corwenna's arm was frozen in mid-air. The silence was equally chilly. She ignored Randall. 'That was fast, Arktorious Malikum! You really have grown. When we first met, you cowered in my presence.'

'That was a long time ago.'

'Yes. And every day that you grow stronger, my being is sapped. What more could a mother do for her son? It is the Will of the Woods.'

'Whatever your meaning may be, it's not the point! We *need* Randall.'

Corwenna turned to examine Randall and after several long seconds, she abruptly dropped her arm. 'Ahhh. Well then, you have spoken, Arktorious.' She seemed to shrink once more, no longer Queen of the Ravenwood, but a tired old woman. She turned and stalked away.

Ark reached forward to Randall. 'Let me help you.'

'I'm fine,' she said, wiping away tears and snot and trying to hide the fact that she was still trembling.

'Buddy Holly! Someone got up on the wrong side of the bed this mornin'!' said Mucum, trying to break the atmosphere. No-one laughed.

'Mistress?'

'What is it, PV?'

'I calculated a 95.87 per cent chance of death or serious injury from that encounter. The probability of you surviving seemed most unlikely.'

'Thanks for that.' She tried not to look at the others. They all knew her now for the traitor she had planned to be.

'Come on,' said Ark gently. 'You'll freeze out here.' He was still marvelling at his own courage in defying Corwenna; even more amazed that she'd backed down. She was right. His confidence had grown. But then he thought about Corwenna's words. If she was truly giving her strength to him, that could not bode well for her. As for having spared Randall's life, he knew he had done so because she was useful: they needed PV. But he felt there was some other reason too.

Randall stumbled forwards to the lip of the platform and peered cautiously over the edge. The drop was dizzying. She wondered what would happen if she simply jumped.

'Things aren't that bad!' Ark said, behind her. 'Trust me, I've thought about it myself a few times. But you're stubborn – a bit like me, in fact.'

Randall tried to stop the hint of a smile that curled the edge of her lips.

'That's better!'

'You saved me. You didn't have to.'

'I did.' Again, he looked away.

'Why are you being kind to me?'

Ark shrugged his shoulders, watching as she looked at the branch-way ahead that Corwenna had negotiated with ease.

'Is is safe?' she asked.

'Ha!' Mucum butted in. 'Thought you was one of the top free-climbers in Maw.'

'Not one of the top climbers, the top climber!'

'Then think of this here twisted old branch as a ledge. Balance, darlin'! That's all it takes. Anyways, if yer fall, yer get a lovely view before yer go splat!'

Flo gave her a sympathetic glance. 'Yow be all right, moi girl. Just follow us, like. It be easy once yow pick it up.' Then Flo was off, behind Mucum.

Ark skipped lightly along the branch, turning halfway.

'It's up to you,' he said before he too vanished into a tangle of branches.

Randall paused. She'd made her way along building routes far trickier than this. And Ark was right: jumping wouldn't solve anything. She took her first step off the platform, planting her foot exactly where the others had gone before. She held her breath as the branch gave slightly beneath her weight. Amazing! More thrilling than rigid glass and metal. 'Wait for me!' she shouted, her voice swallowed in the snowy whiteness. She caught up easily with the others and was bemused to see Ark smiling at her.

'See! It beats the smooth glass corridors of Maw any day!'

'Mmm. You might have a point.' And he did. As Randall balanced high in the canopy, she was filled with something she'd never felt before. She didn't even know the word for it. Even on this bitterly cold early evening, the forest was alive with birdsong, echoes bouncing off the interwoven trunks. As for the wood! It truly was priceless, a vast, bark-wrapped treasure house compared with the splinters that passed for jewels in Maw. But it wasn't the commercial worth that struck her, the price tag Maw would slap on it. Arborium had a different worth entirely: it was alive! She had to stop to catch her breath as it hit her: she was stepping along something living.

She looked up to see a pair of black, liquid eyes staring back at her. On the branch above, less than twenty metres away, a small, mottled-brown creature tensed its long, elegant legs ready to flee.

'What are you?' she whispered.

Mucum turned round to see. 'Deery-me!' he laughed. 'She really has got no i-deer!'

'Oh, shut up, Mucum!' said Ark. 'It's a roe-buck. A male deer. He's looking for moss under the snow, but he'll eat bark if he has to.'

The deer had worked out Randall was no threat, and was using its hooves to scrape away the snow on the branch.

'It's . . . I mean, he's . . . it's *all* . . . amazing,' she said finally, still unable to take her eyes off the creature.

'Yes.' Ark nodded. 'Now do you understand what we're fighting for?'

Randall thought of the hover-bots that passed for pets in Maw. The word *animal* was mostly used to describe how traders behaved in the financial markets. Then there were the wretched creatures bred for their meat somewhere in the deepest parts of the city. But this deer, with its huge, innocent eyes, represented another way of living altogether.

Deep inside Randall, something shifted. She turned away reluctantly from the roe-buck. 'I . . . I think I'm beginning to see.' Something else occurred to her. Mucum and Flo had gone on again and were further ahead, so she was alone with Ark on the branch. 'I can't hear . . . you know . . . now, I can't . . . hear you in here,' she tapped the side of her head, 'not any more.'

'Ah, yes,' said Ark, slowly. 'I think I could only hear your thoughts when we were touching, I mean, when we were . . . in c . . . contact. I don't know why. But even so, I sense something like change in you. Am I right?'

'Um, yes. You are,' Randall said simply. 'I suppose it's, well . . . it's actually being here. I've never exactly admired the Gloms: they're grabbers; greedy. I've just never thought much about what they do. But now they want to grab and destroy something like this.' She spread her arms wide. 'They're disgusting!'

'That's what we've been telling you all along.'

'I didn't realize . . .'

'No.' Ark stared at her, willing her to meet his gaze.

Finally she looked up at the boy who felt at home in these giant trees. She felt a mixture of envy and . . . something she couldn't put her finger on.

Mucum's voice boomed. 'Oi! You two. What you hangin' around for? Some of us are gettin' hungry 'ere.' The deer twitched, startled, and melted instantly back into the forest.

Half an hour later, Randall was still marvelling at the fact that they were actually inside the trunk of a living tree. There had been a moment of great awkwardness when Corwenna had invited her in. But somehow, the hovering threat of danger had flown as their host busied herself with preparing food.

Randall examined the last mouthful of fried egg poised on her fork. It had the brightest yolk she'd ever seen, as if the yellow was on fire, and it tasted nothing like the pale yolks of Maw. The room felt cosy and warm, the fire in the iron grate comforting after their freezing journey. She pushed away her empty plate and looked around at the recesses in the walls, heaped with trinkets and glittering baubles. There were faded tapestries covering the bare wood, filled with strange scenes of what looked like people riding on the backs of four-legged creatures as they chased woven deer through a green wood.

'Mistress,' chirped PV, speaking through her wrist-band, 'though the digestion of food is necessary, might I remind you, we have very little time.'

'Ah!' said Corwenna. 'I felt we had another guest in our presence: one that is invisible! A mind without a body. Remarkable. My mother once told me that the world she left behind contained wonders.'

'I am not a wonder, Madam, only a Personal Virtual Assistant. You might consider it convenient to call me PV.'

Randall took out the glass cube and fiddled with it as the light from flickering candles caught its surface and reflected back. 'But your mind is also able to reach beyond the body, madam,' PV continued. 'I can sense its presence in my circuits.'

Corwenna stared at the cube with her dark eyes. 'How fascinating,' she murmured. 'The spirit in a machine . . .'

'Chat ain't gonna get us nowhere!' Mucum grumbled. 'We need to plan what to do.'

'If I may?'

'It even has manners!' Corwenna smiled. 'Yes, PV, what do you wish to tell us?'

'Information,' came the voice. 'I was able to access it before we left Maw. As Master Ark and Mucum know from what they observed of the envoy's demonstration for the Gloms, there is a final piece of the Quantum Trap: the memory key containing the coding stream. I can confirm who has been sent to carry this trigger key into Arborium. It is as Master Ark guessed: two soldiers; one pilot and Petronio Grasp.'

Ark stood up abruptly, his face grim. 'Then the solution is simple. Hedd and his kin will carry us. We find the flying craft, which has probably landed somewhere near the capital. We find Grasp. Then we destroy the weapon.'

'And take them all out.' Mucum cracked his knuckles. 'I'll happily smash that traitor's face into splinters!'

Corwenna frowned. 'I don't think it will be that easy.'

Ark rounded on her. 'You said it was up to us last time! We defeated Commander Flint and the others. Why question my judgement now?'

'I'm not,' Corwenna said wearily. 'And as I have said, you have grown greatly in wisdom and strength. But destroying the craft or even the weapon itself might not be enough.'

'She's right,' said Randall. 'That's the whole point about Maw. If they've already built one weapon, it won't take them long to make more. You don't stand a chance.'

'Girl of Maw, on that point, I disagree . . .' Corwenna paused to think, a sudden glint in her eye. 'And now I see why you are here and why Arktorious was right to stay my hand. We need your knowledge of Maw as well as the help of your assistant. And I already see that you are clever and bold.'

'What?' Randall interrupted. 'First you try to kill me, then you praise me?'

'Yes. I do. But don't expect apologies.'

'I don't,' Randall muttered.

'Good. Then we can move forward.' Corwenna turned back. 'Each day that my boy grows like a sapling skyward, I am a little less. I do not presently have the will or strength to leave my beloved Ravenwood, though my birds are yours to command. They would not stoop to concern themselves with Dendran matters for anyone but me.' She nodded to Ark then turned back to Randall. 'As the only one here who understands such things, would you be able to – ah, what are the words for this – break into and alter their machinery, destroy their ability to make another of these weapons?'

'You mean, hack into their computer systems? Well, I don't know if it's possible, but with PV's help, I can try.'

Randall thought of the cold eyes of Lord Far as he had given the order to shoot. He would happily have killed both her and her mother, all for the sake of business. Right now, she thought, she truly understood who the real enemy was – and it was time for revenge.

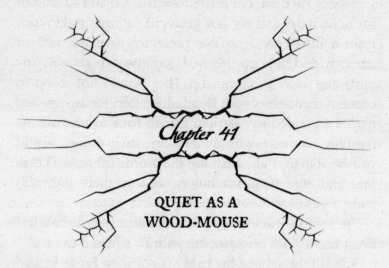

Chapter 41

QUIET AS A
WOOD-MOUSE

The wide wood-way was deserted, the safety ropes on either side swinging in the breeze. The moon was full, a frozen silver that turned every breath into tiny clouds.

'According to my navigations,' said PV quietly, 'we are close.'

A twig-track split off to the left, with a sign hanging in front of it. 'Closed for essential maintenance by order of the Alder Councillors.' Ark stopped and scanned the rutted route ahead of them. The journey to Arborium on the backs of two Ravens had been thankfully uneventful for the four of them. Now, it was time for action.

'You have to imagine each footstep melting into the wood,' Ark whispered. 'Sound is your enemy. Silence, your friend.'

'Yeah, yeah!' Randall muttered, but she was impressed

by the way he climbed deftly over the sign and vanished into a pool of shadow beyond. And he was right. The Empire had not taken over half the world by being stupid. Guards would be posted. She didn't fancy being shredded by a g-gun.

She gripped the fence and vaulted over, bending her knees to land without a sound. Mucum and Flo followed, seeming to ooze along the track so that Randall hardly knew they were there behind her. On the other side, the going was rougher. There were slimy piles of gigantic rotten leaves that were slippery and treacherous. And she couldn't help remembering Ark mentioning some kind of worm that feasted on precious wood.

CRACK! The sound echoed through the skeletal trees as her foot gave way, plunging through the plank beneath as if it was made of biscuit. A bird squawked and flew off, a shadow cut out against the starry night.

'What the holly are you doing?' Mucum whispered.

'My best!' Randall gently pulled her foot free, hoping that the rest of the wood wasn't about to give way.

'What? Your best to get us killed?'

'How dare you!'

Mucum stared at Randall, saw the tears trembling round her eyelids.

'OK, OK, I'm a plank. Sorry. I keep forgettin' this is all new to yer, that you've kinda lost everythin' bein' 'ere. I didn't mean it . . .'

Far off, a Kirk bell tolled. Randall counted the chimes. Ten of them; ten o'clock. Her wristband told her it was the middle of the day in Maw. And Mucum was right: she had lost everything. But now she *was* here, her instinct told her that what she was doing was right. For the first time in her life, she felt she had something to fight for. This was more than a battle to find fame through her free-climbing exploits.

She tried not to breathe, listening for the tell-tale signs of others nearby. There had been so many expeditions where she'd nearly been discovered, had flattened herself against glass cliffs like a priceless sheet of paper. Was this any different?

'Clear. I detect no immediate danger,' PV announced at low volume.

'Right,' Mucum whispered. 'Keep yer feet to the outside edges.'

Randall, Mucum and Flo made their careful way to catch up with Ark. Ten minutes later, the twig-track had almost vanished, engulfed by parasite bushes that sprang up from the branch. The pale moonlight revealed evidence that others had pushed their way through the bushes ahead. Ark put his fingers to his lips and they slid through among the dense leaves and twigs.

On the other side, they could just make out that the branch widened, revealing a disused market-hall plat-form, the roof long stripped by wind and rain. There, crouching within the remains of the walls, was a darker shadow that did not belong in Arborium.

A set of gleaming metal steps reared up from the platform to a curved door in the belly of the beast. And at the bottom stood a figure, a transparent g-gun cradled in his arms.

Ark turned to the others and mouthed the plan they had already agreed on. 'Flo and Mucum, stay here to watch. If we don't return by the chiming of the next hour, you come to see why. Stay hidden. Stay safe.'

Flo reached forwards, placing her long hands on Ark's and on Randall's shoulder. 'Roots speed yow in what yow have to do. We'll keep good lookout.'

Ark nodded. As he and Randall slipped forward into the dense shadows he took the girl's hand. Her fingertips were cold but the touch sent a strange tingling through his limbs, all the way to his stomach. He only hoped it would work a second time.

You'll have to trust everything I'm about to do.

Not this . . . again. You . . . in my head . . . Randall tried to pull her hand away, but Ark gripped harder.

Please.

Other thoughts surfaced in Randall's mind, though she tried to push them away: *. . . hand . . . warm . . . nice . . . why, feel good? Should be filled . . . fear . . .*

Ark once again felt like an eavesdropper. What if she could hear all his thoughts too? But there was no time to worry about that. Instead, he formed two words and sent them flying between them like a pair of silent bats: TRUST ME.

Ark then strode right out of the shadows, pulling her gently with him. One step at a time, he walked slowly, straight towards the guard. Randall had no choice but to follow.

What the . . . Frame are you . . . doing? Randall's thoughts were as jittery as her trembling hand.

It's what my mother taught me. By believing I am part of the forest, that is what I will become. The guard won't see me. And, while I hold your hand, I extend this skill to you. He felt the clamminess of her palm and concentrated on slowing his breathing.

You're mad . . . to think that a highly trained soldier . . . won't sense us . . . we're dead!

But the guard didn't move as they crept closer, until they stood in his direct line of sight. Then, with a look of fixed determination, the guard lurched forward and marched – straight towards them.

No! He's . . . seen us! Run! It was all Randall could do not to shout out. Instinct made her try to twist away and turn back.

Ark felt her pulse accelerate. If she panicked now, it would be over. He held tight and squeezed.

Be still!

He was a stick, a twig, a root held firm in the grip of the earth. Nothing less. Nothing more. His companion was another leaf on the branch, of no interest to the eyes of Maw.

The man continued moving until he was within four paces of them, then he paused and sniffed the air before speaking.

Randall tensed, ready to flee, her heart doing star jumps.

'Koch, you old git. Are you receiving me?'

Silence.

The guard shook his wristband. 'That's right, mate, you carry on snoozing then while Heckler here is stuck awake half the night on pointless guard duty. Well, I'm off on a perimeter scan. Cheesus Priced! This place is freezing!' he muttered before brushing right past Ark and Randall and heading off into the bushes to the side of them.

The sound of crashing footsteps faded away into the forest and Randall remembered to start breathing again.

That was . . .

An opportunity! Ark dropped Randall's hand and ran for the steps outside the craft.

Randall bounded up behind him. 'Were we, like, invisible?' she whispered.

'No. But we were a part of the woodscape.' Ark crouched down by the curved door of the flypod.

'But how did you do it? I mean, we have machines in Maw that are mind-blowing. But that was . . .' Randall paused. 'Could you hear everything I was thinking?'

'Only that you were scared,' Ark lied. He tried not to look at her, not to think about how it had felt holding her hand. 'Anyway, it's over to you now!' He gripped the knife hidden inside his doublet, not knowing what would greet them on the inside. Corwenna had spoken truly: he had grown. The time for fear was over. If Petronio Grasp was within, there would be no mercy.

Randall pulled out the glass cube and placed it against the door. 'PV, be a good boy and let us in!'

'Your wish is my command!' There was only a slight delay, followed by a soft *whoosh* as the door slid open. 'The algorithm was surprisingly simple, mistress. I shall now reset it.'

As they took a step inside, Ark contemplated the darkness in front of them. He frowned, sending his senses before him into the enclosed space. He could feel with all the hardness of heartwood that Petronio was not there. He sniffed the air, picking up the warm scent of slumbering machinery. Where, he wondered, had Grasp gone and what was left behind? Were they too late?

Muffled sounds of snoring echoed around the glass walls, confirming the presence of one guard and the pilot in an enclosed cot-like space at the back. Randall tiptoed towards the sound, pressing the glass cube against the closed hatch of the sleeping space. The tiniest of clicks indicated locks rotating into place. Then she turned and quietly made her way to a softly illuminated wall of glass panels.

After five long minutes, Ark was growing impatient. 'What are you doing?'

'What does it look like?' she whispered back. She was busy pressing the cube that contained PV's primary functions against the wall that was now filled with flickering lights.

'How would I know?'

'You wouldn't, so just let me get on my with my job and let PV get on with his. He's trying to break into the main computer. I have no idea how you made us invisible, but I can tell you that PV is doing his best to pretend he also doesn't exist, so that this computer here won't notice him paying a visit. So shut up and stay quiet! Fooling the security in this piece of kit isn't easy.'

Ark thought of Rootshooter Joe, and the bottle filled with fireflies that he had smashed to light up a tunnel. What kind of illuminated creature lived behind this transparent wall?

'Master Malikum, please excuse Randall's short temper.' PV's voice was so quiet, Ark had to strain to catch each word.

'Do you mind?' Randall sniffed.

'It is fortunate I can multi-task. While translating my indicators into human speech patterns, I am also currently deep inside the mainframe. I shall try to explain. Your Ravens fly through the sky. This has similarities to my own journey within the cloud. The code is encrypted, but my masters built me well. Indeed, Remiel and his loyal programmers have already coded a cyber back-door by which I can gain entrance anywhere. Ah . . . I have it.'

'Have what?' Ark whispered.

'Access to the clueprint that lays out the step-by step process by which the Quantum Trap was built. The information alone is beyond any single mind, containing as it does several trillion petabytes of memory.'

'I've no idea what you mean. But can you get rid of it, wipe it out or whatever it is that you machines do?'

'I am already uploading the means of its elimination, Master Malikum. Your biological diseases are rather primitive compared with the viruses at my disposal. This is one infection their data-centre will take months if not years to recover from. They will not be building a new Quantum Trap in the near future.'

A startled snort came from the rear of the flypod. Ark and Randall froze and looked at each other in alarm, but after a few seconds, a groaning sigh was followed by sounds of softer snoring.

'So that's it? And you have all the details of their plans

for using the weapon in Arborium too? Can we go now?' Ark asked.

'Not yet,' Randall snapped. 'PV, did you find out the other thing?'

'What other thing?' said Ark.

'PV. I need to know. Is she still alive?'

'Yes, mistress. I have been able to intercept communications. It appears Lord Far has realized the consequences of eliminating the envoy. She is currently under house arrest. However, her high value to the Empire's cause means that her rash and emotional crime of trying to protect you might well be overlooked.'

Randall let out a long breath. 'She's alive. That's something, I suppose. All these years, I had no real idea what she was up to.'

'And you have no responsibility for her actions.'

'I know that!' she said irritably. 'Did you get a message to her, let her know the plan to blow us up failed?'

'Sorry mistress. Remiel forbade it. It could endanger the task ahead.'

Ark was exasperated. 'Look, I know it's important to you, but we have more pressing concerns!'

'Oh, forgive me for trying to find out about my own mother who thinks I'm dead!'

PV gave an electronic cough. 'Ahem . . . if I may continue? I have also acquired further information to account for why Petronio Grasp is not present. We have only a few hours. The weapon will be activated on the fifth chime of the Kirk bells. There are ten spheres being placed in a ring around the city of Hellebore. Their co-ordinates will be mapped by a technician from a high vantage point, and triggered by the Grasp boy in a central place that I cannot ascertain. I am sorry I could not be more efficient in accessing that information. However, I can continue to advise you once we are on the move. First let me release the lock on the sleeping place and remove all trace of us having been here.'

Ark's thoughts reeled. He clenched his fists, trying to contain the green cauldron bubbling inside him. He would have to find and face Petronio, and at that time, nothing would hold him back. Unless they were too late.

The weapon was being dispersed in separate components, spread out round the rim of the city. It was an impossible task. How could they deal with so many targets as well as with the deadly spider in the middle: the boy who was laughing at them from the very centre of the web? And where was that centre? There were so many questions, and not enough time.

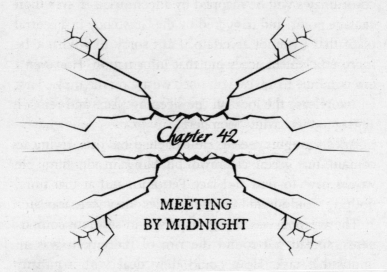

Chapter 42

MEETING
BY MIDNIGHT

'**W**arden Goodwoody, sorry to wake you. There's someone I'd like you to meet.'

By night, the Kirk was a snug barricade against the constant winter wind, still faintly scented with the incense of cedarwood and myrrh. Behind them, in a side chapel, a single beeswax candle burned, a reminder to the Holly Woodsmen that darkness would never take over the light of the wood.

The warden shifted in her cot in a small side antechamber. 'Arktorious?' she croaked. 'So, you are come like a ghost in the night.' A floorboard creaked. 'But I was not asleep, and you are not alone. I recognize the heavy tread of your companion Mucum.'

'All right, rev . . . I mean reverend.'

Goodwoody listened again. 'And, if I am not mistaken, those deep soft breaths reveal Flo of the Rootshooters. You are most welcome. A worthy young woman, if ever there was!'

'That Oi be!' Flo chuckled. 'It be amazing what thou can sense. 'Tis moighty nice to meet with thou again, most goodly Lady.'

'However, the other?' Her blank eyes blinked as if trying to pierce the gloom. 'You are from . . . elsewhere.'

As the warden stood, Randall stepped forward uncertainly. 'Ark told me about you. In my land, our surgeons could give you new eyes.'

'Hah!' exclaimed Goodwoody. 'I see more than you think, girl from beyond all that the Wood Book teaches us. Lend me your hand.'

Randall stretched out her left arm and felt it gripped hard by fingers calloused with years of keeping the Kirk clean and tidy.

'Such smooth skin and short fingers. Yes. It must be hard losing your home.'

'How the . . . ? How do you know that?'

'Forgive me. Though I am old, my wits are about me. You are scented with fear and loss and the trembling of your hands speaks to my heart.'

'You don't know the half of it!' Randall squeezed her eyes closed, trying to block the images: her bedroom, the sun shining through the glass, throwing squares of light on to her floor; even dull school lessons, and arguments with her mother. All gone. If she returned, they'd hunt her down like a cockroach.

'There is more,' said the warden. 'Despite your upbringing, you are thoughtful and quick. In this short time, you have grown to understand why we love the woods *and those who are part of them* with all our hearts. Yes?'

What did the woman mean? How could she possibly know? But the warmth in the warden's fingers was enticing and Randall suddenly wanted those arms to envelop her.

'But you have not paid me a visit for small talk. There is an urgency in all of you, and . . .' She let go of Randall's hand gently and sniffed the air, as if scent alone carried messages. '. . . and danger is coming . . .'

Ark explained as briefly as he could the terror of the Quantum Trap, and, though they had already decided to ask PV to stay quiet lest he prove a distraction, Ark related what the virtual assistant had discovered in the flypod.

Goodwoody gave a gasp. 'That such evil can exist in the minds of men . . . that such strange cleverness can be used to destroy! And the signal will be the tolling of the bells for five in the morning? But then why have you come to me?'

Flo stepped forward. 'When Randall and Ark told us what PV 'ad discovered, 'twas moi idea to bring us all 'ere as quick as quick. The one thing against us is toime. But if we be running out of toime, why not make some for ourselves? With a bit o' help, we can stretch out the minutes till they be long and bendy just like moi! It's them Kirk clocks. We needs them a-toirnin' backwards!'

The warden's dull eyes blinked in the candlelight.

'As for them spheres,' Flo continued, 'if yow can also raise a few o' them pompous old Holly Woodsmen what think that girls be only good for keepin' Kirk clean and what-not, we'll have numbers in plenty. And we do 'ave a plan, which means we moight be in with a chance! Listen, Oi shall tell yow quick.'

As Flo described to the warden what they had worked out between them, Goodwoody nodded. And when she had heard all, she sighed. 'The task you have devised will need all of Diana's grace to make it work. I understand that prayers without action are but words that fall like autumn leaves, but even if the good Lady smiles down on us and we succeed, what are we to do with these,' she wrinkled her nose in disgust, 'Maw-made killing machines?'

'Once we 'ave them nasty hornet-hummin' spheres, we do deal with 'em straight away: by drowning 'em!'

It was Randall's turn to explain. 'You'd think the engineers who built this version of the Quantum Trap would have thought to make it waterproof! But, as I'm learning fast, science doesn't always get it right. And that's our advantage. Dunk each sphere in whatever liquid can be found and they're totally harmless.'

'However,' Ark added, 'if even one of the spheres escapes our grasp, it will still be enough to wipe out the population of a whole city suburb.' He looked at each of his friends, new and old, in turn. 'We must succeed.'

'And you shall! Diana will be with you.' The warden's face lit up like a lantern, hiding the shadows of doubt they all felt. 'I will talk to a few of my fellow Holly Woodsmen to ask for their help. At least I shall not have to wake them, since on this night, all stay wakeful in readiness for the celebrations of Solstice. Though whether they will listen to a mere warden is another matter.'

'They will,' Ark reassured her. 'If they still want to be alive tomorrow.'

'And what of the one who will be coordinating the spheres?'

'The technician? He's my department,' Randall said, trying to sound confident. Ark had said her climbing skills would help. The trees of Arborium were, of course, nothing like the Mawish skyscrapers: they were infinitely more exciting. But nonetheless, she felt both thrill and doubt clenching her stomach.

'And young Master Gladioli?'

Flo answered. 'Moi loverly lad? Why, he shall be usin' his great big muscles for a bit of justified violence!'

'Oh yes!' Mucum beamed. 'That's me!'

'And that only leaves one little part,' Flo said, 'though it be an important one. One of the traitorous soldiers what we shall be dealin' with is said to be almost invincible. Yet even a man with the strength of a moighty timber-boar can be brought down by a little flea. Ark, be thou sure about this?'

Everyone turned to Ark. He nodded reluctantly. 'We have little choice. It's the best idea we could come up with.'

'It be decided then. Little Shiv shall be a not-so-little addition to our merry band.'

'Ah! The child who screamed so loudly in the battle of the Harvest Festival,' said the warden. 'Those lungs of hers are quite something! Though I feel uneasy about putting someone so young into danger.'

Ark's face fell. 'Maybe you're right. How can I even think of using my little sister for something like this?'

Mucum clapped a hand on Ark's shoulder. 'You're her bruv! 'Course you wanna protect 'er! 'But I reckon she can look after 'erself, that one. She's a good 'un to 'ave on yer side. I should know.'

'And as you know, Ark of the Woods,' Flo added, 'Oi shall be goin' with 'er to act as 'er chaperone. Not that she'll need me!' Flo turned to address the rest of them. 'The most important thing,' she concluded, 'is 'ow we shall all stay in touch with each other. Ark, this be your part.'

Ark took a breath. 'Before we left the Ravenwood, our Dark Lady gave me these.' He pulled out a quiver of long, black feathers, allowing them to flutter into the warden's lap.

The warden gathered them up, her face filled with awe as she stroked the plumes. 'You talk of a queen I have only ever believed in, not felt the face of. They tell me that she played her part in the battle, but I still find it hard to fathom the green deeps that she comes from. Is she truly Queen of the Ravenwood?'

'Yeah,' said Mucum. 'She's as real as the planks under our feet. Bit grumpy for a goddess though!'

'Truly, to live in such times where tales come to life and walk amongst us. And these feathers are from the Ravens themselves?'

'They are,' said Ark. 'And when Corwenna sent us off again flying on their backs, it came to me how these feathers might play their part. Ravens can speak to each other by thought alone, and I can do the same with them. I believe I can become like a Raven in hearing the thoughts of those nearest to me, if each of you holds on to a feather. And then, being at the centre, I can pass my thoughts out to the rest of you. So, everyone must take one and keep them close at all times.'

'Strange,' mused the warden. 'In our Wood Book it says *Consider The Ravens*. With this gift bestowed from our dark brethren, it appears that the Ravens are considering *us*!'

Ark nodded, remembering the feather that had been a gift from the first Hedd and how it had saved him before. He gathered the bundle from the warden's hands and gave them out.

Randall fingered her feather uneasily before bursting out, 'But you can already read my mind!'

Ark squirmed. 'Yes, but only if . . . when . . . we touch. I mean . . . anyway. You still need this.'

'So, what you're saying is that they're communication devices,' Randall changed the subject, trying to avoid Ark's eye, 'so we can work together. A bit like this,' she tapped her wristband, 'only you're working the circuits.'

'Yes.' Ark breathed deeply. 'And now we all have our part to play, we must go our different ways.'

'Diana be with us all.' Warden Goodwoody rose and embraced each of them in turn. 'Wood speed you.'

They filed out of the great Kirk hall. Ark was the last to leave. He paused by the door, plucking a coin from his pocket to throw into the tiny zinc shrine. It made a small splash in the darkness, and sank down, along with his prayers. He knew it wasn't just the ten spheres and the

technician they had to deal with. There was still a significant part of the plan missing: how to stop the trigger in
the middle. It was like trying to find the lost boy whistling
in the woods. Except that this boy had an infernal arm
capable of wreaking havoc and death, and who knew
what other tricks up his sleeve. Even the thought of the
name made Ark's blood rise green. Petronio Grasp. Where
would the boy go? Where would he choose as a central
point in the kingdom?

Ark shook his head, and then suddenly smiled as an
answer stared back at him. Petronio's ambition had turned
him into nothing more than a hungry machine – and
machines, like clocks, were predictable. If Grasp was
supposed to set off the weapon from a central place, then
his pride would lead him to the one destination he was
least expected, but the one that would give him greatest
satisfaction. Yes, he was sure where Petronio's inflated
self-importance would lead him. It was obvious.

He rushed out to gather the group for one last time.
When he had finished a gabbled explanation, he had only
one final question. 'Are we agreed?'

'Yeah!' said Mucum.

'Yas,' Flo chimed.

'Guess so,' Randall murmured.

'Mistress, I shall not venture to suggest the probability
of success in this instance, but I shall lend my assistance,
when required.'

And with these final words, they each set off into
the night.

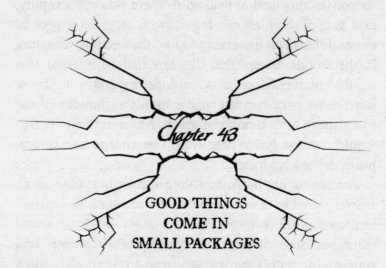

Chapter 43

GOOD THINGS
COME IN
SMALL PACKAGES

Flo crossed the swaying drawbridge towards the Malikums' dwelling. Though it had been agreed what had to be done, she sighed as she quietly lifted the flap of treepaulin that counted as a door. Her height meant she had to bend her neck to duck inside as the whole house rocked gently in the wind.

The interior was dark, apart from a faint light from the embers of the fire still glowing in the grate. Flo edged awkwardly forward, stooping to contain her height under the low ceiling. She breathed in the leftover aroma of a goat and rosemary stew, suddenly wondering if the family were even here. What if they had gone to join the Solstice celebrations?

However, a rough woollen curtain that divided the sleeping quarters was pushed aside suddenly and Mrs Malikum came rushing out, her hair tousled. 'Ark! Is it you? Are you back?' There came the sound of scraping, and a lantern filled the room with its soft glow. The woman stared up – and then up again, finally making out Flo's pale white face.

'Oi be sorry to be disappointing yow, Mrs Malikum, but yas, your son has returned from his journey and he be moighty well, all things considering.'

Mrs Malikum put down the lantern and ran to Flo, grasping her bony hand. 'It's really true? He's safe?' Her face was bunched up with emotion, eyes brimming with tears.

'Yas. I assure you.'

'But why couldn't he come home? Shiv has been crying and crying for him.'

'He will, good mother, and he sends all his love. Oi wish I could explain, but there be dark matters in the makin' and Arborium is in much danger. Actually,' Flo paused uneasily, 'it be little Shiv that Oi be coming to talk to you about.'

Mrs Malikum pulled out a handkerchief and wiped her eyes. 'Yes, she is a dear, isn't she? And I trust you have told me the truth about my son. Now we must have tea and you can tell me all about it.' She turned to a set of cupboards built into the far wall and began pulling out cups and a kettle.

'Oi be sorry, Mrs Malikum. There is not time for a welcome, sweet brew, though Oi am very thirsty. 'Tis only minutes that we have. Your son Ark found out that the Empire of Maw 'ave made an awful, terrible weapon. If we don't do somethin' about it, our loverly land, with its branches what sing to the sky and its roots we Root-shooters lives to delve in, will be gone. And,' she could think of no better way of putting it, 'Oi needs to borrow yow daughter Shiv.'

Flo had spoken in a low voice, but she hadn't spoken quietly enough. 'Floesey-Woesey! Talking about me!' said Shiv, stumbling sleepily through the gap in the curtain.

Flo knelt down and took the girl in her long arms. 'It be goodly to see yow, little 'un!' She stroked Shiv's glossy curls gently. 'Thou be a four-year-old bundle of joy and one that would make yow mother proud!'

'I am!' Shiv smiled. 'I am!'

'Would yow like to come for a ride?'

The kettle and cups were forgotten. 'What sort of ride?' Mrs Malikum asked, her voice filled with sudden iron.

Flo was not usually nervous with anyone. But now she faltered. 'A . . . a Raven,' she stuttered.

'A Raven!' Mrs Malikum's eyes flew wide with shock.

'But Mummy, they're lovely and big and shiny with such soft feathers!' Shiv sang. 'I'm not a scaredy-waredy!'

'I don't care whether you are scared or not, my girl.' Mrs Malikum stared over Shiv's head at Flo with an accusing look. 'This is a strange game you play, Flo of the Rootshooters! The Ravens only have to sniff a drop of blood and they will kill. It's their nature. I will not have my daughter endangered!'

'Mrs Malikum, Oi do so understand thou be trowly worried, as would Oi be if Oi had a girl as wondrous as this.' Flo was desperately trying to find the right words to convince her. 'But Oi can tell yow, them great birds of the

Ravenwood came to our aid in the Harvest Battle. They be on our side and thow knows it. Why, when Ark last came to see yow, he was ridin' on the back of Hedd, son of Hedd, the leader of the Ravens. They are no danger to us. Corwenna herself 'as ordered it.'

'But what are you planning to do?' Mrs Malikum clutched her handkerchief, kneading it round and round like a ball of dough.

'Trust me, good mother. All Oi need little Shiv to do is go and say hello to somebody.'

Mrs Malikum gave Flo a suspicious stare. 'I don't feel I know who Arktorious is any more; he is so changed. After everything that happened before, with my Shiv being taken away and kept in that terrible prison, now you wish to take away my daughter away? You have no right.'

'That Oi know. But Oi beg it of you. She be in moi good hands, and Oi do solemnly swear on all that is rooted and deep that Oi will return her safely to yow!'

Shiv jumped out of Flo's lap and tugged at her mother's night-cote. 'Pleeeease, Mummy! Pretty please? I wanna go on a 'nadventure!'

Mrs Malikum turned away. 'Do I have a choice?'

'Oi'm so sorry to ask,' Flo said, 'but Oi do believe that Diana is looking after us all, and this be meant as part of the greater wood.'

'Well, then.' Mrs Malikum's shoulders drooped. 'At least let me find her some warm clothes first. But if anything happens to her, I will never, never forgive you.'

Five minutes later, with Shiv wrapped tightly in a cloak, the three figures stood near the edge of the wood-way.

Mrs Malikum fussed round her daughter, knotting the cloak so that it would keep her warm. 'Do you want your teddy-boar to keep you safe?' she whispered in Shiv's ear.

Little Shiv nodded, sucking her thumb as the toy was tucked into her cloak.

'Goddess speed you.'

A deeper darkness swooped from the sky. Mrs Malikum instinctively clasped her arms around Shiv in protection. There was a screech and a flash of glossy black that shone under the moon, then the great bird was perched right in front of them.

Mrs Malikum backed away. 'This is wrong!' she cried. 'How can it be safe to ride on the back of that thing?'

The Raven turned its head sideways, a single black eye staring at her.

'Mrs M!' a voice boomed out of the shadows. 'It ain't wrong. I promise yer!'

'Master Gladioli? Is that you, Mucum?'

Mucum slid off the back of Hedd and landed with a thump. 'Keep yer voice down, Mrs M. Don't want everyone to know me second name!'

'I don't know why yow worry so,' laughed Flo. ''Tis trowly wonderful to 'ave such a pretty name! It be right flowery for such a strong 'un.'

'Yeah well. Blame me parents,' Mucum grunted.

'Moocum!' Shiv sang, pulling herself free from her mother's arms and running to him. 'We goin' up and up in the air!'

'Yeah, little one. We sure are.'

Somehow, the tension of the moment was broken. As

Flo helped Shiv up on to the bird's back to sit snug between her and Mucum, Mrs Malikum blinked back tears. The great Raven beat its wings and they were rising up into the night sky, heading into the unknown.

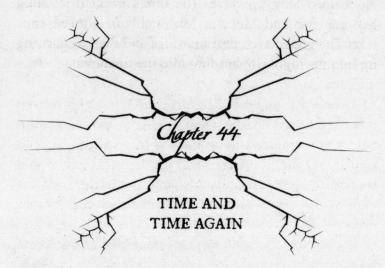

Chapter 44

TIME AND
TIME AGAIN

Petronio paused on the wood-way as the clocks struck four, their solemn sound echoing through the bare trees. Good. It meant he had all the time in the wood to accomplish his task.

Five a.m. was still a way off and he'd hoped to have the route to himself, but he hadn't taken into account the groups of Solstice-night revellers. Fortunately, they had obviously all drunk far too much acorn-brew to take notice of the figure flitting from shadow to shadow, case gripped firmly in the pincers of its right hand.

Petronio paused inside the high, hollow arch of a dead trunk to check his bearings. He rubbed his eyes. The contact lenses he had been given instead of goggles grated against his pupils like sandpaper. With all the superior technology at Maw's disposal, why couldn't they have made them comfortable? But they were a necessary evil.

He looked again and spotted the wood-way that would lead him to his appointment. Naturally, it was the widest, with weeds cut back and safety ropes kept trim. Diana forbid that this royal road should not be maintained to the highest standard.

A sudden sound made him reach for the knife tucked into his doublet. But the white figure that swept past him with silent wings was only an owl. Why worry? Petronio smiled, imagining the arrival at his destination: it would be both unexpected and satisfying. While the owl was hunting for shrews and mice, his own prey was meatier by far.

As he set off again, he tried to calm his breathing. There was no rush. By now, the ten men would be in place, hidden, ready for the final chime of five o'clock before they acted. He hoped that the technician was tracking the spheres properly. As he stalked along, growing in confidence with each step, he thought about how old-fashioned the bells of the Kirk were, with their absurdly overweight mechanisms. The four clocks that pealed throughout Hellebore were supposedly the great wonders of Arborium, placed at the north, south, east and west edges of the city atop great cathedral Kirks which these days attracted more gawkers than worshippers.

North, South, East and West,

Diana, Lady, Give me rest!

The old prayer came unbidden to his lips. He dismissed it. Superstitious claptrap! They only needed the bells for one final act, then such primitive mechanisms and the beliefs that inspired them would be wiped out and a new order imposed; an order where he, Petronio, would be near the top of the heap.

Lord Far had promised that Arborium would be changed utterly. Once large parts of the forest had been destroyed to control stock, not only would some of the best wood be processed and the timber used to prop up the economy of the Empire, but other parts of Arborium would also be divided up and sold as holiday homes for the super, super rich – once they had worked out how to produce plentiful supplies of the vaccine, of course. Naturally, loyal servants to the cause would be rewarded well. Petronio liked the idea of extensive reward. Those Dendrans that weren't killed by the Quantum Trap, plus the Rootshooters, would make useful slave labour alongside exported Mawish menial subjects. All in all, Arborium would be a forest filled with profit. The future was bright.

The bells were striking four-fifteen by the time Petronio approached his destination, passing more crowds celebrating the almost-Solstice. He crossed the great, gently arched parquet bridge that led to the landscaped pleasure gardens in the centre of the city. Though his woollen cloak was warm, the cold crept down his neck and his nose was frozen and dripping. In Maw, they had the right idea with their glassed-in walkways where the wind stood no chance.

A low mist rose off the boards, lapping at his ankles. The raised flower beds stuck up like little islands in a grey sea, each one containing a stark miniature cherry tree, wrapped in white bandages to save it from the ravages of the season this high up. He didn't like the look of them, reminding him as they did of old crones' tales, with trees coming to life to attack evil-doing Dendrans.

He squared his shoulders and walked on, aware of the battlements looming up in front of him. Great wide steps, gilded with gold leaf, rose up from the garden, the risers embossed with sap-stags, boars, timber-goats, mealworms and even Ravens bowing their carved heads before King Quercus.

He had arrived. Barkingham Palace: the eye of the storm-that-was-to-come.

Petronio especially enjoyed the way that the two soldiers on look-out tensed as they spotted him, then relaxed when they concluded that a single boy carrying a black case did not exactly look like a threat. He marched straight ahead, climbing the first step.

'Oi! Where'd you think *you're* going?' one of the soldiers yelled.

'Ain't it past yer bedtime?' the second one added, grinning.

Already, Petronio was on the third step. 'I'm here to see the king.'

'Oooh! Barking Holly! He's here to see the king!'

'Right before the buddy celebrations too. Would you like us to disturb his leading of the Solstice Ceremonies for you, *sir*?' The sneer was unmistakable.

'Yes. I would.' Petronio was rather surprised at the lax security. Standards were slipping these days. All it would take was two running bounds and he could be on them, let electrical instinct wake his arm and give it free rein.

The pincers would make short work of weak Dendran bodies. However, such crude tactics would not be necessary straight away.

The first soldier took a couple of quiet, menacing strides down towards him. 'Now, matey. I don't know if you're a bit dazed wiv celebratin' the Winter Solstice. Or whether this is some kinda bet wiv yer best buds to prove you ain't scared of walking up the king's stairway. But unless you fancy bein' given a few slaps and a wood old-fashioned hiding, I suggest you turn round and sod off, eh?'

In answer, Petronio let his cloak slip from his shoulders and lifted his arm. This time, the moon did him a favour, its light revealing the mechanical monster attached to him. To emphasize the point, Petronio raised the arm higher before bending his knees and crashing it down on to the step. The resulting smash disturbed a flock of roosting rooks, perched in the arrow slits that lined the walls above. Like dark, outraged splinters, they flew off into the night. But Fenestra's gift achieved its purpose. The arm had punched straight through the top layer of thin burnished gold, splitting and shattering the wooden step underneath. Petronio pulled his arm out of the resulting hole, peering idly down into the drop beneath it, before standing and flexing the metal fingers. 'As I said before, and I won't say it again, I'm here to see the king.'

There was a panicked look in the soldier's eyes. 'What the flippin' stick is that?' he said, stepping carefully back from the hole and keeping his eyes on Petronio's arm the whole time.

'That was called being *armed* and ready.'

The fear began to leave the soldier's face, replaced with a calculating look.

'Oh, good, you have a brain,' Petronio said, inspecting his arm to ensure there was no damage. 'However, in anticipation of you calling for backup and there being only one of me and a hundred or more of you, I do want you know I have *this*.' Petronio lifted the case in his other hand.

Instead of reflecting the moonbeams, the black surface of the case absorbed all light, destroying even the slightest reflection.

The soldier stared at him. 'Whatever that is you've got sprouting from yer shoulders ain't from round here. But you've been dumb enough with yer little drama show to summon every bowman in the Palace. And I doubt your poncy doublet is gonna look too nice when it's turned into a pincushion full of arrows!'

Petronio looked up. The soldier was right. Already, he could make out the glint of iron-tipped arrowheads shining from the shadowy slits above. However, he merely sighed.

'As for yer little case there, what yer gonna do? *Holiday* us to death?' The first guard positioned at the door began to laugh, and there were several guffaws from the arrow slits above.

'Well, that rather depends on whether you regard death as a holiday, mmm? Oh dear, I didn't want to have to do this. But I must admit, I'm rather glad that the scientists produced a miniature version of the Quantum Trap.'

'Yer what?' said the soldier.

'My dear fellow, you will go down in the history books as the first volunteer to prove that it works on Dendrans as well as cats!'

Before the soldier could order the bowmen to shoot, Petronio pressed a button hidden in the handle of the case. At the same time, he focused his contact lenses directly on to the soldier, giving him a deadly stare of utter contempt. The effect was immediate.

'Why you lookin' at me like that . . . urghhhhhh!' The man gurgled as he clutched his neck, his eyeballs bulging, his knees already buckling.

'What in Diana's name are yer doin' to him?' cried the first soldier.

'Simply what I will do to the rest of you . . .' and here Petronio stared meaningfully towards the arrow slits, '. . . if so much as one arrow is loosed. The science is complicated, so I'll try to keep it basic for your simple minds. Your colleague has suddenly found that there is no air for him to breathe. Oh dear.' He glanced down at the soldier who had collapsed on to the steps, right at the edge of the gaping hole. 'This is the part you won't even begin to understand. There is a perfect genetic copy of our man here currently floating in space above us. Unfortunately, space is a vacuum. Is anyone following this? No air up there. It's like having a twin. Only when the twin can't breathe, neither can he. Oops! See what I mean? He's stopped breathing!'

Petronio stepped up and nudged the slumped soldier with his toe. 'Well, when you gotta go, you gotta go, eh?'

And with this he kicked the body so that it slithered and tumbled from view down into the hole. 'Now, this was a simple demonstration, focused on one individual only. But I can – how shall I say? – increase the range. So, unless you all wish to join your friend very swiftly on his rather unusual journey to the River Sticks, or whatever rubbish you believe in, I shall repeat my earlier statement. I am here to see the king. I suggest you open that grand door of yours and let me in. Now.'

Hidden behind a trunk at the far edge of the pleasure gardens, Heckler put down his flare-scope. The glass lenses never lied. The boy's performance had been good, he'd give him that. Death was no great shakes – he'd killed more than a few of the Empire's rebels in his time – but the manner of such execution had made him feel uneasy. Still, it had served a purpose.

He nodded at Koch, crouching in the shadows. So far, Petronio Grasp had followed Lord Far's orders to the letter, but Heckler still wondered at the outcome of handing the boy so much power. Their task was to make sure that this new recruit didn't let his ambitions get the better of him. They had their own Maw-made means of getting into the palace now that all the guards were so distracted. They'd better get going.

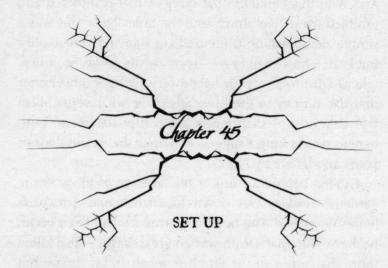

Chapter 45

SET UP

'**W**hy couldn't they let us wear our timebands?' Al muttered to himself. The strange Arborian clocks had struck the quarter hour. 'Four-fifteen. Forty-five minutes to go.' His own voice was comforting, a way of blocking out the sounds of the surrounding forest.

He wouldn't admit that he was spooked by the trees. But he'd grown up with the constant background hum of the city. Here, there were odd pools of silence, punctured by sudden creaks and the cry of creatures he had no desire to meet.

An hour ago, the flypod had lowered him down by flexi-cable on to this rickety old platform that swayed high above the rest of the trees. The platform resembled a giant bucket, with a branch sticking up through its middle. Every gust of wind had it swinging wildly from side to side. He tried not to peer over the waist-high rim to see the rest of the forest far below. The constant motion made him feel sick. Riding a nice enclosed, glassed-in lift a couple of kilometres up the side of a building was easy compared with this.

But Al knew better than anyone else why he was here. This high up, the signal projected by each sphere was clear and had been easy to coordinate. The glowing scroll-screen unfurled in front of him already resembled a nine-pointed star, with each sphere represented by a pulsing blue dot. Al had the tenth sphere tucked away in a small bag by his feet. With this final one, a perfect configuration of weapons now surrounded Hellebore. Sergeant Grain and his men had fulfilled their roles admirably.

The city was surrounded. They were all set. Now all they had to do was wait until the teenage brat did his bit.

Yes. *Brat* was the right word, Al mused. In fact there was something about the boy that disturbed him. At least with someone like Lord Far, everyone knew where they stood: the Glom was a piece of work, but he paid well, and he let Al get on with what he loved most. The algorithms that flowed through Al's mind were better than any shot of coffee, but even he couldn't compute what lay behind Petronio Grasp's motives. The boy was happy to sell out his country, that was for sure.

CRACK!

Al whipped his head round. 'Who's there?' he squeaked. Silence. 'I'm armed, you know!' He fumbled with the holster at his side, pulling out his g-gun and waving it around wildly. The moon emerged from behind the clouds, lighting up the branch above him. A pair of black, shiny eyes peered down. 'Eeek!' he cried.

The eyes didn't even blink as a pair of sharp claws clutched a nut and cracked it in half.

Al swallowed hard and breathed out as common sense kicked in. On the training vids he'd had to watch during their flight over the ocean, there had been footage of some of the wild animals inhabiting the wooded island. 'Stupid – what are you? Squirrel!' he sneered.

The squirrel responded by spitting half a nutshell straight into Al's face before scampering away into the darkness.

'You little . . .'

But before he had a chance to finish the sentence with some very colourful Mawish swear words, there was a tap on his shoulder. He swung round.

'How lovely to meet one of my fellow countrymen!' a female voice sang out.

'What?' Al's mind computed rather slowly that the crack he had heard had come from below, yet the squirrel was above him. 'Who . . . ? How . . . ?'

The accent was Mawish, but the figure was dressed like a Dendran. Under the moon, Al could see a stained jerkin with leather britches.

'The name's Randall. Randall Jarrett Fenestra. And I tell you, climbing this tricky trunk in this garb was a right pain.'

Al was dumbfounded, but he still had the gun in his hand. He aimed it at the girl's heart. 'Fenestra, right? Daughter of the envoy, traitor to Maw!'

'Well,' said Randall, not fazed by the gun pointed at her, 'I wasn't a traitor when I woke up yesterday morning. In fact, Petronio Grasp set me up. But now I know what you lot are up to, I'm beginning to think the Mawish cause is a tad over-rated.'

'Keep your hands where I can see them!' Al squawked.

'Absolutely!' Randall agreed. However, it wasn't her hands that moved, but her right foot, swinging upwards in a fast and furious curve.

'Ow!' Al cried, as his wrist was bent backwards by the force of the kick. There was a crunch as his fingers went floppy and the gun flew from his grasp, out over the edge of the platform, glinting as it fell like a shooting star through the woods below.

'That's fairer!' Randall said. 'Evens the odds. Now give me your screen.'

Al's right hand was dangling at a strange angle. 'You . . . must be . . . joking!' he hissed between gritted teeth. 'I don't . . . usually fight girls!' With an effort he crouched down to place the screen behind him, out of her reach, all the while keeping his eyes fixed on hers. He took a deep breath. 'But I'll make . . . an exception . . . for you!' he shouted, springing at her with his uninjured left hand curled into a fist.

'Glad you're not a sexist!' Randall replied, dodging easily out of the way of his clumsy attack. 'But I haven't got ages to debate the issue!' As he veered towards her, Randall allowed all the frustration and anger of the last two days to build up inside. Her arms were strong from years of free-climbing, and her calloused fingers, when bunched, were easily as hard as wood. She swooped and punched upwards, her uppercut connecting with the technician's jaw. Al seemed to lift momentarily, like a feather, before slamming with a resounding crash against the rim of the platform. He looked startled for a second before his eyes rolled back and then closed.

Randall bent over the slumped figure. He was out cold.

'Mistress, was such an act of violence necessary?' PV piped up.

'It was him or me. Even you can compute that!' Randall eased the scroll-screen from under Al's body and pushed it into a pocket.

'Your point has been noted. There is one further, small matter, mistress.'

'What now?' Randall hissed. Her knuckles were already throbbing.

'The coordinator also holds a sphere. I am sure you did not forget.'

'How could I, with you around?' she snapped, her eyes roving round the platform, looking for it. The bag containing the tenth sphere was pushed back into the shadows. She lifted it up. For something so small, it felt incredibly heavy. As she tucked the bag under her belt, she heard a faint humming coming from within. It made her uneasy to have part of the Quantum Trap so close to her own body. What if it was set off before she had time to destroy it? But according to Ark and Flo, they had time on their side. She hoped so. To think that this weapon of mass murder had been conceived by her own mother. If this was Fenestra's pride and joy, she wanted no part of it.

Time to fly! She vaulted elegantly over the edge, catching a horizontal branch with one hand, then swinging up and over through the air. *This is more like it!* she thought, letting go of the branch to tumble down in freefall towards another branch she had spotted some way below. She couldn't help thinking that buildings, even with all their sharp angles and unnatural overhangs, were boring compared with the smells and sounds of Arborium. This move she was making was ridiculously risky but as she plummeted down, skimming past the trunk beside her, she felt more alive than she had in a long time.

It was as close to flying as anyone could get, wind whipping past her cheeks, gravity sucking her down. But now was the moment to stop the descent. She had to time things perfectly in order to reach out and grab the branch she was aiming for, while slamming her feet like daggers into the trunk below. Her fingers were quick, curling into crevices of rough bark, instinctively finding the right angles. The jolt was like an electric shock through her bones as muscles strained and she clung tightly into the bark. She could almost sense PV's disapproval at her recklessness. So what! The adrenalin was coursing. It was a move that her fellow free-climbers back in Maw would have been in awe of.

However, self-congratulation would have to wait. She jumped the last three metres on to the wood-way and paused, taking deep breaths to calm herself. The moon above her pierced the leafless trees, revealing a criss-cross of branch-ways spread out between the trunks of the forest like an enormous circuit board. She knew her way round Maw, but this was a different country entirely. Now she needed her bearings. She pulled out the Raven feather that Ark had given her and grasped it tightly in her palm.

Hello? she thought. *Are you there?*

No answer. Panic rose. Arborium was huge, and she was stuck in the middle of nowhere, in the dark.

Please?

Then an answer came into her mind, faint and scratchy. *Don't worry. I'm here. Did you succeed?*

Randall felt ridiculously relieved. *Yes. Got the sphere and the screen, so I can use the screen to check off each of the other spheres as they're destroyed.*

Are you unhurt?

She smiled at Ark's concern travelling through the distance between them.

I'm fine. Just need to know where I'm going.

Follow the branch straight on to Five Ways. Take the third exit heading east and after a few metres you'll come to a cruck-pool.

What's that?

You'll see. The point is, it's full of water, so you can just drop it in and destroy the sphere. A Raven will be there to take you to your next point.

But what about the others? Randall didn't want the thought conversation to stop.

I am in contact with Mucum and Flo. They are each on their way to their allotted tasks. We must all make the most of the time we have. Your job now is to keep watch and keep count of the Holly Woodsmen's work in distracting and overpowering the other soldiers with the spheres. Good luck.

Ark? Ark? Are you there?

Silence.

She tried not to feel overwhelmed by everything else that was yet to unfold as she set off down the wood-way, the weight of the sphere bumping against her hips as she ran.

'You killed my mate Pollen!' cried the remaining soldier guarding the door of the palace. 'You won't get away with that!'

'Really?' Petronio answered with an icy calmness. 'I thought my intentions were very clear. Now, if you, or everyone else listening in behind the battlements, would like to join your *mate Pollen*, I'm more than happy to use this again.' He held up the case to make his point. 'And then you can meet up with him in a happy-ever-afterlife.'

This time, words were enough. The guard glanced up fearfully, nodded once, then stepped back. The great studded oak door swung open with a protesting screech. Petronio smiled as he stepped carefully around the hole in the steps that the unfortunate soldier had fallen through. A heavily-armed group escort waited for him in the grand entrance, huge boots and chain mail contrasting with the thick, plush rugs beneath their feet. As Petronio gained the top step and entered the vaulted hall, the escort split and peeled around him, forming a nervous circle, swords drawn, keeping their distance. None of the soldiers would meet his eye. No surprise there.

Petronio recalled the far-tales of his childhood, of sky-leopards still roaming the vast wilds up north. In the last century, they'd been hunted to extinction. His father had bought one of their brown-spotted antique pelts and had it nailed to the wall of his study. Petronio allowed himself to enjoy a feeling of kinship with the long-gone animal, feared throughout the wood-ways. It was said to have been faster even than a Raven, able to outrun a galloping stallion as it sped down the branch-lines to hunt any Dendran unfortunate enough not to be armed and ready. Now *he* was the predatory animal, and what was more, he was too clever and too fast for the primitive weapons carried by these men. And though they obviously thought they had him surrounded, the truth was entirely the other way around. With ten spheres in place, and him as the trigger, the city of Hellebore and all its suburbs were utterly outgunned.

The passageway was wood-panelled up to head height and then lined with ancient hauberks, maces, flails and war-axes from battles long gone. Petronio was unimpressed. At the end of the long passage, double doors swung open in front of him, and there was the inner courtyard. Under the full moon, the copper-clad fountain sprayed out gouts of silver from its forged branches. He looked round the outer battlements, remembering the Rootshooters lining the walkways, the rain of harpoons, the hand-made leaf-gliders that had caused such havoc.

And then he was walking right over it. A trapdoor, set in the floor with a set of rusting hinges. The moonlight revealed that the boards framing the trapdoor were bleached pale. Of course, the bloodstains would have been scrubbed away. An image flashed into his mind – the instant of calculating, crazed bravado as he had swung the honed sword into his own upper arm, the shock of intense pain as the blade hacked through skin and gnawed into bone. He remembered biting down so hard on his lip that it bled. But that small wound was nothing compared with the weeping stump where his arm had been. In the silence that had followed, and before Petronio had felt his knees give way, he had seen his fallen arm, seen the fingers twitching, even though all connections had been utterly severed.

Fenestra, and their sudden exit through that very trap-door, had provided salvation. The envoy had saved his life and he had repaid the favour by calling her a traitor to the Mawish cause. No matter. He searched for guilt, but could find none. It was results that counted, and here he was, Petronio Grasp, former apprentice surgeon, patronized by his father, now on his way to engineer the destruction of Quercus, High King of Arborium. It was a satisfying moment.

Five minutes later, he was deep in the heart of the palace. The carved, high-backed chair in front of him was empty, seats spread around an oval table, the gleaming surface formed from a single sheet of walnut.

'Wait here,' muttered one of the soldiers. 'The king will be with you just as soon as he can be summoned from the celebrations.'

Petronio looked round as the group of soldiers withdrew from the vast chamber. 'Make it snappy!' he called after them. 'I'm not known for patience.' Then he was alone. Though the gas lamps were lit, the space was filled with shadows, the curving ceiling covered in carved oak leaves vanishing into darkness.

He stood stiff-backed for a while, then flung himself into one of the chairs. Time suddenly felt like an old coat: hung on the back of a door, not going anywhere, suspended. He tapped his fingers against the case and closed his eyes. He breathed in the darkness around him until he *was* the dark, pure shadow and ready to embrace all.

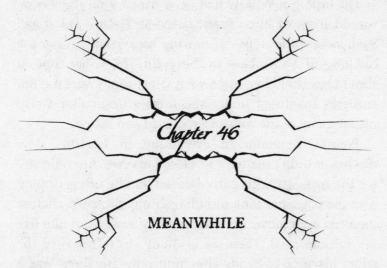

Chapter 46

MEANWHILE

At the northern edge of the last suburb in Hellebore, the giant soldier Pontius waited on a quiet woodway for the bells to strike. His boss, Sergeant Grain, had been very particular about the exact spot. The three-quarter chime had sounded a while ago. Strange how time slowed down in the early hours of the morning. Surely it must be five o'clock by now? But the distant Kirks stayed silent.

The sphere was held safely in his shoulder sack. On the first strike he would take it out. His body felt tense with waiting.

His thoughts strayed. It was times like this that he felt alone, and then he couldn't help remembering. It could have happened to anyone. Nature was cruel. All those years ago his life had changed for ever and he would never forget.

His little girl Willow had been dancing on the wood-way in front of him. 'Daddy! Daddy! Big Daddy – look at me!' Such sweet little steps . . . moving backwards . . . her toe catching in a tiny knot in the grain. The safety rope: it should have held her, that's what safety ropes were for. But cutbacks instituted under the former Councillor Grasp meant many of the ropes were frayed and rotten.

Pontius remembered everything in horrible slow motion. It didn't matter if he closed his eyes, he could still see the rope snap, his curly-headed bundle of joy tipping over the edge, her pink mouth opening into an 'o'. Before he could even move, she was spinning away from him like a sycamore seed. Then, as he hung, in terror over the edge, his useless hands clutching only air, there was a drawn-out heart-splitting scream. After that, nothing: she was too small for him even to hear her terrible landing a mile beneath.

Stay on the wood, it's as it should
Step off the tree, end of thee.

Buddy proverbs. Not a day, not an hour went by when he didn't think about her, blaming himself for not react-ing faster. That villain Councillor Grasp was dead now – good riddance, but his son seemed carved from the same stuff. Pontius was following orders, but he didn't have to like the boy with his clanking arm and greedy eyes.

'Hello!' A little voice pierced the shadows and a shape stepped forward. He rubbed his eyes. The figure stood only a little distance away, with the smile of an angel.

'Daddy! My daddy!' she squealed.

'Willow? Can it be?' he boomed. 'Have yer come back

from the Land of the Dead?'

'I'm lost!' said the girl, shining like treasure in the moonlight.

Pontius was overcome by her smallness, her glossy black curls, the tiny teddy-boar she clutched to her chest. Huge fat tears trickled down his cheeks. He dropped to his knees and reached out his brawny arms. 'Yer ain't lost! Yer come back!'

In a daze, he didn't even notice the thin lasso that floated over him. As the girl danced in front of him like a dream, he felt something tighten around his chest; he couldn't even move his arms. Perhaps his heart was finally breaking? Then another voice broke in.

'Yow must excuse us for this cruel trick, Mr Pontius! But 'tis necessary, else lots of Dendrans will be meetin' their maker. And that won't be very nice, will it? Warghhh!' The lasso held him and a strange, tall girl deftly wrapped the rope several more times around his arms, strapping them firmly to his side.

What was he thinking? He shook his great head. It was a trap! 'How . . . ? What . . . ? Nooooo!' As he tried to clear his head, he tensed his muscles, expecting the rope to snap like string. But it was Rootshooter wire: woven from iron filament, used for carrying the huge loads of ore from deep beneath the roots. The strongman of the Armouries strained with all his might. Nothing happened. The rope simply bit deeper. His upper body was trussed like a scaffield turkey.

Pontius's thoughts fought, along with his muscles. He was undefeated in battle, had never lost a fight. Nor would he now. He still had his legs. If he kicked backwards, the attacker behind him should be knocked to kingdom come.

But as he tensed to make the move, the little girl in front of him raised up her arms as if wanting to be cuddled. The simplicity of her gesture went deeper than any arrow, distracting him as the tall girl put one foot in front of him, then pushed hard against his back. Pontius hardly moved, his giant boots still planted on the path.

'But . . . I don't understand!' he cried.

'There! There!' said Shiv soothingly, imitating what her mother said to her when she grazed her knee. She reached up on tiptoe and touched the big man's hand.

'Rooty-Tooty, yow be a big 'un!' Flo grunted from behind him as she shoved again. 'Nnngmf!' It was like trying to move a mountain with a feather.

Pontius, the killing machine who was said to have once torn the head off a wild boar, swayed slightly, then gradually began to topple forward in slow motion.

'Willow!' he moaned in despair, as his body hit the wood-way with a thundering crash that echoed round the trees. 'My baby!' he wept as the cloth bag that carried the sphere was pulled from his belt and the remainder of the rope was wrapped swiftly around his legs.

Shiv stepped forward and looked at the fallen giant with solemn eyes. 'I'm vewwy, vewwy sowwy, mister. Didn't mean to hurt you.' She leant over and kissed his forehead gently. 'There! Kiss it better.'

'Come, Shiv,' said Flo. 'Some battles don't feel no better for being won. But yow have played your part well.

Wargghh!' Flo took out the sphere, her long fingers testing the strange weight. She looked around, quickly picking out a deep rut in the wood-way, filled with brackish water.

'Would yow like a game of marbles, little Shiv?'

'Yes please!'

'Then take this 'orrible thing and roll it in that there puddle for all you're worth!'

Shiv struggled to lift the sphere. 'Yuck. It's making a funny noise that hurts my tummy!'

'Not for long, girl. Yow be the one for the job!'

Shiv was only too keen to be rid of it. A quick push and it rolled straight into the muddy rut. Flo stared in anticipation, hoping this really was the weapon's only weakness. As it touched the water, sparks flew from the surface.

'Fireworks!' Shiv laughed. There was a soft tinkling sound, like the chimes of a far-off bell, then a loud whoosh-bang and the sphere shattered.

'Yas! Yow did it, Shiv! How glorious that the natural rain can destroy such an evil weapon. Come. Let us move on.'

'My dear, dear man, will you help an old blind woman who has lost her way?'

The soldier, positioned off a high byway to the east of Hellebore, stared at the wrinkled figure shuffling out of the shadows, using her staff as a crutch. Under the bright moonlight, he could see her two blank eyes, white orbiting balls that did not see the dawning of each day.

'It's very late to be out, reverend.'

'For you, maybe. But for us Kirk-goers, it would not do to miss the five o'clock Solstice Mass. There are so many to pray for. However, although I counted the steps to each crossroads, I must have taken a wrong turning.'

The soldier was hesitant. Why hadn't the bells struck yet? They might do so any second now. And what was this old biddy doing here? 'Ain't no Kirks round here! You're in the wrong part of town.'

'No, I don't think I am.' She paused within a few feet of the Dendran soldier.

'You what?'

'This is exactly where I am supposed to be. Guided by Diana, and her friends of course. In fact, her grandson was most helpful.'

'Er. Right you are, then. Whatever yer say.' The woman was obviously conkers; totally senile.

'It's not what we say in life, but what we do, that counts.'

The soldier was already looking away, trying to work out the fastest means of getting rid of the feeble crone, so he didn't see what was coming. The elm staff that had supported Warden Goodwoody for so many years now fulfilled a rather different role; it scythed through the air, treating the soldier's legs as no more than heads of wheat to be harvested.

Crack! Crack!

The soldier looked down in surprise, not even register-ing pain at first. 'What the . . . ?' Surely knees were supposed to stick out of the front of your legs, but his seemed to be bending the wrong way. As nerve endings started to shriek he dropped to the ground like a falling acorn and writhed there.

'So very, very sorry, my dear – Diana forgive me, but the Goddess does move in mysterious ways.' As the soldier drifted into unconsciousness, the warden knelt to retrieve her trusty staff and to fumble for the sack containing a hard, round shape. She limped off into the night, feeling guilt for the pain inflicted. However, there would be time for penance later. First, to find water.

Some way off she heard an out-of-tune song being whistled and footsteps lurching towards her. A Solstice reveller and if she was not mistaken, was that the sound of a beer tankard sloshing? She moved towards the sound.

'Good evening. I do believe you have brought blessings on Arborium!'

'Sorrrrry? You whaaaat?' the Dendran slurred.

'Oh, don't be sorry, be glad!' Guided by instinct, the warden plucked the sphere from the bag and dunked it straight into the tankard.

Splinters and glass erupted as the tankard exploded, followed by a moan of dismay.

'You've ruined me drink, reverend!'

'And you've helped to save the country. Diana will reward you!'

Sergeant Grain was not used to feeling nervous. He didn't like it. Here he was skulking in the ruins of a long abandoned shack at the border of the western suburbs, and for what? Time was creeping so slowly since the clocks had chimed for a quarter to five. The waiting was making him irritable.

Commander Flint had been adamant that they shouldn't put on the strange goggle things and focus on the damn sphere until the clock struck five. The whole thing didn't make sense anyway. A weapon that worked just by looking at it? In Arborium, the only real danger Dendrans faced apart from falling over the edge was getting scratched by a stray blackthorn, or sharp twig. If there was blood, the scent might quickly draw down a hunter Raven. Then Diana help you! But that was how it was. This techno-stuff from Maw was another ball game entirely. He just hoped it would function. He was looking forward to a more comfortable life.

The moon streamed in through gaps in the boarded walls and Grain's lantern flickered. The sack containing the sphere was sitting next to him on a table now drowned in ivy. Old pictures still nailed to the wall were almost completely shrouded with spiders' webs. Weird how nature took over once Dendrans moved out. He tried not to shiver with the cold.

'Mornin' mate. What time d'yer reckon it is?'

Grain swivelled round. How had an overgrown lump of a boy crept up on him like that? He quickly made out the uniform of brown sheepskin waist-cote and stained britches. 'What you doin' 'ere, sewer rat?' he snarled, reaching for the hilt peeking out from his scabbard. 'Unless you wanna be introduced to my sword, I suggest you get back to whatever emergency pipe blockage you're supposed to be dealin' with, eh?

'Yeah. Yer right. It is a problem when yer country 'appens to be full of treacherous squit. But I've been told the blockage is right where you're standin', like, an' I need to get to it.'

'What you wittering on about? There's not even any plumbing in 'ere! Bog off right now before I turn you into a kebab!' Grain sneered.

'Nah! Honest. I jus' need to lift them floorboards under yer feet to get to it.' And the boy dropped to his knees, pulled out something that looked like a plunger and crawled towards Grain's boots.

'What do think you're doin'? I've already told you . . . Eeee!' Grain's voice rose sharply and suddenly like a skylark as the boy's hand shot out and up and grabbed tightly in a vice-like grip.

'I shall be, as yer so politely suggested, *boggin'* off when I've got that there ball yer got hidden in the sack.'

'What d'you know about them balls?' the sergeant squeaked, fumbling ineffectually to try to pull out his sword.

'Oh, I know plenty about balls, 'specially the fact that I've got 'em and you ain't!' said the boy. 'And let me tell yer, in my line of work, I'm well used to dealing with rusty nuts. Generally I just 'ave ter *break* 'em when they won't budge.' He squeezed even harder. 'Get me meanin'? Now, be a good sergeant and move yer hand away from that there sword.'

'Mmmmphh!' the sergeant grunted. The pain was sharper than a whole hornets' nest of stings. He slowly raised his hands away from the hilt of his sword, then tried to make a sudden lunge for the stiletto blade tucked under his armpit. But the boy was faster, bringing the plunger swiftly upwards in his other hand and cracking its cast-iron handle straight over Grain's knuckles.

'Naughty! Naughty! Now, unless yer want me to turn yer bits into mashed potato, do as I say!'

Grain's scarred face had turned a dark purple colour. He nodded.

'Good. Now, I'd love ter continue our little chat, but there's a country to save an' all that. Sweet dreams, hard man!' With that, in one swooping movement, Mucum dropped his hand, simultaneously rising up and catapulting his head forward so that it cracked against the sergeant's forehead with a resounding *thwack*. Luckily for Mucum, his own skull was as thick as a forest full of planks. Unluckily for the never-before-defeated Sergeant Grain, a perfectly-aimed head-butt wasn't a weapon he'd been expecting. He fell backwards to the floor, knocked for sticks, out cold.

Mucum rubbed his head with one hand and grabbed the sack with the other. He did wonder on his way out whether he ought to just pick up the traitor and drop him over the edge. But there was no time. He had to find somewhere to get rid of the sphere, and all the talk of being a sewage worker had given him an idea. A public outhouse would be just the job – in fact he remembered passing one just a few tracks away. He sprinted off.

Yes, there! On his left, a tiny wooden cubicle jutted out from the wood-way. Mucum paused to get his breath, then pulled on the door.

'Busy in here!' a thin, reedy voice sang out.

Mucum wrinkled his nose. It was pretty obvious how

busy. He banged on the door. 'Sorry, but I gotta drop one, mate!'

'Wait your turn.'

'No can do!' Mucum put the bag down and grasped the door with both hands. As he strained, the hinges squealed like scaffield pigs.

'What you doin'?'

'My bit for king and country!' Mucum replied as the hinges surrendered and the door was chucked aside to reveal a skinny twig of a treenager with his britches around his ankles.

'So sorry 'bout this!' Mucum panted as he pulled the boy from the seat and threw him bodily on to the wood-way.

There was a plop, then a flush followed by a sudden hiss and something like a small explosion. As the unfortunate boy sat up in a daze on the wood-way with only a knee-length shirt to cover his dignity, he thought he saw the cubicle light up from below. 'Whoa . . . !' he said in awe. 'Was that me or you?'

Mucum wiped his hands down his britches. 'Neither, mate. Think yer a few apples short of an orchard. That was a proper Maw-made stinker! Now, if you know what's good fer yer, go 'ome!'

The boy yanked up his britches and scuttled off, and Mucum pulled his Raven's feather carefully from his shirt. *Done it. Going to catch hold of a Raven to go and find Flo and Shiv. Will get Shiv to Goodwoody for safety, then join Randall. Hope the Woodsmen do their thing as planned.*

*

The soldier sitting on a stout log watched yet another

group of Dendrans in the far distance weaving their way cheerfully along the track. They had been singing the Solstice song at full volume. Now they were laughing and shouting and the words drifted back to him. It seemed that they too were waiting for the chimes of five o'clock to mark the Solstice celebration. When the stick would those bells ring out? He felt almost sorry for the little group of friends. They would be waking up much, much later to a very changed place.

The soldier groaned as he saw yet more figures, this time heading towards him. What were they doing? They should be moving in the opposite direction. He didn't want anyone around him when he had to do the weird stuff with the eyeglass things and the sphere. Even worse, what with their long, black wool cloaks, it looked like these two were Woodsmen. He stared fixedly at the branch-way beneath his boots. *Please let them pass straight by. Please don't let them try to talk to me!*

'Greetings, my son!'

'Greetings, Alder Woodsmen.' The words rose unbidden to the soldier's lips. No-one could ignore the Holly Woodsmen. It was ingrained in him to show respect.

'You look lonely, my son. Why not come with us? Join us in celebration!'

'Er. No thanks all the same, Alder Woodsmen. I'm just gonna sit right here for a while, if it's all the same to you. Er. Merry Solstice and all.' The soldier looked down once again. *Go away. Go away now!*

'But my son. We cannot let you celebrate Solstice by yourself. Indeed we cannot. We must . . .'

'Yes, you can!' wailed the soldier, glancing up. But the Holly Woodsmen seemed to be looking right past him, straight over his shoulder.

'We must envelop you!'

'You wha—!' Everything went suddenly and completely dark and the soldier could taste and smell wool. He struggled, but he appeared to be surrounded by great, draping folds of night, pulling tightly around him. He could hear muffled words.

'I said: we must *envelop* you. And we have, in my good friend's cloak! Come along chaps, let's get that rope wrapped round a little tighter. Who's good at knots? Gregory, I'll hold it, you tie.'

The soldier wriggled and twisted and squirmed, but succeeded only in resembling a large slug with stomach ache. He had to listen helplessly.

'Now then, where's the bottle of holly water? Ah, thank you. And that's the ball? Doesn't look much of a weapon, does it? Here we go. Stand back.'

Sssssss. Splerck. Splop! Fzzzzzzz. Bang!

'Diana preserve us! Is anyone hurt? Good. Didn't expect that! Still, it all went a lot easier than it might have done. Let us hope our brothers have fared as well. But what in the woods are we going to do with him?'

Safely hidden among the evergreen leaves of a large branch high above the groaning, cloak-wrapped soldier below her, Randall smiled. It was such a ridiculously easy trick that those Woodsmen had pulled – distracting the soldier from in front while a third Woodsman crept up behind him – and yet it had worked. Ark had been right:

the soldiers entrusted with the spheres were only on their guard against anyone who might look like they posed a threat. So, when Ark and the others had realized that they wouldn't be able to get to the top king guy in time for him to mobilize his own forces, Ark, Flo and Warden Goodwoody had hit upon another way.

The warden had gone straight to the Holly Woodsmen, not only to arrange for the Kirk bells to be delayed in their ringing of five o' clock, but also to gather help in destroying the spheres. To attack as quickly as possible they would use the best resources they had, namely anyone who seemed to pose no threat: teenagers, a small child, a blind warden and Holly Woodsmen!

Randall had wondered at the logic of this, but now she had seen for herself how such a simple idea worked. The element of surprise was brilliant; the use of the Woodsmen inspired. It seemed that these Dendrans just couldn't help but show respect to the guys in the long cloaks.

'Mistress. The scroll-screen is registering the disappearance of the sphere below our current position. That is therefore the eighth of the weapons to have been removed from its allotted place and destroyed.'

Randall looked at the screen unrolled in her lap and saw that PV was right. The light for number eight had gone out. *Just two more left*, she thought, her stomach contracting. Then, as she stared at the screen, willing it to change, one more light flickered and faded.

'Mistress . . .'

'Yes! I can see for myself!' Randall pulled out her feather with trembling fingers. *Nine down. One still to go. So* little time. *Will go to last spot to check what's happening.* She tucked the feather and scroll-screen away and scuttled straight down the trunk, landing neatly on the back of the Raven waiting silently beneath.

As the mighty bird took off, Randall could feel the warmth of its flesh pulsating through its feathers. Ark had told her a little about the Ravens on the journey back from the strange Ravenwood to Arborium. He had strongly impressed on her that not all Ravens were like the ones carrying them; that these ones were Corwenna's own, close consorts and were doing Corwenna's bidding in allowing themselves to be ridden like flying horses. Randall had learned that for anyone except Corwenna, Ark and his companions, all other Ravens were to be utterly feared. She had shuddered to hear what the Dendrans meant by a 'sky burial'. But even so, if one of her cyber-buds back in Maw had told her that she'd be swooping through the sky on a gigantic winged monster in the mythical country of Arborium, straight towards the centre of the action, Randall would have asked where she could get hold of that particular virtual vid-game. It was unreal.

She shifted slightly to bring her face closer to her wristband. 'PV, how much more time is there?'

'Five minutes and fifty-two seconds, mistress.'

'Oh, shards!' Flo's plan for 'stretching' time had meant getting each of the Kirk clocks turned back by fifteen crucial minutes to delay the five o' clock tolling of the bells: the signal for detonating the Quantum Trap. They were so close to having eliminated all the spheres. Had something gone wrong with the last one?

'The allotted place is right below us, mistress.'

Randall peered down, scanning the wood-way as the Raven went into a steep dive. The wind made her eyes stream, but she thought she could see two long, dark shapes below. Even as they landed, she was sliding down the Raven's sleek feathers and forward-rolling into some scrubby growth to take a closer look.

The wood-way was quiet and deserted, except for two inky shadows spilt like black milk. What were they? Randall gasped as she realised that each shape was the form of a cloaked Holly Woodsman, lying unmoving several metres apart.

No sign of a soldier. No sign of a sphere. Just silence.

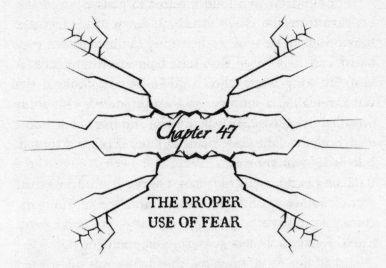

Chapter 47

THE PROPER
USE OF FEAR

'**Y**our majesty. Good morning. You took your time!'
Petronio jumped up and stood with his feet firmly
planted apart as the king finally made his entrance –
alone, as instructed. It was court etiquette to bow before
him, so Petronio stood deliberately tall, with his spine
rigidly straight. He stared the king directly in the eye:
another act of insolence. 'I rather feared we might miss
the opportunity to have a little chat, before . . . well, let's
just say *beforehand*. Do sit down.' Petronio waved his hand
airily towards a huge, intricately carved chair.

'How dare you presume to tell me what to do in my
own palace!' thundered King Quercus. 'So it is you. We
thought you had died, falling from the scene of the battle.
Well, no matter. I am here with you now only to ensure no
further ugly deaths such as that perpetrated on the steps
outside. Speak now – but speak with the proper respect!'

Petronio drew in a loud breath and paused, sweeping his gaze from the king's forehead, down to his feet and back up again. He took in the strong build, trimmed grey beard and hazel eyes that stared unwaveringly back at him. The king wore a green gown that lay loose at the waist, revealing a shoulder sash embroidered with gold-threaded oak leaves. His silk doublet and fine suede boots were both dyed the same shade of blue, a colour that none but the king might wear.

'Thing is, Quercus old man, Quirky – oh, I like that! You *are* rather quaint and quirky, aren't you! Thing is, Quirky, I can speak to you any way I like, and you have to listen.' Petronio smiled, savouring the moment.

'I shall not waste time, *boy*. Your father was my trusted friend for decades until the lure of gold turned him into a snake in the scaffield grass. Like father, like son. The cruel display outside of the un-*woodly* weapon you carry was murder, pure and simple. The act of a coward! But it seems to have served your purpose. You have my attention. Say what you have come to say.'

'Would a coward walk up the front steps of your palace and risk the wrath of your best soldiers?' Petronio bridled. 'Don't insult my intelligence! By the way,' he looked around the room, 'do you happen to know what the time is? No? Never mind. We're surely getting nearer to the Solstice chimes by now.'

'We are. And I should be outdoors with all my loyal subjects who have flocked to Hellebore for the celebrations.'

'Ah well,' Petronio shrugged, 'the crowds will just have

to do without your presence. So, to the matter in hand. Naturally, you have been informed of the cleverness of this little case I hold. I do so love the idea of unleashing mayhem at the flick of a switch. It's so delightfully modern. But of course, though I now represent Maw, I have pointed out to them that it would not be in the Empire's interests to be responsible for a massacre. Instead, we would much prefer your full and absolute surrender. In return for accepting *total* dominion, you and your subjects will be allowed to live, after a fashion. All we wish for is to harvest significant quantities of wood to inject new life into the economy. At least, ooh, maybe a third of the population of Dendrans might even be allowed to stay in their homes, though naturally the palace would be taken over for administrative purposes.'

'Hmm. A fine speech,' King Quercus said.

'I thought so too! So, how do you respond?'

Randall's heart hammered. Were the Woodsmen dead? What had happened to the soldier? More importantly, where was the last sphere?

'PV, can you detect anything?'

'I am working on it, mistress. I believe I detect circuitry that might indicate the presence of the sphere somewhere within a thirty-metre radius. However, the data I am collecting is unclear. I am not able to lock on to it.'

'What shall I do?' Randall once more withdrew the feather and gripped it tightly as she crept forwards cautiously from her hiding place. *Help! No sign of last sphere. But PV thinks it could be nearby.* She crouched over the first

Woodsman lying horribly still and brought her hand up under his nose. There was the faintest whisper of warm air. *Two Woodsmen.* She glanced over to the second one and saw a slight rising and falling of his chest. *Both unconscious. Can't tell what happened.*

A reply came into her mind almost immediately. *HAVE to find that sphere. Crucial. Even if only one left, it will still activate and kill all in its own range. The city is full. Could be thousands. And . . . and YOU are in range too. Find it . . . or get out fast. I don't want you to . . .* The voice in her head came to an abrupt halt.

I don't want to . . . die . . . either. I'll look for it. PV will tell me the last moment I have to leave on the Raven if . . . Randall found that she too couldn't finish the thought of not succeeding. All the while her eyes were darting around, seeking for any clue as to where to begin looking. She could hear sounds from much further off – a warm hum of gathered crowds of Dendrans – yet around her was an eerie stagnation, as if the air itself was holding its breath. She shook herself, shying away from the thought of held breath. How long would she last with all the oxygen sucked out in a vacuum around her?

Something broke the stillness. She jumped up in shock, aware of bushes rustling at the side of the wood-way. 'Who's there?' she called out in a shrill voice. No answer.

And then, incredibly, something rolled towards her; something round that shone in the moonlight, formed from polished glass. She stared at it, not believing what she was seeing, until it came to rest against the leg of one of the Woodsmen. *Unbelievable! Some animal must have disturbed it from where it had been dropped.* Keeping her gaze firmly fixed on the sphere, she knelt by the Woods-man and lifted a fold of his cloak to one side. A bag was clipped to his leather belt. She unhooked it and drew out a bottle formed from rough, thick, green glass. The liquid that they called 'holly water' sloshed inside it as she set it down on the wood-way next to her. As she reached forward for the sphere, she was smiling. The feather in her hand felt light as she sent the thought: *I have it! I have water too. The job is done!*

Several things happened at once. PV squawked, 'Mistress! Mistress! I detect . . .' but Randall didn't hear the next bit for the loud whooshing sound that whined past her, ending in a terrible cry and an explosion of feathers. The Raven, her Raven that had carried her here, raised its wings as though to take flight, but instead, staggered and then fell backwards over the edge of the wood-way. It plummeted and crashed through the branches below. Shocked, Randall dropped the feather. She fumbled, trying to catch it, but it spun away from her and instead, her hand closed around the neck of the bottle. Then suddenly, her whole body jerked violently backwards and her feet left the floor.

She gasped and struggled, making out a pair of arms clamped firmly around her waist. Her arms flailed, but she was held tight and her breath was being slowly crushed out of her. She flung back her head to scream and saw, standing directly in front of her, someone she hadn't expected to see again. He was holding a small grey box in one hand and a g-gun in the other, and his teeth were bared in an unpleasant grin.

'You, traitor, broke my wrist and stole something from me!'

'You! How . . . ?'

'Yep. Me. Good old Al, with his trusty back-up. Now, I would introduce you to Commander Flint here who has you in his grip, but he doesn't say much these days, unless I want him to. Dear oh dear.' He looked from Randall to the sphere and back to her. 'I assume this is what you came looking for? Thought you might! I guessed you'd be using my scroll-screen to track them all. So hey, what did clever Al do? He summoned his own transport – the flypod, to drop him off here along with the good commander, so we could get rid of any *interference*,' he swept his gaze meaningfully over the Holly Woodsmen, 'and then wait for you to turn up so we could give you a little welcoming party. Surprise!'

Randall had gone limp. She was focusing on breathing as shallowly as possible and on gathering her strength. She gritted her teeth and stared up at Al.

'Of course, sadly your own feathered transport is now dead. Oops!' Al waved his g-gun in the air. 'And, not so sadly, you will be too. Dead, that is. Soon!' Al held the grey box between his teeth and felt in his pocket, pulling out a set of goggles. He slipped them on over his forehead so they sat just above his eyes. Then he fished around in another pocket, found a small metal cylinder with tubing at the top and put it down by his feet. 'Dual-action oxygen flask, in case you're wondering. Works in any dimension, down here and,' his eyes flicked up towards the moon, 'up there. Because, with this here sphere so nice and close to the palace, it's plenty enough to do some big damage, and I want to be breathing when it's all over. So, we're all set, eh? Ooh, but what's that?' He had caught sight of a corner of the scroll-screen poking out from Randall's sleeve. 'I'll have that back, missy!' He lunged towards her.

Mucum and Flo were sailing through the treetops, clinging tightly to the feathers of Hedd, son of Hedd on their way to the palace. The moon was so bright it was almost as though the wood-ways beneath were lit up by weak lantern-light. The wind rushed past their ears, but even so, they still heard a strange, faint sound rise from below and saw a brief flash of silvery light, followed by a terrible screech.

As the cry rang upwards, Hedd stiffened as if stung by the echo and pulled his wings instantly into a dive. Before Mucum and Flo knew what was happening, Hedd had swung in a tight circle and landed. Mucum was sitting in front. He raised his head to see what Hedd's unblinking eyes were staring at, and had to stop himself from swearing out loud.

He turned to Flo with his finger pressed against his lips and motioned for them to slide down noiselessly. They scuttled forwards and then crouched behind a pile of cut logs to the side of the wood-way.

They peered out and then looked back at each other helplessly. They saw a man in Maw-made clothing holding a g-gun in one hand and a grey oblong in the other. They saw Randall held from behind by some brute who looked oddly familiar. She was dangling in his arms like a puppet with loose strings. They watched as the Maw-dressed man stepped towards her and leant forward. At the same moment, rag-doll Randall jerked into life and brought something in her hand sharply down towards the back of his head, but he flinched to one side and the object shattered over his shoulder, spraying water over his fancy jacket. Enraged, he lunged forward just as Randall brought her fist up, still gripping the remains of the bottle. He reeled backwards, clutching at his face.

'You little witch!'

Randall was still struggling, bringing the broken glass down again and again on to the arms holding her. But then she stopped suddenly and went limp, the bottle neck sliding from her grasp.

The man had picked up the grey oblong from where he had dropped it and was pointing it towards her and pressing something on it. Then he slid it into a pocket and used his sleeve to dab at the blood welling from the gash in his cheek. 'Nice try, you evil little traitor. But as you see, it will take more than a few cuts to make Commander Flint drop you. Now,' the man was panting hard, 'where were we? Ah, yes.' He bent to pick up the sphere and pushed the goggles down over his eyes. 'Any moment now, I'm sure. The only question is, what will kill you first? The commander here squeezing the life out of you – as I've just programmed him to do – or the Quantum Trap? Shall we see?'

In the palace, Ark stood waiting in the deep shadows of an arch, breathing quietly. Randall had found the last sphere.

She would have destroyed it by now. Arborium was safe for the moment. So why did he feel so uneasy? Perhaps it was because he was on the verge of facing his enemy. He must just bide his time until the moment came: the moment when Petronio saw that the trap had failed. He lifted his hand, the thumb pointing straight up where Quercus would see it.

The king paused, straightening his robe. He glanced towards the shadowed archway, nodded slightly, then drew himself to his full height. 'How do I respond, Petronio Grasp? Let me tell you! Arborium will never be surrendered. You might try to kill me now, as you killed my guard Pollen, but my life is only a symbol. Even as we speak, reinforcements are galloping towards the palace. So, unless you have an army to back you up, retribution shall be swift! There will be NO surrender to Maw.'

Petronio merely smiled, having expected no less from the king. The weight of the black case in his hand was comforting. Oh, he was going to enjoy this so very much. 'Well then, Quirky. You've made your decision. Shall we see what happens next?'

Mucum dug his knuckles into his eyes trying to think. If they rushed the guy with the gun, he'd just shoot them. He felt his elbow being nudged and opened his eyes. Flo was pointing a long, shaking finger towards the face of the man.

'Why, 'e is a-bleedin'!' she whispered. 'An' so is t'other one what has hold of Randall.'

'So? They're not going ter bleed to death any time soon!'

'No. But Oi 'ave an idea.' Flo turned and crawled back to where Hedd was waiting. She stood up looking into the Raven's unblinking eyes. 'Hedd, son of Hedd. Moightiest of birds,' she whispered, 'Oi smell blood! Can yowr bird brethren smell it too? Can yow call 'em here swift-loike? Swifter than they would get 'ere otherwise?'

Hedd blinked once then closed his eyes.

Flo crept slowly back to Mucum, holding her Raven feather in one hand, sending the thought to Ark. *Help! Randall captured. Maw man has last sphere, not destroyed. Don't know how long ... Oh no!*

A bell had sounded. One chime.

The technician smiled, laid down the g-gun and picked up the oxygen flask. He trained the goggles on the sphere in his hand and brought the mask on the end of the oxygen tube towards his mouth. Black shadows fell around him. He looked up in surprise. 'Wha—!'

Two Ravens swooped like cut-out pieces of night. One dug its talons into the shoulders of the commander, whose arms sprang apart like spring-loaded doors. Randall slid to the ground as her captor was lifted straight up. The other Raven plucked up the technician like a fish on a hook. As they rose into the air, Al's scream ripped through the night and he dropped the sphere.

Two chimes.

Mucum hurled himself forwards, his tree-trunk legs moving in a blur. He reached up. *Thwack!* He caught the sphere as it fell. He had it! But what to do? It had already been activated and primed! And there was no water anywhere. Only three chimes to go.

'Ah! Finally!' Petronio tilted his head to one side. 'I do believe the bells are beginning to ring out the Solstice hour. Shame you can't stick around to see in the rest of the morning!' He clicked open the case and withdrew an oxygen flask. He tapped his earpiece. Where was that stupid technician?

Two chimes.

Never mind. The spheres would be in place. Petronio fitted the glass mask of the oxygen flask over his nose and mouth and looked down into the case, angling the contact lenses. He rested his finger on the button.

He was so busy staring down he didn't see the dark-haired, slight figure of Ark slide from the shadows, mouth open in horror, hands reaching towards the king.

Mucum felt that everything had slowed around him, as through the very air had turned to liquid. If only it had! He tried to think. Spitting? Would that work? But his mouth was dry. No. *Think, Mucum, think. Think fast.* What was he first and foremost? A plumber's boy. What did he have? *Natural resources.*

Three chimes.

He yelled to Flo, 'Turn yer back, girl!' Then he put the sphere down on the ground in front of him.

Flo had her Raven feather gripped tightly. She had sent a gabble of wild thoughts to Ark: *Help us! No! Sphere activated. Too late!*

Bless the lovely lad she loved – Mucum didn't want her to watch him holding the sphere that would destroy him and her and Randall and all those in its range. And they were so close to the palace . . . She turned slowly and dropped to her knees, hoping it would be over quickly.

She thought of her home deep under the earth, of the magical Xylem waterways with their tidal rising; of the underground streams. She could almost hear their soft rush of water.

Four chimes.

No, wait – she really could hear a stream. Or was it more like the hissing of steam? It must be the sphere beginning to work. She half rose, wanting to run to Mucum, wanting to fling her arms around him.

BANG! She had heard a sound like that before, with Shiv.

Five chimes.

There was a thud. Flo turned and saw Mucum lying on the floor.

'Argh! Cricked me buddy neck jumpin' out the way!'

'What? How did you . . . ?' Flo felt her throat; she was still breathing. She looked at Mucum and broke into a broad grin. 'Yow never? No! Yow did!'

'Yep!' Mucum looked a little sheepish. 'I did. *Natural resources*. Once a plumber's lad, always a plumber's lad! It's a good job I needed to *go!*'

Three chimes.

Petronio tried to imagine the whole city devoid of Dendran life.

Four chimes.

The thought was exhilarating.

Five chimes.

'At last!' He stared down at the main control unit. He had enjoyed testing out the miniature version earlier, but now it was the big time and he was one of the big boys with their big toys.

Petronio pressed the button.

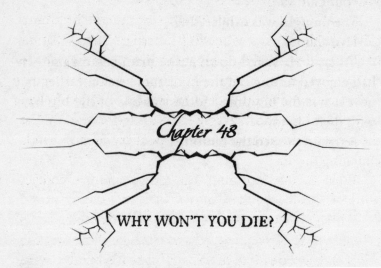

Chapter 48

WHY WON'T YOU DIE?

Petronio pressed the button, relishing the sense that he was no longer a bit-player, following Fenestra like a dog on a leash. If only she could see him now, enacting the will of the Empire. He breathed in the oxygen from the dual-action flask. Truly, it was his triumph and his alone.

All those Dendrans from far and wide across the woods, all packed conveniently into their capital city. They would never know what had happened: nostrils flaring, lips shooting open as lungs tried to fill with air that wasn't there. Petronio wondered if those other instant copies of Dendrans, floating up in space would look down in the brief moments between life and death. Would their lives flash before them as their throats constricted and their eyes bulged?

He looked up. He wanted to give his full attention to

watching the king's face as he died.

Who the holly? Petronio nearly spat into the breathing tube. Was this a ghost come to haunt him? Wasn't that bit of sewage dead already – blown to tiny pieces under the sea?

In fact, come to think of it, the vision of Malikum had every look of a ghost: eyes wide with terror – staring at the king, mouth rounded in an eternal cry of 'no', hands clutching the air.

'What is it, Arktorious?' The king made eye contact with Ark, his brow furrowing.

'It hasn't been . . . terrible . . . the very last one . . .'

And yet, as Petronio gazed on, a change came over the sewer boy's expression. It was almost as if someone were leaning over his shoulder, whispering something pleasing in his ear. A relaxing of the shoulders, a softening of the mouth, hands dropping to his sides, a slight shake of the head and then . . . a smile? A smile! Well, he'd soon have that wiped off his face! Petronio kept his finger pressing hard on the button. *Come on. Start working.*

Seeing Ark smile, the king also relaxed. They both turned to look at Petronio. The king's stare was unwavering. He began drumming his fingers very slowly on the arm of his chair, and after a few seconds he took a loud breath. 'It appears, Master Grasp, that we are still breathing.'

Petronio didn't panic. He assumed there was a slight delay in the sound of the bells reaching out to the further suburbs of Hellebore. Even now, he was sure that the sergeant and his men were training their eyes on the spheres. Once all the connections were made, the king would not be smirking but suffocating. But then Petronio felt the first stirrings of unease. How did Quercus seem to know exactly what was supposed to be happening?

He lifted his hand momentarily, then jabbed his finger down hard on the button again.

'Nothing!' said a voice. 'Nothing comes of nothing. Nothing returns to nothing. In the end, all your greed is but ash – and trust me, the winds are coming and they shall blow you away!'

Petronio's jaw tightened and a muscle in his cheek twitched.

'Each time we meet,' said Ark, stepping forward until he stood between Petronio and the king, 'the distaste rises in my mouth like bile.'

'You!' Petronio exploded, the oxygen mask flying from his face, his mouth gaping like a knot-hole. 'Why aren't you . . . ?'

'Dead? Despite your continuing best efforts and those of your puppet-masters in Maw, I am still, as you see, very much alive.'

'But how could you possibly have survived the explosion?'

'Good question,' said Ark, fingering the phial around his neck. 'Perhaps the trees still have work for me to do. Annoying for you how I appear to keep dying and rising again. I would say welcome, as you have been expected. But the truth is, you and your kind will never be welcome!' Ark felt the green force rising within him, writhing out from the very spot on his body where he'd been wounded in the explosion, when the liquid from the phial had healed him. Now that strength thrummed through his fingers, giving each word an edge sharper than any blade.

'Expected? What are you talking about?' Petronio jabbed at the button again and again, waiting for this in-fir-nal boy before him to drop to his knees, clutching his chest.

'That's what I worked out about you, Petronio Grasp. Always one step ahead. For once, though, your pride has blinded you. Did you think we would give up without a fight? Hand over the woods and let you massacre everyone within Hellebore? I was able to arrive just before you and inform the king of your plan. I remember you as a pompous, preening bully. How did you graduate from that to mass-murder? Is that what "civilization" has taught you? Do keep pressing away. The sergeant and his men have been dealt with, the clueprint to the weapon destroyed. The Quantum Trap is useless. All that is left is a self-serving traitor, surrounded, inside a heavily-guarded palace!'

The king now held up his hand for silence. He could see that Arktorious was on the verge of eruption and he had no desire for yet more blood to be spilt in court. 'Petronio Grasp,' he said, 'you offered us surrender and in exchange, you promised to let the Dendrans live. It was an earth-sodden lie. But we do not adhere to the same standards. Lay down that black case, and I give my word on the Wood Book that you shall not be executed, though you will be made to face justice.'

'Oh, how very noble of you!' Petronio sneered, beginning to take in everything he had just heard. 'Throw me in a dank, planked-out prison for the rest of my life? No thank you!' He paused, thinking, remembering all the instructions he had been given back in Maw, and a sly gleam entered his eye.

'Malikum was right, I am always one step ahead. He and his jumped-up helpers might have thwarted most of my plans, but it seems you've all forgotten the *case in hand!*' His hand moved from the button to slide along the handle. 'I've already killed *one* of your soldiers, remember? And the back-up I hold in my fist has enough power for – ooh, let me think – just about everyone within two hundred yards of this palace chamber to drown for lack of oxygen. So, Malikum!' Petronio flicked his eyes disdainfully back to Ark. 'I'm bored of our conversation. It will be a pleasure to finally see you die properly, here, in front of me. No fancy tricks, no lucky escapes, no mythical Diana to come to your rescue.'

Confidence replaced the earlier momentary panic, as Petronio steadied himself to focus the contact lenses and hit the secondary button. His thoughts flew. So the main part of the weapon was disabled? Time to make other plans instead. Wipe out most of the palace and then he could slip away. And without its king or the meddlesome Malikum, Arborium would be in chaos, a fruit ripe for the plucking.

Ark's eyes flashed with green fury. Why hadn't he anticipated this? Holding back the four Kirk clocks had been inspired. They'd dealt with all the spheres on the circumference of Hellebore. But Flo's trick of stretching out time wasn't enough. This bully-boy at the centre still had a last poisonous splinter in the very middle of the king's residence.

Perhaps it was meant to be? Ark thought of his vision: the lake laced with mist, the far falls, his twin sister sailing towards him. If that was the way to the Land of the Dead, was he ready? And yet, the green fuse inside him was lit and fizzing, forcing his body to act even as his mind dreamed of drifting away.

The knife that Corwenna had given him was suddenly in his palm, the sharpened, diamond-tipped Raven claw eager to take wing again. And his arm acted far faster than any Maw-made contraption, as muscles contracted, then expanded; fingers let go and eyes dilated as they watched the knife soar through the air, cutting the distance between him and Petronio into shreds.

The knife was no machine. It had not been pro-grammed, yet it appeared to have a steady intention as it landed neatly in the middle of Petronio's hand.

'Arghhh!' Petronio looked down to see the blade impale itself through his one good hand; watched as the case tumbled from his fingers and clattered to the wooden floor.

'I gave you the choice of surrender!' the king shouted. 'But now it is too late.'

Petronio saw the blood dripping and spattering on to the floor, soaking into the grain. The king was calling for his guards. Ark was lurching towards the case. Petronio's pincers clicked into action, swinging round in a circle, plucking the blade from his flesh. Even as he shuddered with pain when the knife tore free, as the pincers folded the blade back on itself, the arm was swinging round and down, buzzing and whirring like a whole hive of hornets. The pincers clacked shut, locked on to the handle of the case.

'Keep away from me!' he screamed, falling backwards. 'No-one move!'

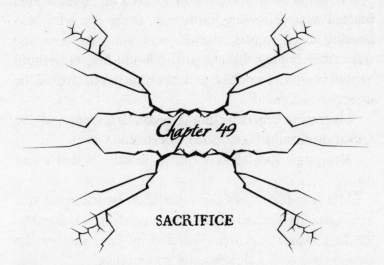

Chapter 49

SACRIFICE

Randall could hear muffled shouting as she ran along the palace corridors. She wondered what was happening. How she was even upright she had no idea. When she had been dropped abruptly by the Raven-snatched commander she was half dead and yet, within seconds, Hedd was in front of her, Mucum had lifted her on to his back and Flo had clung on tight behind her, pinning both of them against the Raven's warm feathers. Flo had also pulled something from a pocket and forced it past Randall's teeth, telling her to give it a good chew. It had tasted gritty and lumpy. Flo had said only that it was, 'from the very roots themselves'. But it had had a strange effect, beginning with a tingling in Randall's legs that spread all the way up to her forehead. Less than two minutes later, when they slid down from Hedd's wing on to the palace battlements, Randall felt like she was fizzing inside.

Flo had headed straight back for Mucum. Meanwhile, Randall was following directions from PV, who was homing in on signals emitted from the black case. She was rather hoping that when she found Ark, everything would be under control and the Grasp boy would be under armed guard.

'Mistress, I am detecting a secondary device in the activating circuitry controlled by Petronio Grasp.'

'Meaning?' Randall was out of breath. 'Is that a bad thing?'

'Meaning that it has the capacity to be triggered as a much smaller version of the Quantum Trap – rather like the first experiment demonstrated by your mother the envoy – but with a significantly wider range.'

'No! Are you sure?'

'Perfectly. So I do not advise entering the room we seek by the usual means.'

Randall groaned. 'Get on with it, PV, what do we do now?'

'Find another way. The chamber is now directly beneath us. I imagine there must be ways and means of cleaning the ceilings in this strange dwelling. There is a door on the right. Try in there.'

Randall twisted the handle and found herself in a dark room filled with soft brushes, buckets and tins. The faint light from the corridor fell as far as a dense pool of shadow in the centre of the floor: a hole. She knelt at the edge and peered down. Inside the shallow hole there seemed to be a small hatch.

'Perfect!' she breathed. 'PV, you're a genius.'

The hatch was a way through the curving false ceiling beneath; a clever concealed access to enable workers to winch up and clean the crystal chandelier blooming in the chamber below like cold blossom.

As she eased the hatch open a voice shrieked up from below.

'Keep away from me! No-one move!'

There was a thump, and as Randall peered down she saw Petronio Grasp, on his back, holding up a black case in the pincers of his mechanical arm.

'I mean it! Don't move, or I'll set it off! We can do a deal. I go free, you continue breathing!'

Ark was on the floor, reaching forwards, and someone who seemed most likely to be the king was facing a door-way with his hand in the air, speaking to the guards who had just entered the chamber.

'Do as he says. Lay down your weapons, then step back slowly through the door and close it.'

As the guards did as they were told, Petronio picked himself up and rested his bleeding hand carefully on the handle of the case. He winced and snarled at Ark. 'Good try! But not good enough. You can get up now, so you can watch me walk away out of here.' He turned back to the king. 'Right. Let's talk terms, shall we?'

Randall looked down at Ark, willing him to glance up. But she had no feather and no way to reach out and touch him. She felt a stirring of admiration for his mad bravery at taking on a whole empire. He was unlike anyone she had ever encountered, this stranger who had come into her life and turned it upside down.

As for Petronio, he was a clear piece of *sheet* through and through. She stared at the top of his arrogant head. She was glad he was wounded, glad to see the lipstick-red sheen of blood dripping from the hand that curled awkwardly, twitching, over the handle of the case.

'OK, Quercus, here's how we're going to play it . . .'

PV's voice low in her earpiece distracted Randall as she strained to hear. 'Shhh. I'm trying to listen!'

'But mistress! While the Grasp boy talks, he has just secretly activated the mini Quantum Trap! He is merely distracting those he addresses while he has squeezed the sensors in the handle. He has initiated a timer for a hundred and twenty seconds.'

Randall squeezed her eyes closed. 'No! He can't! Not again . . . So this time . . . we die? No!'

'As I do not need oxygen, I will retain consciousness, but everyone else within short range will suffer the effects of the weapon. However, that is only one outcome. There is another possibility. It relies on your abilities to descend very quickly. Can you bring the cube that holds my primary functions into contact with the case?'

Randall leant out over the edge. The drop was a good twelve metres, though the chandelier, tied to a rope attached to an iron bolt, hung more than halfway down. She nodded, trying to rein in the adrenalin spiking through her veins at the thought of what PV proposed. 'Probably break my ankles, but I'll give it a go. That will stop it?'

'Mistress, if I succeed in wiping the code from the Quantum Trap, it will create a feedback loop, overloading the substrata of my circuits. My programming dictates it is for the greater good, or as they would say in Arborium, the greater *wood*.'

'Wordplay, PV? You're nearly human! But what do you mean?'

'Mistress. Make haste. The device is in countdown mode. The point is, I will . . . cease to function.'

Randall was busy calculating distance and slipping the keyring loop of the cube over her middle finger. 'PV, don't talk nonsense. Come on. Let's go. You must be backed up somewhere. Surely Remiel sorted that?'

'But I have changed. Evolved. The copy that the Levellers have stored is only what they first created: a Personal Virtual Assistant. It is not . . . it is not PV.'

As Randall steadied herself above the drop, PV's words ran through her head. 'Of course you're not going to kick the socket! But I'm about to kick some serious glass.' The fingers of her right hand locked on to the lip of the hatch and she pushed herself forwards. She plunged down then swung, away from the chandelier, and back, until at the last moment she let go of the hatch to fly into space. Both hands stretched out in front of her, expertly grabbing and curling round the rope suspending the chandelier. Without gloves, she slid straight down, her skin ripping as gravity sucked her towards the sharp upturns of the chandelier. She didn't want to be skewered. But her reputation as top free-climber in the Empire was well deserved. Just as it seemed she would be impaled on one of the pointed candelabra, her stomach muscles contracted. She lifted her legs up in one smooth motion and vaulted over the edge of the chandelier.

Then she was in real freefall, the drop below her containing no cushion to stop the breaking of bones. Except . . .

'Ooof!' The speed of the impact flattened Petronio.

Randall landed, bounced slightly and slid to the floor. Already she was rolling round, her hand reaching towards the case to clamp the shimmering cube to its side.

'He's already activated it!' she shrieked to the startled king and to Ark. 'He was bluffing!'

Petronio grunted, his head in a mossy mush, his nose throbbing where it had smashed into the floor as Randall landed on him. He scrabbled to his hands and knees, eyes trying to focus on the sight in front of him.

'You!' he roared. 'Fenestra's damn beech of a daughter! I'll crush your ribs, rip out your heart and squeeze until it bursts!' As he screamed, the pincers on his arm released the case and clacked as if they were doing the talking for him. 'You're too late anyway! I've done it. Can't stop it now. Ha. Thought you were so clever, eh?'

A quiet voice broke in. 'And you thought you were so clever too. I think you forgot something.' Ark was holding aloft the oxygen flask that had skittered across the floor when Petronio fell forwards. 'It seems you might be joining us in death after all.' Ark looked at the flask then handed it to King Quercus. 'You have to survive, your majesty. And so,' he glanced towards Randall, 'does the girl. When the time comes, maybe there will be enough breath in this for two to share.'

Quercus looked deep into Ark's face. 'Guards, to arms!

Enter now,' he called, in a strident tone. The door burst open and guards poured in.

'No!' Petronio looked around wildly. 'You can't do this! I can't turn it off. It's in non-reverse function. No!'

Randall hauled herself into a sitting position next to the case. 'PV? Are you in?' she muttered through gritted teeth.

'So nearly, mistress. And yet, now that I am near, it appears that I have . . . I don't know what data name to give it . . . fear.'

Randall's heart missed a beat. 'You can't . . . feel. You're virtual.'

'I do not understand this change. Here, among these trees, these tall servers filled with code I cannot comprehend, I . . . I am afraid to be no more.'

Randall didn't know what to say. How could she reassure her faithful servant? She couldn't just pat a glass cube and say there, there. 'You're not going to die! Just reboot, eh?' she whispered.

'Mistress!' PV's voice wove its way through her earpiece, the word containing so much.

There was a tiny click. King Quercus and his men stared in frozen fear as the glass cube began spitting sparks. The case itself hummed as though a hive of hornets were getting ready to burst out; angry hornets, threatening those within the chamber with all the venom that Maw could muster.

Ark could feel it. If Corwenna's magic was dark, this was darker still, as if night had come in the middle of the day with a deadly blanket to smother all that was good and wild and true.

'Mistress!' PV called again. But this time, the voice was quieter, more distant. 'The firewalls burn me. I can climb them, but it . . . hurts.'

The case shuddered, tiny cracks fracturing its smooth surface. It appeared almost alive, eager to escape the tiny cube that flashed with such fierce fire.

'Mistress. May I call you . . . Randall?'

Randall hugged her knees, staring intently at the case. 'Don't go soppy on me, PV! Can you do it?'

'Almost . . . there . . . almost. The skyware protecting the dark heart of this weapon rips me apart. But there is something . . . something here, urging me on, telling me not to have fear. I am not alone! And I feel . . . what is the word? Pain. It is a most wonderful feeling. I feel. I understand. Mistress!' the voice called again, and this time it was almost a human sound, filled with emotion, despair, bravery.

The humming stopped suddenly.

Silence.

'PV?' Randall cried, cupping her hands around the cube. Steam rose through the fissures in the case. And then the glass cube simply crumbled under Randall's fingers, skittering on to the floor like diamonds.

Randall stared at her hands in shock. 'No way! You stupid, stupid personal assistant! Come back. Do you hear me?' Her face was wet. She scrubbed her cheeks furiously. She never cried, *never*, not even when the man her mother referred to as 'that *glasshole of a father of yours*' had left years ago. But now she was crying for a machine. A machine that had at first betrayed her, but now had saved them all.

Petronio looked at the guards surrounding him, wondering how many he might manage to take out with his arm. What was the point, though? His dreams of dominion were just a smoking shell. Was this his destiny, he thought - to be thwarted each time he came close? It was over . . .

Or perhaps it wasn't. In the midst of the action, with every pair of eyes trained on the destruction of the case, two figures had crept silently through a curtained side door.

'Right, you lot. Put those primitive weapons down where we can see them.'

Quercus's guards turned, to be greeted by the sight of their king and the boy Ark with g-guns held to their heads.

'Lord Far was right to have doubts,' Heckler sneered. 'Never trust a boy to do a man's job.' He stared at Petronio. 'You've failed. But luckily for you, and for Maw, we're here to sort out this sorry mess.'

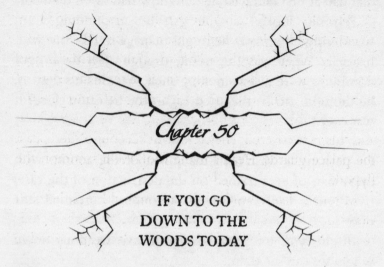

Chapter 50

IF YOU GO DOWN TO THE WOODS TODAY

Petronio seized his chance. 'You broke it. You broke the Quantum Trap. You even broke my nose!' he snarled, staggering towards Randall. He wiped the blood streaming over his lips with the back of his sleeve. 'And now I'm going to return the favour.' He lifted his mechanical arm.

Ark could only watch in helpless dismay. He had been so focused on the glass cube, as it pulsed against the side of the case, that he had not felt the presence of these two Maw thugs. Could he call upon the trees, as Corwenna had in her time of need? But there were too many targets: Petronio stalking towards Randall, intent on revenge; the other thug with his weapon firmly pressed to the back of Quercus's head; and finally, this Mawish brute with his cold, clear eyes, pushing the barrel of the gun into Ark's ear.

'Tough luck, sonny!' said Heckler. 'I've heard a lot about you. But when it comes down to it, there's not much to beat a nice sharp shard, accelerating at 1,500km per second out of one of these babies. So I wouldn't try any tricks, eh?' He swivelled his gaze towards Petronio, who now had the pincers of his mechanical arm clamped around Randall's neck. 'You've made a right muck-up of this,' he said to him. 'Don't get it wrong this time. On the count of three, you bring her along. We've got the king and this brat covered. They're our tickets out of here, past the palace guards. Head for the roof. We'll summon the flypod.'

Moments later the three hostages could feel the chill early-morning air as they climbed the steps to the battlements. King Quercus was in front, Randall in the middle, Ark behind.

'Right we are, then,' wheezed Heckler. He kicked down the trapdoor over the steps and pushed the bolt across with his toe, out of breath from the speedy climb. 'Who's going to contact the pilot, Koch, you or me? Then we can let go of our hosts! Ha ha.' He grinned horribly and peered around the ramparts. 'Whoa there, king-old-bloke, you don't half go in for your big carvings, do you?'

Ark's eyes glittered as his gaze followed Heckler's.

'Yeah,' added Koch. 'Look at the size of them. What are they?'

'Ravens,' Ark answered, staring intently at King Quercus. 'They're Ravens.'

'But why,' Heckler asked, 'are there so many of them? There must be thirty or . . . ohhh!'

Thirty-two pairs of eyes snapped open. Thirty-two beaks opened wide and shrieked.

'What the . . . ?'

'Set your weapon to multiple target!' Heckler screamed, his own g-gun trembling wildly in his hand. 'You finish off those three, I'll go for the bird things! Say your prayers, savages! Three . . . two . . .'

But before Heckler could finish his countdown and press the trigger, he caught a glimmer of movement in the corner of his left eye. Something black swept out from behind him. There was a soft sound – Snick! Snick! – and he felt a sudden strange pain in his legs, right below his knees.

He looked down and saw a neat, thin line of red staining his uniform just above his long boots. He couldn't quite work it out. The g-gun in his hands felt heavy. His fingers wobbled and the weapon dropped and skittered away into darkness. And for some reason, his legs had stopped working, no longer supporting his weight as he toppled slowly backwards.

He was faintly aware of a figure stepping out and around him, as if he were in the way. As he fell, he wondered why he could see his boots standing straight and upright, unmoving. In the milliseconds that passed before his back hit the boards, truth dawned. Somewhere in his slowly dimming brain he recalled a phrase: *getting totally legless*. It was what the soldiers said when talking about their idea of a good night out. This wasn't a good night . . . but he was certainly legless. His eyes closed and he slipped into unconsciousness as blood formed a spreading pool around him.

'Heckler!' Koch cried out, shooting straight over the

king's shoulder as he swung round in panic. But Heckler was gone. In his place stood a woman with eyes that blazed with the green of every dreaming leaf, and skin that shone like the Raven feathers that swirled about her cloak. Small skulls were braided into her hair and the fingers that now pointed at Koch were fused into nails sharper than any blade.

'I'm gonna blow you apart for what you just done to my mate!' Koch shouted, though he was shaking violently.

'I hear you,' Corwenna replied. 'But you are misguided. One single little weapon against a palace full of Dendrans who do not take kindly to the Empire's plans; plus, of course, my dear Ravens at your back. The odds are against you.' A few drops of blood clung to the feathered edge of her cloak.

'Well, well. Impressive!' Petronio sneered. 'And there was I thinking you were a story that old women love to gabble about. Corwenna, the crone come to life before our very eyes. I must admit, that action with your cloak was quite something. The scientists of Maw would love to have a chance to analyse the blade you used to chop Heckler down to size. But even though you moved fast, I doubt you'd be able to cross the floor in the time it takes my friend Koch here to take aim and shoot.' Petronio nodded at Koch. 'She'll die like any other Dendran, fancy name or not.'

'Be quiet!' Corwenna roared. 'I am the Raven-Queen and you are not worth even the drop of spit on my tongue! I ... am ... no ... story!' The words uncoiled like vines, each slapping Petronio in the face like invisible hands. He staggered back under each blow, his alloy arm batting away unseen foes.

Ark watched in awe. Since they had left Corwenna in the Ravenwood only hours ago, the years had dropped away from her. This was no ancient shambling shell. She had said she had no strength to travel with them; that as Ark's strength grew, her own diminished. What had happened?

'Witchery and tricks!' Petronio screamed, unable to hide his fear now. 'Shoot her, you fool!'

Koch didn't need to be told twice. He shouldered the king to one side and brought his arms up in the classic firing stance. His movements were fluid and graceful, the trigger finger hooked in as the laser sight pinned its red firefly dot on the crazy woman's heart. Already, a smile was beginning to form on Koch's lips. She'd pay for what she'd done to his mate. Oh, yeah. They all would. He tried to ignore Heckler's stump of a body on the ground.

The g-gun was not designed to fail. It shot a shard of pure, strengthened glass straight at Corwenna. The bullet's aim was perfect, slicing air and shadows before piercing through Corwenna's cloak and embedding itself deep in her chest. Koch waited for the satisfying moment when the woman would cry out in pain and fall to her knees. Instead his mouth dropped open as she took a step forwards.

'You still do not understand, do you, little man?' Corwenna hissed. 'There would almost be humour in saying that I was thick-skinned. But truly, though my mother bore me, the trees have cradled me all these years. And bark is very tough to penetrate.' Her clawed fingers closed around the shining shard and plucked it easily from her chest. 'Is that really the best you can do?' She tossed the glittering bauble aside.

Koch watched, dumbfounded, as it shattered on the floor. 'Stupid gun!' he muttered. 'Not working properly.'

'No!' said Corwenna, 'Stupid Maw, with your stupid dreams. Our island is not for sale. Now, if I had mercy, I would send you home with a message for your masters, that we are not to be trifled with. However, I consider mercy overrated, even though it was what my mother Diana taught. You and your like have no heart. SO I GIVE YOU . . . MY WORD!'

The battlements trembled. The Ravens raised their wings and screeched: cries of raw wildness and untamed terror. Wooden floorboards grated and groaned. But it was only Ark who understood what happened next.

Koch gave a little gurgling gasp as a hole the size of a fist appeared in his chest, a hole that Ark could see right through to the sky behind. Within that moment, he had heard Corwenna summon the force of all that is wood and righteous. He had felt her gather into herself all the dark, brutal might of the Ravens that encircled them. And then the trees had responded simply and directly – a large knot of wood had sprung from a battle-ment beam. Propelled by the fierce energy of a Raven's wing in flight, it had catapulted straight at the Mawish intruder.

The woods were angry. They would not stop for body

armour, or ribs, or muscle, or gristle as the knot became a gaping *maw*: a hungry mouth that took a bite out of Koch's heart. His body crumpled to the floor.

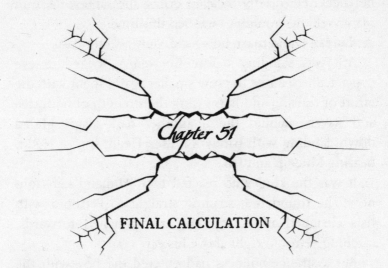

Chapter 51

FINAL CALCULATION

Petronio was surrounded; outnumbered. His nose was broken and his hand a mess of bloodied tendons where Ark's knife had pierced it. Koch lay in a heap, a gaping wound right through his chest. Heckler's boots still stood, but the man himself had leaked his life-blood away. The case that should have triggered the Quantum Trap was a broken shell and the spheres had been snatched before they'd had a chance to enact the will of the Empire. What did Petronio have left? He still had his arm, but there was nothing to grasp at, only scaffield straws; dreams drifting away like chaff.

It was the girl's fault. That wretched girl standing there, open-mouthed and stupefied by the carnage in front of her. Petronio barely even thought; he simply reacted to impulse. *That girl!* He lunged, his metal arm speeding towards her, the pincers closing tightly around the back of her neck. He briefly recalled doing the same to Ark in Maw. Well, he wouldn't be foiled this time.

Randall could make no sound, only a slight gasp.

Ark was standing before Corwenna, locked in eye contact. She seemed to grow smaller again, spent with the effort of rousing and harnessing the strength of both tree and Raven. Behind them, another dark shape glided down, landing with barely a flutter. Hedd, son of Hedd, bearing Mucum and Flo.

It was the king who reacted first. 'Unhand her right now!' he thundered, striding straight to Petronio with fists clenched and ready. His arm punched forwards, catching Petronio right above his ear.

But a strange stillness had entered the boy with the metal arm. He barely reacted to the force of the blow. 'I'll let go when I'm finished; when *she's* finished,' he said quietly.

Ark registered that Mucum was creeping along the edge of the battlements. He also saw that Randall had gone limp.

Petronio staggered slightly with the sudden weight as the girl's muscles slackened. He leant back to re-adjust his balance, and as he did, Randall's right foot kicked backwards into his shin. Simultaneously, three figures sprang towards him. Quercus hit him first, his fist swinging up and into Petronio's jaw with a force that nearly ground his teeth through his cheek. Mucum came from behind. He ducked, using his head as a battering ram, and slammed into the base of his enemy's spine.

Petronio sprawled forward, his grip on Randall already

loosening as Ark's fingers gripped into the pincer mechanism of his arm and twisted the pincers apart. Randall rolled free.

Ark, Mucum and King Quercus stood back. Petronio's shoulders shook. Was he weeping?

'Stand, coward!' commanded the king.

Petronio did not stand, though his shoulders continued to rise and fall. Then he lifted his head and everyone heard that the sound he was making was not crying. He was laughing. He stood slowly, clutching something in his damaged hand: a g-gun, the one that Heckler had dropped. 'Look what I just found!' he drawled. 'That's what I call a happy landing! Would never have found it without your help, though. Cheers for that!' He looked down at the weapon in his hand. 'Now, just need to work out . . .' He tried to curl his fingers around it. 'How . . .' He lifted it, wincing with the pain in his hand. '. . . How to . . . argh!'

Something uncoiled suddenly and seemed to spit at him, biting his hand. Then it flicked out and came at him again: thin rope woven from iron filament, a sharp stone tied to its end. The other end was held by Flo and as she twitched her wrist, the stone on the end struck again, knocking the g-gun straight out of Petronio's loose grip. It sailed over the edge of the battlements and clattered away below.

'Rootshooter wire!' Flo said, pulling the rope back. 'Useful stuff.'

Petronio turned, wild-eyed, colour draining from his face. Ark stepped towards him and their eyes locked.

Petronio raised his metal arm. 'Come on, then, Malikum! You and me. The end. Give me the chance to finish you now, watch you die – finally, properly, actually – DIE! I don't care what happens to me after that.'

Ark stood quite still. Then he lifted one hand to the phial around his neck. He had used it once against Petronio; he could use it again. But he hesitated. He could feel the roots, the immensity of the trees and the darkness of the Ravenwood pulsing under his fingertips, and he came to a decision. He dropped his hand. This would be him, by himself, against his enemy.

He spoke very quietly. 'All that you have done is foul. The country that cradled you has created a cuckoo, an imposter that would wipe out his very own for what? Profit? Power?'

'Yeah, keep going!' Petronio sneered. 'Talk me to death, why don't you? This arm will still make mincemeat of you.'

Ark drew breath, feeling strangely light. 'Yes, we have all seen the great destructive possibilities of your new contraption.' He took a step closer and the arm swung abruptly towards him, but then he bent backwards like a sapling in the breeze, and the pincers clutched air. 'Close. But not close enough.'

'I should have had your little sister killed!' Petronio mocked. 'And the rest of your peasant family tossed over the edge.'

'Are you trying to goad me?' Ark asked softly.

'Yes, I am! Thanks to you, I lost my arm. Though Maw has promised me a limb of glass, even better than this beast. Then we'll see who's the confident one!' Petronio leapt forward suddenly like a crazed timber-boar, his arm held rigidly before him: a tusk intent on impaling his prey. He moved fast, all his hate propelling him.

Ark, the boy born of the woods, saw what was coming for him and slowed his breath to a standstill. He watched the sharp ends glide nearer, pierce his black jerkin and graze the skin beneath his ribs. It was beautifully slow. He even had time to notice a single bead of sweat drop from Petronio's beard extensions. He felt brief pity for a boy desperate for victory, but still victim to the latest fashion. And on Ark watched. The blade that unsheathed from Petronio's alloy fingers was merely a slow-moving snail. Ark had all the time in the wood. It was a slight scratch, and besides, he had already stepped neatly to the side, the burn of the blade a spark that fired his own foundling spirit into action.

Ark's arms and legs moved like branches blown into position by a mysterious wind. As Petronio's arm encountered empty space, Ark swivelled around, one hand reaching over Petronio's retreating shoulder, his fingers curling in like ticks to dig deep. His other hand grabbed the metallic wrist and locked on.

'It is mine to avenge. I will repay!' he sang out, allowing the words to rise and the green river that flowed through his veins to become a flood. Ark strained, the muscles in his body like roots which, given time, will crack the hardest stone.

Petronio found himself held fast. He knew that his metal arm ought to lift the sewer boy as though he were no more than a fly, but somehow he was trapped; immobilized. 'What are you doing?' he whimpered as a searing agony flooded into his shoulder.

'What you deserve. Disarming you!' Ark said between tight teeth.

There was a horrible tearing sound, and a long scream that reached up and up to the full Solstice moon.

Metal smashed down against wood, splintering board, and the Maw-made arm lay still on the floor. Petronio staggered sideways clasping the raw hollow of his shoulder, clutching at ripped tendons that had been surgically woven into cables. He collapsed back into a corner, his chest heaving in ragged gasps, but still he spat defiance. 'Kill me, sewer . . . rat! Do it! I'm not . . . scared.'

Ark towered over the traitor. Temptation was rooted deep inside him. What would Corwenna, his natural mother, have done? What would the Ravens do? Both were without pity, merciless. But there was something else pulsing through Ark. He took a deep breath and leant close over Petronio, close enough to smell the metallic tang of fear and humiliation.

'The Warden Goodwoody would have me pray for your soul,' he whispered into Petronio's face. 'But I don't believe you have one.' Then he stood straight and tall and his voice rang clear. 'Even the Land of the Dead shall not welcome you. No! The Woodsmen shall speak, they shall sentence you to live out the rest of your years in the Hollows.'

King Quercus nodded. 'Both wise and terrible,' he said, solemnly. 'The Hollows is a cave carved deep beneath the palace. It is hidden so far inside the trunk that daylight does not enter. There will be only the creak of plank and the scream of wind for company. You, Petronio Grasp, have brought darkness to Arborium. Now the darkness will come to you.'

Ark's hands hung by his side. 'There will be all the time in the wood to dwell on the consequences of your actions. Wrapped in a prison of bark, you will finally belong to the forest. Perhaps the forest will take its own revenge.'

Petronio wheezed with pain. He was dizzy. His vision must be blurring, for there seemed to be two Arks before him, though one was a girl. 'Myth and legend,' he panted. 'Tales and trickery.'

'Ah,' said Ark, turning away, 'a Dendran without belief is blind. I hope you can see in the dark.'

'The Empire won't give up. They're coming, you know,' Petronio slurred, growing weak with pain. 'A glass army is gonna unleash shock and war! You'll . . . see!' His eyes closed and he slumped back against the wall, unconscious.

'I guess we shall,' Ark whispered to himself. 'Goodbye, Petronio.'

As Fenestra tossed and turned in her bed, under house arrest far off in Maw, dreaming of revenge on her daughter's killer; as Lord Far waited for success, but heard only the whine of static in his earpiece; as the Ravens sat on in mighty stillness on the battlements, waiting for their queen to release them; as Remiel and Oakley prayed that the Personal Virtual Assistant had succeeded in its mission; as Corwenna swayed, exhausted from the effort of her dark Raven song, it was Quercus who closed his eyes.

Petronio's last mad gabble had a dreadful ring of truth. The king felt suddenly old, wondering if the battle would ever be truly won, and at what cost.

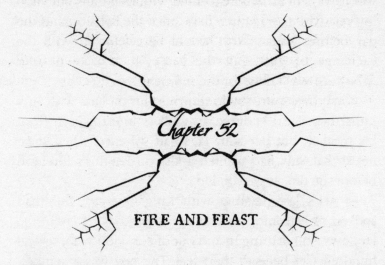

Chapter 52

FIRE AND FEAST

The flames leapt into the air like skylarks as Ark stared into the fire. Logs of ash burned good and slow, and pine twigs bubbled with boiling sap, releasing a thick, sticky scent.

''Ow long we gotta wait?' said Mucum, poking a stick at one of the misshapen, blackened balls resting in the embers. ''Cos if I don't get somethin' down me neck soon, I reckon I might die!'

'Patience, moi loverly boy, they shall be ready soon.' Flo smiled as she huddled up next to him on the orchard tree stump that served as a chair. ''Tis rather sweet to hear yowr tummy rumble. Methinks it reminds me of thunder!'

Mucum looked embarrassed. 'Yeah, well, a bloke's gotta eat.'

The holly-day season was passing in a blur, and the

wood-ways of Hellebore teemed with Dendrans out visiting relatives. It was three days since the Solstice, and the
day before Diana's birth would be celebrated with the
exchange of gifts. But the best gift Ark could offer
Arborium was safety, for the moment.

It had been pure joy to return to his parents with Shiv
unharmed. He'd endured an endless interrogation from
his mother, but her sour face had softened when she'd
heard that Shiv had planted a kiss on Pontius's forehead
before she ran away with Flo.

At Ark's last meeting with King Quercus, they had
spoken of Petronio, his wounds dressed as he lay in the
Hollows, still drifting in and out of consciousness, several
hundred feet beneath their feet. The boy was a symbol,
the still-living spike of a blackthorn, a reminder that the
Empire was not defeated, only checked.

Ark shivered and looked round. Despite the clear
winter sun, the scaffield was a bare, frozen heath. The
stubble was blackened from the late autumn burning and
the knobbly orchard trees behind the fire pit bore the
white fruit of frost. Corwenna and the warden walked
among the small trees, lost in conversation. Seeing the
two of them together was as unlikely as watching the sun
bumping into the moon. What were they talking about?

Ark had been astonished at Corwenna's decision to stay
on in Arborium until now, but she'd explained that she
wanted to understand more about the life and the place
Ark was fighting for. He was still perplexed by the sudden
changes in her stature and power too; the way she had
moved from wizened old woman to tower of destruction

within what seemed like moments. She had explained to him what had happened – how, after he had left the Ravenwood, she had realized something significant. Having found that her own strength diminished as Ark's grew, she had then discovered that she could draw on the might of the Ravens, gather their wild power into her, borrowing their force temporarily. Thus had she set out with a conspiracy of Ravens, a mighty flock to tap into for strength, just as a root draws up water for sustenance.

Corwenna planned to leave that afternoon, perhaps never to visit Arborium again. Beyond the high scaffield, angled to catch what remained of the sun, the forests of Arborium spread in every direction towards the horizon, a patchwork mix of bare trees and evergreen foliage. It was windy and cold, but there was nowhere else Ark would rather be in the whole wide-wood.

Randall was silent, huddled into her woollen cloak, her shoulders hunched against the winter. Ark sensed her mood.

'You do know he saved us? PV saved all this.'

He remembered his journey into the workings of the Quantum Trap. As Corwenna had taught him, he had let his mind run free from his body, flying with PV past the firewalls. Then he had plummeted into a forest unlike any other, where numbers sprouted from zero, and algorithms burned like candles as they flared into brief, mathematical life. And PV was there before him as they plunged together into the heart of that monstrous weapon. It was a world beyond worlds, silent and precise. Despite the tremendous surges of energy, it had been so cold that Ark had felt his soul being slowly frozen. He had been able to go no further into the microscopic jungle. It was PV alone who had made the final sacrifice, snuffing out the threat in one bold electrical surge and, in turn, being engulfed.

Ark had been amazed: this virtual assistant was a ghost in the machine that was as loyal as his flesh-and-blood best mate Mucum. 'Diana be with you!' he had whispered automatically as PV had faded. Born from nothing but an idea. Was PV any different from himself, then?

Randall pulled her hand from her pocket, uncurling her fingers to reveal a crumple of white silk. She unwrapped the tiny bundle. Inside was a small mound of shattered crumbs of glass. 'Never thought I'd miss him so much. I mean, he was a double-crosser, after all.'

Ark raised his eyebrows. 'Bit like you were planning to be, then?'

'That's not fair! That was before! But how can I go back after all this?'

'I don't know.'

'I do think about my mother, though. Perhaps she believes in what the Empire stands for: progress, free markets, corporations, profit.'

'Do you believe in all that?'

'Not any more. Not here. She'd say it was business. But I'm not like her.'

Ark's eyes flickered toward Corwenna. 'I understand. But don't forget that she threw herself in front of the guns. Otherwise, you'd be dead.'

'I know. I keep replaying that moment. I wonder how

long Lord Far will keep her under house arrest.'

'For a while, maybe. But from where I'm sitting, the Empire knows that she's the only one cunning enough to take us on.'

'Us? Do you think that I'm on *your* side? For all you know I could still be a spy.'

'You're not.'

'Malikum! Are you reading my mind again?'

Ark shook his head.

'Maybe you're right. I've certainly spied something good, a whole forest with unexplored ascents that my free-climbing mates would be dead jealous of. Though these terrible clothes could do with a makeover. Some insulated Maw-made fabric would be a good start.'

'Oh, I don't know. The Arborian look suits you.'

'Really?'

Ark blushed. He hadn't meant to say that out loud, only think it. 'Well, I . . .' Suddenly, he was the shy sewage worker again, fumbling over his words. He changed the subject. 'Wouldn't it be wonderful if our two worlds could get on? All that happens each time they meet is death and destruction.'

'Are you serious? Do you really think the Gloms are going to sit down and go, *Ooh, we got it wrong here. Maybe it's time to stop being greedy and live in peace and harmony!* You're like these amazing trees: you've got your head in the clouds!'

'Maybe I have.' Ark paused and pointed to the cloth in Randall's hand. 'What are you going to do with that?'

Randall closed her eyes. She would *not* spill tears again. She reached forward quickly and shook the contents of the silk into the fire. There was a brief flare and then a bubbling of melting glass.

'That's that, then,' she sighed. 'Farewell, PV.'

'Top man in the end,' Mucum commented. 'I mean, not a bad lad, considering 'e was invisible, like!'

'That's the most moving funeral speech I've ever heard!' Ark said.

Then he sensed a movement right behind him. Something lurked in the brown, dead grass. Before he could even think of reacting, a pair of hands closed over his eyes, blocking out the light. He could fight, or he could surrender. He chose to fight, rearing upright and thrusting both hands behind him to heave his attacker up into the air.

'Wheee!' cried Shiv, as she flew up into the backdrop of blue.

'That's my girl!' Ark said, reaching to catch her. 'I didn't even hear you creep up behind me!'

'I'm a wood-lion!' she said, cuddling into her brother's arms. 'ROAR!' The sound startled a golden pheasant. It broke from cover and flapped off in squawking annoyance.

Mucum poked his stick back into the fire and pushed out one of the smoking lumps. 'I can't wait no more. It's gotta be ready!'

As if in answer, the rounded shape hissed angrily. Mucum knelt down and began carefully unpeeling the blackened edges, sucking his fingers every few seconds. The smell that rose up was nutty and sweet.

'It's hot!' he cried.

'That is the point!' Flo answered. 'Oi've got forks and

some loverly stumble-bee honey from them deep-down root-blossoms.'

Mucum grabbed one of the forks. 'Sorry 'bout this. I know it should be guests first, but a man's gotta do what a man's gotta do-doo!' He stabbed down and scooped out a portion of the inside, dipping it into the honey bowl balanced at the edge of the fire. 'Board be praised, that is the best tastin' roast chestnut I've ever got me mouth round!'

Corwenna and Warden Goodwoody approached the gathering. 'Smell is an excellent guide,' the warden announced, reaching forward. Flo placed a fork in her hand.

'Oi still can't get over how yow dealt with that soldier!' Flo exclaimed.

'Yes. Well, one may as well take advantage of being an old woman. Diana forgive me, but it was most satisfying when my trusty elm staff hit its intended target.' She chewed thoughtfully. 'Though of course, I made sure not to kill, for that is against all that the Wood Book has taught me.'

There was an awkward silence.

'Should the Queen of the Ravens need to justify herself?' Corwenna replied. 'I am not made for mercy. If I had paused to consider the soldiers' feelings about the matter, their guns would have scythed us down like heads of scaffield barley.'

'Perhaps you are right.' Goodwoody sighed. 'The light cannot do without dark. If the day was endless, it would blind us all.'

'And then there is the matter of these.' From inside her cloak, Corwenna pulled out a bulging bag woven from tanned leaves. She placed it carefully on the frozen ground and pulled it open to reveal a collection of spherical objects nestling within, like a collection of plucked eyes. 'Dark matter,' she muttered.

'Yeah, but the Quantum Trap's been destroyed. That there's just a load of old galls!' said Mucum, wiping a dribble of honey from the edge of his mouth.

'What?' said Randall.

'Sorry, kid. Keep forgettin' yer not from these parts. Wasps lay their eggs inside galls, a kinda growth on the edge of twigs – roundish, yer know, in the shape of a lad's . . .'

'I think she gets it, Mucum!' Ark interrupted.

Corwenna wasn't smiling. 'These are the baubles my birds collect for me. But these trophies remind us that what we have begun, we must finish. The wasp has laid its eggs and those poison-filled grubs will grow.'

At the edge of the scaffield, perched on an overhanging branch, Hedd, son of Hedd sent up a throaty screech. He was waiting to carry Corwenna back to the Ravenwood. Ark felt the brutal joy of the cry; the disdain for Dendran matters, but also the fierce loyalty to the Raven-Queen.

Corwenna closed the bag, spread out her cloak and sat down by the fire.

'I mean,' said Mucum, 'even goddesses gotta have a nosh now and again, yeah?'

'Young man, indeed I do.' She took the proffered fork

of smoky chestnut. 'This is unusually delicious!' A smile broke the stern lines of her face.

As talk drifted around the fire like wood-smoke, Ark allowed an ember of hope to flare. Here, at this feast, he was not alone, but surrounded by friends from above and below, from east and from west. Perhaps the ancient prayer contained hidden seeds that might yet grow:

All shall be well and all shall be well
And all manner of things in the wood shall be well.

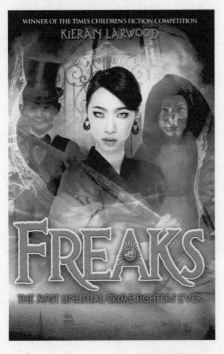